PETALS

AND

LIES

OF PETALS AND LIES

A Wicked and Twisted Tale

J. L. JACKOLA

Paperback ISBN 978-1-960784-44-5
Hardback ISBN 978-1-960784-45-2
Electronic ISBN 978-1-960784-46-9

Distributed by Tivshe Publishing
Printed in the United States of America

Cover design by Dark Queen Designs
Map design by WorldWyrm

Visit www.jljackola.com

Also by J. L. Jackola

AUTHOR'S NOTE

Welcome to the world of thornless roses and golden magic.

Of Petals and Lies is a spicy dark fairytale retelling that takes a Beauty and the Beast villain inspired redemption and weaves it with Rapunzel. This book has dark themes and is intended for mature readers. It contains explicit sexual scenes, language, and scenes that some readers may find triggering, including s. a. situations (not by the mmc), references to s. a., violence, and death.

Hold on to your roses and braids because this retelling is an adventure with twists that will have you clutching the tower window in anticipation.

J. L.

For those who wanted the villain to get the girl.

Chapter One

GARRET

My mind was on the beauty who would soon be mine when the door to the tavern slammed open. Margot burst in, running over to me. My jaw clenched. As much as I feigned interest in her, enjoying the perks of her body while I bided my time to get closer to her sister, I didn't like others seeing her with me.

"Garret—"

I stopped her words, grabbing her arm and dragging her from the tavern.

"What did I tell you about coming here?" I snarled, holding her shoulders. "This is not a place for someone like you."

She recoiled but stayed quiet. There was no backbone to her, which was why she was so easy to manipulate. That was the way I liked my women, docile and obedient.

"What are you doing here?" I asked, releasing her arms and ignoring how she pushed her breasts toward me.

I gritted my teeth, knowing she was just a stepping stone to getting what I wanted: her younger sister, Beatrice. Margot and

Clementine were Beatrice's older sisters, and they were desperate for any man's attention because they didn't hold a flame to Beatrice's beauty. Which was exactly why they were easy to manipulate. They hated their sister, their envy making them prime for my advances and blind to my actual intentions.

"Beatrice has returned to him," she said.

My mouth snapped shut, my fists clenching at the thought. Even before Beatrice's father traded her to that beast beyond the dark forest, I'd worked my way into her sisters' trust to get closer to her. She had repeatedly turned down my attempts to make her mine, but I didn't let that stop me. She was the most beautiful in the town, with suitors who ignored her sisters and lined up for her attention. I was the only one who would have her, though. She was mine whether or not she realized it. She was perfect for me, young, beautiful, pure. Even the thought got me hard.

"What do you mean, she returned to him? Why would she ever go back to that beast?"

When her father had traveled past the dark forest, taking all three of his daughters but returning without Beatrice, I'd wanted to kill him for leaving her with that animal. He claimed he had no choice, that the beast had demanded he keep one, but I knew her father had other motives. He'd traded her for his own safety and the wealth the beast had promised. To think an animal like that had lived so close all these years without us knowing.

I didn't change my plans, continuing to use her sisters while I waited for her return. She may have turned me down, but I knew she wanted me. Who would want that monster over me?

"She says she loves him."

"Loves him?" I sneered as the reddish hue of anger infected my vision.

"She loves him?" Leo asked. He must have followed me from the tavern. Beatrice was his sister, after all. I'd known him for years, latching onto him when I'd first come to town and getting closer to him as Beatrice had aged. Even as a child she'd been beautiful, but I'd been patient, waiting until she was older, all the while using Leo's friendship to stay close to her.

"Yes, Father let her return to him."

"Of course he did," I muttered, knowing the man had gotten himself into financial troubles and that's why he'd agreed to give his most precious daughter to a beast. The promise of wealth and a guarantee of his safety were too much for him to resist. "But I won't." I glanced at Leo. "I think it's time to hunt a beast."

"What do you mean?" he asked me. He was wringing his hands, and I could see him wrestling with his loyalty to me and to the sister he ignored regularly.

"She's clearly under some spell. I'm not letting that animal anywhere near her again. She's mine."

Margot's eyes widened. "Yours? I thought I was yours."

"You're a good fuck, Margot, as is Clementine. But it's Beatrice whom I'll marry. She's not sullied like you two and she'll be perfect for raising my children and warming my bed. Now scurry home. I'm going hunting." I pushed her aside and rushed to the nearest horse.

"Garret!" she squawked. "Are you going to let him treat me like that, Leo?" she asked her brother.

Leo was spineless when it came to defying me. He was too loyal, living in my shadow and doing my dirty work.

"Garret, think about this," he tried, coming after me. "If she loves him, let her be. You can have Margot."

Margot huffed, clearly not liking the fact that she was second choice. I was glad I no longer had to feign interest in her and Clementine. It was time to claim Beatrice for myself. Her sisters could continue to suck my cock while Beatrice cared for our children.

I jerked the reins of the horse. "Are you coming with me or not, Leo?"

"I.... That's not even your horse," he muttered.

"Stay here then. I'm getting Beatrice and this time I won't let her say no."

I took off, hearing him grumble and Margot complain. The sound of hoofs thundered behind me, blending with the sound of the horse I'd stolen, and Leo was by my side within minutes. We raced through the countryside, the dark forest looming before us. I'd avoided going after Beatrice when her father left her, returning to say he'd traded his freedom for hers, giving his youngest to a beast of a man. I hadn't believed such a monster could exist, but both Margot and Clementine had seen him the day their father had delivered Beatrice to him.

I'd waited, knowing she would return. She loved her family too much, even if her sisters couldn't stand her, too envious of her beauty, and her brothers barely noticed her. I spent my time in the skirts of both her sisters who were not as innocent as she was and gladly spread their legs for me, thinking I'd choose them when it was only Beatrice I wanted. And when she returned, I'd cornered her, ignoring her refusal to marry me, dealing with the other suitors who were constantly at her door. Her repeated 'no' didn't deter me, although it irritated me. Now to hear she had returned to him, that she loved him, was the last straw. I would drag her to the altar and fuck the denials from her until she was as willing and compliant as her sisters.

The forest was dark and angry, and I could hear the howling of wolves in the distance. Leo was rambling about how this was wrong and I couldn't force her to marry me. His determination would have impressed me if it wasn't angering me.

I slowed my horse as the castle stood before us. Black roses with gnarled vines and sharp thorns surrounded the gates, and I squinted, seeing glimmers of blood red below their blackened, dried petals.

"Garret, this is a mistake," Leo said, his eyes darting back and forth. "This place looks cursed. We should go back. Marry Margot."

I hopped from my horse, leaving him at the stairs. "I don't want Margot. I want Beatrice, and tonight I will have her."

"She's my sister—"

I whirled to him, grabbing him by the lapels. "That's never bothered you before. I fucked your other two sisters, and you never blinked. I've wanted Beatrice since her tits first formed and you never spoke up. Don't be the protective older brother now, Leo. It's not a good look on you."

I shoved him back and rushed up the stairs, side-stepping the cracks and crumbling stones. Unsheathing my sword, I pushed the doors open, hearing Leo huffing behind me. No matter how he tried to be a man, he was nothing but my puppet and he would always stay by my side.

The gloomy sensation of death clung to the air when we made our way through the lower level of the castle. Strange spirit-like servants scattered to hide, and I had to do a double-take to make sure I wasn't seeing things.

"Were those ghosts?" Leo whispered.

"I don't know what they were," I said, gripping my sword tighter as I climbed a marble spiral staircase that led to the second floor. The staircase held fractures, the banister missing in places like years of erosion had rotted the stone. When we reached the landing, I heard Beatrice's distressed voice.

I ran, trying not to look at the ghost-like figures we encountered, their black wispy consistency threatening to derail my intent. I wasn't the type to rush into battle. Instead, I ran from death, only engaging foes I knew my sword could cut down. Taking my prey from behind and letting my arrows loose as they fled.

Rounding the corner, I found Beatrice sitting on a massive mahogany bed. Beside her lay the most grotesque beast I'd ever seen. He had fangs that sank far below his lips, fur covered every inch of his body, and his hands were paws with thick black claws.

"Get away from him, Beatrice!" I stormed into the room, yanking her from his side.

"No! Garret, stop. He's sick!" she cried, tugging her hands to free herself from my hold.

"Good, it will make killing him easier." I threw her to the side, ignoring her pleas.

"Garret!" Leo yelled as the beast rose from the bed, growling at me.

"Don't turn on me now, Leo. It's time to protect your sister from this beast."

"He's not a beast, Garret! You are!" Whatever cursed magic lay upon this place must have infected her mind. Or perhaps the strange spirits we'd seen were corrupting it.

I gritted my teeth and attacked the beast, sending him sprawling across the room, his body landing near the balcony. If he'd slid any further, he would have gone to his death. Half the stone railing had rotted away. I stomped over to him, hearing Beatrice yell.

I glanced at her. Leo was holding her back, and she was struggling to free herself from him.

"It's time to stop saying no to me, Beatrice. You will marry me and take your place by my side as my wife."

I walked around the beast, looking for any sign that he would fight back, but he looked weak and wounded, like any defeated animal.

"You're going to make this easy on me," I told him, lifting my sword and seeing him struggle to rise.

"You're a cruel, selfish, arrogant beast, Garret!" Beatrice yelled through her tears.

I heard Leo grunt, and I peered up, seeing him doubled over and Beatrice rushing toward me.

"I could never love a monster like you," she sneered, her hands coming out and pushing me.

The force of her push caused me to step back as I tried to

avoid my sword hurting her. My foot caught on the rough edge of the broken balcony, and I teetered, my eyes going wide as the bulk of my body pulled me further back.

"I hate you," she said as my sword fell, my arms swinging to balance myself.

"Beatrice?"

She stepped closer and shoved me again. I stared at her as I fell, in shock that she could hate me enough to send me to my death. She turned away before I lost sight of her, my body falling as quickly as all my mistakes fell with me, dragging me to my death. Right before my world went black, a flare of golden magic spewed from the castle, touching my skin with a tingling that softened the blow as everything went dark.

THE STING of cold water woke me, but it was nothing compared to the sting of defeat. I coughed until my lungs were clear, then rolled to my back and stared at the castle that loomed over me. Dawn had broken and the structure no longer looked like the menacing beast it had been. Home to a creature who had stolen the woman I wanted. I should have easily won a fight with him. But I'd underestimated Beatrice and now I'd lost her.

I lifted myself, ignoring the chill in my bones from the winter air and the ache in my body from the impact it had taken when I'd fallen. That fall should have killed me or at least left me injured, but by some miracle, it hadn't. Crimson rose petals floated on the water as I emerged, reminding me of the roses I'd seen at the gates, their thorns sharp and angry. A deer stood sipping at the water's edge, and it picked its head up, its black eyes evaluating me as I shivered and patted my chest, wondering if I was dead. That fate would have been easier to accept than what I saw when I came around to the front of the castle.

The villagers were celebrating. Their faces beamed with happiness as they hugged and chattered as if a spell had broken and cleared away the memory of the previous night. And in the center, standing at the top of the immense stairs, stood my Beatrice in the arms of another man. Their embrace was a sensual one, their kiss that of two lovers. It was an intimate moment that crushed what resolve I had left.

The voices carried to where I stood, hidden in the shadows. Voices proclaimed the spell had broken, and the beast was the prince. A vengeful fairy had placed a spell upon him for refusing her. A spell Beatrice had broken with her love. Everyone had forgotten him, including his mother, who was returning now that the spell had broken, a fairy guiding her home after years of battling the advancing army from the neighboring kingdom. As their words settled into my mind, the cobwebs of my memory clearing, I remembered as well. The prince who ruled our kingdom, one we'd all forgotten. A man who now held my woman close, his hand touching her like mine should have been.

Anger and confusion overcame me, and I took a step from the shadows, ready to kill the man who had taken her from me until two guards marched Leo up the steps. Beatrice looked away from her brother, not acknowledging him. The prince gave a nod, and they led him away. I stepped back, the sting of defeat returning, the anger simmering until it was nothing but a remnant. Looking back at Beatrice, I knew I'd lost, and so I did what came naturally to me. I ran.

Against the ache of my injuries, I ran. Past the roses that had once been twisted and rotting but now shone a brilliant red, their thorns no longer so menacing, through woods that had been ominous and dark the prior night but now shone bright with sunlight, no prowling wolves to be found. Through the village, keeping out of sight of any villagers who remained. Until I reached my home. I tore through the door, rummaging through my things as I hastily packed what I could. All the while, my mind screamed that I'd lost. I never lost. I cheated, I connived, I clawed my way to victory regardless of who I pushed aside to claim it. But never had I lost.

I didn't know what that made me now. Alone, and from the looks the villagers had given Leo, hated. Things I'd never been that caused feelings in me I didn't understand. I knew anger and jealousy. I knew how to manipulate and connive. But I didn't know what it was like to be hated. The villagers loved me; the women loved me. Or so they had. But the prince was back, some spell broken, and the man who had tried to kill that prince was dead. I stopped and wondered briefly if anyone would grieve me. Perhaps Beatrice's sisters would. I could have settled and taken Margot for a wife and enjoyed the benefits Clementine offered. But I'd been greedy, wanting only their younger sister, the untouchable, the virgin, the beauty. And now I had nothing.

Taking one last look around, I snuck out of my house, saddled my horse, and turned my back on the village, on the past, and on the man I'd once been.

CHAPTER TWO

GARRET

THREE YEARS LATER

I swatted a bug away as I stared at the town ahead of me. My horse yanked at his bridle, telling me I'd been sitting too long, and he was ready to move. But I wasn't ready. Troniere lay on the border of Duntraik, a dark and treacherous kingdom ruled by a king whose hands were caked in the blood of his people. He ruled with a heavy hand and dark sorcery. And I wanted no part in either.

Glancing back at the path behind me, I debated on turning back and heading to another town, but I'd been through the whole of this kingdom, my intention to enter Bira, the kingdom just north of Troniere. I'd been traveling for weeks and was ready to rest, maybe settle down for a few months before people started asking questions and I became bored of answering them with lies.

I urged my horse forward, deciding I would stay here for a spell. As I entered the small town, I wondered at the similarities to my hometown. The vendors were selling bread and essentials. A small tavern and a blacksmith sat nestled within the shops. A melancholy grew, one I'd been shoving aside since the day I'd left my old life behind. Garret of Hiranire was dead, the once proud captain, turned deserter and traitor whom his village had not mourned. News had traveled, however, about the villain who had stalked the young maiden and almost slain her love, the prince who was now king of Hiranire.

The story morphed the further I traveled from Hiranire, the name of the villain lost, changing from town to town. Still, I kept my mouth shut and my head down. Once I'd left the kingdom, my anonymity grew and I could leave the shadows, the alleys, the dark of night without risk that someone would recognize me. Still the story followed me, the title of villain becoming like a second skin even if those gossiping didn't realize the villain was sitting quietly next to them as they shaped his identity.

Tying my horse, I entered the tavern, paying the barmaid for a mug of ale and a bowl of stew. She was curvy, her brown eyes flirting with me, but I remained stoic. I'd had my fill of women in the last few towns, and I wasn't ready to indulge yet. I stared into my ale, contemplating my next move. Even after all this time, it was unsettling to have no direction in my life. Before, I'd been a soldier, rising through the ranks, stabbing my colleagues in the back to get there. I'd had my eye on a girl who would be perfect to raise my children, clean my house, and warm my bed. She was beautiful, with small curves, bright eyes, a mouth I wanted to use, and a youthful body ripe for breeding. I had everything.

The barmaid plopped the stew in front of me, interrupting my thoughts. The interruption reminded me that no matter how perfect my life had been, it was long gone. Now I was no one. I was a stranger roaming from town to town, trying to find his place again. Maybe Bira wasn't where I should be heading. Maybe my travels had brought me this far west for a reason. Duntraik may have held horrors whispered on the wind, but maybe that's what I needed. Running had gotten me nowhere. I was a bad guy, the villain who was no longer welcome in the other kingdoms. Sure, I could continue pretending I was someone else, but I'd been run out of too many towns now for fucking women I shouldn't have touched, conniving to steal power from people who owned it, and robbing to stay fed.

Duntraik was the place where someone like me was welcome. Where I could be the villain they all made me out to be. Even if it was a place that no longer wanted me. One I'd left long ago and never returned to.

I took the last few bites of stew, left some coin for the barmaid, and headed back out to my horse. Duntraik was another day's ride from Troniere, so I'd need a place to stay. And I really needed a break from riding. Cursing myself for not thinking about it sooner, I walked back into the tavern.

"Is there an inn where I can stay a few nights?" I asked the man behind the bar.

"Usually, but it's full."

He turned back to wiping down the bar, his greasy brown hair flopping over his eyes.

"Full?" I clenched my jaw, thinking he was blowing me off.

"The fire festival is this week and people are traveling north to the town of Niscus. We're the closest town, so we're always filled up this time of year."

Fuck. I hadn't expected that answer, but it sealed my thoughts on heading to Duntraik instead of Bira.

"You could try the widow's place," the barmaid chimed in. "She's got extra space and I know she could use some help, no matter how stubborn she is to admit it. She'd probably trade you boarding for those muscles." She squeezed my bicep playfully, and I narrowed my eyes, wondering if it would be worth sneaking off with her for a quick feel of those big breasts that were spilling over her dress.

"That's not a bad idea," the man said, swatting her hand with his towel and giving her a scolding look.

"Widow?" I asked, wondering what the man's relationship was to the curvy barmaid.

"Yes, she lives in the house furthest from town, up on the hill. Her husband died six months ago when a group of stragglers from Duntraik tried to rob them. He killed them but suffered a fatal wound. She's by herself up there now." He shook his head and returned to scrubbing an invisible spot on the counter.

I gave them my thanks and returned to my horse, guiding him through town and debating on my next move. I wasn't certain spending the next few days with an old lady and doing chores for her was something I wanted to do, but it beat sleeping in the woods. And when I wasn't stealing, I'd been working odd jobs. I'd had a few moments where I'd grasped for some way to change my fate, to be a different man, a better man. But each time I tried, I failed.

The small blue house stood just beyond the town, and I could see why the raiders had targeted it. It wasn't large, but the lush garden at the front and side of the house caused it to stand out, and it was just far enough out of town to ensure no one would notice anything unusual.

I tethered my horse to a small tree that stood in the front, my eyes roaming the area. A rundown stable stood at the back of the home, a line with clothes strung near it, the breeze rocking them back and forth. I knocked on the door, noting the weathered texture of the wood and the peeling paint on the house. When no answer came, I wandered toward the back, seeing a dainty hand fiddling to pin a sheet to the clothesline.

"Hello, I'm looking for the widow." I hadn't gotten her name.

The hand froze and I could see the tension in her knuckles before she dropped her hand and pulled the sheet aside.

"Eloise," she said, her voice sweet as honey. Her vibrant blue eyes held creases in the corners. Her silver hair framed a face that looked too young to hold such color. A long scar distracted from her beauty, crossing from her eyebrow and making its way in a vertical line across her face. I'd seen my fair share of scars, but this one seemed distinctly unique, like it didn't sit deep enough on the skin to be possible.

Blinking my eyes against the strange sensation, I said, "The barmaid suggested you might have lodging to offer. I only need a place for a few nights."

"Heading to the fire festival?" she said. The relaxed way she said it came across as forced, and I noted the slight shake in her hands as she pulled a towel down from the line.

"No, just passing through on my way to Duntraik."

She froze, her eyes growing large. "And what would you want in Duntraik?"

Tipping my head, I wondered at her reaction. It seemed exaggerated from any normal response. "I'm not sure we know each other well enough for me to disclose that information," I replied, giving her a coy grin.

She remained unaffected. "What's your name?"

"Garret," I answered instinctively, before I could provide an alias. I was far enough from Hiranire, but I still hadn't taken a chance before now.

"Well, Garret. We now know each other. If you want lodging, I suggest you tell me why you intend to travel to Duntraik." She yanked another piece of clothing from the line, snapping it with a flick of her wrist before folding it and placing it in her basket.

My jaw ticked. I didn't like demanding women, and her attitude tempted me to leave. The woods would be a better option than dealing with her questions.

"Nevermind," I said, turning and walking away.

I heard her mutter something before she ran after me and grabbed my arm. I glanced down at her hand, which looked small on my large arm. In fact, she seemed tiny compared to my six-feet-four stature.

"I'm sorry," she said. "I don't mean to pry, but if you intend to stay on my property, I need to know who you are. Duntraik is the reason my husband is dead. It's not a kingdom I favor."

Understanding passed through me as I remembered the barkeep's story. "I have a goal to travel all the kingdoms. Bira and Duntraik are the last two and as Duntraik is the more treacherous, I thought I would head there next." The lies came easily now, too easily.

She relaxed, the strain in her face fading. Crossing her arms, she stood taller, giving me an appraising look. Her blue eyes were unwavering as they met mine, and I couldn't help but think again how the scar didn't sit right on her skin.

"There's a small building in the back where my husband would...work. It's empty, but there is enough room for you to sleep. I need some help around the property. The shutters are falling, the roof needs patching, and there's plenty more." I was beginning to regret this arrangement, not looking forward to being her lackey for my stay. "You look strong enough to help me, so I'll offer free board in exchange for helping me fix them."

My brow raised. "Help you? Women don't do that kind of work."

She drew a breath through her teeth that were now grinding. "Some of us do," she replied tersely. "Do you want the lodging or not?"

I thought about it for a moment, pondering if I should just head to Duntraik and offer my services there until I thought better of it. I could delay a few days and rest my bones, even if it meant I was stuck doing this woman's bidding.

"Fine, but you won't be helping."

She frowned, her head tilting. "Because I'm a woman?"

"Yes, now show me to my lodging and I'll start your projects."

She didn't move, her hands now on her hips. I could see she was going to be the kind of woman who grated on my nerves just in the look she gave me.

She turned on her heels and stomped away, pushing aside the hanging clothes and disappearing. I followed the trail of her grumbling complaints, finding myself in front of a small wood shack that looked barely the length to accommodate my height.

"This is what I have. I'll bring you a blanket and pillow. I suppose you'll be expecting food with your lodging since you're a man and can't cook anything yourself?" she snapped.

I creased my brows, trying not to laugh at the spitfire. She was plucky, I'd give her that. But plucky women were never my type. They were too mouthy and obstinate. I should have seen that side of Beatrice earlier, but I hadn't until I'd lost her. The thought had my blood stirring and, as if she noticed, Eloise tilted her head and studied me again.

"I can cook well enough to survive on the road, but when there's a home, I expect a warm meal," I said, not caring if I sounded like an ass. I was hoping she'd rescind her offer and give me the excuse of leaving her annoying company.

"I bet you do. Should I spread my legs and moan for you while I'm at it?" she said without missing a beat, her lip curving to a sly grin.

My jaw dropped.

"I thought so." She turned and walked away, leaving me speechless. "You look like that type, but don't get any ideas. I have a knife next to my bed and I know how to carve a man up if you do."

I watched her until the sheet blocked her from my view. I'd never met a woman with such a mouth, other than those who satisfied my sexual cravings when I'd been on the road with the army. This woman didn't strike me as that type, but she had a mouth and an attitude that had me questioning what I was getting myself into.

ELOISE RETURNED with a pillow and blanket by the time I'd pulled out my bedroll and situated it on the floor of the tiny building. For someone who had lost her husband, she didn't seem emotional about me sleeping in the building he had once used for whatever hobby he'd taken up. And there was no sign that told me he'd used it for anything other than storage.

"So, your husband was a crafter?" I asked, trying to determine what he'd used the space for.

"Not really," she said, heading down the small path that led to a woodpile. "I need more logs cut for the upcoming winter. I cut a few, but the axe is heavy, and I suppose my arms are too weak."

"That's because you're a woman," I said, lifting the axe easily and flexing my hand over the handle.

"You are something," she muttered. "It's a wonder there isn't a line of women outside my door waiting for you to marry them."

"That's funny," I said, ignoring the sarcasm that had laced her words. "If you must know," I swung the axe, splitting the log in front of me in one swipe, "I've had my share of women, and most would kill to be my wife."

She snorted. "And cook for you, raise your babies, rub your feet, and warm your cock?"

Again, my mouth fell, the axe almost slipping from my grasp. "How did you ever land a husband with that mouth? Is this a brothel, and you're hiding the whores somewhere?"

Her laugh was wicked and twisted its way into me like a snake coiling around its prey. I wasn't sure what to make of my reaction to that sound or the way her eyes sparkled with humor.

"Cut me some wood and stop thinking about whores," she said, still laughing as she made her way back to the house. "I'll go do my womanly duties and make you some supper."

Shaking my head, I returned to chopping. The entire time, I couldn't take my mind off the feisty silver haired woman in the house. By dusk, I'd made it through the entire pile and hauled it over to where a smaller pile of cut wood sat. Eloise peeked her head from the back of the house, eyeing my work as I wiped the sweat from my brow.

"Not bad. Come clean up and have some roast chicken."

I followed her into the house, where she had a bowl of clean water and a bar of soap out for me to clean up. Rinsing my face, I caught her watching me from the corner of her eye as she chopped some fresh carrots. She'd set a towel aside for me and I rubbed my face dry, glancing around the house. The furnishings were minimal: a small wooden table with two chairs, a lone chair near the hearth which burned with a low flame, a small, cushioned seat near it. A door led to another room where I suspected the bedroom was, but I couldn't confirm from where I stood.

Eloise placed the carrots on the table and motioned for me to sit, giving me a side glance as she brought a pitcher over and poured us both a glass of something that smelled of lemons.

"I presume you prefer ale, but I have nothing of that sort here, so my lemon brew will have to suffice," she said as I sat, thinking it odd to be sharing dinner with a woman I didn't know. I shared beds with women I didn't know, but this somehow felt more intimate, as strange as that seemed.

She took her seat with some hesitation, her eyes guarded as she tore a piece of meat from her chicken leg.

"So, chicken?" I said, trying to make conversation even though I really wanted to avoid it.

"Wild," she said, between chews. "They roam the woods behind my house."

I reached for my drink, trying to chew the overcooked piece of what should have been tender dark meat. The blast of lemon in my mouth erased the torturous experience, leaving a pleasant, cool sensation on my tongue.

"You catch wild chicken?" I asked, looking into my cup and trying to determine what the concoction was.

"Catch, feather, skin, and cook," she said, chomping another piece before grabbing a carrot.

I eyed her over my drink.

"And don't say that's a man's job," she grumbled.

Lowering my cup, I gave her a smirk. "I would, but since even I could roast this meat better, I'm inclined to say the hunting offsets the cooking skills."

She pouted her lips, lowering her fork. "You don't like my cooking?"

"My horse could do better," I teased, enjoying the flare of her nostrils and noticing how the blue in her eyes held a myriad of hues that seemed to shift with her mood. I found it beguiling. "But this drink more than makes up for the tasteless chicken. What did you call this?"

I took another swig, watching her over the rim. She appeared caught off guard until she finally said, "Lemon brew. It's common to my homeland."

"You're not from Troniere?" I asked, noting the sadness that flashed across her features.

"No," she replied, dropping her eyes and stabbing a piece of meat. "My husband and I moved here a few years ago." She brought the piece to her mouth, chewing exaggeratedly. "It really is bad, isn't it?" she asked, grimacing.

"It's a wonder you haven't starved up here."

She dropped her fork and sat back. My eyes took her in once more, the soft skin below the jagged scar, the pert mouth with lips that held a natural stain, the creases that belied her older age, and the thick silver hair that emphasized it. I never turned my sights on older women, but there was something about her that intrigued me, no matter how she had annoyed me earlier.

"I'm sure staring at women with that look gets them into your bed, but don't expect it to get you into mine," she said sharply, crossing her arms as her eyes darkened. The move pushed her breasts up, ones I hadn't taken notice of before but could now see were not as small as her dress made them out to be.

"I don't bed smart-mouthed women. I prefer to use their mouths for other things." I brought my elbows to the table, waiting for her to be taken aback like most women would, but secretly hoping she would surprise me again as she had earlier. I didn't understand why I was looking forward to a snarky comeback or why this woman piqued my interest so. She was nothing like any woman I would have ever approached.

She lifted a brow, and I could see the twitch of her lips as she held back her smile. "So you prefer your cock to keep them silent?"

Good gods, she was something. Chuckling, I replied, "Exactly."

Rising, she took her plate to the counter and rummaged in a small cabinet before returning with a knife, fresh bread, and a jar of jam.

"The baker in town makes delicious bread and his wife makes the jam from her garden. I hear she likes to be kept silent, like you prefer."

I eyed her as she sliced a piece of the bread, slathered it with the berry jam, and walked away. "Don't stay out too late. I expect you up at dawn to help me with the house," she continued as she made her way to her room. She didn't bother turning back to me. Instead, she shut her bedroom door, leaving me to my thoughts.

Sitting back, I wondered about the strange woman who had let me into her life. She didn't know me, yet she was comfortable enough to have me in her home and leave me there while she was in her room, likely stripping out of her dress and into her nightclothes. The thought gave me an unexpected mix of desire and curiosity. Shaking it off, I cut a slice of bread and chomped on it as I walked around her house, trying to get a sense of who Eloise was and why her sharp comebacks had me irritated and hard at the same time.

There was nothing personal in her home, nothing that told me who she was or why she couldn't cook but could kill and prepare a wild chicken or why she had no qualms about leaving a complete stranger in her home. Rubbing my hand over my face, I figured maybe it was simply how the people in this town were. It didn't matter. I would be gone in a few days.

I grabbed another slice of bread, adding some jam this time, and took the cup of lemon brew with me as I left the home and made my way to my sleeping quarters. Staring down at my bedroll, I questioned if I'd be more comfortable sleeping on the ground than in this sorry excuse for a room. With a sigh, I gulped the rest of my drink and saddled up my horse, thinking a few mugs of ale and the attention of a woman would be a pleasant distraction from the bossy woman in the house.

THE ALE WAS smooth as it coursed down my throat and the barmaid eyed me. This was a younger one, her breasts spilling over her dress and a swish to her walk that told me she had a body I wanted to indulge in. But by the time she made her way back to my table, her devious smile telling me she'd easily let me have my way with her, I'd lost my desire to indulge. My mind had wandered back to Eloise, and it ruined all thoughts of spending the night letting this woman worship me because I couldn't stop questioning why Eloise wasn't doing the same. If anything, she seemed annoyed with me, the same reaction Beatrice had always had to me. But with Beatrice I'd ignored it, needing to conquer her whether or not she wanted me to. It bothered me, however, that Eloise wasn't throwing herself at me like all the other women did. And I didn't have that same urge to conquer her like I had with Beatrice. This was different. Like I wanted something else, something more, and I couldn't put my finger on what it was about her that brought that out in me.

"Tell me about the widow at the end of town," I said to the barmaid.

With a lift of her brow, she replied, "I didn't think talking was what you wanted to do when you were devouring me with your eyes."

"I'm no longer in the mood. What can you tell me about her?"

She pursed her lips, disappointment in her eyes before saying, "Not much to tell. She and her husband moved here a few years ago. Quiet folk. They kept to themselves until the night of the attack when he died." She leaned over the table, her breasts tempting me as she whispered, "There were bodies all over that property. Seems to me no normal man could fight off that many men unless he had help."

Creasing my brows, I tried to understand what she was implying. "How many men attacked them?"

"They found eight bodies and that of her husband. She was covered in blood. Said it was his, but...I don't know. There's something strange about her. Nobody is that quiet and nobody lives that far from town unless they've got secrets to hide."

I gave her my thanks and paid my tab, leaving a tip for her time and information. My interest was even more piqued now. Only someone trained could fend off a band of eight men. The odds were too against any normal man. I'd been in the army the whole of my adulthood and I wasn't certain I could hold my own against that many men at once, unless they were complete imbeciles.

So what was Eloise hiding? Had her husband been an army man? Maybe a deserter like I now was, given that I wasn't dead, as everyone back home thought. Or was there more to Eloise than she showed? A reason for that scar on her face, a reason she could kill and skin wild animals for food.

As I squeezed into my inadequate sleeping space, my mind tried spinning the different scenarios, returning each time to the fact that Eloise was a mystery I wanted to unravel. When sleep finally came to me, images of the past filled my dreams, along with falling rose petals and flashes of the mouthy woman who had aroused more than my curiosity.

CHAPTER THREE

ELOISE

Resting my head against the door, I questioned if this had been a mistake. I'd let a man stay on my property and then invited him into my house. A man I didn't know and one I wasn't sure I could trust. There was something about Garret that spurred my interest, like the way his smirk stirred butterflies in my stomach and the brown shade of his eyes, which leaned toward the color of a turning leaf in fall. He was massive, with muscles that were bigger than my head, and I'd tilted my neck to see him clearly. If he'd wanted to hurt me, he could have crushed me in his powerful hands.

I'd watched him as I'd fixed the food, unable to take my eyes from the flexing of each muscle until I reminded myself that the man was a chauvinistic pig. I didn't have to know him to see that. His comments held nothing back, and I considered sending him away just for the assumption that I would wait on him hand and foot. I had enjoyed the look of shock when I'd snapped back with my sassy comments. It wasn't something I did often, nor did I usually use that kind of language, but the longer I lived on my own, the more natural it had become.

Nilan had encouraged it...before I'd lost him. I'd scrubbed the stains of his blood from the floor in front of the hearth for days, trying to convince myself to run. To leave like he'd told me to in his last breath. But I didn't know where to go and I was tired of running.

I heard Garret walk around the house and held my breath as he reached my door. Had I read him wrong? Time seemed to stand still, my lungs burning, my muscles so tense they ached. But he moved away, my breath releasing as I heard the door close behind him. I slid to the floor, hating how weak I'd been in that moment, and trying to call on the strength I now wore as a shield every day. I stared at my hands, seeing the callouses, the rough skin that the past years had hardened, and missing their softness.

Pushing myself from the floor, I removed my dress, changing into my nightdress. I released the spell that covered the truth, running my hands over the skin below the illusion of scars that forced men's eyes from me. All but Garret, who seemed to see past those scars, his eyes not judging or avoiding them. I combed my hair out, letting my fingers drift through it and remembering when it had been so long that it had cascaded across the floor. The strands had fallen away, scattered on the wind with the life I'd known, one I could never return to.

With a sigh, I climbed into bed, closing my eyes to the past and thinking of the man I'd let into my life and hoping I could keep my secrets from him.

I heard Garret ride off a short time after and a strange sensation like jealousy slithered through me when I thought he was likely leaving for a drink and a woman to warm his bed. It seemed assumptive of me, but he looked like that kind of man. It had been a long time since a man had touched me. I hadn't indulged since Nilan's death. There wasn't anyone worth bringing into my life, and it was too dangerous to even think about. Each day brought another sense of relief that no one had come for me yet, but the fear of it lingered strongly so that it permeated every part of my day.

I squeezed my eyes harder, trying to shut the memories of the past out and the worry of the present. Trying not to think of the handsome stranger who'd sat so comfortably at my table as if he'd always been a part of my life.

The sound of Garret's horse returning woke me, the pitch black of night telling me it was late. I buried my face in my pillow, aggravated that I cared if a man I didn't even know stayed out late and had sex with whomever was willing in town. From the looks of him, I could name a few who wouldn't hesitate to take him for a ride.

Cursing myself for the thought, I laid in my bed, trying to go back to sleep but failing. I wondered if he was drunk or if he'd satisfied his male appetites in town. Again, envy snaked through me, and I shoved it away, annoyed that it was even present. This man meant nothing to me, and I knew it was simply the male attention I'd grown accustomed to with Nilan that I craved. Garret wasn't the type I should have even thought about, not with his expectations of what a woman should be. I rolled my eyes and sat up, cursing my inability to sleep.

The moon was bright, adding a sheen to my room, and my eyes fell upon the few pieces of jewelry I'd had on the night we'd run. I left them out as a reminder of my past, to not forget where I came from. I missed my life, but living on my own had changed me, making me value the freedom I now had and the woman I'd become. With a sigh, I flopped back into my pillow, eventually slipping to sleep, the scent of rose petals and the touch of golden magic permeating my dreams.

I WOKE JUST BEFORE DAWN, dressing hastily and applying the façade of age that I'd carried for three long years. The morning air held a chill, and I bustled out to grab some firewood, spying the open door to the small cabin where Nilan had stored his weapons and where Garret's large feet stuck out. It was a sight that had me laughing and questioning if other parts of him were just as large. I felt the blush fill my cheeks and looked away, grabbing two pieces of firewood and hurrying back into the house.

I stoked the fire and sat on the floor before it, losing myself to memories that Garret's appearance had stirred. It made little sense that he should have had that influence, but I supposed having another human to talk to reminded me of the days when it was more than just me. Before my life had turned to chaos. I touched the spelled scar on my face, wishing for the day when I no longer had to hide, when I could live freely, but this was as free as I thought I'd ever be.

As dawn lit the world more, I rose and headed out, hoping Garret would be awake but finding him still snoring away. I peeked in on him, my eyes widening when I saw he wore no shirt. He'd unhooked the top button of his pants, and I followed the trail from them up to the muscles that lined his chest. I had the urge to run my hands over those muscles, then down his muscular arms. A scar sat on the inside of his bicep, dark like an infection had festered there at one point. I dragged my eyes away and trailed his chest again, turning quickly when I saw the large bulge in his pants. Shit, he was bigger than Nilan, but I should have expected that since he was such a massive presence.

I walked away quickly, shaking the thought out of my head and reminding myself that the man had probably used some woman the night before after drinking his way through the night. He wasn't the kind of man I wanted around for long, and the sooner he was gone, the better. I was fine on my own and I'd been doing just fine without a man around. I glanced back, looking at his feet with the socks that had holes in them. He really did need a wife. He looked like the needy kind of man. Not one I would ever want because I didn't want men like that. I didn't want their possessiveness or their protectiveness. I didn't need their demands and their expectations. Especially a man like him.

I picked the eggs from the few hens I kept, convincing myself that I was strong and capable, all the while knowing a part of me missed being coddled and spoiled. That I missed being treated like someone special, missed being loved. But those were things of the past and they weren't who I was now. I'd lost that woman and there was no room for her to return, no matter how she wanted to.

As I rounded the front of the house, intent to trim some flowers from my garden, the baker's wife walked up the lane. I brushed my loose strands of hair back, feeling the need to look presentable as her heavy stare judged my disheveled appearance.

"Delphine," I greeted her. "What brings you this far from town so early?"

I really didn't have to ask. She was being nosy about my boarder, always flirting with men, even when she had a devoted, attentive husband. Her attempts to seduce Nilan in the time we lived here were overt and embarrassing. I could only imagine what lengths she'd go to for a taste of the handsome beast of a man with the big brown eyes and thick auburn hair. I bit my cheek, hating how that thought had invaded my mind.

"I brought you a loaf of honey bread with some fresh berry jam." She handed me the basket, surveying the yard and the house.

"I still have plenty, but thank you for the kind gesture. I was intending to go into town on the morrow," I replied, hoping she would leave. I wasn't much for talking, preferring the solitude of my life to the gossip and chatter of the villagers.

"With your new guest, I thought you might need more. I heard he's a large man and men like that need to be fed well."

"I'm feeding him well enough." That hadn't come out the way I'd intended, and she lifted her brow.

"Where is your guest?" She strained her neck, looking toward the house.

"He's staying in the outer shed and still sleeping. Can I get you some coin for your kindness?" *Please leave*, I wanted to add, as the anxious feeling I knew too well crept into my chest.

"Outside?" she asked, trying to move around me.

"I'd prefer you not wake him. He was out late."

That brow lifted further, my head throbbing as my irritation grew. "He was at the tavern. I don't know if he was out fucking anyone, but if he were fucking me, I'd gladly tell you if that's what you're curious about, Delphine." I put my hands on my hips, the basked thumping against my leg.

She brought her hand to her chest, her eyes wide. "I would never...and please don't use that language, Eloise. The men don't like—"

"Gods, Delphine. I don't care what the men like. I'm not interested in bedding any of them, nor inviting any into my bed. If my language offends them, I will gladly go into town and tell them what I think of their opinion."

Her lips pursed, and I knew I'd gone too far.

With a sigh, I told her, "Stay here," and hurried into the house, placing the basket on the table. I emptied it, then placed the eggs I'd gathered earlier into it. Rushing back out, I spied her creeping further toward the back of the house.

"Here," I said, trying not to laugh when she jumped. I handed her the basket. "Take these to your husband for his baking. They're fresh, picked just this morning."

She peered into the basket.

"Thank you for thinking of me and bringing the bread and jam. The berry is my favorite." I was trying my best to be polite, especially after shocking her.

She thinned her lips before saying, "A lot of strangers have been in town and passing through for the festival. I would be careful out here all alone, perhaps keep your boarder here until the travelers have returned home."

I furrowed my brow, wondering why she cared. She barely spoke to me anytime I went into town. "Is there something I should be concerned about?"

That anxious pounding started in my chest again, the air in my lungs thinning. I squeezed my hands, hoping it would pass.

She moved closer, her voice low. "A couple passing through yesterday told my husband of a disturbance in Sirak. A husband came home to find his wife gone, taken, the house in shambles." My legs shook, my knees threatening to give out. "They found her the next day." Her eyes darted around as she leaned even closer to me. "Dead," she whispered like the killer would jump out and grab her if she spoke too loudly. I swallowed, the spit sticking in my throat. "With so many strangers in town and on the road, you should take care."

I didn't know what to say. The act of kindness was in contrast to how she usually behaved toward me.

She tucked the corners of the towel around the eggs and moved the basket further up her arm so it sat in the crook of her elbow.

"Best to keep your boarder from leaving you alone until the festival travelers have all gone. But be sure to send him into town to see me," she added, her serious expression turning as her eyes lightened. "I have some special jams I keep in the house and I'd be delighted to give him something sweet."

Even with her change in demeanor, my tension didn't fade. "Tell your husband I said good morn, Delphine. And perhaps you should give him something sweet instead."

Her smile hung unflatteringly on her face before she gave me a last look up and down and walked back down the lane to where her horse and buggy waited. It was a pity, her husband doted on her, giving her everything he could afford, attention other wives didn't get, and she looked everywhere but at him.

I turned back to the small garden of flowers that lined the front and sides of the house. Dropping to my knees, I pulled the clippers from my skirt and snipped a few of the pink roses, my finger pricking on the thorns. I brought my finger to my mouth, sitting back and missing the thornless roses that grew at home. I could almost smell their scent and see the fields that covered the land like an ocean of crimson. It was the only color that bloomed in Bira.

I brushed the thought away and rose, taking the flowers with me, my mind returning to Delphine's words. Sirak was a few towns south of us, far enough away for my worry to be minimal, but that didn't mean my nerves weren't on edge. The familiar tingling in my chest worked its way down my limbs and into my hands as I tried to fight the oncoming attack. Leaning over, I rested my hands on my legs, trying to steady my breathing. I'd been getting better at controlling the panic that would creep into my body like a predator ready to pounce. The months without Nilan to help me calm had forced me to grapple with it myself, something I'd never had to do since they'd entered my life like the strike of a snake, embedding its fangs into me and refusing to let go. My brother had called them fear's touch when we'd been younger and he would hold me through them. Nilan had called them weakness. Whatever they were, they were always unwelcome, and I'd yet to conquer them.

As the sensation passed, I picked the fallen roses back up, careful to avoid the thorns and trying not to notice the way they shook in my hands. Whatever had happened in Sirak had nothing to do with me. But no matter how I continued to tell myself that, I couldn't shake the unsettled sensation that had crawled into my bones and screamed for me to run.

CHAPTER FOUR

GARRET

Something was bumping my foot, and I shoved it away, grumbling, "Leave me be woman, I told you I wasn't in the mood," before realizing I hadn't bedded the barmaid.

"Well, you'd better get in the mood, or you'll be sleeping on the road tonight."

I sat up, wiping the sleep from my eyes and running a hand through my messy hair. Eloise had her hands on her hips, her silver hair sparkling in the early rays of the sun.

Giving her a smirk, I said, "I don't think you want me in the mood." I was hoping she'd come back at me like she had the previous night and hit me with a snarky remark. I didn't know why I enjoyed the banter between us so much.

Her eyes perused my bare chest, a slight pink hue filling her cheeks.

"And why would that be?" she asked after a few moments of silence.

My smile grew as I anticipated her response to my next words. "Because you couldn't handle me, Eloise. But if you'd like to try, I might be willing to give you a taste of me if it means I'll be sleeping in your bed and not the road."

Her mouth fell open, and I noted how cute she looked with her pink cheeks and gaping mouth.

"You will be sleeping right where you are, and I can guarantee I won't be tasting anything you have to offer."

I let out a hearty laugh as she walked away, her skirts swishing in an aggravated fashion. I should have followed to convince her how wrong she was, but I didn't want to upset the witty rapport we were building. Maybe I should have looked to older women earlier if this was what they offered.

Pulling my boots on, I went behind the shed and relieved myself. As I came back around, pulling my shirt over my head, I saw her climbing the vines along the side of the house. I stopped, staring at how she swiftly clambered up them with no trouble and hoisted herself onto the roof. Who was this woman? I rubbed my eyes, thinking maybe the ale had gone to my head from the night before, but she was still there, tentatively poking at a loose tile.

"Do all your socks have holes in them?" she called down to me, not looking up.

I glanced at my feet, saying, "I haven't found the right woman to darn them yet."

"Pfft, are you sure you're looking for a woman and not a servant?"

I'd made my way over to the vines and was yanking on them to see if they'd hold my weight. "Aren't they the same?"

She remained silent, and I peered up to see her poke her head over the side of the house.

"What is it they teach you men these days?"

"That we need a good woman to settle down with," I answered with a shrug.

"Finally, a decent answer," she muttered, turning back to her prodding.

"One who can wait on us hand and foot and bear us children. Are you still young enough for that?"

A strange squawk came from the roof. It was a mix of a growl and a confounded scream.

"Are you all right up there?" I asked.

"I will be once I'm over the urge to strangle you," she muttered, backing her way down the vines with the same precision she had shimmied up them.

I watched, unable to take my eyes from the view she offered me up her skirts. I arched my brow upon seeing the bare legs above her short boots that led to an equally bare ass.

"Do you not have any panties on?" I teased, trying to ignore the way my length twitched at the sight.

"Why you!" she reached back and pulled her skirts around her legs, the move throwing her off balance. Her other hand slipped, and she fell. Without hesitating, I moved under her, catching her in my arms and pulling her in against me, fear hammering my chest that she'd be hurt.

Her arms flew around my neck, her blue eyes meeting mine. An unfamiliar sensation flittered through me, along with a desire to keep her in my arms. Her lips parted, her mouth perfectly poised for a kiss, until she said, "Is your hand on my ass, Garret?"

I squeezed my fingers, enjoying the soft flesh within them. "Damn, I think it is."

She tried to look indignant, which was the normal response to such an unintended situation, but I detected the tug at her lips as she fought her smile.

"It's not a bad ass considering your age," I said. She pushed at my chest, and I released her, letting my hand slide along her thigh until it was hooked beneath her knee. She teetered and fell against me, her eyes searching mine for just a moment.

"I'm not old," she groused. "And I'm certainly no older than you."

Letting her leg go, and missing the feel of her supple skin, I gave her a coy grin. "I beg to differ," I said, pulling a strand of her silver hair out and letting it slide through my fingers. It was soft, and I detected a scent of rose petals from it.

She swatted my hand away, smoothing the loose strand back into her bun. It was the same style she'd worn her hair in yesterday, but it didn't seem right for her.

"It's always been that color," she muttered, dropping her eyes.

"Really? Silver like that?"

"No, bla—" she started, but stopped mid word.

"Black?" I eyed her hair again, detecting no color but silver.

"It used to be black," she said hurriedly, turning from me and abruptly changing the subject. "There are a few tiles on the roof that need fixing. I'd like you to work on them while I go hunt for today's meal."

"More overcooked wild chicken?" I asked, following her with my eyes as she disappeared into the house without answering.

Maybe I'd pushed it by calling her old or by insulting her cooking again. It confounded me that a woman didn't know how to cook. I'd never met one who didn't.

She emerged a few minutes later with a bow and some arrows, tucking a dagger into the waist of her dress. I dropped the hammer I'd found and stared at her.

"You were serious."

"Maybe if you stopped assuming women were only good in the kitchen, you'd have believed me," she said, marching past me.

"They're good for more than that. Sewing, cleaning, raising kids, fucking."

She shot me a look as I followed her path.

"What are you doing, Garret?"

"I'm following you. This I have to see."

She huffed but didn't respond.

"The patch of wood beyond the river is the best place to hunt," she said, pointing to the trees in the distance. It looked to be a good distance, and I now understood why she was getting her horse from the small stable.

As we saddled our horses, I asked, "Did your husband do the hunting before?"

"We would go together. He didn't like leaving me alone..." She trailed off, and I figured the memory must have triggered some emotion. He'd only been gone six months.

"Yet here you are, all alone," I commented.

"Conceited, chauvinistic, and heartless," she said, mounting her horse. "You keep adding to that keeper list."

"I'm not heartless," I said, feeling attacked and trying to figure out what the other two words meant.

"But you're not denying the rest. Interesting."

This time, it was me glaring at her as she rode off. That witty banter had shifted ever since my comment about her cooking, and I missed it. We rode in silence, and I stole a glance at her, thinking once more that her hair didn't look natural the way she had it piled on her head. It seemed more like it needed to be free and wild.

"So the roof needs fixing. What other chores do you have for me today?"

"Did you go into town and drink last night?" she asked, as if I hadn't asked her a question.

"Yes. Why?"

"I'd prefer you didn't," she said as we followed a trail into the woods.

"What does it matter if I go to the tavern? A man has needs, after all."

Her narrowed eyes were hard when she peered at me, their blue dark and mysterious.

"Keep your womanizing and drinking to a minimum while you're staying with me. I don't want you bringing unwanted attention to my home."

She pulled her horse to a stop and dismounted, drawing an arrow from her quiver.

"How does my fucking and drinking bring attention to you? Are you joining?"

The daggers in her eyes were almost lethal, the darkness in them stirring a need in me. I wanted to touch that darkness and see what it brought me. Shaking away the thought, I waited for her to respond as I dropped from my horse.

I tethered him next to hers as she said, "I'm not joining anything and I don't give a damn if you fuck and drink." Once again, she caught me off guard with her language. "But you'll do it after you leave. And stop staring at me like that. Women swear where I come from, and fuck is a fun word to say." A bit of mischievousness glimmered in her eyes. "I slipped and said it in town one time, and one woman actually swooned and fainted."

"That's not unexpected. It's very unladylike to swear, and you seem to be quite adept at it."

She slowed down, and I followed her line of sight. A buck was grazing across from us, too far to notice our presence. Eloise stooped down and aimed. It seemed an odd position to take the kill, but I kept my eyes on the deer, sensing her let the arrow loose but not seeing it hit its mark.

"I'm unladylike because I have to be," she said, her words hushed. "And ladies can't do what I just did."

I gave her a funny look. "Miss your mark?"

"I did not miss my mark," she hissed, pointing away from the deer. There in the brush lay a rabbit with her arrow through its neck. A direct kill, but wasted on such small prey.

"Are you serious? That's a rabbit."

"That's dinner."

I grabbed her bow and an arrow. "I'll get us dinner. I'm not chewing on tough rabbit when I can have deer."

I aimed, nocking my arrow.

"No!" She tackled me, the arrow flying so far off its mark it landed in the tree, the deer fleeing.

Eloise collapsed on me as I hit the ground hard.

Anger burned through me like a searing heat, and I flipped her, hovering over her and pinning her arms.

"Don't you ever attack me again or you'll wish that arrow had hit me."

Her hair had freed from whatever she'd had it pinned up with and it lay in waves around her face. There were different depths to it, tempting me to run my fingers through it, but my anger stopped me.

"Don't threaten me. I'm not one of your defenseless damsels and I'll gut you so fast you'll wish the arrow had done the damage."

There was pressure under my rib, and I looked down to see her dagger aimed at inflicting pain. Peering back up at her, I raised my brow, impressed at how stealthy she was.

"You know how to use that thing?" I asked, relaxing but not moving.

Her eyes sparkled, the blue dancing in them. She'd had the dagger positioned perfectly, as if someone had trained her to kill. The arrow had hit so that the rabbit had a swift death, something that would have taken skill and training. I thought back to the story of the night her husband had died. Eight men had come for them. All eight had died, and she'd survived.

"Are you going to continue to stare at me or get off me so I can breathe?" she asked, taking me from my thoughts.

I rose from her, wondering why I noticed the absence of her warmth the moment I did. I offered my hand to help her up, but she swatted it away, hopping up gracefully and wiping the dirt from her dress.

"Don't touch the deer in this forest, Garret. I will kill you before I let you harm one." She stomped away to retrieve the rabbit, her silver hair flipping back and forth with her steps.

"What's so fucking special about a deer, other than how much meat we can get from it?"

Stopping abruptly, she swiveled toward me. "We? There is no we." There was fire in her eyes, and I wasn't sure what to make of my reaction to it. Women who weren't subservient and quiet never attracted me, but something about Eloise reached in and jerked me by the balls. She had a spirit I normally would have squashed, but with her, I wanted more of it. "You are here for a few days and then you'll move on to whatever it is you're seeking. You will not leave me with the repercussions of your greed."

She went back to stomping away from me, leaving me baffled about the mouthy woman who was stirring a part of me that had never wakened.

CHAPTER FIVE

GARRET

Dusk was slowly making its way to the horizon and for once, I was glad to see the end of the day. Eloise had worked me hard, her temper short after the incident in the forest. She was demanding and any other time, I would have walked away and continued my journey. I didn't know what it was about her that both rubbed me wrong and captured my interest. It was a conflict that hadn't resolved itself by the time I finished fixing her door.

"Looks good," she said, coming to stand next to me.

"I'm not much of a craftsman, but I'm happy with it."

"What is it you do, Garret?" she asked, brushing at a spot of dirt on her dress. It didn't seem worth her effort considering dirt covered her dress from the work she'd been doing in her garden.

Not thinking, I reached over and brushed my thumb over her cheek to clean off another spot. Her eyes searched mine as my thumb lingered, tracing the path of her scar until it met the corner of her eye.

We remained that way, both frozen until she reached up and

removed my hand, her fingers lingering on mine before she took a step back, the unexplainable moment lost.

Clearing my throat, I answered, another lie slipping easily from my lips. "I was in the army, but I retired after I served my time."

Her eyes perused me, her lips pursed. "You don't strike me as a soldier."

"No?" I said, raising my brow. "What do I strike you as?"

Crossing her arms, she brought her fist up and rested her chin on it while she thought. "I don't know," she said with a shrug.

"That's insightful," I noted, seeing the smile form on her lips, and liking how it warmed my chest.

"I do know that you stink." She put her fingers on her nose and waved her hand in front of her face. "Come inside and I'll warm some water so you can clean up."

"Will you be scrubbing me down?" I couldn't help asking.

Her lips thinned before she frowned. "I can make you clean up in the stream if you'd prefer."

I put my hands up in surrender. "I'll scrub myself."

Her laugh was like the hum of hummingbird wings, sweeping through me and weaving its way into that space that was slowly becoming hers. The profound truth of that realization almost knocked me off my feet as I watched her walk into the house. She glanced over her shoulder at me, giving me a questioning look, but I couldn't move as the reality of everything I'd ever searched for in a woman unraveled and reshaped to become the woman who stood there waiting for me.

"Garret?" she said, her voice sweet like the drops of honey my mother would give me as a child.

Shaking the thoughts and uncomfortable emotions from my head, I followed her in, not sure what to think of my revelation. I helped her build a bigger fire in the hearth, then went out to the stream to retrieve water. While it warmed above the flames, I sat at the table, throwing my boots off and propping my feet until she gave me a scolding look.

"Get those nasty things off my table," she said, washing her hands up in the small basin on the counter.

As I dropped them, grumbling about where I would stretch my legs, she wandered into her room. When she didn't return for a few minutes, my curiosity became too much and I peeked in, spying a bed with a worn quilt, a small vanity with a surprising array of jewelry on it, and in the corner, a mahogany wardrobe which she was currently bent over and rummaging through.

She emerged with a handful of men's clothing, jumping when she saw me.

"Did I say you could come into my room?"

"Don't get all prissy on me. You're not one of those women. You told me that yourself," I returned as she shoved the clothes into my hands.

"Nilan wasn't as big as you, but he was tall, so these should fit. Since he's no longer here to wear them, you might as well. Your socks are about to fall off your feet with all those holes."

I stared at the clothes of a man who had given his life protecting his wife, who had touched her and loved her long before she'd come into my life. I didn't know why the thought left me jealous, but envy knotted in my gut.

"The water should be done. I'll wait outside while you wash up, as long as you give me the same courtesy."

"Of course," I said more hastily that I normally would have because the opportunity to see a woman bathing was usually one I didn't pass up. But no matter how playful our remarks had been, I suddenly wanted to protect this woman, just as her husband had. Even if she didn't need it. And again, the reality of that desire to keep her safe was unsettling. I didn't care about other people, I never had. I'd put myself before everyone else, living only for my wants and desires so that it had cost me everything.

As I sat outside on her porch, squeezing the water from my

wet hair, I thought about the confused jumble of emotions and thoughts that were going through me. I couldn't control them and since that moment in the forest, they'd been constant. This woman had done something to me that I couldn't explain. I'd only known her for two days and I barely knew her, but there was a connection along with a sensation I could no longer deny. No matter how distinctly different she was from every woman I'd ever been with or wanted.

I leaned back against the wall, contemplating if I should just pack up and leave. Run away while I could before these emotions grew to something I couldn't contain. I'd only intended to stay a few days. Maybe moving on now would be wise.

The door opened, and I glanced up to see Eloise in the light that poured from the house. Her wet hair gave it a black appearance that enhanced her blue eyes. She'd changed into a purple dress, the sleeves short enough to leave her arms bare, and I noted the scars that lined her arms. That need to protect her from whatever had caused those scars screamed through me again. Rising, I had the urge to pull her into my arms and kiss her, because that's what I would have done to any other woman—assumed my dominance and assumed they wanted my kiss. But Eloise was different, and I knew she'd likely punch me if I did.

"What are you laughing at?" she asked, as I snickered at the thought.

"Myself," I answered, thinking how true it was.

I took her hand, and she squinted as she tried to figure out what I was doing. Letting my fingers trace the long, jagged scar on her arm, I asked, "Where did these come from?"

She jerked her arm from my hold, her demeanor changing. It wasn't anger; it was more like an uncomfortable, nervous reaction. "None of your business," she snapped, heading into the house.

Her abrupt attitude change left me miffed. It seemed a common thing with her, as if she had two personalities. Again, I thought of how her hair seemed more natural left down and how the scar on her face sat as if it weren't flush. My fingers twitched as I remembered how it had felt below them, rigid but not quite natural.

"What is it you're hiding, Eloise?" I dared.

She ignored me, motioning for me to help her with the tub of dirty water. Scowling, I took the other side and helped her carry it out, waiting for an answer that never came. When we'd emptied the water and placed the tub back in its resting spot, I grabbed her arm, stopping her from entering the house.

"Let go of me, Garret."

"Not until you tell me what you're hiding. Eight men came to this house for something, and your husband died protecting you, fighting eight men and killing them even though they had mortally wounded him. That's not something a normal man can do. And why eight? That's not a simple robbery. That was something more."

"Leave it be." She tried moving from my hold, but I wouldn't let her. I wasn't sure why I was pushing her, but I wanted to know the truth.

"No. Now tell me the truth."

She glared at me, her eyes dark. "Why don't you tell me what you're running from first? Why you're roaming the kingdoms, pretending like you're on a mission to see the world? What are you running from, Garret?" She spat the words as if they held venom in them, and I could sense the ire that was raging in her, just as it was in me.

"I don't have to tell you anything, Eloise."

"Then neither do I. You have your secrets, and I have mine."

I stepped closer into her space, seeing the conflict in her eyes, the flash of desire that clouded them. Her breaths were coming fast, and I could feel her heart pounding. My own was racing uncontrollably, and I wondered if she could hear it above hers. Loosening my hold on her arm, I brought my hand up and pushed her wet hair aside, wrapping my hand around her neck and bringing her closer to me. She didn't resist, her lips parting temptingly. They were so close to mine that I could smell the sweet scent of jam on her breath.

We remained there, our eyes locked, our bodies needy until I released her. The air filled my lungs again as I stepped back, trying to get a hold of my emotions.

"Keep your damn secrets," I muttered, walking away and questioning why I had when she'd looked more than willing to let me kiss her. "I'll leave in the morning."

I stormed off, not bothering to look back. The door closed like a dam, stopping the rampant flood of emotions she'd stirred in me. I saddled my horse and rode into town, turning the situation over in my head, running through all the options I had and all the reasons I needed to leave like I'd threatened. Eloise was tearing at a part of me I didn't recognize. A man attracted to the strength and fierceness in her, the fire that sat in her eyes, the wicked words that fell from her lips, the scars that sat upon her skin less subtle than the creases at the corner of her eyes. The way her silver hair glinted in the sunlight and shimmered in the moonlight.

She was everything I usually turned from but was now what I craved. Hitching my horse, I made my way into the tavern. I kept my head down, finding a spot in the corner. When the barmaid came over, I ignored her flirting, using the last of my coin to buy a bowl of stew and a few pints of ale. I had nothing left and no place to go but back to Eloise. Part of me questioned why I didn't find a woman to ease the frustration in my dick while the other cursed me for getting myself worked up over her.

When my coin was gone, I headed back to my small shed, determined to pack up and leave before dawn so I wouldn't have to see her again. I would run because that's what I did best. I wasn't a good guy, someone she could depend on, someone who would treat her right and protect her like I wanted to. I was the bad guy, the villain. And this wasn't some fairy tale. This was about me and my need for self-preservation, and I wasn't about to let Eloise crack that part of me.

I WAS LOADING my bed roll onto my horse, glad I'd tossed and turned enough to rise at dawn, when I heard Eloise's footfalls.

Sighing, I kept my focus on readying for the trip into Duntraik.

"The scars are a reminder of a past I have to forget," she said, her voice barely a whisper. "The reason for them is irrelevant except to know they remind me every day of what I lost and what I left behind."

I stopped, listening to her, but not quite understanding what she was trying to tell me.

"My history is convoluted and...it's not one I can share. Just like I believe yours is."

I glanced over my shoulder. Her eyes held nothing but sincerity, just as her words did.

"But," she continued, "I enjoy having you here. It's nice, and you're welcome to stay as long as we can leave our pasts where they belong. Behind us."

It was exactly what I wanted to do with my past. I dropped my head on the saddle, thinking about her offer. "I'm not a good man, Eloise," I admitted.

"Maybe you weren't, but that's not who I see. We all change, Garret. Whatever lies in your past, I don't need to know because I like the man you are today."

I looked back over my shoulder at her, unsure of what to say. Never had anyone said those words to me. Sure, I had my share of compliments from women who wanted me to sleep with them and from my best friend who gave them too frequently. My former best friend, who I was sure cursed me daily now...if he still lived.

"I'll leave it up to you," Eloise said, giving me a slight smile before she walked away.

"Will you leave your hair down if I stay?" I asked, uncertain why that had been my response when there were a dozen snide remarks I could have made before I rode away and retained my dignity.

I turned around, crossing my arms and seeing her halt in her tracks. She reached up without looking back at me and pulled the few pins she had haphazardly shoved in her hair to keep it in place. It released, falling like a waterfall over her back as she started walking again.

Chuckling, I decided it was worth taking a chance and finding out more about the mysterious woman who had worked her way into my mind and soul. And discovering if the version of me she saw was one I wanted to embrace. It was uncomfortable on my skin, as if it didn't belong, but perhaps I'd get used to being the good guy.

By the time she'd gone back inside, I'd unpacked my few belongings. Eyeing her bow and arrows that were resting on the side of the house, I knew she was planning on hunting again. I grabbed them and mounted my horse.

"You are not going hunting without me," she said, just as I was about to ride off.

"I am. You stay here and do whatever it is women do, and I'll hunt."

She put her hands on her hips and stomped her foot. "No."

"Yes. Are there any other animals to avoid besides deer?"

Her eyes went wide for a moment before her lips thinned.

"You're not changing my mind. This is my thing," I said, thinking of all the deer heads I had mounted in my home and wondering what she'd think if she knew how many had died at my hands.

"Fine, although I doubt you can shoot as well as I can."

"I can shoot just fine. Although maybe not as cleanly as you."

She made to protest, but I pulled the reins to let my horse know it was time to go.

"No deer and no fox," she blurted.

"Are you shitting me? No fox either? No wonder you're so skinny. So the only things I can hunt are the small rodents and wild chicken?"

"Boar is fine. They're nasty things."

"Damn right they are. Fuck, I'm going to have to gnaw on your dried chicken legs again tonight, aren't I?" I teased, liking that our playful banter was back again.

"You're not gnawing on anything of mine."

With a laugh, I directed my horse toward the river.

"Follow the deer. They will show you where to hunt. Just don't hurt them and please make clean shots!" she yelled as I rode away.

I shook my head, finding her rules humorous. Never had I hunted and avoided deer, but I didn't want to piss her off. Not that I had any reason to avoid pissing her off. I ran my hand through my hair, annoyed at the thought.

The ride to the forest's edge was long without Eloise by my side, and I pondered why I suddenly found riding by myself to be a tedious thing. Tethering my horse to a tree, I gave him a pat before heading into the forest, careful to leave markings with my knife so I could find my way back.

"Follow the deer," I mumbled, remembering Eloise's words. I thought of how she'd watched for the deer, then shot the rabbit, the deer not moving even though it had to have heard the arrow hit its target. Maybe an enchantment sat upon the forest. I'd heard tell of such things and after the situation with Beatrice, I knew there were things in this world that were unexplainable.

I leaned on a tree, wondering if Eloise had an explanation or if it was something to do with her past. If so, it would remain unexplained. I wouldn't push the conversation into her past again. We would leave it there just as we would leave mine. I searched the forest ahead, waiting for some sign of life and thinking about my past. Doing wrong was all I knew. The cheating, backstabbing, exaggerating. The pride, the women, the drinking. All were part of my identity, the man I knew, the one the people in my village knew. But that wasn't the man Eloise knew and what she'd seen she liked. I hadn't turned on my charm for her, exaggerated my prowess in the battlefield and in bed, hadn't taken advantage of the moments when we were close enough to read an invitation. I'd been me. Plain, uncomplicated. A man with no money, no job, no past, and no future. And she'd accepted me that way. The thought warmed my heart, giving me a comfort that settled in my chest.

Movement distracted me from my thoughts, and I spotted a magnificent buck gracefully walking through the trees ahead of me. It turned to me, and my fingers itched to pick up my bow and kill it, but my promise to Eloise weighed heavily and I stayed still as it appraised me. Those seconds seemed to last forever, and I vaguely wondered if it was looking into my soul, judging me. I held my breath, afraid to move until it returned to its path, walking out of my sight.

The breath filled my lungs again, and I stood, following its path just like Eloise had said to. After a few minutes, it stopped by a stream, dipping its head down and licking at the water as if I weren't there. I glanced around, looking for any sign of other creatures, but found none. I was getting frustrated when the water rippled across from the buck. I dared to move closer, seeing a school of fish circling near to the edge.

"I'll be damned," I mumbled. I lowered the bow, pulling an arrow from my quiver. Aiming, I released the arrow, watching as it plunged into the largest fish, piercing it all the way through, then hitting a second fish. The school swam away, leaving the two for me to harvest. Lowering the bow, I peered over at the buck. It lifted its head and wandered off. I stared at it until it was gone. I wasn't sure what to make of what had happened, but I would take it for what it was and reap the benefits. Pulling my boots off, I waded into the water and retrieved the spoils of my hunt, content that we'd be having a delicious meal of plump fish for our dinner. The anticipation of showing Eloise what I'd done sent a flood of excitement rushing through me, and I didn't care that it wasn't from selfish pride but from the thought of the smile it would bring to her face.

CHAPTER

SIX

ELOISE

rubbed my arms as I watched Garret ride off. I'd tossed and
turned the night before. His questions, the touch of his
hands on my arms, and his closeness stirred feelings in me I
wasn't ready for. Ones that made no sense, considering I didn't
know the man, and he'd only been in my life for two days. But
there was something I couldn't deny building in me, and every
time his chestnut eyes cast upon me, a strange flitter tickled my
stomach.

Maybe I should have let him leave and been done with all of
this...whatever this was. I'd had my chance, watching him from
my window while he'd been packing up his horse. But something
stopped me, an instinct that crept below my skin and buried itself
there. And so, I'd asked him to stay, relief slipping in to sooth the
discomfort the instinct had given me when he agreed. His one ask
was that I let my hair down.

It seemed an odd request, but it was one I gladly accepted. I
hated binding my hair up the way they expected women to, especially married women. I liked my hair loose, like I'd worn it at

home, unless I had it braided. Only when my mother expected me to be present and respectable, when I was on display and reminded of the caged life I led, did I have to wear it up. But that had been before the restrictions, before my freedom had slowly shriveled, my hair growing with every day that passed without the touch of the grass beneath my feet or the breeze along my skin. My days spent wondering why that was my fate, why the gods had intended it to be so.

Walking back to the house, I fingered a few strands of my hair as I thought of Garret and wondered if he'd respect my wish about hunting. It wasn't a wish; it was a necessity. Deer were rare in our kingdom and their appearance signified a special favor from the gods. Not as food, but as a sign. The buck that wandered that forest had appeared when we'd settled here, leading us to food on each hunt, granting permission for us to take the lives of the smaller creatures that roamed those woods. Only with the blessing of the gods could I harm another. Before my life had changed so drastically, I'd only eaten meat on the rare occasion the stag had shown itself to our hunters. When Nilan and I had run, the stag had appeared as if the gods were watching us. I had to wonder why they hadn't been watching me before my life had taken a turn.

It was still early, but I needed to run into town, and I knew the mercantile shop would be open. Grabbing some coins from where I kept them hidden in the bottom of my wardrobe, I pulled my hair back up, styling it so I wouldn't shock any of the towns-folk. They already looked at me suspiciously, steering clear of me when I went into town. A few, like Delphine, made idle chatter to cover their curiosity about me.

Garret would be gone for a few hours, so I'd have time to pick up some supplies. Delphine's words repeated through my head the entire ride into town so that by the time I walked into the mercantile shop, my hands were stiff from gripping them so tight and my heart was racing. Every word I spoke while the shopkeeper exchanged pleasantries came out hollow. As he loaded the few items into my saddlebag for me, the need to hurry home was rushing through me like a thunderstorm. My hands were tingling, numbness shifting through my limbs down to my feet.

"Are you all right?" he asked, giving my horse a gentle pat once he finished.

"I'm fine, George. Delphine visited yesterday and told me of the trouble in Sirak. I suppose it just left me shaken."

He furrowed his brow. "Now she shouldn't have gone worrying you about that, Eloise."

"No, she should have. I need to be extra careful with Nilan gone."

He shook his head, and I could see how he wanted to do what everyone else in town always did and remind me there were men in town who could take care of me. I tried not to roll my eyes as he said just that.

"I'm doing fine on my own—" I started.

"What about that fellow you took on? I hear he was in the tavern last night. Is he causing you any trouble?"

Trouble? That was the perfect word for what Garret was causing. Stirring trouble in my mind and working my body up with each flex of his muscle and smirk he threw me.

"No, no trouble at all. He's been a big help."

He looked around, then stepped closer to me, a little too close, and if it hadn't been George, the gentle shopkeeper who wore a fresh flower that his wife tucked into his apron every morning, I would have said something. But he was harmless and sweet.

"Sirak isn't the only trouble," he said in a hushed tone.

My mouth went dry, the tremble in my hands increasing.

"Soldiers from Duntraik have been crossing the border. There have been several sightings of them."

"Duntraik?" I said, hearing how my voice wavered.

He nodded. "Those men who killed Nilan. They—"

"Thank you, George," I said, climbing quickly on my horse, not wanting to hear any more.

"Eloise, please be careful. If you think that man who's boarding with you is a good man, keep him there. At least until all this passes over and the festival is past."

"What good is a man going to do? It didn't help Nilan. It won't help any other man." I turned my horse toward home, saying, "Tell your wife I said hello and thank you again, George."

I didn't wait for his reply, urging my horse forward, my body quaking too much to do more than hold on. The entire ride, I couldn't clear my mind and by the time I arrived home, my panic was so high that I had to lay my head on my horse for fear I would pass out.

"Control it, El," I told myself, taking big breaths to calm the fear that gripped me.

I wanted to cry, to pack everything and flee. But I couldn't. I had nowhere to go, no one to help me, and I was tired of running. This was the first time I'd taken root anywhere for more than a few months and as much as it wasn't home, it was all I had.

Sliding from my horse, I held on to the saddle, waiting for my legs to stop shaking. I had to be strong, to be the fighter Nilan had trained me to be. Garret would be back soon and the thought of him calmed my nerves. I took a few minutes to breathe through the panic, soothing the tingling, the numbness that sat in my chest as the rest of my body vibrated.

I walked my horse to the stable once I put my packages in the house, the entire time wondering why the thought of Garret had done what nothing else could—it had soothed the fear. He would be back soon and as I unpacked the few staples I'd bought, I fingered the sugar, thinking I'd make him something special. I'd never cooked well. No one had ever taught me. It wasn't something expected of me. The only things I could make well were the two things my mother had taken the time to share with me: lemon brew and rose drops.

With Garret on my mind, I went about making him rose drops. They were something I hadn't made in too many years, since the last sliver of tenderness my mother had shown me. Rolling the dough out in paper-thin strips, I cut it into petal shapes before coating each with a layer of sugar. I crushed two rose petals and scattered them over the sugar before warming the candied petals with a touch of my magic. They turned a rich shade of red as they curled into shape. Gently, I took the petals and formed two rose buds. When they were ready, I sprinkled more sugar onto the petals, letting a small dusting of magic trickle from my fingers, just enough to seal in the sweetness. Then I laid them out on the counter, letting the magic take hold as my eyes glazed over. I wiped my arm over the tears, knowing I couldn't let them fall, that I had to leave the memories where they'd been, lying dormant and buried with the life I'd fled.

With a heaving sigh, I brushed my hands over my apron and pushed the tears back in their cage. I turned my back on the petals, knowing they would need time for the magic to work its way into the treats before I could share them. As I hung my apron, I questioned why it had been important for me to make them for Garret. I bit my lip, my hand in stasis on the hook where I'd been placing the apron, not understanding why my chest twisted with the thought of him or why I wanted to see the glint in his brown eyes and the curve of his sly smile. My insides grew warm, and I shook my head, baffled by the strange effect he was having on me.

Going about the remaining morning chores, I tipped my head to the morning sun, thinking it was perfect weather for the last day of the fire festival. Nilan had taken me when we'd first settled in town, but he'd kept me guarded, not allowing me to enjoy myself like I'd wanted. I'd seen the festivities every year when I'd been home, but never from the vantage point that festival goers had. Having Nilan take me had been memorable. As memorable as it could be with his hand on my elbow, guiding me too quickly to take in all the wonderful items the vendors offered.

But Nilan was no longer here to keep me from enjoying myself, and having a few moments to live free of the burdens that rested on my shoulders would heal my tired soul. It could prove risky, however, if there was anything behind the gossip I'd heard this morning. I rubbed my arms against the nerves that were still bouncing through my body. Perhaps I could convince Garret to accompany me, so I wouldn't have to travel alone. I brushed a few strands of my hair back, remembering how he'd requested I let my hair down. Unfastening it, I decided to ask him when he returned. It would be good to get away for a few hours and, although I could fend for myself, having him with me would ease my nerves some. He was a large man with muscles that warned other men to avoid stirring trouble with him. My fingers absently traced the air, following the path of muscles I'd seen on his chest as I contemplated how firm they would be to touch.

Shaking the image from my head, I returned to the rose drops, delicately placing them on a plate and hiding them in the cupboard. The sound of Garret's horse sent anticipation cartwheeling through me, and I imagined the sexy smirk he would throw me when he greeted me.

"Gods, Eloise. He's just a man," I scolded myself, noticing my cheeks grow hot.

For a moment, I worried he might not have heeded my warning about the deer. The thought had crossed my mind earlier in the morning, but with my focus on the rose drops, I'd forgotten about it. Now, it settled in my forethoughts, everything else set aside as I exited the house, brushing my hands on my skirts and praying he hadn't gone against my request. If he had, it wouldn't matter how many sexy grins he flashed me, because he would be my undoing in more ways than the pleasurable kind.

CHAPTER SEVEN

GARRET

I hopped from my horse, intent on showing my kill to Eloise. Excitement coursed through me, and I felt like a small boy again, bringing my mother the rose I'd plucked from the thorny vines outside our home. My hands had borne the wounds from the attempt, and she'd taken them in hers, kissing each one. The memory was one I cherished, my mother taken from me too soon, the moment then tainted as my father discovered my act of kindness and tore the rose from her hands, stomping it to tattered remnants below his boot. He'd dragged me back to those vines, shoving my small hands into them, the blood seeping from the wounds until he was satisfied he'd thoroughly punished me.

I shook the memory away, burying it back in the recesses of my mind with the others.

"You're back," Eloise said, and I turned to see her wiping her hands on the front of her dress. A flush stained her cheeks, enhancing the depth of her scars but also her beauty.

"I am. And I've brought us dinner." I held up the two fish.

Her smile was reward enough, and it erased the memories that had stirred moments earlier.

A look of relief accompanied it, and I wondered if she'd been worried I would betray her trust and bring home the prize buck I'd so wanted to kill. A pang of hurt ricocheted through my chest as she took the fish from me. I stood there while she continued into the house, contemplating my reaction and how that one thought had morphed my mood completely.

"I have an idea for today," she said, returning shortly after. "I had intended to make you climb to the roof and fix those loose tiles, but I think maybe we both deserve a break."

She was chatting away excitedly until she noticed I was still standing where she'd left me.

"What is it?" she asked, turning her attention to me.

How did I tell her the doubt she'd carried had left me wounded? I couldn't even explain it to myself. My reaction should have been a sharp retort, an insult on her frail woman-hood, anything but the weak emotion that sat in my chest.

"Nothing," I grumbled, finally moving and taking my horse by the reins to lead him to the stable.

"Don't put him away," she said.

I turned back to her, throwing her a questioning look.

"I have plans..." She suddenly seemed unsure of herself, and it juxtaposed the strength she usually carried. "What's wrong?" she asked.

"I said it's nothing. What plans do you have for me today?"

She studied me, her eyes intense. "Thank you," she said unexpectedly.

"For what?"

"For not harming the buck. For bringing us dinner."

"Yeah, well, I'm sorry you were sitting here stewing over it."

Her head snapped back as if I'd slapped her. She no longer looked unsure. The feisty woman I knew returned as she thinned her lips, her eyes narrowing.

"Is that what you're upset about? That I worried you might not heed my request?" Her hands went to her hips.

"I'm not upset," I spat.

"Oh yes, you are. We don't know each other, Garret. Not well enough to have complete trust. You need to earn that, especially with me."

There was a flash of something behind her eyes that I couldn't make out. A vulnerability that sat within her anger. And I questioned who had hurt her in the past that she hid from me. I wanted to ask her, to find out and drive my dagger through their heart. Gritting my teeth against the reaction, I replied, "No pasts, no trust. Got it."

Her jaw twitched, and I could see her irritation growing.

"Changing your mind about letting me stay?" I asked, giving my horse a pat and leading him away.

"Dammit, I'm not changing my mind. You're just being a bratty child."

I halted, my mood souring completely as I turned my head back to her and snarled, "Better than a weak female. Go clean the fish and make me something to eat."

Her fists bunched, and her teeth clenched so tight I could hear them grinding. I returned to walking, contemplating if I should have left like I'd intended, when something smacked the back of my head. Releasing the reins, I swirled to face her, spying the rock on the ground.

"Did you just hit me with a rock?" I asked, rubbing my head as my irritation transformed to ire.

"Yes, I did. It's better than the log I had in mind."

I gritted my teeth, trying not to grab her and smack her like I wanted.

"I was trying to do something nice," she continued, "and you're being a big baby."

"A baby?" I said, moving closer to her, my muscles so tense it was hard not to punch something.

"Yes, a big baby. You and your chauvinistic remarks and your oversensitive pride."

I still didn't know what that word meant, but given the way she spat the words at me, I knew it was an insult.

"I'm not oversensitive," I replied, now so close I could see the darkness in her blue eyes.

"You're not denying the other part?" she asked, throwing me off.

"Fuck off. I'd rather sleep on a pile of rocks than deal with your ugliness." As soon as the words left my mouth, I regretted them because I knew they had come out wrong. I saw it in the startled hurt that appeared in her eyes. Eyes that grew watery before she grabbed her skirts and stormed away.

"Dammit," I grumbled, knowing I'd fucked up completely. "Eloise!" I called to her, chasing after her.

I snagged her arm, her body slamming into mine as she turned. A few tears had fallen down her cheeks and I could see she was trying to hold back the rest. This was the first time I'd seen her vulnerable, and I wasn't sure what to make of it.

"Leave, Garret."

"I'm sorry," I said, reaching up to brush a tear away. She pushed at my hand, pulling her face back, but I tightened my hold on her arm and forced her closer to me. Too close and having her body against mine had been a mistake. "I didn't mean it that way."

"No?" she said with a sniff as she looked away from me. "I know I'm not pretty, that I'm...damaged and old, but you didn't have to remind me of that."

"You are not damaged and you're not that old...well maybe you are. How old are you, anyway?" I asked, hoping to change the tone.

From the frown she gave me, it hadn't worked.

"You don't have to lie. The scars are...." She sighed, her eyes glancing away again, looking at something in the distance.

"They're superficial, but they cover marks I can never remove. Even if they weren't there, I'd still be ugly."

"Ugly?" I took her chin in my hand and turned her face back to me. "You're beautiful, Eloise. With or without the scars or the gray hair—"

"Silver," she said, as if it made a difference.

I laughed, saying, "Silver hair. You're one of the most beautiful women I've seen. And trust me, I've met a lot of women."

Her brow arched enticingly, and I struggled to find my breath, questioning how that one move had me wanting to pull her further into my arms and kiss her.

"Still want me to leave?" I asked, brushing the drying tears from her cheeks with my knuckle.

"If you continue to flaunt how promiscuous you are, I might."

"Promiscuous?" Gods, she kept using these words I didn't know. She was too smart, and it made me feel small. Beatrice had been like that. A bookworm using big words to insult me. I'd blown it off, not caring. But with Eloise I cared.

Her smile grew, and she leaned up on her tiptoes. For a moment, I thought she was going to kiss me and my heart thudded against my chest. She put her mouth against my ear and whispered, "It means you sleep around, big boy."

The way my dick jumped at the nickname confounded me, but I didn't have time to question it.

"Are you over your tantrum?" she said, and I scrunched my eyes, crossing my arms as she backed away from me.

"It wasn't a tantrum," I grumbled.

"We'll agree to disagree." She turned on her heels and entered the house, leaving me with the scent of roses that seemed to linger on her skin and a sense that she'd gotten the last word. "You're taking me to the fire festival," she continued, as if nothing had happened. "Niscus is only an hour from here and they have festivities and vendors. Nilan let me go one year and I've always wanted to go back. You're going to take me." Her voice carried from the house.

I shook my head as her words sank in. "He let you? What does that mean?"

She peeked out, her hands deftly weaving her long hair into a braid. A pink ribbon was between her teeth and she took it and tied it around the end of the braid. "He didn't let me go far," she said, her face dropping just enough for me to notice.

"Wait. You had a controlling husband who didn't let you go places, yet you harass me for my comments about a woman's place in the home?"

Her lips pursed before she snapped, "It's not the same."

"The fuck it's not."

She grabbed a cape, leaving the house and brushing past me. "It's not. He didn't expect me to serve him hand and foot. He let me be who I am."

"And who is that?" I asked, following her to the horses.

She lifted her head before she climbed on her horse, her eyes holding a sadness that was palpable. "Someone I can never be," she murmured.

She was riding away before I could respond, leaving the comment tumbling around in my head.

Catching up to her, I looked at her from the corner of my eye, trying to determine what secrets she held. Small pieces of her dropped bit by bit, but I couldn't put the puzzle that was Eloise together. And perhaps I wasn't meant to yet. Yet. That word resounded through my body, like a confirmation that I wanted more than just the smiles and word-play we had. That I wanted to discover who Eloise was and who she thought she couldn't be.

As we grew closer to Niscus, the road became more crowded with travelers flocking to the town.

"Tell me about the fire festival," I said as we rode.

"The kingdom of Bira holds it for two days each year to give thanks to the gods for the blessing of magic the gods granted to them," she said, her voice distant. I peered over at her, seeing the shift in her emotions, the distinct melancholy of her tone reflected in her features. "They allow a limited number of visitors to witness from within the kingdom. The rest celebrate in Niscus. Today is the last day."

"Which is where we're headed," I said, wishing the smile would return to her face.

She only gave me a curt nod. I'd noticed the shift in her mood the nearer we grew to Niscus, which sat on the outskirts of the main road into Bira. It was the only way into the kingdom that wasn't barred by thorny bramble. Myth claimed the gods had stripped the thorns from the roses in the fields of Bira and planted them along the border to protect the land from intruders...all but the border into Duntraik, which was too treacherous to brave.

We rode in silence the rest of the way until the crowd spread out. Vendors and food merchants lined the fields ahead of us and I took in the breathtaking sight. I'd never seen so many people in one place. Travelers had set up camp beyond the vendors so that it gave the appearance of a mini town. The town itself sat just past the festivities.

Eloise hopped from her horse, walking it the rest of the way, and I followed her lead. I knew my eyes were wide, unable to decide where to land. There were too many things to look at. She led us to a hitching post and threw the attendant a coin. As much as I hated that she'd paid, I had no money left, so I bit my tongue, holding back my comment.

She was looking around, her eyes bright and as wide as I suspected mine were. Her smile warmed the recesses of my soul and was infectious. She wandered through the vendors, picking up small things and holding them to the sky as if the sun would show her the answer to what each one was. Her fingers danced over the material on cloaks and dresses, lingering on a corset that my mind automatically pictured her in. I looked away quickly, the image not fading, my pants growing uncomfortable.

I kept my eyes turned away, setting them on a juggler who was tossing six balls hypnotically between his hands. When I turned back to Eloise, she was gone and my heart pounded as fear streaked through me, nerves colliding like the strike of lightning to the ground. I swiveled, my eyes searching every face as the fear grew. I wasn't certain why it was so strong, but an instinct to protect her barreled through me and without her next to me, I was failing.

A delicate hand took mine, small and fragile yet calloused from labor, and I spun around to find Eloise, her blue eyes sparkling with amusement.

"Come on," she said, tugging me behind her.

I didn't have time for my relief to settle as the sensation of her hand in mine overcame it. I couldn't get over how perfect it felt in mine.

She dragged me to a tent where a woman was selling painting stones and brushes. Eloise picked up a brush, her fingers running over the bristles, a faraway look in her eyes.

"How much for one?" I asked, knowing I wouldn't have enough coin.

"One silver and if you want to paint, it'll be another silver."

I pulled the ring from my pocket, the only remaining reminder of my heritage, rolling it in my fingers before I handed it to the woman.

"Garret, no," Eloise protested. "I can pay."

"No, it's my treat," I said, something driving me to let her have the items. "I should have let it go a long time ago."

"That'll do," the woman said, pocketing the ring and wiping the last of my connection to my father away. She gave me two silvers in return, which didn't seem enough for the value the ring held or the tainted memories that sat upon it. "Is that the brush you want?" she asked Eloise.

Eloise nodded, her eyes still on mine.

"Here," the woman pulled out a large, flat, circular rock and handed it to her. "The paints are through the other side."

I followed the direction of her finger and thanking her, took Eloise's hand and led her out.

"Garret—"

"Consider it payment for the chewy chicken you made me." I gave her a devilish look and a wink.

Her smile spread to her eyes, causing butterflies to flip through my stomach irritatingly.

Several children were in the grass, an array of paints out for their use. Eloise flopped down in the middle, placing her stone in front of her. She reached over and took a jar of red paint and a jar of white as I sat next to her.

"My parents sheltered me," she mumbled, dipping the brush in the red. "I had a lot of time to kill and painting helped pass the time. I painted the walls of my room, the door, and even the ceiling before they took the paint away."

"Took it away?" I asked, wondering why her parents would do that.

"I haven't painted for a very long time," she said, disregarding my question. She leaned forward, and I watched as her initial strokes became more confident and fluid. She grew immersed in painting, her hand moving deftly as the shape of a rose bud formed. From it, petals floated as if a breeze had picked them up, tearing them from the bud and leaving it vulnerable and open, its protection stripped from it. White paint tipped each petal, highlighting the rich crimson within.

I didn't move, mesmerized by Eloise's actions until she sat back and wiped her forehead with her wrist. The red and white paint had blended on her fingers, leaving them with streaks of pink. A smudge of it smeared on her forehead with her movement and I lifted my thumb to wipe it away.

"A rose, huh?" I asked, trying not to think of how it reminded me of the roses on the night I'd gone after Beatrice and her lover.

She shrugged and stood. I watched as she walked over to a small child who stood looking over at the other children. Eloise stooped before the child, peering up at the parents, who nodded. She handed the brush and her paint to the girl, then took her hand and led her to a space where she helped her sit. She ran into the tent, returning with another rock. Squatting down, she gave it to the girl, whose smile beamed.

I couldn't help but wonder why Eloise had no children. She had to be in her late forties. I wanted to ask her, to find out how long she had been married and if they'd chosen not to have children. But it was part of the past and, as so, it was off limits, just as mine was.

Standing, I wiped the dirt from my pants, thinking she would have made a wonderful mother. That had we met years before.... I let the thought go, not understanding why it had formed.

A purple flower was tucked in the grass where she'd been sitting, and I leaned down and picked it just as she returned to my side.

"Ready?" she asked. I pushed a strand of hair from her cheek and tucked the flower in her braid.

She brought her hand up to touch it, giving me a beautiful smile.

"You don't want to take your painting with you?" I asked.

"Let someone else enjoy it."

I held my hand out, hoping she'd take it and loving how, when she did, our hands fit perfectly together again. I didn't know how we'd progressed to that level of comfort, but it seemed right. I let her guide me through the festival. The small things she did charmed me—the laughter that fell so easily when she relaxed, the way her eyes shone with excitement when she saw something new, the way others seemed to gravitate to her as if she had some magic they couldn't turn from. Each moment seemed to slip into me, taking hold of another piece of me and claiming it as hers.

She smiled up at me, the sun shimmering in her silver hair, and something woke in me that went deeper than the surface of attraction I'd had to Beatrice. This peeled away the parts of me I hated, the ones that had defined me and made me the reviled villain others saw. A sudden need to be something different for Eloise, to be a good man, screamed through me and I didn't understand it.

Eloise looked away, the moment gone as if she'd felt the same things and wanted to deny it as much as I did. Her fingers slipped from mine and a lump formed in my throat as I struggled with the loss of it. I watched as she swayed to the music from two men playing their instruments, their music filling the air with a joyful melody. Letting my feet guide me, I took her in my arms and danced with her, twirling her around and letting her laughter and the smile that brightened the world around us fill my heart more.

I'd never been so free, so happy. She clung to me as I twirled her through the group of people who had joined us. I brought her completely against me, knowing it was inappropriate with so many others around, but not caring. Her eyes were bright, and they seemed to see so far into me I worried she'd see what she was doing to me. How she was breaking down the man I'd been, the exterior I'd built, the opinions I'd carried, the heart I'd sheltered.

The music stopped, but I kept her there. Time seemed to halt around us, and we remained frozen, and the instinct to kiss her barreled through me. It accompanied a need to keep her in my arms and to never let her go. Her eyes searched mine before they dropped, the moment lost. Hesitantly, my hands released her.

"We should head back before it gets dark," she muttered, brushing loose strands of her hair from her face. Her cheeks held a pink flush, and I thought of how it enhanced her beauty. It struck me that I'd always been superficial, choosing women for their outward beauty, not caring what they were like as I conquered them. With Eloise, scars marred her features, but somehow they made her that much more attractive to me. In the past, I never would have paid any attention to her, had never looked at an older woman and definitely not one whose face wasn't perfect.

"What?" she asked, wiping her cheek as if she had something on it.

"Nothing," I said, bringing her hand back down and keeping it in mine. I led her away from the musicians, walking us back toward our horses.

On our way, I spied a woman weaving fresh flowers into headpieces. Letting Eloise go, I ran over to the woman, taking the last two coins from my pocket and trading them for a headpiece with pink and purple daisies weaved throughout it. I rushed back over to Eloise. She questioned me with her eyes as I placed it on her head. As she reached her fingers up, touching the flowers, her eyes grew misty.

My face dropped at the reaction until she whispered, "Thank you. It's beautiful."

Relief washed through me, and I took her hand again, thinking of how she carried the headpiece like a crown she should have been wearing.

As we headed out from the festival, I peeked over at Eloise, wondering how this day had twisted everything I wanted in life to just one thing: Eloise.

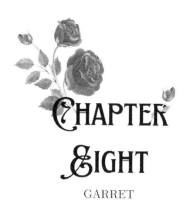

CHAPTER EIGHT

GARRET

The fire flickered gently, casting its light in Eloise's eyes and lighting the blue in them to a dusty hue.

"Where did you learn to debone and filet a fish so perfectly?" she asked me, licking her fingers clean.

We'd returned from the festival at dusk, and I'd gone right to preparing the fish, realizing we'd barely eaten while we'd been there.

I smiled, thinking the sight was a cute juxtaposition to the woman she was.

"Part of the past," I said with a shrug.

"Oh, sorry. Don't tell me then."

"My best friend joined the army because I did. He wasn't the army type." No, Leo was a conniver and a thief, and between the two of us, we made the perfect pair. I'd just never realized it before now. "And he was terrible with a sword, so they put him on cooking duty. At first, the meals were horrendous," I continued, thinking of the slop he'd made the first day. "It was a wonder the other men didn't kill him. But he was a determined ass, always looking for approval..." I stared into the fire, thinking of how Leo always wanted my approval, doing everything I asked, no matter how cowardly or sneaky. We'd been like brothers, but I'd taken him for granted, using him to get closer to Beatrice.

"He taught you to cook fish?" she asked, and I met her eyes, seeing the understanding there that this was delving into the forbidden we'd both agreed to leave forgotten.

"He did. On a trip home, returning from battle. The idiot had gotten himself cornered by an enemy soldier, and before I could reach him, the soldier had injured him. Nothing life threatening because I gutted the man in time, but he was in no shape to cook. So, he walked me through it and I cooked the rest of the ride home. And when he healed, I taught him how to fight properly so I wouldn't have to save his ass every time."

She stayed quiet, her eyes seeing too deeply into me until I broke the contact, looking down at my hands.

"Well, he did a good job because that was definitely better than my dry chicken. I think you'll do the cooking from now on," she said with a laugh.

"Oh no, I don't think so," I replied playfully. "Cooking is woman's work."

She tossed her boot at me and I dodged it as I gave her a menacing look that I couldn't hold because her laugh was infectious.

"I will break you of that notion, Garret," she said, rising and fluffing her skirts out to cover her bare feet. She'd taken her boots off as we'd settled before the fire, surprising me with the comfortable move.

"Will you?" I asked, thinking she was already breaking me. "Because that's years of training you'll need to unwind."

Her eyes twinkled in the firelight. "I promise, I will." She said it with such surety that I believed it myself. "Stay here," she said. "I have something for you."

She rushed off into the house and I puzzled over what that

could be. Returning within minutes, she plopped down next to me, saying, "Put your hand out."

I did as instructed, watching as she placed a delicate rose with loose red flowers in my hand. The sight brought images of that night back, the rose petal that fell from the blackened rose, the petals floating in the water when I'd come to. It was the same reaction I'd had when she'd painted the rose, only this time more intense.

"Be gentle," she said, bringing me back to the present. Her words stopped my instinct to crush it, reminding me that I didn't need to go back to that night. Peeking over at her, I realized I hadn't lost everything because that night had offered me a chance to find something new.

"What is it?" I asked, looking back at the flower, which was brandished with a sparkly coating.

"A rose drop. I used to make them with my mother," she said absently, playing with a loose petal of the one in her hand. "We would sneak down to the kitchens after dark and she would teach me the intricacies of shaping the petals and adhering the sugar so they would be perfect replicas of roses."

In those few words, I learned more about Eloise than she likely wanted me to know because commoners didn't have kitchens or levels to their homes. Eloise came from aristocracy and my curiosity about how she was living by herself in a run-down home was now tenfold.

"How do you eat them?" I asked, knowing I couldn't pry. I liked what we had too much to risk pushing her away.

She shook her head slightly, as if clearing away the memory. "Like this." She picked it up and opened her mouth, sticking her tongue out as she shook the rose. The petals fell, landing on her tongue and dissolving until only the center of the bud remained, which she popped into her mouth. It seemed such a dainty move and my hands were twice the size of hers, if not more.

"Now you try," she said. I eyed her from the side, then looked back at the flower, knowing there was no way I was pulling this off as gracefully as she had. With a giggle, she took the flower from my hand. "Here, let me help."

She scooted closer, turning her body to mine, and my chest leaped at the closeness.

"Open your mouth."

"Isn't that what I'm supposed to say?" I asked, unable to resist. Her eyes grew wide, a deep crimson filling her cheeks.

"You are a dirty man. Do you talk to every woman like that?" Her voice was hushed, as if someone might hear.

"Just the ones I want," I said without thinking. Shit, I hadn't meant to say that and now it was out and I couldn't take it back. I'd flirted and been suggestive to her early on, but this I'd said with a certainty I knew I couldn't walk back.

"Well, I can see why you're alone then," she said. "That suggestion would shock any decent woman."

"Maybe that's why the decent ones avoid me," I said, thinking how true that might have been.

"Open your mouth and stick your tongue out. I should clean your mouth out with soap instead of something sweet."

"You know you're setting yourself up for more of my dirty comebacks if you keep that up," I replied, loving how the blush climbed higher in her cheeks and noting how she hadn't blushed when we'd first met and exchanged words like this. The blush had only begun tonight, and I wondered if it was for the same reason that my heart was now pounding so hard I didn't think it would stay in my chest much longer.

"Just do it, Garret."

I obeyed, locking my eyes with hers as she leaned up and dropped the petals on my tongue. I would have focused on how close our bodies were if not for the sudden burst of flavor on my tongue. The sensation was like a punch of sweetness softened by a delicate floral taste that awakened my senses and calmed my soul. She let the bud fall, instructing me to close my mouth and not chew. Nothing I'd ever tasted matched the flavors that lit my senses with their power before gently fading and leaving me wanting more.

"What was that?" I asked when I could finally talk.

"Magic," she said before quickly adding, "the magic of flavor." She backed away like she'd said too much and I tucked that notion away with the other small things I'd discerned and heard from her. I was still trying to piece together who Eloise was, determined to find out. "It's a delicacy in my homeland."

She stood, and I disliked the distance it put between us. "I think I'll head to bed," she said, giving me a quick glance before walking toward the house. "Goodnight, Garret."

I couldn't take my eyes off her and continued to stare at the door long after it closed. I didn't want the night to end. I wanted more of Eloise. To hear her laugh, to see her smile and the way the light hit her eyes. I needed those things because they woke a part of me I was starting to like.

After dousing the fire, I started toward my small shed, only to stop and turn back to the house. I was taking a chance, but it was one I needed to take. Knocking on her door, I looked down at my hands, seeing how I'd nervously gripped them. Nervous? I was never nervous. I was confident and sure of myself, and no woman had ever made me nervous. But when Eloise opened the door, wearing a long white nightdress, with no sleeves, the swell of her bare breasts clear beneath it, I could barely find my voice.

"Garret?" she asked, her eyes searching mine.

"I don't want to say goodnight, Eloise. We don't have to do anything. I don't care if we talk more or if we sit quietly next to each other. I just want to be with you." I sounded so weak and vulnerable, and I thought of running, hating that she'd seen that side of me, the one no one saw.

"Then don't say goodnight," she said, grabbing my shirt and pulling me to her. I hesitated. For the first time in my life, I hesitated to touch a woman, unsure of what this would do to us if I did. But she didn't hesitate. She reached her hand around my head and pushed my lips to hers. Everything in that moment fell into place and a completeness washed over me as I wrapped my arms around her and pulled her body to mine. That kiss was the most profound, life altering kiss I'd ever experienced. It reached in and embedded itself in my heart and soul, claiming them as hers.

I threaded my fingers through her hair, reveling in its lushness as I lost myself further to our kiss. She tugged me closer, dragging me into the house. I kicked the door closed, hoping I was reading the hunger in her kiss correctly. I couldn't stop kissing her and as she tugged my shirt free, I took it as a sign she didn't want me to stop. She pushed my shirt up, her hands roaming my chest as mine discovered her curves, caressing their way over each one and loving the way they felt in my hands. There was a haste to our touches and as much as I wanted to let my hands linger, to slowly explore every inch of her, the hunger I had for her was too great. She shoved my shirt higher, and I took the hint, pulling it over my head and breaking contact with her. I threw it aside, taking her face in my hands and seeing the lust that sat in her dusty blue eyes.

"Are you sure?" I asked, cursing myself for being such a wimp. Since when did I stop and ask? I took what women gave me and they always gave it up for me. But I wanted to hear her say it, to tell me to take her, to touch her, and hear her screams as I filled her.

"Yes, fuck me, Garret."

Good gods, that mouth was enough to make me lose it before I even entered her. I brought her mouth to mine, kissing her again and bringing my hands down her neck to push the straps of her gown off her shoulders. Excitement sparked through me at the thought of seeing her body, of touching every part of her and owning her. Her gown dropped, and I pulled her closer, her breasts warm against my skin, intensifying my desire to have her. Her hands were touching me with a confidence I only experienced when I indulged in whores, which was rare. I usually took women who were inexperienced, ones who fooled around with boys and not men like me, asserting my dominance and teaching them what it was like to have a real man.

But Eloise was an experienced woman. She'd been married, and she was older. And damn, did she know what she wanted. She had no hesitation in unhooking my pants as I walked us further into the room, bumping into the table. I caressed the supple flesh of her firm breast, her nipple puckering below. My pants dropped, and I picked her up, placing her on the table, ready to have her wrapped around me, to have her cry out my name as I fucked her, but her hand encased my dick, throwing me off my game. She stroked, moaning through our lips, and I jerked in her hand. She was so sure of her moves that it was turning me on even more. I should have known with the way she talked, the strength she had, and her independent spirit that she wouldn't have any shyness about touching me just as much as I was touching her.

"Gods Eloise, you're going to have me coming in your hand," I muttered, pulling her hair to stop her.

She moaned more, tipping her neck back, and my desire for her flared through me. I shoved her hand aside and pushed through her folds, grunting at how wet she was.

"You're not coming until I come," she said, putting her hand on my chest.

I halted my movement just as I was about to sink into her and gritted my teeth at the ache the move caused.

"Women don't come. Now move that pretty hand off my chest so I can feel you."

She narrowed her eyes, pushing me back more.

"Eloise," I scolded, not understanding why she wasn't worshipping my cock with her body like all women did.

"You've never made a woman come?" She sounded so incredulous that I questioned myself.

"Of course I have," I replied, not sure if that was the truth because I'd never even thought about it.

She ran her hand down my chest. "How do you know?"

"Are you really doing this now?" I snapped, hating how my dick was throbbing painfully. She was so wet it was coating my tip and it was torturing me.

"How?" she asked, titling her head and licking her lips.

"Damn, you're a bitch. I don't know. They moan and cry out my name, so I guess they come."

"You are so full of shit," she said, slapping my chest.

I grabbed her by the wrists and yanked her against me, sinking further into her. "Women don't need to come," I said.

"The fuck we don't. Now make me come, Garret, and I can promise you'll want me coming all the time."

She confounded me. This was about me, not her. Women were for my pleasure, and they were lucky I chose them.

Leaning forward, she pulled my bottom lip into her teeth and dragged them along it. "Make me come." And the way her words reached in like a claw, dragging its talons around my balls and squeezing, made me want to obey.

I pushed her wrists behind her, shoving her against me and kissing her, pushing further into her warmth, needing to thrust into her so badly that it took all my strength not to. But my mind was trying to figure out what she wanted me to do. I only ever took what I wanted from women, and they responded, fuck if I knew if they came or not. I really didn't care. I wanted the thrill, the ecstasy of release. But that something that drove me nuts about Eloise, drove me to put aside my need.

I threaded my fingers into her hair again, pulling the way I had earlier, and she grew wetter. She liked it hard, and I could deliver hard. Releasing her wrists, I grabbed her ass and shoved her body forward, thrusting into her at the same time. My body came alive, the feel of her around me sending jolts of ecstasy through it. Her legs wrapped tight around me as she took my hand from her hair and guided it to her chest. She kept her fingers wrapped around mine as I caressed her breast, pushing harder so that I was squeezing. I took her nipple between my fingers and she turned them, twisting as she cried out. Capturing her cry with my mouth, I wrapped my other hand around the back of her neck and yanked her back from me.

I needed to hear more of her cries, cries that were almost feral and that dug into my core like a nesting snake coiled and ready to strike.

"Show me what you like," I growled, not caring if it made me less of a man, if it stripped me of my control. The desire to hear her scream for me had hold of me and I couldn't free myself from it.

She met my eyes, guiding my hand up her neck. The fire in my belly blazed as she tightened my fingers, her eyes rolling back as I took over, spreading my fingers over her delicate neck and feeling the pulse of her life below them.

"Fuck," I muttered as she grabbed my head and shoved my mouth to her breast. Her hands pulled my hair while I sucked her nipple into my mouth, grazing it with my teeth. Dropping my hands, I gripped her waist tight and increased my thrusts. She'd summoned the aggression in me and it coursed through me, ready to answer her call.

She pushed at me and laid back on the table, her body sprawled out for me to see. My eyes surveyed her, noting the scars that covered her body in ways that made no sense, almost as if they formed a pattern.

Pushing me back with her feet, she said, "Show me what that tongue can do."

I froze, not understanding what she wanted.

"Damn, Eloise, let me back in," I said, forcing her legs back and penetrating her again. My sigh was loud, and she laughed, bringing herself up on her elbows. She had her feet pressed against my chest, so I gripped her calves, noting the strength within them.

"I come first and then I'll come with you," she said, her feet pressing me back.

My growl rumbled through my chest.

"Keep that aggression up, Garret, because I guarantee I can meet it." Her eyes shimmered with hunger, and she sucked her bottom lip between her teeth. "Get on your knees and I'll return the favor later."

The jump of my dick was muted only by my confusion. "My knees? You're the one who should drop to your knees."

She threw her head back and laughed. "Taste the forbidden fruit because I can guarantee you won't think twice about doing it next time I ask."

I glanced down to where I was still embedded between her legs, raising my brow before I looked back up at her. I'd heard men talk about it, but never had I bothered to indulge because when I wanted sex, it was hard and fast.

She held my eyes, not wavering. "On your knees, big boy, and make me come."

Her command was like a chain around my cock, and it jumped so hard she sighed and dropped back down to the table. I didn't take commands from women...but I pulled out and fell to my knees, staring at the most intimate part of a woman who was nothing like any other woman I knew.

She was dripping, and I slid my fingers through her, seeing the muscles in her thighs quiver before I brought my fingers to my mouth and tasted. She was sweet, and I craved more, shoving her thighs further apart and sinking my tongue right into her. I'd thought the roses she'd made were delicious, but this was a delicacy I wished I'd enjoyed years earlier.

Each swipe of my tongue had her shivering, her fingers weaving through my hair and pulling it when I hit a spot she liked.

"There," she said as I flicked my tongue over a raised spot I found fascinating, just like her reaction. "On my clit."

That word I'd heard but had never wanted to admit I didn't know where the damned thing was. Now that I did, I sucked on it and she bucked, making me grow harder, which I didn't think was possible. She pushed my face further into her and I brought my arm under her thigh to balance myself, slipping a finger into her and grunting at how tight she was as she clenched around it. Her legs were quivering, her body pushing against me as I continued to taste her until she cried out, her hands steadying my head while a burst of flavor filled my mouth.

Her body convulsed erotically until her grip on my hair relaxed. She released my head and pulled me up, her mouth crashing into mine as I plunged into her. Rapture wasn't the right word for the way her muscles spasmed around me, pulsing so tight it edged me closer to release. She clung to me, kissing me with a desperation that rippled through me like a storm, a need for her that shredded through me and left me riven. I continued to drive into her, twisting my fingers around the locks of her hair until my body rebelled on my hold over it and my climax tore through me, eviscerating me with the intensity so that all I could do was hold on to her.

With the last flood of my release, I loosened my grasp on her body, tipping my forehead to hers and waiting for the tremors to stop.

Bringing her mouth to mine, I kissed her again, uncertain if I wanted the kiss to end or the touches to stop. This was where I usually left, leaving them splattered with my essence, their satisfied eyes begging me to stay. Apparently, I hadn't really satisfied them. But perhaps they hadn't realized that, thinking as I did that sex was really for the man to take what he wanted from a woman.

Reality dawned on me that I'd never made the mistake of coming in a woman, that I'd always pulled out and used their bodies or their mouths to capture my release. Eloise didn't seem concerned, and I'd wanted her so intensely that I'd neglected to stop myself. But coming inside of her had taken my release to a level I'd never experienced. The pleasure outweighed any thought of the consequence, and I knew if I took her again, I wouldn't give it a second thought because it had been too perfect.

Eloise let her fingers drift through my hair, and our lips separated.

"That's how you make a woman come," she breathed, her chest still heaving.

"Is that all it takes?" I asked, truly hating that I sounded and looked so naïve, as if I hadn't had sex before and she had been my first.

She nipped at my lip, her smile lighting every part of my soul. "It's a start."

Laughing, I unlatched her legs from me and pulled my pants up. Her legs dangled over the edge of the table as she creased her brows.

"What are you doing?"

I peeked up at her. "Going back to my bed, or maybe to the tavern for a drink."

"You're running," she said. The words stopped me. "That's what you do, isn't it? Run."

"I'm not running." But I was because she was right. Running away was what I did best.

"Then stay. Don't go to the tavern, don't sleep outside. Stay with me."

It wasn't a command or a plea. It was simply a request, one that went against everything I was. Fuck them and leave them. Run from everything that can harm you. And women, no matter how docile and dependent I thought they were, could hurt me. Only one woman had tempted me to settle down and that had been for just as selfish a reason as leaving them always was. There was no love there, nothing more than physical attraction to her beauty. I would have married her and continued my ways, taking what I wanted from her and leaving her at home while I took it from other women.

But if I stayed with Eloise, if I turned my back on the man

who wanted to run, to drink off the feeling that had slinked into my chest and was owning it even now, I didn't know who that made me. Her eyes were on me, holding no judgement but seeing into me in ways that in the past would have guaranteed I'd run.

"And what would we do if I stayed?" I asked, deciding I liked the man she was bringing out in me. I stepped forward, parting her legs again and sliding my hand up her thigh.

"Oh, I believe we could think of a few things to occupy our time." Her brow arched seductively.

"Better than a mug of ale?" I teased, bringing her body against mine.

"Much better."

I brushed my thumb along her cheek, following the line of her scar before lingering on her lips. They parted, and I pushed it further, her tongue circling it. My length sprang back to life as if she had some magical hold on it.

"Time for you to drop to your knees?" I asked, giving her a coy grin.

"If you're a good boy."

Shaking my head and laughing, I threaded my hand through her hair and yanked her head back, the sigh she emitted lighting a fire in my balls. Leaning in, I murmured in her ear, "I'll give you tonight to show me what I need to do to break you further, then the control is mine again."

She shivered delectably, and I knew I was going to enjoy this new version of me she was bringing out, especially if it meant I could watch her fall apart for me repeatedly. Picking her up, I carried her to her room, prepared to spend the night pleasing her in every way she wanted.

CHAPTER NINE

GARRET

Eloise was in my arms, her body pressing into mine, my hands wrapped around it. I'd held her in our sleep, not letting go, and I wasn't sure what to make of that as I blinked the sleep from my eyes. She'd taken me to new heights, teaching me how to make her completely soaked and doing things to me that had me coming so hard I almost blacked out. She was magnificent, and I didn't think there was a woman out there like her. She was free, bold, confident, and so experienced that it had me seeing red with jealousy if I stopped and thought about how she'd learned those things.

I drew my arm from her waist, but her hand stopped me.

"Running, Garret?" she said, pulling my hand back and placing it on her breast.

My body woke, my erection pressing into her ass.

"Only if you want me to." I nuzzled her neck as I squeezed her breast, pulling at her nipple. "But this doesn't feel like you want me to," I said, pinching it and loving the quiet moan it caused.

I'd never spent the night with a woman unless I'd unintentionally passed out drunk after fucking one. I would have said I'd been missing out, but I was glad I never had because it made waking up to touch Eloise even more special. As my hand skirted over her body, it hit me that this was how I wanted to spend every morning. Touching her and hearing the cries that had hastened my release the prior night.

I slid my finger through her arousal, feeling how wet she already was. "And what were you dreaming about?" I asked, teasing her clit. Now that I knew what soaked her, I'd take every chance to do it.

"A muscular, broody man with an amazing dick," she replied playfully as she dropped her head to my chest and wrapped her arm around my neck.

"Should I be jealous?" I asked, licking her neck and shoving my finger into her. Her body bucked perfectly.

"Probably," she breathed. "Unless you can make me come better than he can."

"I promise you, I can."

I reached my other hand around her neck, spreading my fingers over it, the move stirring the aggressive part of me just as it soaked her more. That was the beautiful thing about her. She may have been controlling and commanding—teaching me and guiding me, changing me as she slowly had in the mere days I'd known her—but she welcomed the aggressor in me, the part of me that had fed the bad boy in me. In fact, she brought him out when he'd always been in the background, waiting to be dominant. I'd never embraced that side of me. Sure, I'd known it was under there, waiting to lead me to be the man I should have always been, but I'd left it buried, choosing flight over fight. Running from threats I knew I couldn't beat, and only letting the aggressor free when I was certain I could win the fight. That side of me had been leading me the night I'd stormed the castle and attacked Beatrice's lover. But the day I'd run, letting them think I was dead, it had been silent again.

Eloise had awoken that part of me, feeding it and giving it power, but balancing it with her own power. And between the two of us, we played a beautiful dance. She empowered me, recognizing that my façade of the womanizer was just that, a façade I wore to impress others. It was only a shell of the man she'd released.

She cried out as I gently pinched her clit.

"You know you've set the beast in me free," I slipped two fingers into her and fucked her with them until she was right on the edge, "and now I can't put him back."

Her body convulsed, tightening around my fingers as she climaxed, a cry escaping her. "That's it, Eloise, come for me." She cried out again, her head digging into my chest as her back bowed. Every muscle in her body was trembling, and I held her through it until she relaxed.

"Gods, I've created a beast," she muttered.

"You just let him loose and now he wants to play." I nipped at her ear, freeing my fingers from her.

As I licked my fingers, she turned and pushed me over.

"That's the tastiest thing I've ever had," I said, cleaning the last one and savoring the taste.

She straddled me, enveloping me in one swift move that tore a growl from me. Grabbing her waist in reaction to how good she felt, I asked, "And what do you think you're doing, Eloise?"

She leaned back on my thighs, her silver hair spread out behind her in a glorious wave. Her breasts were bouncing hypnotically, and I couldn't stop staring at them.

"Taking back my control," she said, dropping over my chest and raising her body before dipping so low that I bottomed out. I grunted, tightening my grip on her waist.

Shoving her forward, I took her breast in my mouth, sucking the supple skin, then dragging my teeth over her nipple. She rode me, her nails digging into my chest, until I was close to losing it. But I wanted her to come with me like she had when I'd taken her the second time the prior night. The feeling of her tightening around me had taken me over the edge as I'd chased it, and I wanted to experience it again. I wouldn't let her rip my climax from me until I did.

Stopping her, I dealt with the aggravated look she gave me as I flipped her and yanked her ass back. She giggled, the sound digging its way into my chest and taking hold of whatever it was she'd awakened in me. Parting her legs with mine, I thrust into her, shoving her head down as I fucked her hard the way she liked. And I wasn't complaining because I liked it just as much. She groaned, and it tugged at my dick as I thrust so deep it jerked her body forward.

Pulling her hair, I rammed harder, her muscles shaking, her cries raking through me and calling to my release. She clenched around me and with a muted scream she broke, the spasms around me summoning my climax which exploded with such force that I let her hair go and grabbed her hips, pulling her back into me as ecstasy surged through every pore of my body, leaving me numb and empty by the time I had control of my muscles again.

When I could finally move, I released her, dropping next to her and scooping her into my chest. I nuzzled her hair as she kissed my chest, and I couldn't help but think about the intimacy. Nor could I deny how perfect she felt in my arms. She peeked up at me, her silver hair slipping in her eyes, and I brushed it back, kissing her nose.

I followed the line of her scar across her cheek and down to her lips, her kiss heating every part of me.

"You'd better stop," she muttered between kisses, "or I'll make you please me again."

Chuckling, I bit her bottom lip, which curved as she smiled. "That's not a threat that holds much power, Eloise."

She rolled from me and rose from the bed, her ass rocking seductively with each step. She was the sexiest thing I'd laid eyes on, and my body woke again at the thought of what I'd done with her and how my cum was leaking out of her with each step she took.

"Where are you going, princess?" I asked as she wrapped a blanket around her shoulders and walked through the doorway.

She halted in her tracks, turning swiftly to me. "What did you call me?" Her demeanor had changed, fear flickering in her eyes, her voice shaking.

"Princess," I replied. "Is there something wrong with that?" Shit, I'd fucked up and I couldn't figure out why that thought hammered at me like it did. The nickname meant something to her.

"Don't call me that," she said tersely.

I wanted to ask her if her husband had called her that, but I didn't want to make the tension in her jaw any worse, so I refrained, assuming he had.

"Noted." I rose, going to her and lifting her chin, seeing her in an entirely different light. Gone was the strong, confident woman who had guided me last night and in her place was a fragile one. "What about El? Can I call you that?"

She chewed her lip for a moment, then nodded.

"All right. Then let's start over. Where do you think you're going, El?"

She relaxed, but there was still something in her eyes I couldn't name. "To stoke the fire. It's chilly in here, and we need to get moving. The fish is gone and since you didn't bring any other meat back, we'll need to hunt again and—"

I brought my finger to her mouth. "You get back in bed and rest. I'll throw wood on the fire and hunt."

"But there—"

"Is nothing that needs to be done that can't wait." I turned her toward her room and gave her a gentle push. "Rest that body so I can ravage it more when I get back."

Grabbing my pants, I dressed, her keen eyes watching me.

"I need to go into town and get more sugar from the general store."

Raising a brow, I asked, "Making me more rose drops?"

Her smile lifted my spirit and eased the worry that had settled in me. "Maybe."

"Then I'll head into town once I return," I said, snatching my shirt from the floor where she'd torn it from me.

After pulling my boots on, I ran a hand through my hair and moved to her, taking her in my arms and kissing her. The kiss was gentle, and my heart leaped with an emotion I didn't want to define. One that seemed too soon to recognize.

"Keep that body ready because when I get back, I plan to use it the rest of the day," I told her.

Her laugh followed me out the door and left a residual that lingered in my mind as I prepared my horse to leave. I paused just before I rode off, a disconcerting apprehension simmering in my bones. Glancing back at the house, I thought about going back in and telling her we could do without meat and even without the sugar. But I ignored the inclination and headed to the woods, my mind on Eloise and how she was changing me with each passing minute.

THE WOODS WERE QUIET, and it seemed like hours before I found anything to hunt. The buck finally appeared as the mid-morning sun was upon me, but there were no other creatures around it. Confused, I stepped closer, thinking perhaps it would be chipmunks or even mouse for dinner. It wouldn't be the first time I'd suffered such scraps, but I wanted something worthier of Eloise, something to impress her.

"I see nothing," I finally said out loud, as if the deer could understand me. Its beady brown eyes stared at me, and I questioned my sanity, glad no one from home could see me now.

It moved closer to me, its ears flicking quickly, a sudden nervousness showing in the shake of its legs. It stopped, pawing at the ground like a horse before it raised up on its hind legs and kicked at me. I didn't know what to make of how agitated it seemed, but even when it dropped back down, it didn't calm. Instead, it kept moving closer, backing me down the light trail that I'd left to get back to my horse.

I glanced behind me, hearing it snort before I turned back to it. "You want me to leave," I said, and it pawed at the ground again in agitation. "Fuck, what are you trying to tell me, and why am I talking to a fucking deer?"

I raked my hand through my hair, wondering what Eloise would say about how foolish I looked.

"Eloise," I mumbled, and the deer stopped, its eyes meeting mine again. "It's something to do with Eloise."

I remembered that sense of foreboding I'd had before I left, like a need to stay behind with her.

"Dammit!"

I ran, bumping into trees and scrambling over debris as I made my way back to the horse. I threw myself on him and rode him hard through the field and river, my bow and arrows bouncing on my back. Fear raked through me, that uneasiness becoming a torrent of desperate need to reach her. I thought of what the barmaid had told me. Eight men had come to the house, eight dead and her husband with them. But there was no husband there to protect her this time. No matter how strong she was, there was no way she could fight that many men. And if more came, she would die this time.

CHAPTER TEN

ELOISE

I pulled the blanket around me tighter, crawling back into bed as I heard Garret's horse take him from me. Tracing the space where his body had lain, I thought about how he'd taken me, butterflies skittering through my stomach. Turning to my back, I stared at the ceiling, wondering how I'd gotten to this point. How I'd let him in so far that I didn't think I could push him away. The thought terrified me because it would only bring him harm and destroy my heart. He would run when he discovered the truth. No matter how bad his own secrets were, they couldn't possibly be as devastating as mine were.

Rising, I cleaned myself up and dressed, running my fingers through my hair as I walked to my kitchen. Leaning against the cupboard, I smeared jam on a piece of bread, my thoughts only on Garret and his touches. I couldn't help smiling at how such a man hadn't known how to please a woman. He'd let me lead, let me show him and tell him everything that made me crumble, then he'd taken that lead back and demolished me. I shivered, thinking of how easily he'd made me climax before he left.

Licking the remnants of jam from my fingers, I set to my morning tasks. Garret wanted me to stay in bed and let him do everything for me today. It seemed an odd juxtaposition to the man who had boasted that a woman was only there for his needs and use. Perhaps I'd been responsible for that change.

My hand brushed the scars on my face, and I stopped, thinking of how he wanted me despite the scars and the wrinkles, despite the silver hair I wore to cover my true identity. He didn't want to use me for who I really was because he knew nothing but the lies and magic I'd woven to disguise myself. My heart pounded in my chest, a sensation I didn't want to recognize floating in the periphery, just as it had when he'd been touching me. I shoved it away, knowing it was a dangerous emotion to even consider.

My eyes fell on the floral crown he'd bought me, trading a ring that had clearly meant something to him for it and the painting time. I fingered the delicate flowers, wondering who the ring had belonged to and why he had traded it for my happiness. Lifting the crown, I nestled it in my hair, making my way to the small mirror in my room and staring at my reflection. The woman who looked back at me was the one I'd been since the day I'd run but she was a woman forged from her pain and circumstance, not the woman she'd been before who had worn delicate dresses and braided hair that fell to the floor as servants embellished it with jewels. No, the woman in the reflection was hard, her hands calloused, her face and body scarred to hide the truth. She could fight, she could fend for herself and survive on her own...and I'd lost my true self to her long ago.

I bit the inside of my cheek, refusing to let the tears free because I couldn't cry. I'd told myself years earlier, when I'd left the woman I'd been behind in the tower where she'd spent her days, that I wouldn't cry for all I'd lost. That I wouldn't dwell on the past. But Garret's presence had caused that past to surge forth. Before, I could go through my days not thinking about it, pretending to be Eloise of Troniere, the widow in the house outside of town who shied from the others. But Garret had awoken something in me and with it, my heart.

I turned from the mirror, removing the headpiece and tossing it on my vanity. I needed to get to work, no matter that he wanted me to rest. I was no longer the resting type, and I needed to stay busy. I tended to the hens, collecting the few eggs they left, all the while thinking about Garret, my spirit lifting with just the thought of him.

As I was dusting my hands on my skirt, having cleaned the debris from our fire the prior night, my senses tingled, my intuition telling me something wasn't right. My breath stuck in my chest, my heart beating hard in its cage, all thoughts of the prior night and Garret pushed aside by a need to run. Panic built in me like a storm brewing, but I ignored it, knowing to give it life would only be the death of me. Slowly, I walked back to the house, my eyes flicking to my periphery, looking for any motion. The crack of a branch broke the silence, and I pretended not to notice, fully aware it had come from behind me. I feigned bending over to pick up something from the ground and pulled my knife from my boot, glad I'd thought to tuck it there.

My breathing was shallow as a noise behind me told me my attacker was on the move. I clutched the knife, remembering Nilan's training and his words—'strike without hesitation and stop to question later'. Straightening quickly, I turned and slashed my knife, meeting the firm feel of flesh as the blade sliced through the face of my foe.

"Fuck," he grumbled, grabbing at my wrist. Blood poured from the wound, but it didn't stop him. I switched hands, appreciating Nilan's insistence to train me with my weak hand, and drove the knife just under his rib. He let my wrist go as another man came at me. Grabbing the sword from the man in front of me as he staggered away, I took a defensive position.

"Get her," the wounded man growled.

The new man rushed me, but I swung the blade deftly,

meeting his sword with a loud clang that vibrated through my wrists. I kicked him in his balls, sending him doubling over, and drove my sword into his back. I fought his body's movement as he fell, trying not to topple over with him. The second man came barreling toward me as I was applying pressure on the dead man's body with my foot to free my sword. The second man tackled me, and I went flying, the sword still in the dying man's back.

"Why, you little bitch." Spit flew from his mouth, and he wrapped his hands around my neck.

"You can't kill me," I said, barely able to get the words out. "He'll kill you if you do."

His jaw clenched. His fingers loosened but not enough for me to break free. My hands scratched at the ground, trying to reach for something to use as a weapon until my fingers touched a rock from the fire pit. Wrapping my fingers around it, I smashed it into his skull.

He yelled, his body rolling from mine, and I ran, praying I could make it inside to my other weapon. There was no grabbing the sword, which was still embedded in the back of the other man. I crossed the entrance into the house and made it inside right before it occurred to me that the door was wide open when it hadn't been before. It now hung loose from the hinges. Someone snatched at my arm as I faltered, throwing me across the room, my hip bouncing painfully against the table before I toppled to the ground.

A man stomped from the bedroom, another from behind the door where he'd been hiding. They'd been waiting, letting me believe I was winning the battle when they'd had control the entire time. I hadn't even heard them break the door.

"Dammit," I grumbled, scooting across the floor as they gained on me.

"Grab her," he grumbled to his partner. The man I'd fought outside hadn't entered the house, and I presumed he was waiting to see if he'd need to deal with me again if I gained the upper hand on these two. Exactly what I would have expected from soldiers of their sort. Duntraik soldiers may have relied on their king's magic, but that didn't mean they weren't lethal and strategic on their own. And these were Duntraik soldiers, not even bothering to hide their uniforms this time.

My hand hit the hearth, and I fumbled for the poker, finding the cold metal within my reach. Wrapping my fingers around it, I waited until he drew close enough. His confidence in his bare strength was his mistake as I drove the poker into his eye.

His scream was one from the depths of the underworld and it stung my ears.

"Are you going to let a woman beat you?" his partner yelled.

"Fuck!" he roared, pulling the poker from his eye. Bile surged in my throat, but I swallowed it back, my hand finding the loose stone in the hearth, remembering how Nilan had complained about it one too many times but never fixed it. Leaping to my feet, I lunged at the other soldier, slamming it into his head and knocking him off balance. I bashed the stone at his head as he fought to throw me from him.

"Fucking bitch," he growled, shoving me from him. I rolled to a crouch as both bloodied men approached me. I absently wondered if their colleague was laughing at their attempts to round me up as he nursed his wounds.

"You can't hurt her," the soldier with the missing eye said, his hand covering his socket.

"I'm going to do more than hurt her."

I tried backing my way to the door, but they were corralling me away from it. My heart was pounding so hard it thudded viciously in my chest.

"I would leave now while you have the chance," I threatened them.

"You're a fragile woman—"

"Says the man with the wounds," I said, my back hitting the counter where I kept my long dagger stashed.

He pulled his knife from his belt.

"You hurt her, and he'll kill us."

"I won't do too much damage. I just want to make sure it's her," he said, tossing the knife between his hands. "The last one wasn't, even though she was a fun distraction for my dick."

The woman from Sirak. They'd thought she was me and she'd suffered when they discovered she wasn't. Tortured and dead because of me.

"It's her. Look at the eyes and the path of her scars."

I clenched my fingers around the dagger, weighing which soldier would be the easier target. I could take on one, but both would be hard, especially since they were both armed. Releasing my grip on my dagger, I felt around on the counter behind me, finding the eggs I'd brought in earlier. Latching onto two, I made my choice.

"You're not touching me and you're certainly not taking me anywhere."

I lobbied the eggs at the one with the knife, grabbing my dagger as he blocked them, and I lunged at the one with the hand over his eye just as he came at me. I dug my knife into his chest, my full weight on it as I twisted it up under his rib. His head hit the floor hard, the loud thud dulled by the cracking of his skull. His body convulsed below me as he died, but the other soldier hauled me from him, his thick hands around my waist. I kicked and clawed as he dragged me across the room, my foot hitting his kneecap.

"Damn whore!" he screamed, shoving me to the ground and pinning me. "I don't give a fuck what that asshole wants with you. I'm going to kill you myself."

His hands came around my neck and I scratched at them, trying to free myself as my throat closed from the pressure. As much as I didn't want the last soldier to come in, I hoped he would, if only to stop the man on top of me whose crazed eyes showed no sign of granting mercy. This was it, all the hiding, the fighting, the lies, the running lost to this one moment. As my life slipped away, the fringes of my sight growing dark, I thought of Garret, wishing I'd had more time with him. Wishing our destiny had been more than a mere moment of time that would fade away as quickly as the air was fading from my lungs. My fingers slipped from my attacker's hands, and I took a final attempt for air, praying the gods would favor me in death unlike they had in life.

CHAPTER ELEVEN

GARRET

Every minute that passed was like a knife twisting in my gut, the unknown of what I'd find barreling through my mind like a windstorm. As I reached the house, I jumped from my horse, throwing the bow and arrow from my back and running. Someone had kicked the door in, and I pulled my knife, irritated my sword was in the shed, but ready to kill anyone who had dared touch Eloise.

I ran past the dead man on the ground and burst into the house, leaping over another dead body and spying Eloise on the floor. The sight of the man on top of her with his hands around her throat sent my adrenaline surging higher. I raced over and yanked him off her, slicing his throat and throwing him across the room, where he struggled to close his wound with his hand as his life bled from him. Eloise drew in a deep ragged breath, coughing on the floor as I scanned the room for any further danger. I scooped her up, resting her on the table and looking her over for any other injuries, my fear driving me and blinding me to anything but her. Her neck was raw, with bruises forming.

"Are you all right?" I said, touching her neck.

She didn't answer, her eyes darting behind me. She grabbed my knife and threw it. I heard it hit its target before I even turned to look.

"Shit," I muttered as she scrambled from the table. I held her back, approaching the man who was pulling himself from the floor. Eloise kicked him so that he was back on the floor as I eyed the distinctive clothes he wore, the insignia branded into his bicep.

"You can't escape, Princess," he said. There was that word again, but this time it meant more than a playful nickname.

I should have killed him, but his words had me curious, as did Eloise's reaction. She marched over to the dead man and yanked a knife from his body. I punched the wounded soldier, stepping on his arm to keep him from going after her. He let out a pained scream as bones shattered beneath my foot, but I disregarded it as I stared at Eloise. She stomped back over to us, her eyes hard.

"There's no running from him," he spewed, thrashing under my hold.

"Fuck you," she said before plunging the knife into his chest. The fierceness of the move left my jaw dropping. It was like watching a private conversation that I shouldn't be part of at the same time as I was watching the woman whom I'd held in my arms and taken just hours before, kill a man. I lunged toward her as he grabbed her hand.

"Rikeri will find you," he said, blood pooling in his mouth.

"Rikeri can rot in the underworld where you'll be rotting." The vile venom in her voice almost stopped me from dragging her from his grasp. I pushed her back and grabbed his head, breaking his neck in one swift move. Anger was seething through me at the thought of them hurting her, of his hands on hers. But along with it was confusion.

"Are there any more?" I asked, staring at his insignia and the all too familiar uniform.

"No," she mumbled.

I looked at her, seeing the understanding in her eyes. I'd witnessed too much. Her secrets could no longer be secrets and I had a suspicion her secrets were even deadlier than mine.

"Talk," I said.

She turned from me and hurried to her room. "You need to leave. Get as far from here as you can and as far away from me as you can."

By the time I caught up with her, she was stripping from her dress. I snatched her by the arm and turned her to me.

"What are you doing?"

"Let me go, Garret."

"Not until you tell me what the fuck is going on and why Rikeri's men are after you."

Rikeri was the king of Duntraik. He was a brutal, power-hungry man who dealt in black magic and death. No one crossed him and no one escaped him.

"It's not your concern," she snapped, freeing herself from my hold and rummaging through her wardrobe.

"What do you mean it's not my concern?"

Clothes were flying from the wardrobe until she emerged with a pair of pants and a shirt that looked too tight for any decent woman to wear. Not that pants were something most women wore.

"You don't know me, Garret. One night of sex doesn't oblige you to be my protector. Run like you wanted to."

She had pulled the pants on, the shirt still in her hands, her breasts bare when I turned her to me. "I'm not running. But I need to know the truth."

"We said no truths, only secrets between us," she said, struggling to free herself from my hold.

"That was before those men came to kill you and I learned Rikeri is searching for you."

"And he'll continue to search once you let me leave."

"I'm not leaving you." The statement came out with such absolute certainty it stunned me. "Now tell me why Rikeri sent his soldiers after you."

She screwed her face up in anger, looking almost like she would have a tantrum, then huffed, "You're a stubborn fool."

"So I've been told."

Her eyes searched mine, and I knew she could find no doubt, no wavering of my conviction to know the truth. The skin under my fingers tingled, my breath stolen from me as I watched her hair slowly darken to an ebony the color of night with thick streaks of gold through it. Her eyes sparkled with flecks of the same gold, her wrinkles disappearing. My jaw went slack as her scars faded to reveal the black markings they hid. I dropped my hands and took a step back, knowing my wide eyes gave away my shock.

The markings formed delicate patterns from her shoulders down to her hands and curved down her chest to spread in a fragile line to her belly. On each of her cheeks sat a cluster of tiny rose petals scattered as if the wind were blowing them.

I tried forming the words, but my stunned mind was attempting to comprehend the sight and the magic that had revealed it. This was why she'd reacted so defensively to the word princess and why the scars never looked right to my eyes. She was the second born to the king of Bira. A title that held more power than even the firstborn who would inherit the throne. The power of the gods in physical form and from her markings, they had blessed her with magic far beyond any other.

"That's why Rikeri is after me," she said, pulling her shirt over her head. "And why you must follow your instinct and leave me."

She snatched a pair of riding boots and a cape from her wardrobe before shoving me aside and leaving the room.

Rikeri wasn't hunting her to kill her. He was hunting her to use her.

"Fuck," I muttered, swiping my hand over my face and hearing her banging around. The mess she was in was far worse than mine. And this was way over my head. My kingdom didn't have magic. We were small and sheltered, separated from Duntraik by many other kingdoms. But now I stood in the corner of two powerful kingdoms, where magic was the source of that power. My curiosity had driven me to this moment, the inclination that I belonged in Duntraik, where dark magic ruled and people like me thrived, bringing me to Eloise.

A cabinet slammed, waking me from my thoughts, and I chased after Eloise. She was wiping the blood off a knife, her things slung in a cloth bag over her shoulder as she made her way to the stable.

"Eloise, stop," I said, catching up with her.

"I need to leave. Nilan warned me to do this when the last men came, but I didn't listen. I was too afraid to run again. But I have to run now, Garret."

I stopped her and turned her to me. She dropped her eyes, but I took her chin in my hand and forced her to look at me. "Let me help," I said, my thumb brushing over the petals etched on her skin. She looked so different now and I missed the silver hair and age that had hidden her true identity.

"It's too dangerous. Nilan was a trained warrior and even he couldn't stop them."

But he had and her words explained how he had downed so many men. From the bodies that now layered the house, he had trained her well enough to fend for herself.

"I'm coming with you."

She went to protest, but I placed my finger over her lips and stopped her.

"Saddle up and wait for me," I instructed, before heading to my shed to pack up my things. My horse was still grazing where I'd left him and I snagged his reins, guiding him closer. While I was tying up my bedroll, I heard Eloise gallop away.

"Dammit," I groused, irritated at her stubbornness. I turned and watched her ride away, debating if I should follow or just let her go. If she wanted to be on her own so badly, I should let her. This wasn't who I was. Some noble man who risked his life for a woman. This wasn't my problem and had nothing to do with me. The last thing I wanted was to stand in the way of something Rikeri was hunting.

I rubbed my hands down my face, cursing the circumstances as I put my things on my horse and climbed on him, sitting at the crossroads of my future. I could turn away and continue my journey, living a life on the run with no center, no identity, no constraints. Or I could take the other option and follow her, accepting the man that decision made me. One who risked his life for a woman he barely knew, a woman who was the most coveted of her people and was now stubbornly running from me.

"Fuck," I muttered, guiding my horse in the direction Eloise had gone and taking off after her. I had no explanation for why I was following her except that letting her go was a choice I couldn't make, no matter what consequence it held.

CHAPTER TWELVE

GARRET

Eloise was a fast rider, and it took me some time to catch up with her. She threw me a glance before staring back ahead. As the silence continued, the muscles in my jaw clenched, my irritation growing. I was risking everything to accompany her, more than she knew. Because I'd been to Duntraik before, at a weak point in my life...yet another. And I'd kneeled before Rikeri, giving him information I'd gathered for him on Bira. Exchanging it for my freedom. I scratched at the scar on my arm where he'd burned his brand from my skin with his magic.

I'd been young, and it had been the first selfish act I'd committed, the start of many. Any prior acts I could blame on poor parenting or the abuse at the hands of my father, but that last act had been nothing more than self-preservation and with it, I'd fled Duntraik and never returned.

We rode through the morning, the silence heavy between us. It wasn't until I saw the black tipped mountains in the distance that I reached over and snatched her reins, stopping her horse.

Even with her cape on and hood up, I could see the glare she gave me.

"Don't give me that look. The horses need to rest, and you need to explain why we're riding into Duntraik when that's the last place you need to go."

She hopped down from her horse and I guided both to a patch of shaded grass where a small stream sputtered lazily through the ground. We were off the road, so I had no worry that anyone would spot us. Even so, I surveyed the area, looking for anything out of the ordinary. We were a day's ride from Duntraik, so that could mean anything.

"Why are you here?" Eloise asked, her hands on her hips.

"I'm here," I said, moving to her and pulling her against me, "because I am." I couldn't tell her I was there because the thought of not being with her was painful, that not seeing her brilliant blue eyes would be like being blinded, and not having her smile light my heart would be death.

"But you shouldn't be," she murmured as I pushed her cape down and brushed my knuckles over the markings on her cheek.

"Yes, I should. Now tell me why Duntraik lies ahead of us when we should be heading far from its border and into Bira."

Tension filled her body, her eyes seeming to darken to the shade of night. "I can't run anymore—"

"Running is exactly what you should do," I argued, not understanding why she would ride to her death.

"I'm tired of running, of hiding. It's been three years of moving from town to town, changing identities, pretending to be something I'm not. I'm tired of being this strong, fearless woman because I'm not."

I wiped the tear from the corner of her eye. "You don't have to be that, Eloise. You don't have to be anything but who you are. I just wish you'd let me know who that is," I said, hearing the hypocrisy in my words and hating it.

"You know who I am." The response was terse, her words frigid.

"Princess of Bira, second born to King Stefan, marked by the gods and blessed with their magic. Did I leave anything out?"

"Curse to my family and people—"

"That's not the way I heard it." I pushed a strand of her hair aside, letting my fingers slide along the dark lock. "You're a blessing to your people. Your existence ensures the magic of your land continues. It touches every part of your kingdom so that it flourishes."

Her eyes dropped.

"Eloise, huh?" I asked her, not knowing if that was her real name, but not remembering what the king's second born was called. It had been a long time since I'd been this far in the world and my memory of it had faded the further I left it in the past. Most people referred to her as the vessel, nothing more, as if she were a thing and not a person.

She glanced back up at me. "Named for my grandmother. I fought Nilan to keep my name so I wouldn't forget where I'd come from...but who can forget when a madman steals you from your home in the middle of the night and cages you in his dungeons?"

"Rikeri did that?"

"Yes." She moved from my arms and searched through the saddlebag, pulling out a water bag and some bread she'd packed.

I observed her as she sat on the ground, her legs crossed, her eyes trying to avoid mine. The golden strands highlighted in her ebony hair emphasized the distinct markings on her face.

"What does he want, princess?"

She swiveled her sight to mine.

"Don't give me that look. Now I understand why you didn't like that nickname, but the truth is out and I'm going to claim it. Tell me what he wants."

The pout of her lips was perfect, and my heart swooped as I

thought of how beautiful she was. Even with the scars she'd stolen my breath, but now with her true appearance revealed and the black markings upon her skin, she was stunning.

"My power."

I tried not to react to the force of that statement, but it was hard not to, and I teetered slightly before I walked over and took a seat across from her. I'd suspected he wanted to use her for her magic, but her answer implied there was more to it.

"Tell me more," I said, grabbing the water and taking a gulp, then wiping my mouth with the back of my hand.

"You ask a lot of questions," she complained.

"And you have a lot of secrets."

"As do you," she countered, humor touching her eyes. "How about for every question you ask, I get to ask one?"

Damn, she had me, but I wasn't ready to give away my secrets, to see the disappointment in her eyes, the judgement they would hold if she found out what kind of man I really was.

"I'll play along," I said, the lies already forming in my head.

She ripped an end off the bread and handed it to me.

"But answer my question first. What does Rikeri want, and how did you end up in his dungeons?"

"That's two questions," she grumbled.

"Phrased in one. Now answer them." I shoved a piece of the bread into my mouth and waited.

She reached into her boot and pulled her knife out. Raising my brow at the smartly concealed weapon, I waited to see what she'd do.

"Do you know why the second born heir to the throne of Bira is so treasured?" she asked, skimming the knife over her hand.

"Your birth ensures the magic of the gods continues in your people and land," I said, repeating what I'd always heard.

"Textbook answer."

From someone who'd never picked up a textbook in his life, but I wasn't about to admit that.

"But that's not exactly it," she continued, the knife blade sliding along one of her markings. This one started at the tip of her index finger and curved down to her thumb like a vine before spreading to her wrist. Tiny thorns lined it until it climbed up her arm where it intersected with more vines, their own thorns prominent. "Yes, my birth continues the blessing of magic in our land. The power that runs through me connects to the land, keeping it fertile and to those who have the gift of magic, ensuring it continues. There has never been a generation where a vessel of the gods has not been born."

"Not since the first kings," I mentioned, remembering snippets of the history I'd picked up in my travels.

"Correct. They say the gods favored Bira and gave us their magic as a gift imbued in the countless fields of thornless roses. Their power seeped from the roots into the land and their scent carried it to the people, gifting them with various levels of magic." I wanted to take the knife from her, my nerves flinching each time the blade tip touched her skin. She seemed unaware that she was doing it. "When Duntraik's king discovered their favoritism, he grew jealous and crossed the border into Bira, cutting down a field of roses and taking them into Duntraik. He syphoned the magic from them, harvesting it for himself and in doing so warped it to be the dark magic that still runs through the veins of each of his ancestors." She peered up at me, her eyes sparkling in the mid-day sun. I wondered how much of her story held truth and how much had morphed through the generations of retellings.

"The gods grew angry with him," she continued. "They punished him with the blight that is Duntraik to this day—harsh, mountainous terrain, the land not fertile, the people suffering. And to protect Bira, they created the vessel. The second born of every king, no matter how many children he has, will always bear the burden of protecting the magic of Bira."

She brought her hand out and sliced into her marking, enough to draw blood. The sight triggered the need to stop her, my hand reaching over and grabbing the knife from her instinctively. But I halted my movement, my hand mid-air with the knife in my grasp as I stared at the blood that trickled from the wound. Golden slivers danced within it, lifting into the air and becoming a mist that floated away.

Dropping back in my seat, I blinked my eyes, thinking I'd been seeing things, but the gold remained, sparkling in the red blood. I lifted my eyes to hers, knowing my astonishment was clear.

"My blood is the blood of the gods in mortal form. Every step I take, every word, every laugh, every tear, is a bit of their magic seeping into the world to fuel the magic bearers in my kingdom. No matter how far I am from them. Magic seeks other magic."

She dragged her finger along the wound, and my eyes grew wide as it disappeared. "You have healing magic?" I asked. There were a dozen questions forming in my mind, but that was the first that I blurted out.

Eloise gave me a half smile. "Only on myself and only where my markings are. Any other wound can still leave me injured or killed, just like any mortal, because I am mortal. But cut me on my markings and I will only bleed, never die."

I took her hand, running my finger over the healed wound. "But your magic bleeds with you," I observed, thinking of how it had seeped from the blood.

"Yes."

My mouth grew dry as the realization of why Rikeri wanted her settled in me. I tightened my hold on her hand, my heart racing. Magic seeks other magic, she'd told me. "You're not going to Duntraik."

"I must," she said, trying to pull from my grasp.

"No," I said. "He knows, doesn't he? Knows he can leech your magic from you. A continuous stream of power at his beck and call."

The thought was terrifying, gripping my chest like a vise.

"Yes." The fight in her fled, her hand going limp in mine. "I was in those dungeons for days before Nilan came for me. My father sent him, ordering him to find me and run with me. But that was enough time for Rikeri to torture me and discover the secret of the markings."

I released her, an anger I didn't understand coursing through me with a need to go to Duntraik and tear Rikeri apart for touching her, for hurting her. Clenching my fists, I rose and fetched the horses. The red-hot streak of ire burned through me, and I couldn't stop it. There was no way I was letting her anywhere near that man again and I would hunt him down and kill him once I had her safe.

"Garret," she said, her voice quiet. I felt her hand on my back, resting softly on the tense muscles.

"You're not going back there. I'm taking you as far away as I can." Even if it meant taking her across the kingdoms to Hiranire and facing my punishment for the things I'd done there.

"I can't keep running—"

"Then return to Bira. Let your family protect you."

She shook her head adamantly. "No, I won't risk it. I have to face Rikeri. I can't continue to live like this."

Turning on her, I took her by the shoulders, saying, "Yes, you can. I won't let that man touch you again." The words had come out so quickly that I couldn't take them back. It was an admittance I wasn't ready for. A need to protect her because the thought of anything happening to her killed me.

She brought her fingers to my face, tracing the tension in my jaw. "I've lost too much already, Garret. I don't want to lose anymore."

My heart thudded as I pulled her to me. "Then don't. Stay with me and I'll take you far from here. I can keep you safe."

Her head shook, her eyes growing sad. "No, you can't. No one can. Nilan was captain of my father's deadliest warriors and even he couldn't keep me safe."

"You can't go into Duntraik, Eloise." I heard the plea in my voice, the emotion that belied the feeling in my chest. Placing her hand on my chest, she lifted on her toes and kissed me. Her kiss was tender, and it called to that emotion I was trying to deny, the one that told me this was more than I'd expected it would be. Calling to a place in my heart that wanted to let her in, to stake a claim that I'd let no one have because it signified an ownership I'd never wanted. I ran my fingers through her hair, pulling her closer as I lost myself to those emotions.

A sound in the distance distracted me and I broke the connection, missing it the moment it ended. Looking to the west, I saw riders barreling toward us.

"Shit," I mumbled. "Hide your marks and your hair, princess."

"They're too close," she said. "They'll grow suspicious if we ride off, especially if they're Rikeri's men."

I kept my eyes on the riders, hearing her adjust her cape.

"And I can't use my magic, they'll notice."

Fuck. She was right; they were too close. The golden haze of her magic would be a dead giveaway. I grabbed her, throwing us both to the ground and crushing her under me.

"Garret, what are you doing?" she complained, struggling to get up.

"Play along and don't question me."

I kissed her, pushing her cloak aside and pawing at her shirt to free her breast while I glanced up at my horse, spying my sword tucked in the saddle. I had my dagger on me and she had hers, but I was hoping I wouldn't need them.

"Not exactly my way of getting out of a sticky situation," she mumbled as I caressed her breast.

I pinched her nipple, joking, "I bet it feels better."

"Gods, yes," she moaned as the riders drew closer. But the quivering of her body below mine belied her nerves.

I pulled her leg up, rubbing my hand along her thigh and

cursing how my dick was now throbbing just at the mere touch. I needed to focus, but I was praying this would work. Avoiding danger was always my first choice, especially if Rikeri's killers were indeed coming.

"Wouldn't it be better to fight them?" she said rather breathlessly.

"This is more fun."

I heard them approach, bringing their horses to a stop. Keeping my hands in place and Eloise below me, I brought my head up and looked over my shoulder at them, but keeping my head at an angle that blocked her face. Her heart was pounding, her breathing halted. She was tense, her body trembling, something that struck me as odd since she'd faced four of Rikeri's soldiers at her house.

"Can I help you, gentlemen? If not, let me go back to taking my woman."

They looked at each other, one smirking.

"Couldn't find a more private spot?" one asked.

"Where I fuck my woman isn't any concern but my own and we were alone before you two showed up to aggravate my hard-on."

Shaking his head, the other spurred his horse, saying, "Let's leave the two lovers alone."

He rode on, the other following. I released the breath I was holding, sensing Eloise relax below me. I turned back toward her, only then seeing the gold and black locks that had slipped free of her hood. My heart raced, my body tensing as I crept my hand from her leg to my belt, where I had my dagger tucked. I gripped the handle, hearing a horse slow.

Eloise's eyes held mine, the intensity in them making them a bright blue.

"Hold on," I heard, and I gritted my teeth, knowing they'd spotted my lapse. "Both of you up," he said. From the corner of my eye, I watched him turn his horse.

"Ready?" I mumbled to Eloise.

She gave me a quick nod. I knew she could fight. I'd seen what she'd done at the house to the other soldiers, but I didn't want her fighting. It went against everything I thought of women, everything I believed. But she was constantly twisting my view of women and their abilities, showing me how I'd underestimated them.

After adjusting her shirt, I rose, keeping my body blocking hers as much as I could and calculating the time it would take me to reach my sword.

"It's her," the soldier said, and I reacted quickly, catching him in the chest with my dagger as he leaped from his horse. He staggered as the other jumped down, his sword in hand. I lunged toward my horse, hating that I needed to leave Eloise unguarded for those few seconds, but knowing she could hold her own.

Pulling my sword free, I heard her scuffling with the soldier, but I caught sight of the one I'd injured darting toward me. I met his sword with mine, the metal clinging loudly. Fuck, I needed to get back to Eloise, and this asshole was slowing me down.

I may have cheated my way up the ranks of the royal army, but I was still a trained fighter, lethal when I wanted to be...even if I stabbed men in the back instead of looking them in the eye when I killed them.

I heard Eloise grunt as she fought the other soldier. My need to protect her surged forth, and I pushed the soldier back with my next move, throwing his footing off. Taking the advantage, I curved my next strike, slicing through the muscle in his arm. His sword fell, and I plunged my sword into his abdomen, using all my strength to rip it through his sternum. His body fell backward, his eyes wide as death took him. Using my foot, I tore the sword from his body and turned to save Eloise. Only to find she had disarmed the soldier, his sword now hers and slicing through his stomach. His body crumbled as she took the killing blow, plowing down his spine with a strength that had my mouth gaping.

She stooped and took her dagger from where she'd lodged it in his shoulder during the fight. Meeting my eyes, she gave me a shrug and proceeded to wipe the blood from her dagger using the dead man's uniform. Realizing I had a goofy grin on my face, I cleared my expression, giving her a scolding look. I should have known she didn't need my help, but seeing her destroy a man two times her size was intimidating.

Her brow arched, her smile mischievous. "Does that turn you on, big boy?" she asked, seduction lacing her voice. "Should I make you drop to your knees again?"

My cock lurched painfully.

"Admit it," she said, walking over to me. "It turns you on that I can fend for myself."

It shouldn't have because those kinds of women had never turned me on, but everything about Eloise defied what I normally found attractive in women.

"Maybe," I admitted.

She kissed my cheek and walked toward the horses. "Was your last girl independent?" she asked.

"Are you my girl?" I countered, not sure I wanted to talk about Beatrice and how wrong I'd been. I stooped over the soldier. "I thought you were my princess?" I didn't know why I said it, inferring ownership over her.

"I'm not anyone's to own," she said, and I peered over at her. "But I don't mind being your princess."

I gave her a lopsided grin, liking the way it sounded. My princess. It had a ring to it that nestled in my soul. Rising, I pulled a knife from the soldier's belt before heading to the other soldier.

"So was she?" Eloise asked, and I clenched my jaw, annoyed that she hadn't let it go.

"In a way," I said. "She had a mind of her own."

I found a dagger on the second soldier that had a nice grip to it and tucked it into my belt.

"And?" she asked.

I met her curious eyes, knowing she wasn't changing the subject. "And I wanted her to be something different." I returned to my horse and mounted him. "Come on, we need to get off this path. There will be more where those came from."

"You're changing the subject," she said, climbing on her horse.

"I'm not changing the subject."

"Then tell me about her."

I threw her a look, but she didn't flinch.

With a huff, I answered, "She was beautiful, sweet, book smart, young—"

"How young?"

I stared at her, thinking of how different she was from Beatrice, yet similar in ways.

"Young enough...eighteen."

"Are you serious?" she said with a snort. "And you're what? Thirty?"

I rolled my eyes at her.

"Twenty-nine," I grumbled.

"You fell for a girl when you needed a woman," she said with a laugh.

My teeth ground, the sound drilling through my ears.

"Shouldn't we be talking about getting away from this open space?" I asked.

"No, I like this conversation better."

I held the reins tighter, annoyed with the humor in her voice and the questions that forced me to admit what kind of man I'd been. "What do you want to hear, El? That I fell for her beauty, expecting her to fall for me because of my looks and muscles? That I was foolish enough to think she would marry me, serve me, bear my children? That she fell in love with another man when I was so certain she was mine?"

She studied me, her blue eyes seeing so far into my soul that I could almost sense their weight. Looking away, the intensity too much for me to bear, I said, "We travel through Bira and along the border until we get closer to the capital city. I'm not risking another run-in with Rikeri's men."

I urged my horse forward and rode away, not wanting to admit my flaws and mistakes anymore, to dwell on a past that held nothing but mistakes that were revealing themselves every second I spent with Eloise. She caught up, leaving me to stew in my silence. Each minute that passed reminded me more of who I'd been and how I'd chosen wrongly, trying to force a woman who hadn't loved me to be mine, convincing myself she would jump at the chance to have me like so many other women did. Waking up in that river to discover how wrong I'd been about everything.

CHAPTER
THIRTEEN

GARRET

The silence remained until we were a half day's ride from Bira's border, the sun descending and the moon taking its place above us. The mountains of Duntraik hovered in the distance, an ominous reminder of what awaited us. I found shelter for us along a raised bit of land that sat beside a small stream.

After settling the horses, I leaned down and splashed my face with the water. It was cool and upon tasting it, I found it to be a clean source that would refill our water bags for the next day's trip.

"This stream sources from Bira's longest river." Melancholy sat in Eloise's voice, and I remembered she'd been away from her home for years, running from demons that made my own seem childish. My anger at her invasive questions faded.

"Come," she said, reaching her hand out to me. I took it, rising and following her as she walked us further up the stream to where it pooled as the land dipped, forming a lake that shimmered in the fading sun.

Eloise pulled her boots off and shimmied out of her pants, throwing a glance over her shoulder at me. Her eyes shone a dusty blue in the reddish-orange of the sunset and I questioned how I'd ever thought anyone was as beautiful as she was right then. My eyes followed her movements as she lifted her shirt over her head, her breasts falling free. I licked my lips, my body buzzing with anticipation. She gave me a playful smile before wading into the water, and I watched her ass move, mesmerized by the motion until the water covered it.

Lifting her finger, she motioned for me to join her, and I didn't hesitate. I stripped quickly and made my way to her, the water cool and refreshing.

"Still mad at me?" she asked as I drew closer.

Pulling her to me, the feel of her skin against mine erasing all traces of what remained of my irritation with her, I said, "I'm not a good man, Eloise. I'm not the knight in shining armor, the one who rushes in to save the world."

"No?," she said, tilting her head as she studied me. "You rushed in to save me."

Her words hit me like the blunt end of a sword upon my head. I had done just that. Rushing back to her house, not thinking of myself, only thinking of her.

"And you saved me again today."

Chuckling, I said, "I beg to differ. I kept a man occupied while you hacked his friend up. You don't need saving."

"Yet you still wanted to. And that tells me you are a good man." She ran her fingers down my jaw. "Maybe you always have been. You just never set that side of you free."

"You set it free," I admitted.

"I don't think I have that kind of power, Garret."

Smiling, I pushed her hair back and brought her closer to me. "I think you have more power over me than I want to admit."

"Is that a bad thing?" she mumbled, her lips brushing mine.

"Before, yes. But now…" I thought about how she made me feel, how my heart leaped when her eyes met mine, how just being near her made me complete, and how she'd woken a part of me I'd never realized was there. "You make me want to be a better man, princess."

Her smile reached in and claimed another piece of my heart that I wasn't ready to give up.

"You are a good man, Garret," she said.

"You don't know me, El." I hated the lies that sat between us, the ones I kept weaving to keep her with me. Fear sat in my chest. A fear of losing her, of having her turn from me if she knew the truth of who I really was. Of what I'd done in my kingdom, the way I'd been intent on tearing down a man I'd thought was a beast when it was really me who had been the beast. And Eloise was slowly peeling away the layers and revealing the man below the beast. The lies remained, however, and with them the fear that she would leave me when the truth came out. But I was so far under those lies that peeling them away like petals of a rosebud was impossible. They were stuck tight and there was nothing I could do to rip them away.

"I don't know who you were before," she said, her fingers tracing the path of my jaw, "other than what you showed me when we first met, but I see who you are now."

I nuzzled my face to hers, then kissed her, quieting her words, stopping the talk because it hurt to hear. I wasn't the man she thought I was, even if I wanted to be that man for her. As the force of that thought hit me, I kissed her more passionately. Because I wanted to be that man. I wanted to be everything I wasn't for her. To change and be what she saw in me.

Our kisses grew more heated, and I ran my hands the length of her body, letting the worries and the events of the day fall away so that only the two of us existed. My hand weaved through her hair, pushing her lips closer, needing to hold her as tight as I could, as if I never wanted to let her go. The power of that thought washed through me because it was the truth. I didn't want to let her go, to ever have her away from me again.

Her hands skirted the muscles in my back, and I scooped her up. As she entwined her legs around me, I entered her, groaning at the feel of her around me and the perfection of her body fitting with mine. With a squeeze to her ass, I tilted her and thrust deeper, her head falling back as a moan slipped from her lips. I slid my hand up her back and twisted my fingers in her hair, pulling it so that she arched into me further. Her cry lit my body on fire, and I dropped my mouth to her breast, needing her to come undone around me.

There was a tall ledge of rock where the stream fed into the lake, the water trickling over it and smoothing the stone over time. I walked us to it, pushing her back against it and grasping her ass tighter as I drove into her. Her body quivered delectably. Every cry, every tremble brought me closer to the edge, her body spurring mine on.

"Garret," she cried, almost breaking me. She dug her heels deeper into my back and I grunted as I went deeper.

"Gods, you feel so good, princess," I said, sliding my hand between us and playing with her clit.

"Be a good boy and call me princess again," she commanded, her thighs shaking.

Chuckling, I pinched her clit, and took her nipple between my teeth, flicking my tongue against it before I said, "Come for me, princess," against her skin.

She broke, her body a flurry of glorious trembles. Her muscles spasmed around me, the sensation coaxing my climax free. It tore through me like a storm that battered me to the core, leaving me clinging to her as it ravaged me.

When I could finally breathe again, I released the tight hold I had on her and pushed her hair back. Her eyes were hazy with satisfaction, and I smiled, kissing her again. She wrapped her arms around my neck and bit my bottom lip, skimming her teeth along it.

"You're a quick learner," she breathed.

"I had an excellent teacher and, to be honest, watching you come is enough to ruin me for any other woman." I cringed at the honesty of my words, hating how they sounded but knowing they were true.

Kissing me again, she mumbled, "Good, because you've ruined me for any other man."

That sensation in my heart returned, a tightness that sat in my chest as her words carved more of her place into it.

I carried her out of the water and laid her on my bedroll, kissing every inch of her markings and watching as they sparkled with my touch, a shimmering gold that lit the darkness around her body. Her eyes shined with touches of it.

"You're gorgeous, princess," I told her, running my hand up her body.

Spreading her thighs with my leg, I sank into her, ready to take her again. I took her hands, pinning them above her head, and looked into her eyes. Each move intensified my need for her, the emotion I held for her. The connection between us grew until I couldn't tear my eyes from her, watching as she fell apart for me, her body curving into mine as I came undone, my release a wave so powerful that it stole the breath from me. When we both calmed, I released her hands, smoothing my hand down her hip and pushing into her once more as the remnants of my release slowly faded.

Her eyes saw deep into me, and I wondered if she could see what she'd done to me. Aside from changing me, from waking the man in me, could she see that she'd stolen my heart? That it now belonged to her.

My fingers drifted through Eloise's long locks, my eyes watching how the gold merged with the ebony.

"Did you love her?" she asked, and I peeked down at her.

Her fingers stroked my chest in a soothing motion that had been lulling me to sleep.

"No," I said, admitting the truth for the first time. "I didn't know what love was. I loved the idea of what having her meant."

"And what was that?" she asked, studying me.

I swallowed back the urge to change the subject, hating how vain I'd been, how conceited I'd been to assume Beatrice would want to marry me simply because we were both the most attractive in the village. Basing my entire attempt at having her on her looks and innocence, ignoring the fact that we had nothing in common. Refusing to accept her rejections and feigning interest in her sisters to get closer to her, taking pleasure in their bodies as I did. As if that would have won Beatrice over. By that point, my desire to have her had turned from winning her hand to forcing her to be mine and manipulating her. I'd threatened every other suitor, making it known she was mine, expecting she would come to her senses and be my wife. Until the moment I learned of the other man, the beast that sat beyond the dark forest, a curse upon his head, forgotten with time and enchantments until Beatrice broke the spell and me.

Sighing, I replied, "Marriage, a wife to service my needs, to wait on me hand and foot, to bear my children. Love was never part of it."

She kissed my chest and leaned over it, resting her hands next to my head as she hovered over me. "I won't wait on you, but I'll service your needs as long as you service mine."

Smiling, I tucked her hair behind her ears. "And the children?"

Her smile faded, her eyes growing sad and dropping from mine. "I can't have children," she murmured, her words like a punch in my gut.

I'd lived almost thirty years with the notion of eventually settling down with a wife, children running around my feet, one resting on her hip as I kissed her goodbye before leaving for duty. Eloise must have read my expression before I could hide the disappointment. She rolled from me, the hurt in her eyes fracturing the hold she had on my heart. I laid there for a moment, contemplating her words and why they'd affected me so...as if I'd filled her in as the wife I was kissing, our children running at my feet, our babe on her hip. Now I understood why she hadn't been concerned with me coming in her each time. I was so enraptured with her I hadn't cared if I got her pregnant because seeing her that way would have only endeared her more to me.

The vision dissolved and reality set in that everything was different now. My desires had changed, my view of what I wanted in a woman, my situation, who I was. All of it had shifted and with it, that vision shifted because I knew in that instant that if she weren't in it, then I wanted no part of it. The children at my feet didn't matter, nor did the babe on her hip. The only thing I knew with certainty was that I wanted Eloise to be the one I was kissing, to be the one I came home to, the one I lived my life with. The rest we could figure out.

I drew her to me, turning into her, and tipping her chin up. Her eyes were shadowed with the hurt I'd caused her because she wanted something...that same something I wanted. A thought occurred to me, burning through me like a wildfire looking for a way to escape.

"Is Rikeri the reason?" I growled, my hold on her tighter.

She shook her head. "No. Vessels can't bear children. We live until the one to take our place is ready to be born and at their birth, we die. The magic comes with a price—endless magic, but no children. We live our lives secluded, sheltered and protected, never experiencing love or sex, the joy of children."

"Yet you're different," I said, my ire fading.

"Yes," she said with a smile. "My great aunt was the last vessel. My brother told me that when my mother became pregnant with me, she made my father promise to let me experience life like a normal child."

An immense respect filled me for the king of Bira because, in doing so, he'd let life shape Eloise into the woman she was today.

"I played with my older brother, ran in the fields, climbed the hills and the trees. And in embracing life like she wanted me to, my power flourished."

"Because the gods never meant for your kind to be locked up like some untouchable treasure, hoarded and hidden."

"Exactly," she said, her eyes twinkling with her magic. Her smile faded. "But I'm still broken, not like other women—"

"You're not broken, Eloise," I said firmly, pulling her further into my hold. "I don't care if you can't have children."

"But you—"

"Only want you." The words were out before I could catch them. And with them, there was no need to question the sensation in my chest or the way her presence lit my soul, giving me a peace I'd never had. "If there is no you, then the rest doesn't matter. So if I can only have you, that's all I need to be happy."

Her eyes searched mine, tears pushing behind them. I didn't want to divulge the feelings for her that sat in my chest, ones I was still struggling to contemplate because they were far deeper than anything I'd ever experienced.

But the words fell from my mouth before I could catch them. "I love you, Eloise. And you're all I want, all I need."

Her breath hitched, a tear slipping over the rose petals etched on her skin. I swiped one away.

"I know it's soon, and you just lost your husband. But I can wait until you're ready—"

She stopped me with a kiss that tore at the last pieces of my heart, claiming them and ingraining her essence on them for eternity.

"Oh, you foolish man. He wasn't my husband, and I didn't love him," she muttered between kisses.

I pushed her back, and I was certain she could see the confusion on my face.

"I told you, Nilan was captain of my father's private guard. My father sent him to protect me."

"He wasn't your husband?"

She laughed, throwing her head back. "No." And her answer caused my heart to leap hard in my chest. "He was there out of duty. We were stuck living together for over two years before they found us." My fingers had drifted up her neck when she'd tipped it back, and I spread them around it, seeing the fire that lit in her eyes and stirred my desire to have her again.

"Did he touch you?" I asked, the sting of jealousy lashing at me.

She arched her brow, giving me a coy smile. "Are you asking if I fucked him?"

"Well, I was asking if he fucked you."

Her laugh was deep this time, and I squeezed my fingers gently, feeling how it rumbled below them. She inhaled temptingly. "We were two people stuck with each other, lonely and seeking comfort in each other."

"Did you love him?" I hated the way the question had come out with a plea laced in it.

"Only as a friend. He was much older than me. We fucked and enjoyed each other's company because we were all we had."

"How much older?" I asked, raising my brow.

"Old enough to teach me to please a man and to show me how a woman should be pleased," she replied, her fingers wrapping around my hand and tightening it. My cock twitched and her lips curved seductively when she noticed it.

"So I have him to thank for the demanding woman who likes me to take her hard and commands me to my knees?"

"Damn right you do."

Chuckling, I pulled her lips to mine. "Remind me to thank him later. After I take you again."

"And how will you be taking me?"

I released her neck and brought both hands to her ass, squeezing it tight before smacking it. "Hard. Now get on your knees, princess."

She shivered before pressing her hands to my chest and saying, "Not until you're on your knees like a good boy."

My dick throbbed so hard with that command that I flipped her, draping my tongue down her body and following her order until she was coming so hard that her screams filled the quiet night.

CHAPTER FOURTEEN

ELOISE

My body simmered with the aftershocks of my climax, but Garret's tongue didn't stop. He had his enormous arms wrapped around my legs, his tongue smoothing the pulsing in my clit. Gods, I really had created an unstoppable beast and now that he knew how to make me crumble, he did it as often as he could. Not that I was complaining.

He flattened his tongue and ran it over me once more before he kissed my inner thigh, sliding his lips along it and groaning.

"Fuck, princess, I could feast on you all day and still want more."

I couldn't stop my giggle, and he peeked up at me, his eyes glinting with desire. He ran his tongue over my stomach, following the path of my markings. I'd always hated the vines that scarred my body, evidence that it wasn't mine. That I belonged to the gods, to the kingdom, to the monarchy. There had never been a time when I'd felt beautiful, my body marred with that ownership, my face blotched with the black petals on my cheeks. Only my brother had ever seen past the markings. Everyone else saw me as nothing more than the vessel the gods had made me.

But the way Garret touched me, his fingers always following the path of my petals as his brown eyes held mine, his mouth worshipping my body, kissing my markings, made me feel like I was something more. In his eyes I was beautiful and the way he looked at me as if I were the most breathtaking woman in the world, seeing past the patterns that had defined me since the day I'd been born assured me that his admission of love had been true.

His mouth lingered on my breast, sucking my nipple into his mouth as his hardness pressed for entrance, slipping along my folds and teasing me. I bowed my back, sending my breast further into his mouth, a moan falling from my mouth. He was insatiable, and I was ready to meet that insatiability.

His hand tucked below my knee, drawing it up as he entered me, a low rumble coming from his chest. I loved how full I felt when he was inside of me. His mouth covered mine, silencing my cry, his body moving mine with his thrusts. I wrapped my legs around him, running my hands over the muscles that lined his chest and loving the strength below them. Our lips parted, his eyes holding mine, and in them sat the love he had for me. He loved me. Not for who I was, but despite it. He'd wanted me before he discovered I was the vessel and before I'd lifted the façade of age. And he loved me despite hearing that I was barren, that I'd never give him the children he'd envisioned, that a madman hunted me and I was about to hand myself to him, that I was only a thing, not a woman to be loved and cherished.

The thoughts in my mind morphed, the assuredness his touch and love had given me now repressed as doubts and fear took their place. There was no future that held a happy ending for Garret with me because there was no happy ending for me.

He slowed his thrusts, his fingers pushing my hair back as his eyes questioned me.

"What's wrong?" he asked, lifting his chest from mine.

I swallowed, hating that my mind had turned from such a tender moment to something worrying.

"El?"

"It's not fair to you," I murmured, wishing I hadn't thought of what he was giving up for me. Or that my future held nothing but pain and despair. That he would lose me because I wouldn't be able to stop Rikeri.

"What's not fair?"

"For you to love me when I can't give you what you want." I sniffed, hating that I suddenly appeared so weak, even with all the strength he offered me. My strength was faltering from the crushing weight of reality. "That I—"

He stopped my words with a kiss, his arm moving under me to pull me to his chest, holding me securely just as the swell of panic bloomed. I clung to him as it dragged me under with its viscous claws, Garret the only thing grounding me.

"Shhh," he whispered against my lips. "I told you, there is nothing more that I want than you."

"But I'll only disappoint you," I said, my voice so low it was barely a whisper. "And you'll lose me."

He drew back, his eyes darkening. There was something more behind them than the protectiveness that lay on the surface as he said, "No one is going to take you from me."

He hadn't said he wouldn't lose me, and I wondered at his reaction because I saw it then, the fear that sat below that bravado. There were secrets he kept from me, just as I kept my own still, and within those secrets lay the explanation of that fear. My lip quivered as the force of my attack hit me. The worry, the trepidation, the futile impossibility of my situation that I'd dragged him into came slamming into me like a rush of waves pounding the surf and I felt myself drowning.

"El," Garret said.

I tried to breathe, to remind myself that he'd been making love to me, that he was still nestled deep inside of me, waiting to bring my body over the edge once again. But it was useless, and I dug my fingers into his back.

"Eloise," he said, lowering me and coming up on his elbows. His hand pushed my hair back as I tried to focus on him in the desperate struggle to not pass out. "Eloise, I am not going anywhere. I will not leave your side, and if you insist on facing Rikeri, then I'll face him with you."

He dropped his forehead to mine. "Or we can turn around now. I'll take you away. We can get a small house for just the two of us and live our lives fucking until the gods take us." His words were soothing, the intensity of his eyes pulling me from panic's hold. "If you want children, we'll adopt. If you don't, we'll get a cat."

This time I laughed, the reaction calming my body and lifting me from the drowning thoughts. I nodded as his expression relaxed. He kissed my nose, nuzzling his nose against it.

"It'll be okay," he said, and I wondered if he was trying to make himself believe it, too.

"Did I ruin the moment completely?" I asked, my confidence still gone.

"Well, I can't say I'm as hard as I was a few minutes ago, but I'm sure a few moves of those hips will have my cock straining to reach the deepest parts of you."

I pulled him to me, kissing him and wanting to go back to the moment when the excitement of hearing him say he loved me was blazing through me. But he stopped my kiss, glancing at me with concern in his eyes.

"I'm fine, now," I said, reassuring him. "Make love to me, Garret."

"I thought that's what I was doing," he said, giving me a sexy smirk. "I've had plenty of reactions to the way I fuck, but that's one I haven't seen."

My eyes dropped, guilt that I'd ruined the moment coming through.

"I'm waiting," he said, and I peeked back up at him.

He wanted an explanation. He'd seen me at my weakest and now he wanted answers to why I wasn't as strong as I tried to be, that below that show of confidence was the scared girl who feared the world was swallowing her whole as the burdens of her destiny erased her potential.

I looked down at his chest, running my fingers over it and feeling the heaviness of his eyes as he waited for answers.

"I've had them since I was a teenager. They grew in intensity with each passing year until they became so overwhelming I could no longer find my way out from under their hold. I'm sorry, Garret. I know I'm not perfect. I'm not strong like I pretend. I'm really—"

"No, princess." I glanced back up at him, seeing that darkness in his eyes again, but along with it was a playfulness that met the smirk he gave me. "That's not what I was waiting for."

I searched his eyes, looking for an answer, not understanding what he wanted. He leaned closer to me and took my lip between his teeth, dragging them over it.

"You're fucking perfect, El. And if I ever hear you say you're not strong, I will flip you over and smack that ass so hard that every time you sit, you'll remember you're the strongest woman I know." My heart flickered back to life, the cobwebs of my anxiety swept away with his words. "Now, I'm waiting to hear some witty comeback about my ability to please a woman after my last comment."

Relief surged, my body relaxing completely into his as my confidence returned with the simple knowledge that this man thought I was strong, that he didn't care that I'd lost my grasp on reality, that he hadn't stopped holding me through it, and he hadn't judged me for it.

I laughed, threading my fingers through his thick hair. "And what kind of reactions have you had when you've fucked women?"

"There's my girl. Why don't you let me show you?" His eyes twinkled with amusement, all worry gone from his features.

"So, you're saying I'm just like any other woman you've fucked? Spreading my legs and satisfying that hungry cock like a good girl?"

"Fuck, yeah. But like *my* good girl and," he pushed into me, his length growing thicker, "I've never had a woman who reacted as gloriously as you do, princess."

I yanked his lips to mine, kissing him, my body reawakening as his hand drifted over it. "That's because you didn't know what you were doing before me, big boy." He jerked inside of me, and I pressed my pelvis up, sending him deeper.

"You keep calling me big boy, and I'm going to come before I get to rip that reaction from you."

My moan was loud, and he captured it before it could fully escape. I let myself go to his touches, the way his body felt against mine, and how his every kiss was like he was kissing me for the first time. This man was mine, and he loved me. That was all I needed to know. It was enough. And as the waves of my climax tore through me, I held tight to him, knowing my heart was his and that he would protect it.

GARRET HAD his limbs tangled with mine, his enormous arms holding tight to me even as he slept. I turned my head and took the time to look at him. This handsome man who had his pick of women, who came with mistakes and poor decisions, some of which I still didn't know, loved me. No man had ever loved me. Nilan had touched me and fucked me. We'd shared a bed, but there had never been love between us. It had been nothing more than friendship and sex.

But Garret loved me, and I loved him. I understood that in the deepest recesses of my heart and yet I hadn't said it back. His confession had left me shaken, the force of it triggering the racing of my mind until his love had brought me back.

I let my fingers linger on his face, his stubble rough against my calloused skin. Maneuvering from his arms so as not to wake him, I made my way to the stream to wash up. Collecting my clothes and Garret's from where we'd left them, I returned, dropping his beside him before dressing. As I fixed my shirt, I thought about how different I looked from what anyone at home would find acceptable. Anything but a heavy dress with layers of the finest materials would have given my mother an excuse to chastise me.

A lady didn't dress like this, nor did a princess. But a woman on the run, who rode for days leaving her past behind, needed to dress like this. I remembered the day Nilan had bought me the outfit, helping me out of the torn and bloodied dress that had been a constant reminder of Rikeri's abuses. I'd shed my identity that day, ignoring the pain it had caused, the finality of it that sat on my chest like the hooves of a horse.

Brushing my fingers through my hair, I looked toward the horizon, following my instinct, the draw of my magic to my homeland. I left Garret and followed the incline of the land until Bira sat in the distance. My chest clenched, tears pressing for freedom. A swell of homesickness overcame me, and I teetered slightly.

I could see the border wall of impassable thorny vines that kept my kingdom safe from invaders, the treacherous mountains of Duntraik to the left, and past the thick bramble far in the distance lay the fields of thornless roses. A sea of crimson that defined my kingdom as the blessed land of the gods. I could almost smell their sweet scent in the air and it brought a blend of warmth and sadness to me.

Garret didn't want me to go to Duntraik, and I'd noticed his tension as we grew closer. He wanted to run, to take me far from

Rikeri's reach, but there was no escaping him. I chewed my lip as I thought of Bira. I couldn't go back, it was too dangerous. I was a liability to my homeland now, a risk that would bring nothing but ruin. But how did I keep Garret from insisting I go back? He still had his secrets, and I still had mine. I didn't want to see the disappointment in his eyes when I told him the truth, the same disappointment that had sat in my father's eyes. Why I thought Garret would be anything but supportive, I didn't know. He hadn't judged me for my panic, hadn't told me how weak it was like Nilan had, or insisted I stop being childish like my mother had, or looked at me with eyes that told me I was being a nuisance like my father had before sending me back to my tower. Locking away the embarrassment, the truth that I wasn't like the vessels before me. That I pushed too much, that I feared my destiny too much, that I asked for too much freedom. Freedom that had lessened with each passing year until the sun only touched my skin for mere minutes a day. Locked away to do my duty for the kingdom, to be the vessel, a thing to worship, a thing to respect, but not a thing to touch, not a thing to love, only a thing to use.

I wrapped my arms around myself, shoving the thoughts away. I wouldn't let the past own me when I was this close. But I couldn't ignore the tremble in my hands as I squeezed them tight. My eyes stayed fixed on the roses, the sight of them reinforcing me. Relaxing my arms, I brought my hand out, perceiving the tingle of magic in my fingers, the call of magic to magic. The land of Bira and the thornless roses both linked to my magic, blessed by the gods. A gold dusting sparkled on my fingertips as I closed my eyes and let my connection to Bira feed my strength and praying it wouldn't signal to my father that I was close and that I didn't cause more damage than I already had.

CHAPTER FIFTEEN

GARRET

Dawn came too soon, the morning light forcing my eyes to open. I rubbed the sand from them, stretching before realizing Eloise was no longer in my arms. She'd fallen asleep as I'd held her, but now there was no trace of her. Sitting up, I looked around, still not seeing her. Fear snaked through me, striking me in the chest like a viper's sting. I grabbed my clothes, throwing my pants and boots on while my eyes searched for her. The horses were still where I'd left them, and I would have woken if anyone had come for her.

Nevertheless, my fear remained. I checked the lake, then ran back to where we'd slept, running past and around the cluster of rocks, my tension fading when I saw her. Coming to a halt, I stood back and watched as she tilted her face to the rising sun, the orange glow giving a blush to her cheeks that highlighted her markings. The gold in her hair sparkled, her markings glittering as if dusted with the gold of her magic.

She stood on an incline, Bira before her in the distance. The wall of thorny vines rose far into the sky, delineating the border between the two kingdoms. From where I stood, I could see into Bira where a field of thornless roses rested in the morning sun far beyond the bramble. They were a rarity that only bloomed in Bira, said to be touched by the gods. The same unique roses Rikeri's ancestors had stolen to gain his power.

I stood enamored as petals lifted from the field and floated in the air. An unseen breeze carried them toward the border, lifting to eclipse the wall, a golden essence streaming from Eloise and reaching for them. A few nested in the vines, blooms spreading from them, transforming the gnarled, twisted throng of thorns so they became something almost delicate and beautiful. The petals that floated on the air dissipated at the contact with her magic, transforming to a glittering dust carried away on a breeze I could not feel.

I held my breath, enraptured by the vision as her magic spread along the field, on a course to bless those gifted with what little magic the gods allowed mortals. Mortals other than Eloise, who was the vessel that fed all other magic in her kingdom. An immense pride filled my chest. This woman whom I loved, whom I'd admitted what I'd never admitted to another woman, for whom I would risk my life to protect, was the most powerful being in our world. Her gift was so cherished that her kingdom protected her above all else, their most lethal warriors in charge of her.

Until that one fateful day...my heart stopped, tension slinking back into my muscles.

"Eloise," I called to her.

She turned to me, her markings brilliant in the morning sun, her magic surging through them. Her eyes were cornfield blue, a startling color that stole my breath. Her smile was glorious, and my heart pounded with the weight of the lies I'd weaved, ones I could never reveal to her now because if my suspicion was right, there was a reason Rikeri had broken through the defenses that had kept each vessel secure for centuries.

She ran to me, her hair flowing behind her as she jumped into my arms. I pulled her close, needing the solidness that was her, the reality that she wanted me in this moment, before the truth mangled the bliss I wanted to hold on to.

"Good morning," she said, giving me a kiss.

I brushed her hair back, putting off what I knew I had to ask for another second.

"El, I need to—"

"No," she said, stopping my words with her finger. "I need to say something because I didn't last night." I went to talk again, but she halted my attempt, narrowing her eyes as if scolding me. I was happy to see she was back to her confident, strong spirited self. Seeing her so broken last night had hurt, because she wasn't fragile, she was a force. And I loved that about her. But she had layers to her, ones she was still revealing to me, and that had been another layer. A side of her I hadn't seen but a part of her I would keep safe and love just as much as I loved the other parts of her. Until the day she no longer wanted me, a day I feared was closing in on me.

Bringing both her hands to my cheeks, her eyes gazed into mine, the emotion behind them palpable. "I don't understand why or how it could be after just these few days, but I love you, too."

I wanted her to take the words back, to unhear them, but they were there, in the air like a heavy load under which I was faltering. The way they weaved into my heart, matching with the force of my love for her, made it too real to bear losing. And I would lose it. I would lose her if she ever found out the truth, the lies I couldn't climb from under.

She frowned, studying me as I grappled with my emotion.

"Did you change your mind in the span of one night?" she asked, backing from my arms.

Forcing myself to put my worry aside, I drew her back to me, leaning my forehead on hers.

"No, I just didn't expect it," I answered honestly. "I thought you'd stubbornly mock me for being weak."

"Love isn't weakness," she whispered.

Tracing the petals on her cheek, I tipped her lips to mine, relishing the feel of them and wishing I could take so much back, so many of the mistakes I'd made, the steps I'd taken, choices I'd made. But it was too late and in some ways, those mistakes had led me to her. Leading me to the woman who would change me, making me a better man before she walked away from me. Because that's what she would do if the truth ever revealed itself.

"You wanted to say something?" she asked, nibbling my bottom lip. The pinkish hue of the sun sat on her cheeks, reflecting in her eyes.

My heart sank as I formed the question that would change everything for me once she answered it.

"How did Rikeri kidnap you?" I asked, knowing he wouldn't set foot in Bira. His power juxtaposed the light in the magic that ran through Bira, and the gods had ensured he couldn't corrupt their favored kingdom any more than his line had when they'd warped their blessing. He stayed in Duntraik, avoiding the discomfort being in Bira caused him.

"His men got in through old servant tunnels that had been closed off. A servant had sneaked her lover in years earlier and my father sealed the openings off, but somehow they knew of them and got through." My chest was so tight I could barely form a thought other than the one that screamed that I knew who that lover had been.

"They struck in the dead of night, killing the guards outside my door and the few they encountered as they made their way to my tower. I remember seeing their dead bodies, the gag in my mouth muffling my screams." Her gaze slipped from mine, landing on something in the distance as her memories returned. Memories marred by my own. Because I had been responsible for that night as much as those men who had taken her. Buying my freedom from a man who had enslaved me from birth and exchanging that freedom for Eloise's.

I had been that lover, seducing the servant girl with my charms and false words. Fucking her in those tunnels, muffling her cries as my eyes memorized each detail of those tunnels. Lying to gain access, letting her take me deeper into the castle as I manipulated her with sex and false words until the day I'd left her heartbroken because I had what I needed. Turning to the scullery maid who had even more access, twisting my words so that she let me take her in the second set of tunnels, pushing her against the wall and fucking her hard as I continued to memorize the routes, the weaknesses in their defenses. I'd left her just as heartbroken because I hadn't cared for either girl, using their bodies and their hearts because they were a way for me to achieve what I'd always wanted. My freedom.

I rubbed the scar that remained on my arm where Rikeri had burned away his brand with his power, granting my freedom for the sacrifices I'd made for the kingdom. Upholding his end of a bargain he'd doubted I could uphold. I'd left Duntraik that day and never returned. Barely a man but shaped to be the man I'd been before Eloise had changed me.

"Garret?" she asked, noting how I'd become lost in my memories.

"Why now?" I asked. "Why take you three years ago?" Because I'd given him that information twelve years ago. Twelve long years where I'd worked to forget where I'd come from, settling in Hiranire as far from Duntraik as I could be, climbing to captain in the king's army, establishing myself as something other than the enslaved boy I'd been.

She looked toward Bira. "I don't want to cut through Bira, Garret."

"Don't change the subject, El. Why only three years ago? Why not take you earlier?" When those tunnels had been open, unguarded because the servants would use them to sneak out or sneak boys like me in.

She tried walking away, and I stopped her. "What does it matter?" she asked.

Because it mattered, but I couldn't tell her I knew that he'd sat on that information for years.

"Call it curiosity."

With a sigh, she said, "Few people know..." She rubbed her hand over the markings on her arm. And I suspected I was one of the few who knew because I'd delivered that piece of information to Rikeri, not understanding its importance. "The markings stretch as we grow. We're born with them, but they aren't complete. They continue to grow with us until our thirtieth birthday, when they meet in one continuous design except for the blessings on our face."

"How old are you, El?" But I knew. Because Rikeri had planned it based on that significant detail I'd overheard but not understood.

"Thirty-three. He took me on my birthday."

I stepped back, the impact of all I'd done slamming into me like a rusty knife, twisting and rotting until I thought I might die.

"There's nothing you could have done to stop it, Garret. We didn't even know each other." But there was something, everything, that I could have done differently.

I'd been on my knees, his power encasing my body, waiting to strike as I'd poured out all the details I'd memorized, all the information I'd gathered, and the one piece that the servant girl had said as I pretended to care about anything more than her words, asking her what the engravings on the tunnel walls meant. And her answer had supplied Rikeri with the most important piece. 'They mirror the markings on the vessel. When she turns thirty, they glow as the full power of the gods merges in her.'

A vessel growing stronger with every passing day until the day the gods filled her completely, leaving her ripe for Rikeri's taking.

I staggered back, running my hands over my face as the reality of all the damage I'd reaped with my selfishness pummeled me.

"Garret?" The concern in her voice wasn't something I deserved.

Her hand touched my back. "I'm not that much older than you," she said.

I looked at her, her comment causing me to smile amidst the anger and frustration that was gripping me. "No, you're not," I said, running my fingers through her hair. "I rarely pay attention to women my age." I played along, too afraid to tell her the truth, to tell her it was my doing, my selfishness that had left her in this situation. That I'd used those girls for my gain, that I'd in turn used her for my gain, trading her freedom for mine.

I grasped my hand around her neck and brought her against me. "I don't care how old you are. It's only a few years and you are by far the most amazing woman I've ever been with. I fell in love with you when you had silver hair and wrinkles. If you were twenty years older, I'd still be in love with you, princess."

"Then what's wrong?" she asked, her hand cupping my cheek.

Swallowing back the truth, I did what usually came naturally. I lied. But the lie was the hardest yet, each word burning another scar on my soul. I accepted it because, faced with losing her, it was all I knew to do. "I want to kill Rikeri. To rip him to shreds for disrupting your life, for daring to put his hands on you, for hurting you, and hunting you. For taking you from everything you knew." There was truth to my words, but the anger I directed toward myself because not only did I want to punish Rikeri, I wanted to punish myself.

Her eyes softened, turning a lush navy. "There's no taking back what happened. No going back to change the past. And if he hadn't done the things he did, the gods wouldn't have put you in my path."

The certainty of her words lightened the load of my guilt but didn't ease it. Her thumb brushed over the tension in my jaw.

"Let's go back," I said. "Turn back and head to the other side of the world, far from Rikeri. I can keep you safe there. We can settle down—"

"Raise a family? Live a normal life?" she asked, the sadness in her eyes killing me.

"I didn't mean that."

"But it's what you want, Garret." Her eyes dropped, and I hated that she'd read into what I was saying.

I tipped her chin. "It's not what I want. I told you that, El. I don't want anything if you're not by my side. But I want you safe. And going to Duntraik isn't safe. It's suicide. If anything, we should go to Bira."

She swallowed. "Then go, Garret. Run far from here and go someplace safe because anywhere with me can never be safe. I'm not some trophy to hide away."

"That's not what I said." This was turning, and I wasn't sure how to bring it back.

She freed herself from my arms and stormed back toward where we'd slept.

"Eloise!"

She ignored me, irking me at the same time. She was frustrating, but then she'd been frustrating from the moment I'd met her.

I ran after her, grabbing her arm and forcing her to look at me. "Where you go, I go."

"Then we go to Duntraik. Straight through and not through Bira."

"No." I stood firm, folding my arms and glaring at her.

"No?" Straightening to her full height, which still stood many inches below mine, she put her hands on her hips. "This is my journey. Not yours. If you insist on coming with me, we go the way I want to and I'm not wasting any more time."

"Wasting time? Like last night?" I barked, the sting of her words causing me to flinch. How had this turned? Gods, she could be irritating at times.

"No," she said, scrambling to fix her words. "That's not what I meant."

"Then what exactly did you mean, Eloise?"

Her lips thinned, and she scowled. My lip twitched, the look too cute to stay mad at her.

"What?" she spat.

My smile grew as the reason I loved her came slamming back into me. It was the fire in her, the free spirit, the strength that I loved, the independence that challenged me.

"You know you're cute when you're angry."

"Are you serious right now?" she asked, her eyes wide.

"Deadly."

She huffed and stomped away, leaving me chuckling as I followed.

"You are so frustrating," she grumbled.

"As are you," I retorted, my mood calmer. "I like the way your ass jiggles when you stomp like that."

She stopped and turned to me, her face contorted with aggravation. Stalking over to me, she poked my chest, saying, "You're not twisting my words around, then joking about my ass."

I snatched her hand, grabbing her other one and pushing them behind her so that her chest smacked against mine. "I didn't twist your words around. You said we were wasting time, which I took to mean fucking me was a waste of your time." I jerked her wrists, pinning them in my one hand while I guided my other into her pants. "Now, just for that, I think I want to waste more time before we ride into Bira on this blasted mission to kill ourselves."

"I'm not riding into Bira. We're going into Duntraik," she replied, her voice husky.

I squeezed her ass, slipping my fingers to the front of her and dipping them between her legs. She drew in a breath, her breasts pushing further into my chest.

"Bira," I said, forcing her legs open with my knee and thrusting a finger through her wetness.

"Duntraik," she moaned.

"I'm not giving on this one. We skirt the border of Bira and then move into Duntraik when we're closer to the capital."

I plunged a second finger into her and she cried out before saying through gritted teeth, "And how do you know where the capital is?"

Fuck, that was a question I didn't want to answer, but I'd have to come up with something. Freeing her hands, I threaded my fingers through her hair and smashed her mouth to mine, kissing her with the need that was flaring through me. My fingers were so drenched as they fucked her, I questioned if I could wait for her to come before selfishly taking her.

"I studied all the kingdoms before I set out on this journey," I said, between kisses, another lie falling too easily from my mouth. "Now come for me, princess."

I pulled her hair and dropped my mouth to her cleavage, running my tongue over her skin as my fingers worked her body into a frenzy. She grasped my back, her nails digging into my skin. Pushing her shirt down, I freed her breast, pulling her nipple into my mouth and sucking at the same time I retracted my fingers, playing with her clit. Her body was trembling so hard she could barely stand and when I plunged my fingers back into her, she shattered. I caged her cry with my mouth, kissing her through it, her body clamping down on my fingers so tightly that it had my cock aching.

Pushing my hand up around her neck, another wave of release shivered through her. I was so hard by now that I knew I needed her to ease my pain. She was clinging to me, her breathing rapid, and I tightened my hand around her neck, dragging my lips over her cheek and murmuring, "Now drop to your knees, princess, and relieve the hard-on you just gave me."

The gorgeous quiver that racked her body was one I committed to memory. She released my back as I pulled my fingers from her, and dropped to her knees, her blue eyes watching me as I licked each finger clean.

"Damn, that tastes sweet," I muttered.

She worked me free, and I wondered at the dynamic between us. As if she noticed, she flicked her tongue over her teeth and said, "I'll let you dominate me now, like a good princess, but I can promise you'll be taking my commands later like a good boy."

"Fuck, yes I will," I said, twisting my fingers into her hair. Anticipation surged through me as I watched her mouth settle over my tip. No matter how I enjoyed the way her commands turned me on, the sensation of commanding the most powerful woman in our world was a rush I couldn't ignore.

"Take your shirt off, princess. I want to see those tits jiggling while you take me." The aggressor in me was ready to play, and excitement surged through me as she sat back and pulled her shirt over her head, her breasts springing free. I played with one as she descended on my hard-on, her tongue circling my head enticingly. And when she dropped her mouth, taking almost my full length, my groan broke the silence. I tangled my hand in her hair, trying to breathe as I lost myself to the sensation of her mouth. She dipped lower, her quiet gag accompanied by my grunt. I wanted to hear more of those gags, to have them take me over the edge, but I'd never been the aggressive type, not until Eloise. She invited it, her moans deeper when my hand wrapped around her neck or I pulled her hair. Her body falling apart when I took her hard. And somehow, I knew if I used her mouth the way I was craving, the way I'd held back in the past when other women had gone down on me, that Eloise would invite it.

Grasping a handful of her hair, I shoved her forward, fucking her mouth so hard her gags drove me close to breaking. I jerked her back, my dick releasing from her mouth with a pop, strands of saliva dripping from it and her mouth. She took a deep breath, her eyes watery, and I questioned myself, thinking I'd become too unhinged and pushed her too far.

"Shit, princess. As sexy as that is, I don't want to hurt you." And I didn't. No matter how many times I'd found pleasure in women over the years, I'd never hurt one, never forced one, never left a mark. As much as I had thought women were there for my pleasure, to take care of me and wait on me, I still valued protecting them. They were fragile, delicate things. At least that's what I'd thought until Eloise had come into my life.

She brought her finger up and swiped the spit from her bottom lip. "Do you like it when I gag, big boy?"

"Fuck, do I ever, princess."

"Then fuck my face like a good boy and use me until your cum is sliding down my throat."

My jaw dropped. For someone blessed by the gods and meant to be treated like a holy treasure, she had a mouth on her. A dirty, sexy mouth that I was about to finish using.

"As you wish, princess."

I took a fistful of her hair as she opened her mouth and grasped my cock again. I rammed into her so far that her gag sent a raging inferno through me. I couldn't stop. The beast she'd unleashed in me took over and used what she'd offered so hard that spit was dribbling everywhere and tears were running down her face. But I was too lost to halt my oncoming climax, its hold too strong on me, and as it tore through me, I shoved deeper, hitting the back of her throat as my release flooded from me. My growl rumbled through my chest. My body was a rush of sensations that rocked me as I held her there, pumping the last currents from me until she left me spent. Her eyes met mine, and I released her hair, her tongue gliding over me as she heaved breaths my actions had kept her from. Brushing my thumb over her cheek, I wiped away the tears, hating that I'd caused them, but with a mixed sense of accomplishment that I had. She dragged her finger from the corner of her mouth and licked it clean, and I shook my head.

"You are amazing," I said when I could finally speak. I reached down and picked her up, her legs wrapping around my waist. She leaned her chest into mine, the warmth of her breasts accompanied by the dampness of the spit that lingered on them. Her arms entwined around my neck, and she gave me a smile that lit my spirit.

"I like your aggressive side," she said playfully, a sparkle in her eyes.

"Do you now?" I took her bottom lip between my teeth and nibbled on it.

"I do. But you have me so wet again I don't think I can get on that horse without some release."

Raising my brow, I chuckled. "Again?"

She nodded, her hands running through my hair.

"Tell me what you want, princess." I was ready for her to take the lead back, to command my next move.

"I want your tongue on my clit as I ride your face until I come. Then you're going to fuck me before we ride into Duntraik."

I lowered her to the ground and hovered over her. "We're going to Bira." Pinning her hands over her head, I added, "Or I won't obey."

Her jaw ticked.

"How badly do you want to come, princess?" I rubbed her nipple between my fingers, watching the rapture contort her expression.

"Duntraik," she said meekly.

Sucking her nipple into my mouth, I twirled my tongue around it before I scraped my teeth over it. Her moan was sensual, and my dick sprung back to life.

"Bira and I'm not discussing it again. I will not take you directly into Duntraik yet."

"Why wait?" she asked. "He'll find me either way."

"But Bira offers us more time." I tweaked her nipple, running my tongue up her neck. "More time to play and watch you fall apart for me."

"I can't—"

I pinched her nipple, stopping her words. "Tell me where we're going, princess, and I'll satisfy that ache between your legs."

"Gods, you're not right," she muttered.

"I told you, you created a beast who likes to play."

"Fine. But don't say I didn't warn you. We'll go to Bira."

I released her wrists and dropped to my back. "That's better. Take those pants off and get over here, princess. I want to hear you scream."

She sat up and gave me a look I couldn't quite read before she muttered, "I thought I was the one in control."

"You're welcome to take that control back at any time." I put my hands behind my head and watched her take her pants off, my eyes devouring every inch of her.

I moved my arms to embrace her as she climbed over me. Settling her ass in my hands, she looked down at me, saying, "Make me come, like a good boy."

"That's more like it," I said, ready to obey every word as I sank my tongue into her and prepared to make her screams fill the air.

CHAPTER SIXTEEN

GARRET

It was well into morning by the time Eloise and I started to the border. She'd left me so depleted, I didn't think I'd make it very far. I hadn't wanted to stop touching her, knowing what awaited us, and I hoped making the trek into Bira would delay the inevitable. With each stride we drew closer to our destination, the urge to force her to turn back grew. But I knew there would be no changing her mind, no matter how much I wanted her to. If it was one thing I'd learned about Eloise in these past few days, it was that she was stubborn headed.

I was dreading returning to Duntraik. It was the last thing I should have been doing. I'd promised myself I would never return, never look back once I'd crossed the border, leaving my past behind. It was a past I'd wanted to forget and yet here I was staring it in the face. In my desperate moments before fate had put Eloise in my path, I'd considered returning. Thinking it best to accept the villain I'd become and find a place in Rikeri's ranks once again. I was no longer a child or even a teen to be abused and manipulated. I was a villain—a selfish, vain, conniving villain. Or, at least, I had been. That man was slowly transforming, becoming someone who regretted the actions that had made me the bad guy. And with that transformation, my need to avoid Duntraik had returned.

I could see the mountains of Duntraik looming ahead of us, the wall of thorny vines that lined the border of Bira casting a constant shadow on us to our right. My chest tightened, nerves tingling as a sense of confinement overwhelmed me. The past was a mountain pushing toward me and the future was an unknown, towering over me with its sharp thorns and tangled paths. Neither seemed worth daring, and my desire to lead Eloise far from there was storming through me once again.

As we neared the border of Bira, as close to Duntraik's as we could get, I sensed the change. The air grew lighter, a floral scent filling the air. The thornless roses of Bira, the gods' blessing on the kingdom, stood on the other side of the thorny barrier. There were nights the wind picked the smell up and spread it deep into Duntraik, a reminder of the transgression Rikeri's ancestor had committed. Those nights had been brutal, his temper tenfold, and it was rare there wasn't at least one body to dispose of the next morning. Whether it be a woman who fell victim to his hungers or a servant in the wrong place at the wrong time, there was always death expected those nights.

I blinked away the visions that were obstructing my view and turned my attention to the thorny wall. Running my hand down my face, I thought about how to break through the damned thing. I didn't want to cross into Duntraik and enter Bira that way. Stepping into Duntraik was something I wasn't ready for, and I wanted to keep Eloise from it for as long as possible. I was delaying the inevitable, the day she would call me on my diversion, my insistence we stay in Bira before breaching Duntraik. The longer I kept her from Rikeri's reach, the longer she was safe and the more time I'd have to figure some way out of this nightmare.

I glanced at Eloise. She was chewing her lip, her eyes focused on the vines, her hands clenched tight on the reins. There was something more she wasn't telling me. She hadn't given me a reason for not returning to Bira, but she was adamant that she not. Her family was there and even if her father had wanted her to run, being in Bira's capital under his protection had to be safer than having her hand herself over to Rikeri. I wouldn't push her. We both had our secrets.

"How do you suppose we get past this?" I gestured to the thorny bramble, not seeing any light seeping through to indicate its depth.

"Me," she said, jumping down from her horse.

I followed her lead, not sure what she meant. "Mind explaining what you mean by that?" I asked, scratching my head.

She walked closer to the vines, the sharp thorns too close to her delicate skin. I snatched her back. "Don't touch them," I warned. "Let me see if I can get us through without you hurting yourself."

I tried not to cringe at how that had sounded like she was some fragile woman. I knew it irked her when I talked like that, but this was a man's job, and I wasn't about to let her get hurt. She narrowed her eyes at me, and I could see the anger behind them.

"Don't give me that look, Eloise." I pulled my sword out and returned to the wall, noticing how she'd crossed her arms, her scowl turning to amusement.

The vines bent to my strength, shredding as I hacked away at them. I peered over at Eloise. "See, this was a man's job."

Her lip twitched, her brow raising. "I see. How assumptive of me to presume I didn't need a man."

I grimaced, knowing it was a dig at me. She walked over to me, placing a hand on my bicep and squeezing it. "I hope I didn't tire those muscles out too much last night. You're going to need them." She pointed at the vines, and I followed her finger, seeing them reform until there was no sign I'd even touched them.

"Fuck," I grumbled.

"I think this might be a woman's job," Eloise said with a coy smile, humor lighting her eyes. "But feel free to keep showing me what a powerful man you are. I don't mind watching those muscles flex, although I prefer them flexing on me."

I shot her a look, annoyed that my unruly dick had reacted to her comment and that she'd once again shown me that my ways of thinking were wrong.

Leaning on her tiptoes, she gave me a kiss on the cheek. "I love you, Garret, but I'm going to continue challenging that backward mindset of yours."

And I knew she would because she had since the day I'd met her. "I welcome it, princess. Now, since my brawn can't cut through those damned vines, what do you have in mind?"

She gave me a smile, her eyes brilliant in the sun's rays, before she turned back to the wall. "Did you know there's a myth that the goddess Fauna took a mortal lover?" She took a step closer, and my muscles strained to bring her back to me. "Her father forbade the affair and cursed the mortal. He blinded the man so he could no longer look upon the goddess. But she continued to love him, disobeying her father despite his warnings." Eloise brought her finger out and touched a thorn which pricked her finger. I clenched my fists, fighting the need to rip her away from the danger. "She loved him, despite his imperfections. Her father found out and lured the man to the fields of roses that cover Bira. At that time, thorns still sat upon the stems and her father imbued his magic upon the roses, sharpening the thorns and enlarging them. He put a stone in the mortal's path, tripping him and sending his body into the roses. The thorns tore him apart, his blood seeping into the ground by the time Fauna found him."

Eloise sucked the blood from her finger as I impatiently shifted my feet, waiting to see what she would do and wondering what the point of the story was. It struck me that so much myth surrounded her kingdom, much more than any other kingdom.

"So what happened?" I asked, not having heard the story before and wondering if it was one distinct to Bira.

"Fauna cried for days, holding her lover's dead body as his blood coated the field. In her agony, she ripped the thorns from the roses but instead of destroying them, she buried them in his blood and when the gods raised the wall around Bira, those same thorns emerged on the vines. The roses in Bira never again carried thorns, our roses always a shade of red deeper than anywhere in the world as if they hold his blood to this day." She brushed her hair from her eyes and looked up, her markings changing so that a path of gold sat in the ebony, a dusting of that same gold seeping from her body toward the vines.

"Fauna still wanders the field. She takes the shape of a deer, and they say if you see her, it means she's blessing your path forward, watching you and protecting you like she couldn't do for her lover."

I wanted to respond, understanding now why she wouldn't kill the deer, why her people cherished the animal, but her golden power had bled to the vines causing them to shrivel, forming a path large enough for the two of us and our horses to walk through. I couldn't help staring at her, knowing my eyes had creases as I once again tried to comprehend how the woman who had fallen apart at my touch held such power. I swallowed, my mouth going dry, words escaping me.

She turned to me, seeing my response and reading it wrong. She dropped her eyes, fidgeting with some invisible string on her pants. I took her hands, not liking how insecure she seemed. Her eyes lifted to mine.

Giving her a playful grin, I said, "You think you could use some of that magic dust the next time you're riding me, princess?"

Her eyes widened, her expression shifting as a smile formed. "I can try, but what do I get in return?"

My hands circled her waist, and I drew her to me. "I can think of a few things that involve my fingers and my tongue."

"Not your cock?"

I tipped my head back, eyeing her. "We need to work on that mouth of yours."

She licked her lips, causing the bulge in my pants to leap like a trained pet. "I thought my mouth was just fine."

"Damn, princess, that mouth is perfect for putting things in it, but what comes out of it, that's another story. You've got a dirtier mouth than some of the men I served with."

She giggled, leaning into me. I thought she was going to kiss me, but she mumbled, "We need to move before my magic wears off. We can talk about my dirty mouth later when you're fucking it."

I groaned, my pants now painfully tight. Pushing her into me, I wrapped my hand in her hair, keeping her close to my lips. Memories of that mouth on me burned through me.

"We need to go, Garret," she breathed.

I held her there, weighing my options and wondering if I had time to bend her over and satisfy the throbbing that was aggravating me. But I knew it wouldn't be something quick, not like it had been before her. With Eloise, I needed more. I needed to touch her, to hear her cries, to have her come undone for me. There would never be a quick fuck with her. I didn't think it would be possible.

Releasing her neck, I dragged my hand down her body, torturing myself even more.

"Come on, I'll take care of this," she cupped me, and I twitched in her hand, "when we stop again."

"Fuck, you better. It'll be a miracle if I can get back on my horse with it so hard."

She lifted on her tiptoes and gave me a quick kiss before freeing herself of my hold. I followed the sway of her hips as she walked to the horses. Shaking away my naughty thoughts, I looked back at the walkway she'd created, noting how it had closed slightly. Her magic was holding the vines back, but it wouldn't hold against the magic of the gods.

"You should go through first with the horses," she said. "I'll follow in case it starts to close since I'm smaller."

"Nope. You go through first, guide the horses and I'll follow."

Her lips thinned, the grinding of her teeth revealing her aggravation. "Don't get all protective on me—"

"I am protective and as the man, I'm going through last in case anything happens. Plus, I'm not leaving you back here unguarded."

"I can handle myself," she grouched, putting her hands on her hips.

"I know you can, but I'm still going through last. Think of it as me letting you take the lead," I said with a wink.

She rolled her eyes and began to speak, but I stopped her, pointing to the vines. "The longer we stand here arguing, the tighter that walk is going to be. Now get that ass moving before I smack it."

A blush crept below her markings, making me wonder just how hard my princess liked it. She huffed but led both horses to the opening. Her golden magic sparkled against the vines, but I could see it fading as if the magic of the gods was fighting it. I tilted my head, wondering how that could be if her power was from the same source.

"Hurry up, big boy," she said, and my cock twitched. Every time she called me big boy, it was like a chain that jerked me.

She'd led one horse through and was leading the second by the time I cleared my head. The vines were closing in and I cursed myself for wasting time. The way the remnants of her magic flickered over the black vines was captivating, but I forced my eyes away, heading into the thick tunnel she'd created. I had to duck, and the further I walked, the lower I had to dip my head. I hadn't realized the vines were so dense and they were encroaching on me, closing in like a collapsing wall. My breathing constricted, my body freezing as memories of Rikeri's magic entombing me returned like a nightmare that fogged my senses.

"Garret!" I heard Eloise call to me just as the thorns dug into my arm. My eyes flew open, seeing the vines blocking my way.

"Dammit," I groused, pulling my sword up and slicing through the recent growth in front of me and the thorns that were reaching toward me like massive claws.

Each swipe of my sword only allowed me one step forward, and I had several steps to go that were now buried below the vines that separated me from Eloise. They pushed at my back, and I was thankful the thorns weren't tearing through my skin. My need to escape both the vines and the memories they were releasing tore through me, and I swung my sword frantically.

"Garret, stay still!" Eloise cried.

"And end up like that man in your story?" I yelled back.

"Trust me!" I wanted to so badly, but that need for self-preservation that had driven me all these years screamed for me to run. There was nowhere to run to, however. "Please, Garret, stop moving!"

I closed my eyes, imagining her in front of me, and my breathing calmed. Fear still barraged me, but I fought the need to open my eyes and fight. The vines behind me pushed me forward, thorns poking into my clothes but not ripping. One pressed so close to my eyes, I swallowed back the urge to move. Within seconds, the tingle of Eloise's magic touched my skin, the thorns retracting. I let out the breath locked within my lungs and opened my eyes, seeing her standing there on the other side, the gold streams running through her markings, slivers of it twinkling in her eyes.

The tension fled my body, and I relaxed the grip on my sword, taking the final steps to her. I hated that she'd seen me so weak, that my reaction had been so uncontrolled, and I looked away, making a smart comment to recover. "If you wanted me tied up, princess, you could have just asked."

The concern in her eyes disappeared, and she grabbed my shirt, pulling me to her. Her kiss was intense, and I dropped my sword, pulling her into my arms.

"I might take you up on that," she said between kisses. "Dominating you completely is a tempting offer."

I laughed against her lips. "I'll let you play, but only so you think you're in control." Dragging her bottom lip between my teeth, I continued, "When it's really me who's in control, princess."

"We'll see, big boy. Let's go so I can find some rope and see if you can handle it." She maneuvered out of my arms, my length so hard from her words that I had to adjust myself. With her playfulness, she'd swept away all thoughts of the bramble behind us and the memories from my childhood.

Shaking my head, I grabbed my horse's reins and followed her into Bira with the promise of release leading me.

CHAPTER SEVENTEEN

ELOISE

S tepping into Bira, my magic stirred along with emotions that threatened to undo me. If Garret's struggle in the bramble hadn't distracted me, I may have turned and run. A myriad of emotions coursed through me as I stared at the field of thornless roses that stood in the distance. Each step closer caused them to increase so that I could barely take the next step. Anxiety riddled my mind, my chest uncomfortably tight as if the vines were constricting it.

"The gods' flowers," Garret said.

His words should have distracted me, but they weren't enough. I couldn't breathe. The reality of my life, of what my stepping back into Bira meant, hammered me so that my step faltered. I shouldn't have let him talk me into returning. My presence was a curse, a death sentence to the magic that made Bira so unique.

I stepped back, shaking my head, my breathing erratic, all the strength I'd been carrying fleeing like a moth escaping a spider's web.

"I...I can't," I mumbled, stumbling away and running back toward the wall.

"Eloise!" Garret yelled, running after me and grabbing hold of me. He turned me into him, holding my shoulders, his eyes creased with concern.

"I can't return, Garret. I can't go back. We shouldn't be here." I looked to our right, knowing we weren't far from Duntraik. I'd been ready to face my destiny, to face Rikeri and end this. Going to Duntraik was what I'd wanted, and I'd let Garret talk me into Bira. "Duntraik isn't far. Let's cross the border today." I pleaded with him, knowing he was seeing the vulnerable side of me I'd left behind the day I'd run from Rikeri. It was the second time he'd witnessed me lose control of it. "Please, Garret."

His brows furrowed and I could see his own struggle reflected in his eyes. He was avoiding Duntraik; he didn't need to tell me that. I'd heard it in his voice, knowing it was part of the secrets he kept from me. But staying in Bira, especially this close to the border, was dangerous for us, for my people, for my family. I just couldn't tell him that without giving away more than I already had.

"No, we stay here. I won't cross into Duntraik yet."

His obstinance was frustrating.

"Then I'll go. This isn't your fight, Garret. Stay here and let me go."

His jaw clenched, his brown eyes growing dark. "You're not going anywhere."

"I'm serious. I can't stay in Bira—"

"And you won't tell me why?" Hurt sat in his eyes, and I wanted to alleviate it, but I couldn't.

"Just trust me."

He shook his head. "Not this time, princess. We both have our reasons for wanting to be in Duntraik or Bira, but I'm winning this argument."

Before I could protest, he hoisted me over his shoulder.

"Garret, put me down!"

He held me tight, my kicking and hitting not fazing him. He was too solid, an immovable beast I couldn't persuade, no matter how I tried.

"You're not getting rid of me that easily, princess, and there's no fucking way I'd let you out of my sight. Plus, I have plans for you when we finally camp."

I couldn't stop the flutters that ravaged my stomach, my thighs instantly squeezing.

"That's right, El. You keep your mind off where we are and on how you're going to be clenching around my cock later."

Damn, I really had created a beast. Now that he knew how to satisfy me, he did so every chance he could get. And I loved it.

Giving up my fight with a sigh, I said, "Can you put me down?"

He was quiet for a moment. "No, I like having your ass in my hand. I may even play a little while I walk."

"Don't you dare," I protested. Although the thought didn't help the wetness that sat between my legs.

He pushed his hand down my pants.

"Garret!"

"What, princess? There's no one around for miles and I can smell you."

I hissed, smacking his back. "You cannot!"

My cheeks were burning, and when his hand caressed my ass, I squeezed my legs together.

"Loosen those legs, El," he said. He stopped walking, and I thought he'd let me down, but he tightened his hold on my ass and rounded up the reins of the horses with his other hand. Bringing that hand around my back, the hand on my ass slipped between my legs. "That's it, princess. Let me feel how wet you are."

"Gods, Garret." My words came out broken as his finger slipped into me.

"Don't fight me or I'll use these reins to tie you up before you get the chance to try that on me."

I shivered, the thought of dominating him like we'd discussed calling to the side of me that reveled in her strength. The other part of me melted more as his finger slipped to my clit. My body was a slew of embers that were spreading like wildfire. I gripped his back as he plunged two fingers into me. My cry was feral, and I dropped my forehead into his back, biting him as pleasure tore through me. His fingers were large, filling me almost as fantastically as his dick did, and my climax climbed until he removed them and smacked my ass hard.

"Ouch!" His back muffled my cry.

"Don't bite, princess. Although I enjoyed smacking that ass, so maybe you should bite me again."

I tried kicking my legs, but his hand didn't move. His fingers plunged back into me, sending a rabid cry from me. I gave up fighting, my body awash with the rapture he was bringing to me. With each swipe over my clit followed by the thrusts of his fingers, my release surged until it was an inferno ready to flare through me, leaving me wrecked. And as I came undone, it surged, drowning me in the flames of ecstasy that only Garret had ever brought to me with such intensity. I clung to his back, screaming as I lost all control of my body.

He removed his fingers, chuckling before he dropped me. My legs were weak, and I wobbled until he reached for me and pulled me into his chest. I was breathless and knew my cheeks remained flushed. He gave me a coy grin, his eyes dancing with humor as he brought his fingers to his mouth and licked them clean.

"Damn, princess. That taste is as close to the gods as anything I've ever tasted."

I couldn't respond, too weakened by him to do anything but remain standing. He lifted me onto his horse, mounting it after me and scooting me in the saddle so his hardness pressed into my back.

"What are you doing?" I asked, finally gaining some sense of control over my body.

"Keeping your body close so I can feel you tremble more. My dick is hungry for you right now, and this is as good as it's gonna get until we make camp, and I can fuck you."

"Gods," I said, flopping my head on his chest, barely able to hold it up. "You get dirtier by the day."

"Ha, I've always been dirty, El. I just save it for when I'm out of earshot of a lady. But since your mouth is as foul as mine is, I can talk dirty to you whenever I want."

I bit my lip, hating the effect his words had on me because I liked it when he talked dirty.

"You rest that pretty little body of yours, princess, because I plan to use it the rest of the night."

I should have come back with a snide remark about how he was assuming I was some dainty woman who lived to spread her legs for him, but I didn't have the energy and as much as I didn't want to admit it, I wanted him to use me that way, to take me to oblivion until I couldn't walk.

I shivered in anticipation, and he squeezed my hips with the hand holding the reins. His other hand slipped down my shirt and cupped my breast. I didn't know how we would make it any further if he kept touching me this way. But he didn't move his hand, keeping it around my breast as if it were a comforting thing. Leaning my head back again, I relaxed, listening to his breathing, feeling his chest rise and fall with each breath, and forgetting all about my reasons for avoiding Bira.

"Stop," I said, as we came to the field of roses. The sway of the horse and the strength of Garret's hold on me had been lulling me to sleep as we eclipsed the distance from the wall to the roses.

Garret removed his hand from my shirt, its warmth lingering on my skin.

"What's wrong, El?" he asked, pushing my hair back and kissing my neck. It was a gentle move that made my heart race.

"I want to get down and see them."

He tipped my head, and I peered up at him. The speeding of my heartbeat grew, and I brought my arm around, drawing his lips to mine. His fingers weaved through my hair, the kiss becoming more passionate until our lips parted.

"I don't know if I want to let you go," he said, and the vulnerability of his words threatened to shatter my resolve to face Rikeri. He dropped his eyes as if realizing what he'd said held more meaning than simply releasing me from the horse.

Again, I wondered at what lay below his bravado, the exterior of the vain, handsome man who boasted of a woman's place to serve him. There were layers to him, ones I questioned if any others had seen or if he'd reserved them for me.

"You don't have to let me go, Garret." I heard the deceit in my voice, knowing I couldn't let him anywhere near Rikeri.

His expression shifted, his eyes hardening to cover the vulnerability. He took my waist in his hands and lifted me from him, gently placing me on the ground before he dismounted, his eyes averting mine.

"Garret—"

"No, El." He ran his hands through his hair. "I've kept quiet, going along with your intent to go into Duntraik and trying to think of a way to keep you from facing that madman. This is madness. He kidnapped you and hurt you. And you want me to let you walk back into his kingdom and hand yourself over to him?"

"I need to. This will never stop if I don't."

He took my face in his hands. "We can go to the furthest

corner of the kingdoms, we can cross the ocean and live on another continent, we can—"

"No, we can't. Do you think Troniere was the first place we fled to?" His face dropped, and the memories returned like phantoms I couldn't shake. Running from Duntraik in the dead of night, hearing the hounds in the distance as we ran. My body was so weak I passed out, days of coming in and out of a fog I couldn't lift until my body recovered. The months on the road, looking over our shoulders, making our first home in Mesok, the furthest from Rikeri's hold, thinking we were safe.

I rubbed my arms, shoving the memories away. "There is no escaping him."

"And what will you do if you return to him? Let him take you? Use you?" His voice was raising with each word and I tried stepping back, but his hands moved behind my neck, holding me in place. "Fuck you?"

"Stop it, Garret," I tried pushing his hands from me, but he was too strong.

"No. Eloise, this is madness. He will hurt you and just because he didn't touch you that time, doesn't mean he won't. Because I know he will. He'll force you..." He let me go and walked away, rubbing his hand over his face.

His words had such surety to them. It was almost as if he knew Rikeri, but that made little sense because he'd never been to Duntraik.

"Garret," I said, placing my hand on his back.

"Can you destroy him with your magic, El?" There was a desperate plea to his voice that cracked the heart he'd claimed.

I sucked in a breath, knowing I couldn't but not wanting to admit it because he would pick me up and steal me far from there. "I won't let him take my magic or hurt my people."

He peered over his shoulder at me, and I thought maybe he noticed I hadn't answered his question directly, that I'd avoided the truth. Not quite telling him a lie, but not giving him the truth. He came back to me, his thumb brushing over the petals on my cheek, and I closed my eyes to his touch, thinking of how our relationship seemed to be built on nothing more than petals and lies.

He studied me for a moment, and the heaviness of his gaze made me uncomfortable. I turned away, knowing I could give him no more. The truth was too hard to admit. And I didn't know if I had answers for him. Something was driving me to return to Duntraik, to face Rikeri even though I knew I couldn't beat him, that I couldn't hurt him, that I was offering myself to a life of enslavement as he twisted the power the gods had given me. I didn't know what else to do. I was tired of running, tired of him taking the people I loved from me. Staring into the field, I wrapped my arms around myself as my emotions began to unravel me.

"They really exist," Garret muttered, coming to stand next to me, and relief swept through me at the change of subject.

"The roses of Bira, holding the magic of the gods, made thornless by the pain of the goddess, Fauna," I said.

I breathed in the floral scent that filled the air of my homeland. The smell brought a melancholy that threatened to pull me under and bury me so far I didn't think even Garret could save me. I lifted my hand, sensing the call of the magic to my own and watched the petals lift, carried by an unseen breeze that brought them closer to me. My magic surged, the burning intensity of it tingling through my body like it did each time. It streamed from me, and I heard Garret's inhale as the line of golden sparkles touched the petals, which disintegrated into more golden shimmers that floated away.

I bit back the tears that were bullying their way to freedom, knowing my father and my brother would sense my magic, that they would know I'd returned. A tightness squeezed at my chest followed by a need to escape Bira, the same that had sent me running when we'd crossed over the border.

Garret stepped behind me, wrapping his arms around my waist and burying his face in my hair like he sensed my distress. His strength fortified me and I held tight to his arms as panic surged through me, my heart racing, my limbs tingling even though my magic had faded. I tried breathing, my lungs devoid of air, and he held me closer.

"Shhh, whatever happens, I'll be with you, El," he murmured.

But how did I tell him my fear of Rikeri was a distant thought to what my magic was doing to my people, to my father, and to my brother? How did I tell him my magic had been tainted, corrupted, and it was destroying the magic of Bira the longer I stayed in its borders? I couldn't because I still had my secrets, just like he had his.

I clung to him, waiting for my panic to subside, waiting for the breath to fill my lungs, for my limbs to stop tingling, my heart to stop its erratic beats. And as I did, I spotted a stag in the distance. A graceful, strong one that turned its black eyes to me, lending a sense of calm that swept through me.

"Do you see that?" Garret whispered, his cheek leaning against my hair.

"Yes," I breathed, afraid to move and disturb it.

The stag came closer to us, both of us frozen until it was so close, I could reach my hand out and touch its muzzle.

"Fauna," I said, my voice hushed.

A tear fell from its eye, confirming my suspicion. A tear for the lover she'd lost all those eons ago. Or a tear for the future that lay before me, the sacrifice I was making to save my people. One that would likely hurt the people of the other kingdoms unless I could find a way to kill Rikeri. If I could find a weakness or somehow get my knife close enough to gauge his icy heart out.

Because that's what I intended to do. If I had to let him touch me to get close, if I had to suffer the pain, the violation, I would if it meant I could kill him. But I wouldn't tell Garret that. Wouldn't tell him I would do anything in my power to stop

Rikeri, even if my power was something I couldn't use to accomplish it. I was hoping the stag was a sign of the gods, a blessing for me to kill him, but I couldn't be sure and without that certainty, I wouldn't risk using my magic. It was yet another secret I would keep from Garret, because having him discover that even with the magic of the gods coursing through me, I was still powerless would surely cause him to stop me. And I thought nothing would sway him once he knew that truth.

CHAPTER EIGHTEEN

GARRET

I held Eloise, the tension in her body fading. Her need to face Rikeri frustrated me, and there was something she was hiding, another lie that layered the foundation of what we had. I didn't push, not when I saw her almost break down again. She was terrified, but she wouldn't admit it, too stubborn to let me know. She had her own secrets, and the thought lessened my guilt, but not by much.

Watching her interaction with the roses had been astonishing. My mouth had dropped as the roses had reacted to her, her magic reaching out to touch the petals that floated in the air, carried away on an invisible breeze to scatter her magic to those in Bira. Just like they had before we'd crossed into Bira. Even as she'd approached the roses, they seemed to lean toward her as if seeking her essence.

Ahead of us, the stag stood with an intensity to how it observed Eloise. My fingers twitched to pull the bow out that was stashed behind my saddle, but I remembered the story of the goddess and her lover, Eloise's words confirming she thought the same. I wondered what it was waiting for.

"You can really see it?" Eloise asked.

"Of course. Why?"

"The goddess doesn't show herself to everyone," she said, her voice a gentle stir in my ears. "The legend of the vessel says she was first seen standing in the nursery of the first vessel, the infant reaching its hand to touch her snout. She was in doe form that day, but over the centuries she has taken both forms. Her preference is the stag. After that first sighting, only vessels or those touched by magic saw her."

I swallowed back my surprise, not sure what to make of that fact. I glanced down at my hands wrapped around Eloise's waist, her own clamped tight over mine. Magic had touched me, but it had been corrupt and twisted as it had burned its way through my body. Rikeri's only intent had ever been to bring harm to me, and his magic had been only one of the weapons he'd used to do so.

When I looked back up, the stag was gone, as if it had been nothing more than an illusion. I squeezed my eyes shut, thinking of all the stags I had hunted in my lifetime. The antlers that lined the walls of my former home, the hides I'd skinned for nothing more than the sport of the hunt. There was no question I was just as bad as I thought I was, and that only left me confused as to why the creature would show itself to me.

Eloise turned in my arms, her fingers running over my cheek. "She let you see her, just as the stag in the forest did. Maybe you're not as bad as you say you are, Garret." She leaned up and gave me a kiss before skipping to her horse. The weight she'd carried earlier, the fear and tension, was gone as if the deer had lifted it from her. I wished I had that ability to wipe away all her worries, but I didn't.

"Catch up, slowpoke," Eloise called, climbing onto her horse. "And don't think you're tormenting me with your hand on my breast for the rest of the ride. That was just cruel."

167

Shaking my head, I let my thoughts go and mounted my horse, saying, "That wasn't cruel, that was fantastic. I need to find another excuse to have you that close while we ride. Kept me hard the entire time, and I'll be ready to take that body and use it when we stop for the night."

I urged my horse forward, guiding him to the path around the flowers, unsure if I wanted to risk the wrath of a goddess by trampling her roses.

WE RODE FOR ANOTHER DAY, camping in a cluster of trees just beyond a slope of rock that passed over from Duntraik. The mountains were gaining in height the closer we came to where Rikeri's castle stood, wedged within the menacing mountains. As I lit a fire, Eloise stopped me.

"Don't, we're too near the border. Rikeri has hounds that case the border at night."

"Hounds? Why? This is Bira, the most peaceful of the kingdoms. It's no threat to Duntraik."

She pursed her lips, her eyes dark.

"I'm not inferring that your kingdom is weak. It's simply no threat to a kingdom like Duntraik. I'm actually surprised he hasn't run Bira down by now." He would never risk the wrath of the gods, and striking Bira would be an insult to them. His ancestor had suffered the consequences, his magic warped, his lands cursed, but I didn't want Eloise to know I knew enough about Rikeri to know that fact.

I hadn't thought her eyes could grow a darker shade of blue, but they did.

"Still not the right answer?" I asked, taking her silence to mean she didn't approve.

"Bira is not weak. And Rikeri hasn't struck the kingdom because he knows how strong we are. The protection of the gods sits upon Bira." Her smug tone told me she had won the disagreement.

"So why do his hounds patrol at night? To keep people from crossing into Duntraik?" It must have been a recent addition to his forces, because there'd been nothing of the sort when I'd crossed the border with the news that would lead me to this point in my life.

"It's to keep his people from crossing into Bira."

My brow furrowed, the tension returning to me. "Has it gotten that bad?" The way into Duntraik from Bira was treacherous except for a few paths that passed through the mountain range. His army blocked passage into Troniere, so no one ever dared take that route, leaving the passages into Bira as the only alternative. Bira hated outsiders, but the chance for freedom was still enough for people to have hope. And hope was enough to drive a desperate person to do the unthinkable.

She studied me, her head tilting. "You said you hadn't been to Duntraik."

Shit, the lies were hard to keep up with. "I haven't, but that doesn't mean I don't know the news of other kingdoms."

She remained silent, her gaze steady, before she finally said, "Rikeri is starving his people, using all of his resources to build an army."

"An army?" That made no sense. "Rikeri is a force on his own with plenty of capability to protect his kingdom."

"Yes, but my father thinks he wants to expand. Nilan told me that my father and his advisors surmised Rikeri has intentions to attack the other kingdoms."

"So with his power and an army to back him—"

"He'll take over this part of the world. And if he ever gets hold of my power, there will be no stopping him."

"Where do the hounds come in?" I asked, completely

confounded and even more concerned about her intent to face him.

"He's training them."

My hands clenched waiting for her next words because I had a suspicion I knew how he was training them.

"With his people," she finished, and my stomach knotted, the horror of what she'd said souring the already acidic taste I had for Rikeri. "He's starving the towns outside the capital city, and he offers an escape. If they can make it to the border, he'll reward them. But only if they make the attempt at night."

"Gods, they never even get close, do they?" The idea of it was revolting, and I swallowed back the bile.

She shook her head. "If they go during the day, his men block every route into the kingdom from Bira and kill them. If they go at night, they think they're escaping and the hounds attack at the border, hunting them, then playing with them until they're ready to eat them. Nilan said the shrieking carries through the night sky the closer you are to the border."

"How did he get across that border to rescue you?"

"They only hunt at night. He fought his way through a passage, losing the two men he was traveling with."

I sat back, the sun's last rays cascading around her, casting a godlike aura on her. I wasn't sure how close we were to the border, but the thought of hearing those shrieks didn't bode well for a good night's sleep.

"That's why you didn't want to travel along the border of Bira," I said, realizing she'd had reasons for the fight about it and for the panic that had struck her.

Her answer didn't come quickly, making me think there was still something she hadn't told me.

"Yes."

I wiped my hands down my face. I'd fought a beast before, thinking I was undefeatable, that I was a god who held the power to judge him for taking what was mine. Thinking I could beat him when he'd already won. I'd lost then and I would lose now.

"Grab the horses. We're not staying here tonight. We'll ride east."

"But east will put us closer to the towns," she argued.

"And offer us a chance for a comfortable bed and more than stale bread and scrawny rodents to eat."

"No one can see me. I can't risk my brother or parents finding out I'm here."

It still seemed insane to me that she wouldn't return to the safety of her family, but she knew the power dynamics of this region better than I did. If her father had sent Nilan to keep her far from Bira, then he feared Rikeri would come after her again, and that put Bira at risk. That answer didn't seem right to me, not with what I knew of Rikeri. He might have risked stealing Eloise, but he would never risk the wrath of the gods by invading the holy lands.

"No one will know it's you if you use that spell you used to disguise yourself. Go fetch the horses. The sun has gone down and I'm not taking a chance that one of those things ventures over the border."

As if on cue, the low distinctive rumble of a growl filled the silence. I froze as Eloise's eyes grew wide. In the darkness, a pair of red eyes watched me.

"Don't move," I whispered between my teeth.

Eloise was the strongest woman I knew, but fear shone in her eyes so distinctly that every part of me wanted to shield her from it. Her breaths were coming fast, her eyes darting to get a glimpse of the creature.

"And don't look," I told her.

My years of training spanned through my mind as I went through all the scenarios, none of which left us unharmed. The hound may have blended into the night, but from the position of its eyes, it was massive.

"Garret," Eloise said, and the eyes shifted to her.

Dropping my hand slowly, I gripped the handle of my knife, wishing I'd set my sword nearer.

"I'm going to distract it, El. I want you to run for the horses."

"But—"

The eyes followed our conversation, and I noted how they seemed to grow closer. It was hunting, prowling steadily closer until it could play with its food.

"Just do it," I said, drawing the attention back to me. "Run for the horses and don't look back. Now, princess."

I whipped my knife at it, perfectly aimed for its eyes, and lunged for my sword. Eloise ran, the beast roaring as my knife hit its mark. It reeled back but recovered quickly, stalking from the shadows. It was enormous. Well over six feet tall, it looked like a beast from nightmares. Hound seemed a strange name for what was now lunging at me as I stood with my sword ready for the attack, and I prayed the goddess who watched over Eloise was watching her now. It leaped, the enormous black paws with claws that were extended and ready for the kill were each the size of my head. Its legs were thick like any dog's, but the joint extended upward, giving it a spiderlike appearance.

A shiver scurried up my spine as its fur stood up, revealing black feathers with quills at the ends. It was horrific, and it was in the air, mid leap. My heart stuck in my throat as fear pounded through me. Time seemed to stop, my mind screaming for me to run, to do what I did best—choosing only battles I could win was my way, not this. This was something I couldn't win, but then I thought of Eloise. She was why I was here, watching as death came for me in the form of a mangled beast once again. But this time I stood proudly with no selfish intent, only a need to protect the woman I loved and ensure she lived.

I clutched my sword, aiming for its belly and bracing for impact when it screeched, its path veering off course as it landed next to me, its body sliding to a stop. It stood, wobbling slightly before it roared at me, slobber dripping from its huge teeth. Its paw had an arrow embedded in it. I heard the release of another arrow, feeling it pass right by my cheek and watching it land in the center of the beast's eye. It was a better mark than my knife had been.

The creature shrieked, dropping its head and pawing at the arrow. Another arrow flew by me as I took my opening. Running toward the beast and jumping upon its nose as it reacted to the second arrow, I drove my sword into its skull and used my body weight to force it deeper. The hound thrashed, but I hung on tight, catching sight of Eloise as she shot arrow after arrow into the hound, her aim steady, her focus unwavering. I twisted my sword, the fight fleeing the hound, its body going limp right before its legs buckled and it collapsed, sending me sprawling across the ground.

Picking myself up and stretching the soreness from my back, I ran to the beast and, after a brief struggle, extracted my sword.

"We need to move. Now," I said, grabbing Eloise's elbow and guiding her to the horses. I helped her up and smacked her horse on the rump.

"Garret!" she yelled.

"Go. Head east. I'll be right behind you. I need you far from this border, princess."

Thankfully, we had unpacked little, just my bedroll, which I hastily threw onto the back of my horse. Guiding my horse, I trailed after Eloise, pushing our steeds to put as much distance as we could between us and the border. Fear drove my sense of urgency, and I wrestled with what Eloise would think. Wondering if she would judge me for running from the threat, for making her run with me. If she would discover that was the man I'd been and want nothing more to do with me.

THE MILES CLOSED BEHIND US. I kept the horses at a steady pace, but no matter how I wanted to push them, I didn't, knowing I would only wear them down too soon to make it a safe distance. The light from the full moon was bright enough to make travel easier. I preferred to travel during the day, but this was safer.

As the night sky lightened, I knew we needed to stop. The hastened pace had worn the horses out, and Eloise had fallen asleep an hour before, flopping forward on her horse. I'd taken his reins and guided him, ensuring she didn't slip off. Ahead of us, I could see the outline of a village. As much as she wanted to avoid the towns in Bira, a warm bed and a hot meal were what both of us needed. We'd been on the road for too many days.

"Wake up, El," I said, slightly nudging her. She grumbled at me and swatted my hand away. "Stubborn woman, wake up."

"Let me sleep."

"Don't make me push you off that horse, princess."

She picked her head up, squinting her eyes at me.

"We're close to a town and we need to stop," I told her, pointing ahead of us.

She followed the direction of my hand and rubbed the sleep from her eyes. "I can't go into a town. Someone will recognize me."

"How often did you get out of the castle grounds, Eloise?" I doubted she had ever been past the protection of the castle until the day Rikeri took her. She was too special, even if her father had let her live a freer life than the vessels before her.

"Rarely," she murmured. Her voice carried a sadness to it that suggested even that was an exaggeration.

"And did you ever come this far west?" I knew I had her, that there was no arguing her way out of this.

"No."

"Then it's settled. Use your magic to disguise yourself again and pull your cape up."

With a sigh, she closed her eyes and her features transformed, bringing her back to the woman I'd fallen in love with. Her eyes opened, and she questioned me as I gave her a lopsided grin.

"What?" she asked, running her fingers through her silver hair.

"Just thinking of how beautiful you are, no matter what age you are."

A pinkish hue filled her cheeks, increasing my smile.

"You just like your women older and never wanted to admit it," she teased. "Running around chasing girls when women like me were out there, knowing how to satisfy you better than you could have imagined."

"Not just any woman, princess. Just you." The words had come out naturally, and I didn't mind if they made me sound weak. They were the truth. Her mouth parted, and I gave her a wink, urging my horse forward.

Dawn lit the small town by the time we arrived, and I guided us to an inn, handing the reins of the horses to the stable boy. Eloise threw him a coin, and I was thankful she'd remembered I was out of my own. I didn't like depending on her for money, though. That was my job, and it rubbed my sense of worth wrong. Eloise had already skewed my view of the hierarchy in our relationship, and this distorted it more. Men worked, men paid for things, men provided while women worked in the home, raising our children and cooking us meals before warming our beds. But once again, Eloise was in the dominant position and as much as I enjoyed it when we had sex, I didn't want other men seeing it.

I ran a hand through my hair and pulled her aside before we

entered the building. She tilted her head, her eyes holding an understanding as she dropped her pouch of coin in my hand. I looked down at it, then back up at her.

"I wasn't born like this, Garret, nor was I raised this way. Bira doesn't differ from any other kingdom, as much as I hate it. My parents raised me to obey the men in my life, to know my place. And with who I am, everyone drilled that need to be obedient into me." She looked tired, and it wasn't only from the lack of sleep. Her life hadn't been any easier than mine had, even with the riches and pampered lifestyle. "My brother took the time when my father gave me freedom to push those constraints, to understand that there was more to me than the constructs our society made me. My situation, my time in the dungeon of a madman, my life on the run, have forced me to be who I am now." Her expression grew melancholy, and I reached over to touch her cheek. "That doesn't mean that I don't miss being feminine and delicate. That I don't want to be protected and cherished."

I gave her a smile, taking a few coins from the bag and handing it back to her. Giving her the power back but taking some for myself. "Then I'll protect you when you want me to and when you want to fight, just tell me and I'll step back to fight by your side."

She drew in a breath, her eyes growing misty. Her mouth opened like she wanted to say something, and I didn't need to hear the words that wouldn't come out, because I felt them in my core, that connection we'd built snapping into permanent place. I drew her to me and kissed her.

"Ready to go in and get some sleep, princess?" I murmured.

"I'm not sure we'll get much sleep," she teased, and those words sent my anticipation climbing because the thought of touching her pushed all other needs aside.

I opened the door to the inn for her, mumbling, "We'll get sleep, but not until you've come enough times to satisfy me."

She shivered, and I rubbed my hands together, looking

forward to spending the day in bed with the most powerful woman in the kingdoms while she owned every inch of me.

The man behind the counter gave us a judgemental look, turning my mood instantly.

"We need a room," I said, assuming the authority.

His brow pinched, his beady eyes making assumptions I didn't like.

"I don't run that kind of establishment," he said, and I clenched my jaw, trying not to knock him on his ass.

"Well, it's good that you don't because I wouldn't want to bring my new bride to a place that wasn't respectable," I retorted, liking how it sounded to claim Eloise as my wife.

He looked over at her, his eyes surveying the gray locks and aging spell she wore, her hood not far enough forward to hide them.

"Do you have a problem?" I asked, dropping my fist to the desk with a loud thump.

I was an intimidating presence, and I stood well over five inches taller than him.

His lips pinched, and he said, "You're not from around here and your accent hints of foreigner—"

"The kingdom allows visitors during the rose season to bring tithes to the gods," Eloise said. "We wish to ask favor of the goddess of birth to bless us with child."

Gods, I loved her more each day. She was smart and quick on her feet. Where I had muscle, she had wits.

"A little old for that, aren't you?"

I reached over and grabbed him by the collar, pulling his body over the counter. "You will apologize to my wife quickly or I'll use your face to warm my fists up." I shoved him back, my glare penetrating.

He cleared his throat and said a quick apology to Eloise. It wasn't sufficient for the punishment I wanted to give him, but it would have to suffice. I didn't want to draw unwanted attention to us. He handed us a key, and I paid him for the full day. Taking Eloise's hand in mine, I followed the man to our room.

"No bags?" he asked, the sarcasm not disguised well enough. My fist jerked with the need to punch him.

"We stayed in Kinat last night and had expected to return, but I'm not feeling well, and my husband was sweet enough to suggest we rest today and travel to the fields tomorrow before we return to Kinat."

I tried not to let my awe at her skills show, but damn, she was a natural and for a moment I questioned why she was so adept at lying.

He gave her an appraising look before taking his leave. As I closed the door behind me, I leaned against it, crossing my arms and staring her down. She removed her cloak and set it on a small chair in the corner of the room. Her golden magic sparkled to reveal her markings and natural hair color, and when her eyes met mine, the shimmer of gold still flittered in them.

"What's that look for?" she asked, brushing her fingers through her hair.

I gestured to her with my finger, and she came to me, looking up at me with large eyes.

"Why is it you lie like someone who's been doing so her entire life?"

Her smirk was tempting, and I almost pulled her to me and devoured it.

"I come from royalty, Garret. My brother trained me in the fluent exchanges kings and queens use daily. He would take me through the lessons his tutors gave him as well as those of our father. They may have locked me away, expecting me to sit quietly and obediently as life passed me by and my magic blessed the kingdom, but I didn't want to do that. And my brother knew it. He was my co-conspirator," she said with a smile. Her fingers danced along the string on my shirt, slowly untying it. "Besides, I've lived a life of lies for three years. I'm as good as anyone at lying."

I snatched her waist and yanked her against me.

"Are you intimidated, Garret?"

"Not in the least. In fact, I think it's sexy as fuck."

"People in Bira are suspicious of outsiders, and lying was necessary. Besides, if I hadn't spoken up, you would have beaten the shit out of him."

I let out a hearty laugh, giving her a kiss as I wrapped my arms around her. "Damn right I would have. No one insults my princess."

"Let's forget about the nosy innkeeper," she said, dragging her teeth over my chin. "I remember something about me coming enough times to satisfy you."

I slipped my hand up her back, pushing her shirt up. "I believe I may have said something like that."

"Then get to work, big boy."

Giving her a sly grin, I scooped her into my arms and tossed her on the bed, ready to ravage her the remains of the day until she completely drained me, and I left her body thoroughly exhausted.

CHAPTER NINETEEN

GARRET

I rubbed my eyes against the late morning light as we stepped from the inn. We'd spent the day in bed and the evening sleeping, our bodies too worn and our eyes too tired for anything more. But that hadn't prevented me from taking Eloise again when I woke, kissing every part of her waking body until she was so soaked I couldn't deny my need to be deep inside of her.

I rolled my neck and surveyed the town which had come to life. Eloise pinched my ass, and I gave her a sly grin, grabbing her ass and pulling her against me.

"You know I can't have it looking like my woman dominates me, princess," I said, squeezing it tight.

"Wouldn't want the men to be jealous?" she teased, nipping my lip.

Someone cleared a throat, and I saw the disapproving eyes of a woman guiding her child away from us.

"Play the part, El, and you can force me to my knees when we're alone again." I kissed her roughly and released her, thinking of how different I was from the man who had run from Hiranire.

"You'd better," she said, bringing her fingers to her lips and touching them. "Although I might enjoy letting you manhandle me again."

My crooked grin made her giggle, and I adjusted my now prominent hard-on before taking her hand and leading her into the village. Neither of us had eaten in over a day, and we needed sustenance. A tavern sat next door to the inn, and I led her there, my stomach grumbling at the smell of food when we entered.

"Tell me your plan," I said to Eloise once the tavern maid left us. We'd chosen a corner table, set off from the other part of the tavern.

She glanced around nervously, and I placed a hand on hers to calm her.

"I'm going to face him," she said, leaning toward me, her voice barely a whisper.

"That much I know, but how do you intend to do that?" It was a question I'd been asking myself since we began this journey. "You can't just walk in there."

"Why not?"

I bit my tongue because as much as I loved her, she frustrated me to no end. "Because he will capture you and kill me." And he would. He'd told me as much the day he'd given me my freedom, threatening to kill me if I ever stepped foot back in Duntraik.

When I'd met Eloise, I'd been intent on testing that threat. On seeing if he'd take me back, and if I could make my way in Duntraik with people who were just as irredeemable as I was. But Eloise had changed me and with that transformation, I knew I could never go back and be what he expected of me. It was the reason I'd begged for freedom in the first place.

The tavern maid returned, setting down the plates and giving me another questioning look as her eyes darted between me and Eloise.

"Thank you," Eloise said, her tone terse.

With a shrug and a teasing look, she left us alone. I peeked over at Eloise as I shoveled a pile of hash in my mouth, savoring the taste while my stomach growled in anticipation. She stabbed a potato, her brows knitted.

"You know people don't like things that are out of their norm, right?" I asked, the food muffling my words.

Her eyes shot up. "If I wasn't hiding my identity, she'd be on the ground groveling to me," she snapped.

It sounded like something I would have said, so it didn't sound right coming from her.

"Since when do you worry about who bows to you?"

With a sigh, she stabbed another piece of potato and shoved it into her mouth. I'd questioned why she hadn't asked for any meat, but she'd mumbled about blessings and the gods before changing the subject quickly. There was something she wasn't telling me, and it would have bothered me if I wasn't still hiding my own secrets.

"I don't," she said between chews. "I just don't like the judgement. Is it so wrong for me to be an older woman and for you to love me?"

"You're not an older woman, for one...even if you have a few years on me. And no, it's not wrong. It's simply not something most people see, so they make assumptions about why someone as gorgeous as me would fuck someone as old and wrinkled as you." I gave her a playful wink and ducked just as she whipped a potato at me.

Yanking her chair closer to me, I twisted my fingers in her hair and drew her face to mine. "Throw something at me again and I'll no longer obey my feisty woman and test her obedience instead."

"Gods, that's tempting," she breathed. It was tempting, but I wasn't so certain that was a role I wanted. As much as having her on her knees as she worshipped my cock had been a turn on, I'd never been into dominating a woman.

"Fuck, eat your meal so I can settle my dick down, woman." I released her from my hold and rolled my neck, wishing I hadn't touched her because now that was all I could think about.

"Let's get back to your lack of a plan," I groused, irritated at myself.

"I told you my plan—"

"That's not a plan. I didn't argue with you about this when we left Troniere, but now that we're so close, I'm going to. You can't go to Duntraik. We're in Bira. You're safe here. Why don't you return home instead?"

She lowered her fork, her eyes growing dark. "That was your intent all along, wasn't it?"

My teeth gritted at the accusation before I said, "No, it wasn't. But you're here now and there are people here who can defend you better than I can." I hated that I'd lied again because it really had been my intent, but I didn't want to aggravate her any more than I already had.

She scooted her chair back and was out of it before I could stop her. Damn, I hadn't meant to piss her off and now my stomach would need to wait further. I threw some coins on the table and ran after her. Catching her elbow, I dragged her into the alley next to the tavern.

"What are you doing, Eloise?"

"Leaving you to fester in your boorish backward thinking," she snapped.

"Boorish backward thinking? For trying to keep you safe? To keep you alive?"

She yanked her elbow from my hand. "I've done a fine job of staying alive without you."

I clenched my jaw, wanting to snap back at her. Instead, I placed my hands on the wall, pinning her between them. Her brows creased, and the pouty look she gave me would have turned me on if I wasn't so annoyed with her.

"Give me three reasons you shouldn't return home, and I'll ride into Duntraik with you."

Her mouth fell open before she slammed it shut, glowering at me. "Rikeri will attack, and war will break out."

"He won't risk war in the favored land of the gods. Try another."

She made a sound between a growl and a scream, reminding me of a child having a tantrum.

"I won't risk him hurting my family, Garret. I need to do this on my own."

Those last words told me everything I needed and confirmed that I would never let her ride into Duntraik. With a sigh, I relaxed my arms, bringing my fingers to her face and tracing the rose petals hidden beneath her magic. "You don't need to prove yourself to anyone, El. You're an amazing woman, strong, powerful, intelligent, frustrating at times—" she punched me in the chest, trying not to smile, "—and more than capable of surviving on your own. Go home. You've been gone three years."

"I can't," she said, looking past me at the people walking by.

"Why?" There was something more, just as it seemed with everything about her. There were layers to Eloise that complicated her, and I was slowly peeling them away.

"Because it's my fault Rikeri took me."

I stepped back as if she'd slapped me. The guilt I'd harbored that I had been at fault teetered as I waited for her to explain.

"I left the castle on the day of my birthday celebration. There were so many people, so much bustling and noise. I only wanted to escape for a few minutes." She dropped her eyes, and I could read the guilt she'd carried since that day. "I snuck through the old service entrance. There was a space for me to squeeze through. When I was young, I would use them to hide from my brother."

My stomach turned at the thought that she'd been down there, the same place I'd manipulated the servant girls, taking my pleasure from them while stealing secrets. I swallowed back the mixed emotions, wishing I'd wandered further, that I'd not stopped to trick them, and found Eloise instead. It was some warped dream that if I'd only found her then, I could have protected her, that I wouldn't be here lying to her and trying to keep her from heading to her undoing. That she'd met me before those deeds had shaped the man I would be and before every step I'd taken after that time had further changed me.

"I sat on the castle wall and watched the sky, not knowing my parents had kept me inside that day for a reason." She rubbed her arms, and I could see the heavy toll her remorse had taken. "I was born at the full moon of the summer solstice at the stroke of midnight. And as I sat there that night, waiting for the stroke, my family thinking I was safe in my bed, the channeling occurred. That's when the true power of the gods blesses the vessel. It was like a blast of lightning that lit my soul, my body paralyzed with the force as every dormant cell of magic woke, calling out to the magic of Bira like a beacon."

"A beacon...for Rikeri," I said, once again stunned by her power.

She nodded. "The castle has stood since the first of my kind. Years of protective magic stand upon it, shielding others from that transformation." Her brows furrowed as she wrung her hands. "I was outside, free of those barriers, and when it struck, a wave of magic flooded across the kingdom." Her voice dropped to a low whisper. "I sensed him, Garret. The corruption that warps his magic, the way it seeps from him like some twisted infection. It answered the call of my magic."

"Because his magic derives from the same source as yours."

"Yes. It snaked its way into Bira and just as my magic touched my people, so did his." She sighed, her eyes looking past mine. "My action weakened my kingdom. For the first time since the first of the vessels, the blessing wasn't as secure, our magic not as strong."

I gave her a puzzled look, wondering how that could be. It made little sense that she'd caused such a thing.

"How do you know that happened?"

"Because I felt it, as did all those who bear magic in our land. Rikeri's magic latched onto mine as it woke completely, and he sensed my power and how his had weakened it."

I thought of the reaction of the roses in the field to her, the way the magic had floated out to bless her people. "You're not weak, Eloise. Rikeri took you because that was his plan all along."

She shook her head. "No, he experienced my surge in power. As did everyone in the kingdom. My brother found me and dragged me back into the castle, but it was too late by then. His magic was faltering, not heeding his command, the same with my father and the guards. All because I wanted to be independent, to get away from the castle for the last time."

"Wait, the last time? I thought you said your father let you have more freedom than the prior vessels." A sense of dread was building in me, a suspicion that there was more to the peaceful kingdom of Bira than we were told on the outside.

"Once the full power of the gods awakens, the vessel must remain within the castle, protected and under guard from any who might try to manipulate the magic. My father had already limited my time outside my tower to a few minutes a day. That was my last day of freedom. They would have locked me away in my tower for good, treated like some fragile object."

I couldn't help but gawk at her, not comprehending how they could think of doing that to her after teasing her for years with small glimmers of freedom.

"Do you see why I can't return home? I am the ruin of Bira. I have Rikeri hunting me and as soon as he knows I'm here, he'll do what he's wanted to do for years, destroy my family and over-throw Bira."

Rubbing her arms, I pulled her into my chest. "That's not what will happen. Even Rikeri respects the gods' land. He won't come here." Attacking Bira would risk his power and that was something he would never give up, no matter the prize.

"If he respects the gods, why did he have me kidnapped? Why

steal the vessel of the gods and torture me so? He will bleed my power from me, Garret, and destroy my kingdom if I don't—"

I pushed her back, holding her arms. "He will bleed your power and destroy your kingdom if you go to Duntraik. Your father had Nilan hide you for a reason. They want you nowhere near Rikeri."

"And nowhere near Bira," she said, crossing her arms.

Releasing her shoulders, I backed up, leaning against the opposite wall and thinking. "Why?" I asked. "If you're safest in the castle, safest in Bira, why not bring you home?"

"I told you, they were worried Rikeri would find me again and raise Bira to get me."

"No, there's something more." The image of her with the petals came back to me again. The way the gold magic floated over the field, heading to bless the people. People who only had magic because Eloise did, because the gods blessed them through her. A people who selfishly hoarded that magic, never leaving their kingdom. Carefully guarding their secrets. So why wouldn't they want her back once rescued from Rikeri?

Because she'd done something that night, destabilizing what had been in place for centuries. Her presence now risking the magic that had been theirs to covet since the first blessing.

"Shit," I muttered, wiping my hands down my face. "We shouldn't have come here."

"I told you—"

"No, Eloise. You don't see it. Nilan didn't keep you away because your parents wanted to keep the kingdom safe from Rikeri. They ordered Nilan to take you because they were protecting the kingdom from you."

She stepped back, bumping into the wall. Her eyes had grown large, and I could see the struggle for her to grasp what I'd said, the disbelief that sat in her eyes.

"No, that's ridiculous."

"Is it? As ridiculous as locking you in a tower for the rest of your life?" I took her shoulders again, forcing her to look up at me. "They locked the vessels away because the magic here feeds from you. You did something that night that upset their hold on the magic, and I suspect it remained unstable until Rikeri took you. They didn't want you back because it risked further destabilization of their magic. They couldn't leave you with Rikeri because he would use your power to destroy them, but they could keep you away."

Her head shook as she tried to free herself from my hold.

"We're leaving, Eloise. I'm taking you far from here and from Duntraik. Neither is safe for you."

She was trembling and the strong woman I knew looked defeated as the truth settled. I hated being the one to break her like this. I wanted to break her with my touches and my words, but not these words. Not like this.

"We've already risked them realizing you're here." The image of the golden magic on the air returned, something about it nudging me. "Does your magic touch every part of the kingdom?"

"Yes," she said. "The land, the animals, the people."

So where had that magic gone? There was something I wasn't seeing, but there was too much I'd already discovered, and Eloise looked too shaken to dump more on her.

I took her by the elbow, leading her out of the alley and to the inn to collect our horses. As we waited, I rubbed her back, hating how her eyes had lost the life I loved so much in them. My mind churned through what I'd learned so far and how much I didn't know. Bira was a respected kingdom, placed on a revered level because the gods had blessed it with their magic, magic that didn't flow past the borders, not until Rikeri's ancestor had stolen it and suffered punishment from the gods.

That was the story, but what if that's all it was? A story to cover something.

"We should get some provisions," Eloise murmured. "We

can't go back to Troniere and it's a long trip to the next kingdom."

I shifted my gaze to her. "Are you giving up on Duntraik?" I asked, relief flooding me as I felt some of the tension flee my body.

"No, but I don't think this is the time. I need to think about what you said and...I can't do that here."

"I'll travel as far as you want, princess."

She gave me a sad smile. I threw the stable boy a coin and led the horses to a post near the vendors as Eloise wandered to a vendor selling fruit. I watched her for a moment, seeing the defeat still present in the way she carried herself. The confident, strong woman I loved was nowhere to be found, and I hated that.

I walked toward her, movement catching my eye from the periphery. Glancing over, I halted in my tracks, my chest tightening. Standing behind a stand of bright scarves was Leo, the best friend I'd left behind the day I'd run, leaving the past and everything in it behind. He looked up, seeing me, his eyes hardening as much as his jaw. Peeking back at Eloise and satisfied she'd be safe where she was for a few minutes, I marched over to Leo.

"You've got a lot of nerve even coming near me, Garret!"

I pulled him into a hug, giving him a hearty pat as he went stiff in my arms. "It's so good to see you, my old friend."

He shoved me from him, giving me a confused look. "How are you alive?" he asked. "And why the fuck did you leave me to rot in that prison? You're such an ass, not worth all the years I dedicated to you. Everyone turned on me because of you. Even my family. You don't deserve friends."

I listened as he ranted, my eyes flicking to Eloise to ensure she was still safe. I didn't like having her so far from me, but I didn't want her bumping into my past. She was grappling with too much as it was.

"I woke up in the river below the castle," I said. "And I ran."

"Of course you ran. That's all you ever fucking do unless you're fighting someone you know you can stab in the back. Go away, Garret, before I call those guards over here and tell them the scum of Hiranire who tried killing the prince is here."

"Don't even think about it. Look, I'm sorry I left you. It was a shitty thing to do, but you're free!" I gestured around us to emphasize my words.

"No thanks to you. It was Beatrice who talked the prince into releasing me, saying you manipulated me into being that way. Which wasn't a lie. She's my sister, Garret, and you used me to get to her. Gods, I was so blind, and you were so manipulative and selfish." He rubbed his hand over his face and my guilt grew. In all my devious attempts to get Beatrice, I'd never considered what I was doing to Leo.

"I'm sorry, Leo. I really am. For everything." He gave me a doubtful look, his brows knitted. "How are you here?" I asked him, hoping we could move forward from the past.

"Although the prince granted my freedom, he banished me from the kingdom. Beatrice worked it out somehow for me to come to Bira, and this is where I live now." It was a special privilege since they rarely allowed outsiders to stay, and it didn't surprise me that Beatrice had been behind it. She was kind to a fault.

I rubbed my neck, thinking of how that kindness had faltered when she'd pushed me from the balcony. My actions had forced her hand, changing the sweet, innocent girl she was into a hate-filled killer. She was only protecting the man she loved, doing the same thing I would do to anyone who threatened Eloise, but villainous acts had already tainted my soul, while hers had yet to bear the same scars. It was yet another example of the destruction I reaped with my selfish ways.

I glanced over at Eloise, thinking of all the damage I'd done to her that she had yet to discover. She'd moved farther from me, and my fingers twitched to be closer to her. She was talking to a woman who was sitting at the fountain in the center of the town. The woman was clutching a lumpy bag, her face tear streaked and etched with heartache. Eloise had stooped before her, holding her hand in hers.

"What are you doing here?" Leo asked, pulling my attention away.

"I'm here with someone."

He raised a brow. "Someone?" Peeking to where my sight had lain, he said, "She's a little old for you, isn't she? Unless you mean that teary-eyed one."

"No, and she's not. She's perfect." I turned to him. "And she's special. Leo, I need you to keep my identity secret. She doesn't know about my...mistakes. I'm a different person now and she's the reason."

He studied me, his green eyes judging me in a way only someone who'd known me since we were younger, the only person who knew what escaping the bounds of Duntraik had done to me, would do.

"Fine," he huffed. "But you owe me. A lot."

"I do and once I have her safe, we'll sit down with a mug of ale, and you can berate me until you run out of air."

"And what is he berating you for?" Eloise's sweet voice drifted through my ears, causing goosebumps along my neck.

"For being an old friend who lost touch with him for too long," Leo said.

"This isn't the friend who taught you to make fish, is it?" she asked, her smile lifting my spirits.

"Why yes it is," Leo said, turning on the charm and giving her a polite nod. "Leo—"

"Of Bira," I finished for him quickly, not wanting her to know where we'd come from and risk the chance she would piece my secrets together.

"Well, Leo of Bira. I'm...El." And her lies came as easily as mine. She hadn't really lied, but she'd deceived, using the nickname to avoid revealing her identity.

I glimpsed the guards Leo had referenced as she and Leo chatted about how he'd gained access to be in Bira.

Guards. My alarms went up, my heart hammering. I'd insisted Eloise come to Bira, insisted we needed to skirt the border, then stay in town. Every minute she'd been here was a beacon to the king. If her magic was indeed negatively affecting the magic of Bira, they would have noticed her presence the moment she stepped into the kingdom, triggering whatever effect they'd stopped when they'd had their guard steal her away.

I randomly wondered why they hadn't left her with Rikeri, but then remembered he would have bled her power, keeping her life in stasis as her magic fed his and made him an unstoppable foe. A threat they couldn't counter, especially if their magic had indeed been affected.

"We need to go," I said to Eloise.

"Running again?" Leo said, and I shot him a look.

"He knows you well, doesn't he?" Eloise teased, her smile fading as she read the tension in my body.

"Now," I said. "Leo, I'll find you when this is over. El, pull your hood up."

I ushered her away, hearing Leo grumble about making it up to him.

"What were you doing talking to that woman?" I said, my voice hushed as I kept my eyes on the guards.

"She needed help, so I helped her."

I glanced at her. "How did you help her?"

"I gave her some advice and..." I knew instantly what she was going to say and seeing the guards move toward us, I had a feeling they knew as well. Because they'd felt it. The royal insignias on their armor told me they were more than patrol men, these were royal guards.

I steered Eloise from their direction. "You used magic, didn't you?"

"Just a little to give her something small to guide her."

"Dammit, El, each time you use magic, it draws more attention to us."

"The horses are the other way. What are you doing?"

Two guards stepped into our path, and my grip on Eloise tightened as I backed us up. A tall man with ebony hair and blue eyes that matched Eloise's stepped between them. "He's trying to keep you from us," he said as I shoved Eloise behind me.

"Garret, stop," she said, and I noted how the man's brow lifted at my name. "He's my brother."

He drew his fingers up, a trickle of hazy magic dancing between them. I'd only ever seen Eloise's magic, and this seemed a dismal mimicking of what she had. "Yes, take your hands off my sister, and I might let you keep them."

I didn't shift my stance, not trusting him after what I'd discovered earlier. Much to my dismay, Eloise pushed past me and ran to him. He pulled her into a big bear hug, her feet lifting from the ground as he kept his eyes on me, trained and guarded. If Eloise had taken any of my revelations to heart earlier, she'd forgotten them with the arrival of her brother. And I'd lost any ability to get her to safety.

"You're alive," he said, placing her feet on the ground and looking over her. "But what is this?" He dragged his hand over her scars, the magic lifting with his touch. Her hood had fallen, and I watched as her silver hair faded to reveal the ebony and gold below. Those who had noticed the prince in their presence had already moved back from us, but with the fading of Eloise's façade, the town went silent. I looked around as they all dropped to their knees, their heads touching the ground.

They were in the presence of the closest being to the gods, and it was likely the first time a vessel had ever been past the castle grounds. I caught Leo's eyes, his expression confused and concerned. "What have you gotten yourself into?" he mouthed.

I shook my head, turning back to Eloise and her brother.

"Nilan was supposed to keep you from Bira, El. Where is he and who is this man?"

I didn't like the way he gestured to me as if I was some common beggar, latching onto his sister to take advantage of her. But I couldn't rightly tell him I was a captain of Hiranire's army, a deserter, a dead man, a manipulative, conceited, arrogant man whom his sister was changing to become something more. So I lied, the lie not slipping out as easily this time.

"My name is Garret of Southkent."

"Southkent? You've wandered far from home, haven't you?"

"He's traveling the kingdoms," Eloise said. She tried to move back to me, but her brother kept his hold on her arm.

"Let's get you home before we draw more attention. If Rikeri has spies here, any word of your appearance will risk danger to the kingdom and the capital. Where is Nilan?" He looked around, his brow wrinkling.

"Dead. Killed by Rikeri's men six months ago."

His expression shifted, concern now sitting on his features. His eyes darted around nervously. "We need to go. Garret of Southkent, thank you for escorting my sister home. I'll ensure my father rewards you generously."

"I don't need your reward, and I'm not leaving her side." I stood taller, the two inches I had on him showing as my muscles tensed below my shirt.

"My sister does not need—"

"I do," Eloise said, jerking her arm from him. "He comes with us."

"What?" I said, shifting my eyes to her quickly. Going to the capital of Bira and rubbing elbows with royalty who likely knew of the mess I'd made in Hiranire was the last place I wanted to be. "No, we're leaving Bira. That's what you and your family wanted, isn't that right, your highness?" I looked pointedly at her brother.

"Because she was safer far from Duntraik. But now, it's too late. You brought her back here, setting off a signal for Rikeri."

I moved closer, the guards going rigid as they watched my moves. "I was keeping her from riding into Duntraik. I didn't realize Bira was just as dangerous for her."

His head picked up, his jaw ticking, before he looked down at Eloise. "You wanted to go into Duntraik? After all we did to ensure you escaped." He dragged her from me, and I snatched her arm.

"You're not taking her anywhere without me." His head snapped back at me. Eloise was struggling to free herself from his hold, mumbling about pig-headed men and stubborn asses.

I would have chuckled had the situation not been so tense.

"Fine. You can go," he said. "But my way."

The blow to the back of my head came too fast for me to react, and I heard Eloise yell as everything went black.

CHAPTER TWENTY

ELOISE

"N o!" I screamed as Garret collapsed. My brother held me back as the guards gathered his limp body and dragged him across the town center.

"Calm yourself, Eloise. Your people are watching you. Remember your place," Tristan said, his hands tight on my wrists.

I pulled my sight from Garret, trying to calm the ache seeing him like that caused. He was such a large presence, so strong and confident, that it gutted me. I met his friend's eyes, seeing the distress there. He wanted to help, and I could see him weighing his choices, but there was nothing he could do. Not against my brother and the royal guard. I shook my head to tell him to stay where he was and snatched my arms from Tristan's hold.

"Eloise," he scolded.

"Don't use that tone with me, Tristan," I said, stomping from him and following the guard. "I'll go, but don't hurt him."

"He's trouble, El."

I laughed, thinking of what Garret had figured out just before

Tristan had found me. "No more trouble than you are," I snapped.

"What does that mean?"

I ignored him as the guards hauled Garret up and threw him over one of their horses. It took three of them to lift him and I couldn't help but stare. I knew he was big, towering over me, his muscles huge, but watching them struggle opened my eyes to just how massive he was. Tristan grabbed my arm, spinning me to him. I couldn't read his eyes. They were a guarded mix of anger and relief.

"What does that mean, Eloise?"

"Your people are watching, Tristan. Wouldn't want them to see us for who we really are." I yanked away from him, snatching the reins of a royal horse and climbing into the saddle. "Take me home. I know that's why father sent you. Put me back in my tower where I belong."

I turned my sight from him, staring ahead and hearing his frustrated sigh. Spurring my horse forward, I followed the guards, Tristan beside me. The silence was heavy, and I could sense his eyes peering over at me as we traveled, but I refused to look at him. I kept my eyes on Garret, worried that he hadn't woken. With every minute that passed, my fear grew, but as mid-day came, he stirred, picking his head up and grumbling.

"What the fuck?" he grouched, looking back at me and Tristan. His eyes narrowed at Tristan. "You knocked me out?"

"I had my guard knock you out."

"You better be glad I value your sister's feelings over mine, or I'd have my knife buried in your chest by now."

"I doubt that," Tristan said, and I glanced over at him, hearing the amusement in his voice. He didn't look at me to see the glare I was giving him.

Garret lifted himself further, trying to maneuver to a sitting position. "Stop your horse, El. You're not going back there."

Tristan nodded, and a guard moved his horse closer and brought the blunt end of his sword to Garret's head.

"No! Dammit, Tristan," I yelled as Garret's eyes rolled back and he flopped back down, slipping from the horse and landing in a lump on the ground.

I jumped from my horse and ran to him, rolling him onto my lap and running my fingers over the lump on his head.

"How could you?" I said to Tristan.

"He's not a good man, El."

"And you know this from the few minutes you spoke with him?" I cradled Garret's head in my lap. Tears burned behind my eyes, but I refused to let them fall. "Please stop hurting him," I said, my voice cracking.

Tristan dropped from his horse and strode over to me. I looked up at him, his hard features softening.

"Please, Tristan. I love him."

The fight fled him, and a conflicted look crossed his face before he stooped next to me, searching my eyes.

"If he keeps his mouth shut and behaves himself, I'll leave him be. But if he doesn't, I'm shutting him up."

"I hate you," I said, the words coming out like the strike of a snake bite before I could stop them. The look of hurt that flashed in Tristan's eyes wounded my heart, but he'd lied to me, used me just like my parents had. Garret was the only one I had now.

Tristan's lips thinned before he stood, straightening his shirt and saying, "Get on the horse, Eloise."

He motioned for the guards who scooped Garret from my arms, the three struggling again to toss him over the horse. I tried to climb on his horse, but Tristan jerked me back.

"You ride on your own horse, or I'll make you ride with me," he snarled, the sound crushing what faith I had left in him. The tears built, the pressure behind my eyes almost painful. Betrayal dug its talons into me, bringing a pain to my chest that was worse than anything Rikeri had done to me. I kept my eyes on Garret, praying he would stay quiet, that he wouldn't complain or try to save me when he woke. I didn't think there was any saving me now. My family didn't want me, yet Tristan was taking me back to them. The thought sent the panic storming through me like hail pounding against a tin roof. My limbs went numb, my mind filled with thoughts I couldn't escape, the beating of my heart was so hard I struggled to breathe, and the world spun as the relentless, uncontrollable circumstances of my life weighed upon me.

"Eloise?" I heard Tristan, but I was trying to force the breath from my lungs, my heartbeat so loud I could barely hear his words. I tightened my grip on the reins, thinking of how Nilan would calm these attacks when he'd been with me, before our relationship had been strained by the passing of years, before we'd agreed that love wasn't something for us and our physical needs and his duty to me were all that kept us together. And how Garret had stepped behind me, his presence a soothing balm to the panic that owned me in these moments, twisting my grip on reality and shredding it.

My vision spun without Garret's strength to hold me up, and the last thing I saw was Tristan's hand flying over to catch me.

THE CRACKLING of a fire and warmth on my face woke me. I opened my eyes, staring into the fire until I noticed Tristan across from me, his eyes intent on me, concern etched in the creases on his brow.

"Thank the gods," he muttered, rising and moving to stoop in front of me. He brushed my hair back. "You still have those attacks?" he asked.

I jerked from his touch, sitting up too quickly, and he grasped my arms to steady me. I averted his eyes, hating that I wanted him to hold me like he had when we were young. When I would sneak from my tower and find him, crawling into his bed when thunder boomed outside my window and lightning crackled across the dark sky. Or when the attacks first started as my magic increased, along with the burden of the reality that faced me, and the looming confinement in a tower removed from everyone, never experiencing the things other women experienced. No first love, no first kiss, no friends, no children... nothing to make me anything more than the piece of property I felt like. Those moments would strike, and I would find my way to my older brother, letting him wipe away the fear that tore its ugly talons into me. Holding me until it passed, and I could breathe again.

"Yes," I said, searching for Garret and finding him passed out, two guards standing watch over him. I went to move toward him, but Tristan stopped me.

"The asshole went feral when he saw you passed out and we had to knock him out again."

"How could you?" I hissed, knowing my words carried more than one meaning.

"He wouldn't shut up and he beat through two of my guards before we put him down."

"Like an animal?" I snapped.

"Yes," he said, the word blunt. "He's protective of you, I'll give him that. But I can't let him take you from here."

"No?" I asked, my anger rising. "Isn't that what you want? To take me far away so I don't hurt your precious connection to the gods' power?"

He looked as if I'd struck him, backing up on his bent knees and almost falling backward. "What are you talking about, El?"

"I know why father sent Nilan. It wasn't to keep Rikeri from Bira like he said. It wasn't to protect me, to hide me where Rikeri couldn't find me."

"El—"

"You and father needed me far from here to protect your power."

His face dropped, confirming Garret's suspicion, and I sucked back the sob that threatened to spill from my throat.

"You used me, both of you, and Mother let you."

I tried rising, but he grabbed my hands, holding me in place. "El, listen to me. There are things you don't know."

"Clearly," I said. "I thought my brother loved me, but I was wrong."

He flinched. "I don't care about the power, El. I wanted you safe. That's all I've ever wanted. How could you think otherwise?" The hurt in his eyes killed me, causing me to doubt my accusations.

"Then why—"

"Not everything is as it seems, El," he said with a sigh. He glanced over at the guards, then at Garret. "I'll explain when we get home. And when we do…" He looked so distraught, the worry in his eyes almost palpable. He dropped his eyes to my hands, flipping them over and rubbing his fingers over my callouses. "I never meant for any of this to happen, El. All I ever wanted to do was to keep you safe. And now that you're back, I can't. Father knows you're here and I have to take you home."

"But you don't want me there," I said, my voice so low it came out as barely a whisper.

"It wasn't me, El. It was never me." He let my hands go and rose, looking down at me with such a pained look that it nearly crushed me. "Get some sleep," he said, walking away and leaving me with the confusion of thoughts that were so tangled in pieces of truth and lies that I couldn't find my way out.

I watched him walk away, his head down, the strength I'd always seen in him no longer there. Tristan had always been the person in my life who grounded me, who let me be me. He would sneak me out of the tower after father stopped my daily freedom, as the door remained closed to me more and more. It was Tristan who brought me the paint and brushes to occupy me when he couldn't, who looked at the murals I created with eyes filled with wonder. He was the one who would bring me books about adventures and fantastical creatures, places I knew I would never see, but he promised he'd take me to one day. And it was Tristan who knew when the thunder shook the walls of my tower that I would be afraid, that I could no longer sneak into his room because the lock and the guards kept me contained. He would come to me with a candle and a book and read to me through the noise and the streaks of light that lit my room with their force.

Tristan had been my strength before circumstances had forced me to find my own. But it was because of him I had that strength to draw on.

I stared into the fire, wishing I had him now. Wishing I could trust him, that I could crawl into his arms and have him tell me everything would be fine. Instead, I crawled over to Garret, ignoring the looks from the guards, and I curled into his body, feeling his chest rise and fall in the forced sleep that left him unable to hold me. I leaned my head on his chest, closing my eyes and wishing I'd listened to him, that I'd let him take me far from here. But I hadn't and now the remaining pieces of my life were crumbling around me, and I knew not even the magic of the gods that coursed through my veins could keep it from fracturing completely.

THE NEXT DAY I stayed quiet, but Tristan was just as quiet. It was nearly nightfall when we crossed into the castle grounds. I gripped my reins, a strange sense of foreboding assailing the calm I was struggling to maintain. My home looked no different from the last time I'd been there, but I was different, seeing it in a new light. The massive walls that surrounded it, keeping me in and others out. The acres of land around it with no thornless roses to grace the space like there were right outside of it. The tower standing tall and distinct in the back of the castle, with one small window where a girl once stared out and wondered what the kingdom looked like beyond the wall, dreaming of one day escaping, of finding love, of experiencing life outside the confines of her life.

She had escaped, and she had found love. Yet now she was back.

My father's advisor met us at the gates, giving an obligatory bow to Tristan and me as we dismounted.

"Princess, it's such a relief to see you safe and healthy."

Healthy seemed a strange term, but then all of this seemed strange and unreal.

"Who is this?" he asked, gesturing to Garret.

Garret, my burly protector who fought each time he woke. Even when they bound his hands, he never stopped trying to get to me and so the guards had knocked him out so many times I worried he would never wake again.

"Take him to the dungeon," Tristan ordered.

I swiveled to him, my hands on my hips. "No, you will not take him to the dungeon. He needs to be cared for. Your bullies hit him so many times it will be a wonder if he wakes up sane. You'll take him to my tower."

Tristan balked, his mouth dropping. "You will not have a man in your quarters, Eloise."

I walked up to him, getting so close I could feel the heat of his anger. "I am not a child, and the man I love is hurt. You will take him to my room so I can tend to him and pray that he wakes."

"It's not fitting—"

"Oh, fuck fitting!" The gasp from the advisor was audible, and the guards shuffled their feet. "I am not the woman I was when Rikeri took me from here. I've had him in my room before, and you will not deny me that request."

He grabbed my arm and dragged me out of earshot. "Did he touch you?"

"Yes," I hissed. There was a strange blend of relief and anger in his features. "I am not a child, Tristan. I'm a woman."

"I know that, Eloise. That doesn't mean I like to think of any man touching my little sister."

"Now you get protective? Where was that man when you were using me for my magic?"

"I wasn't—"

"You've found her." My mother's voice interrupted whatever Tristan was going to say. It was just as cold and distant as it had always been.

I turned to her, seeing her standing there as stiff and uncomfortable as normal. I didn't know what I'd expected. There were only a handful of memories I had where she'd been something more, almost as if she were a different woman. Not the woman who locked her daughter away in a tower, never hugging her, never soothing her, never showing her any signs of love. Not the kind she showed to Tristan, not even close. I was nothing more than an object she avoided.

"Yes, Mother," Tristan said. "She's home."

"Make sure you clean up before your father sees you, Eloise. You look like a commoner." She turned and walked back into the castle. A familiar shallow sensation returned to my chest, one that had escaped me for the years I'd been away.

I felt Tristan's hand on my shoulder, but I shrugged it off, not needing his support, not like I had before life had changed me into someone he no longer knew.

"Escort the princess to her quarters and..." I waited, breath held, to hear what he'd do with Garret as I moved to take Garret's lifeless hand. "Take him, too. If my father asks, he is in my wing. I want two of you outside of her door. Lock them in. No one goes in and no one leaves."

I snapped my eyes to his.

"I have no choice, El."

"You had a choice, Tristan. You could have left me there with Garret and never brought me home." I turned my back on him, not wanting to look into his sad eyes anymore. I followed the guards, ignoring the curtsies of servants we passed and wondering where my father was and why he hadn't come to greet me.

As the hallways led to my tower, my breathing grew shallow. I fought back the panic that grew with each stair I climbed until I could barely move, frozen as I stared into the room that now seemed much smaller than it had. The rounded walls, the canopied bed against a curve that held vines and rose petals I'd painted and repainted over the years. Thornless vines that climbed to the height of the ceiling where a star-filled sky with a crescent moon stood in dark contrast to the bright colors I'd adorned the walls with.

The guards threw Garret unceremoniously onto my bed, giving me a sideways look as they left the room. I heard the door lock; the sound echoing through my mind and reminding me I was a prisoner. Now even more than I ever had been. I sat by Garret's side, praying he would wake but he didn't, even as the maids in waiting came in to clean me up, erasing the woman I'd become and replacing her with the woman I'd been the day my life had changed. Stripping away the strength, the confidence, the spirit I'd gained and bringing back the heavy sense of futility, the caged spirit, the obedient girl who didn't question, didn't fight back, didn't know how to escape the expectations that society and her father placed on her.

I sat on the side of the bed, my skirts fluffing around me, my long hair swept up and tightly bound to the top of my head, the corset restricting my breathing like everything was restricting me.

I took Garret's hand in mine, waiting for him to wake and take me from there. To run like I knew he always did, but this time with me.

CHAPTER TWENTY-ONE

GARRET

My head was pounding, but the cool touch of fingers running through my hair soothed the ache. Blinking my eyes open, I waited for them to adjust as a pair of brilliant blue eyes, creased with worry, looked down on me.

"That's a sight for anyone to wake to," I said, hearing how my words slurred.

"Thank the gods," Eloise said. "I didn't know if you'd ever wake again. Tristan had no right to do that to you."

Tristan must have been her brother. It sounded like a pompous name, fit for a prince.

"How long have I been out?" I asked, trying to rise. She stopped me with a hand to my chest.

"A few hours the first time, then they knocked you out again. And again...and you stubborn fool, I don't know why you didn't keep your mouth shut after the first time. Rambling about how you wouldn't let them bring me here and spouting colorful words about my brother."

The memories were slowly returning, moments of lucidness

where I remembered waking to find myself flung over the back of the horse, my hands tied at one point, a gag in my mouth at another. I rubbed my head, noticing more than one knot, and grumbled my sentiments about her brother's brutality.

"He doesn't like you much. I'm not sure why, but I doubt he'd like any man near me."

"Were you a virgin before your fake husband?" I asked.

"Which fake husband?" she said with a wink, and I couldn't help smiling as I remembered our story for the innkeeper.

"Your first," I said, rubbing my fingers over hers.

"Yes," she replied with a blush. "It's hard to lose your virginity when everyone is afraid to touch you and even if they wanted to, you're guarded like a rare treasure."

"Well, you certainly were a fast learner," I said, giving her a sly grin.

Her blush deepened, highlighting her markings, and I reached up and touched the petals, following their path down to her lips.

"Three years with a husky, older man taught me a thing or two about how to please men and how I expected to be pleased."

"Nothing wrong with that, princess." I pushed her hand aside and slowly sat up, my head dizzy. "Damn, that's gonna sting for a few days."

"I'm so sorry, Garret."

"Don't be. I'm the one who dragged you into Bira. Not that Duntraik would have been any better." I would have felt more welcome there, even with Rikeri stealing the life from me with his magic. "So if you're so precious, why did your overprotective asshole of a brother let you in here with me? I'd have thought he'd have you locked away in your tower and me in the dungeon."

She gave me a scolding look. "My brother is no more overprotective than you are."

I shrugged, looking around the room. It was massive, larger than my house had been. A fireplace sat across the room, a deep burgundy rug in front of it. One small window sat within the rounded wall. Paintings adorned the walls—thornless roses with their petals dipping lazily to where they folded onto the floor, vines of rich green climbing to a ceiling where the night sky sat dusted with stars, their golden light streaming as if reaching for something.

This wasn't just any room, it was her tower and the evidence of her seclusion was striking. I tore my eyes from a chestnut wardrobe painted with a myriad of flowers and from which I could see the bottoms of elegant dresses. I absently wondered if she ever wore any of them, since she rarely left her tower.

"Not overprotective enough," I muttered.

She lowered her eyes, staring at her hand in mine.

"So this is the infamous tower," I said, hating how down she seemed. "I like the way you decorated it." Her eyes lifted, a small smile forming. "How did you convince your brother to let me in the same room as you? And alone?"

"I can be quite persuasive when I want to be." She gave me a devious smile, and I squinted as I tried to determine what else she'd done. "My parents think you're in Tristan's wing, locked in one of his guest rooms."

"Aren't you a sneaky princess?" I fell back onto the bed, regretting it the moment my head hit the pillow. Its down softness didn't help the pain. I grimaced and Eloise climbed over me. Only as she shifted the skirts of her dress did I realize she had changed. The dress she wore was of the finest material, its color a light pink that brought out the blush in her cheeks and the blue in her eyes. The corset below pushed her breasts up just enough to make me want my hands on them. Someone had done her hair and twisted it up in multiple twists that met in the center, where it curled into one lush pile of ebony and gold. She was stunning.

She leaned over me and I brought my hands to her face, taking her in as she truly was—a princess, revered vessel of the gods, the most powerful woman who walked our lands, and the woman who held my heart even before I knew she was any of those things.

"You clean up well, princess," I said, brushing my thumb over the petals on her cheeks. Of all her markings, those had become my favorite.

"I had no choice. Mother made it clear my other outfit wasn't appropriate. Only rough commoner women wear things like that." The last statement she said in a mocking tone.

"I'd hate to hear what they think of me," I muttered.

"It doesn't matter," she said, her lips touching mine. The moment they did, everything else fell away and only the touch of her kiss existed.

I pulled her against my chest, wishing I could run my hands through her hair.

"Don't mess me up," she breathed between kisses.

"But I'm hungry and I really want to devour you right now."

She giggled and freed herself from my hold before rising and smoothing out her dress. "You need a bath and—"

"Will you be joining me in that bath?" I asked, struggling to sit up without my head pounding.

"No, she will not." The door had opened without either of us noticing and in it stood a broad man, his presence intimidating, his stance threatening. His blue eyes held the same intensity that Eloise's often held.

"Father." Eloise rushed over and gave him a hug. His embrace was warm but not as tight as I would have thought for a father who hadn't seen his daughter in three years.

"Eloise," he said, bringing his hands to her arms and inspecting her like she was an object and not his daughter.

I stood, holding onto the bedpost for support, until my head stopped spinning.

"You have a man in your room." He glared at me, that look telling me everything he thought of me.

"Garret of Southkent, your highness." I bowed, keeping my eyes on him.

"Southkent? Yes, I hear you're a traveler. One who I was told was nowhere near this part of the castle." There was disdain in his tone, and it put me even further on edge. Every instinct in my body screamed for me to take Eloise far from him. "Southkent is quite beautiful. Do you hail from the coasts of Linia?"

He was testing me, like any good father or king would. But I'd been on the road for years, and I'd chosen Southkent because I knew it well. "Begging your pardon, but Linia sits in Hiranire." And that told me he suspected my identity, although this far from Hiranire I wasn't certain how he would. Eloise's brother had seemed suspicious as well. If Beatrice had bargained Leo's admittance to Bira, then it stood to reason her prince knew Eloise's family well enough to gain that favor. "I hail from the northern cliffs of Sathin that overlook the ocean. It is breathtaking, especially in the warm season."

He looked me up and down while Eloise looked between us.

"You shouldn't have anyone in your room, Eloise," he said, dropping the subject and his interest in me. "Especially not a man."

I expected her to come back with something witty but she merely said, "I'm not a child, Father."

Where was the brash, foul-mouthed woman who could trade words with the best of men?

"No, but you are the vessel." His response was curt and held no emotion. I wanted to grab her and run, but there was nowhere to go. He looked back up at me. "Did you touch my daughter? Spoil her with your common hands?"

My jaw ticked. "I didn't spoil her. You have your loyal captain of the guard to thank for that. But I won't deny I've touched her."

His jaw went rigid.

"Father, what does it matter?" she said, too meekly for the Eloise I knew.

"It matters because you are an unwed woman!"

"I'll marry her," I said without thinking, the words coming

forth naturally. And I accepted the truth in them. I would marry her in a heartbeat, not just to keep her safe.

Eloise swiveled her sight to me, her eyes dancing with emotion. Her lips had parted to form a surprised *oh* before they curved into a wonderful smile. Her father studied me, that intensity in his eyes growing twofold.

"A vessel does not marry—"

"Nor does she indulge in matters of the flesh," I said, really wanting to say fuck, but knowing this man would surely have me thrown from the castle if I said I was fucking her. Better to stick with the fancy words with layered meanings.

"Yet it seems she has," he said, his voice gruff. He turned from me as if I was no longer worth his attention. "While your guest washes up, you will come down for supper, Eloise. We have things to discuss." He glanced my way, his eyes roaming up and down. "Your guest will join as well after he washes and changes into something respectable. I'll have water and clothes sent to the room."

He took Eloise by the arm, intent to leave with her.

"Father, may I stay..." He snapped his head to her, anger etched in his features. "...just until the water arrives. Then I'll be down, I promise."

I watched as the muscles in his jaw tightened further. "It is a privilege for you to join us," he said, and again I wondered how a father could keep his daughter locked away like an untouchable piece of property.

"I know, Father. I won't tarry."

I wanted to strangle the man for the effect his presence had on her.

"Fine." He looked back at me. "Keep your hands off her."

I gave him a nod, waiting for him to leave before I said, "I can't make any promises."

Eloise didn't react. She stood at the door, her head down.

Going to her, I tipped her chin up. "Why do you let him treat you like a child?"

"He's my father, Garret." She tried to pull away, but I brought her against me.

"And you're a grown woman, not a child."

"It's different here."

"No, you're different here." Her eyes met mine, stealing my breath once more. "Out there, you're free spirited and feisty. But in here? Where's the woman who ordered me to my knees, who climbed the vine on the side of the house to walk around her roof, who killed Rikeri's most deadly assassins? That's the woman I love."

The hurt in her eyes wounded me, and I wished I'd worded that differently. "You don't love me like this?"

"That's not what I said. I love you however you are, but this isn't you."

The sadness didn't leave her eyes, and I wasn't sure how to erase it. "But it is me. This is who I am. Circumstances shaped the woman you know. But that's only one side of me."

I didn't believe her. This place repressed the woman she was, the expectations placed on her and the protective shell they kept her in dimming the most amazing parts of her. I drew her closer, running my hands down her body and squeezing her ass. "Then I love both sides of you, but being here represses that fiery, confident side, and I miss her."

She sighed, her fingers draping over my mouth. "That side of me would only upset my parents."

"Not your brother?" I asked, curious why that wouldn't be the case.

She shook her head. "Where do you think I learned all those vulgar words that make you so hard?"

That surprised me and I scrunched my eyes, trying to figure out why he would have encouraged a side of her that didn't fit the expectations of a vessel.

"Tristan is more like you than you think, Garret. Don't judge him just because he's overprotective."

"Or because he had his guards hit me on the head multiple times to shut me up?"

She laughed, her head tipping back, and I dragged my tongue up her neck, loving how she shuddered.

"Don't start that," she warned, trying to free herself from my hold.

"Start what?" I replied, nibbling on her earlobe. "Bringing my princess out to play?"

Her sigh was delectable and did nothing to stop me. "How long will it take for them to bring the bathwater here?" I asked, my body coursing with the anticipation of fucking her.

"Long enough," she breathed.

My head was suddenly better and so I pushed her against the wall, muttering, "I'm going to make a mess of you, princess."

She seemed to wake at my words, taking my shirt in her hands and pulling me to her, our mouths crashing into each other. She was ravenous, and I was no better, my need for her consuming me. Her fingers tugged at my shirt, and I pulled it over my head, taking her face in my hands and resuming my desperate kisses. I skirted along her neck, pushing at her sleeves and cursing the damned corset that held her breasts in. Laughing, she bit my lip, saying, "Leave it and fuck me, big boy."

"There's my girl," I said, pushing her skirts up as she dug at my pants to free my length, which was pressing so hard to reach her I thought it might burst from my pants. My hand hit the bare skin of her leg and I drew back, smirking. "Nothing underneath, princess?"

She stroked me, her hands giving just the right pressure to cause my entire body to ignite. I slid my hand over her ass, gliding my other up her body and squeezing her waist as I drew her closer. She grabbed my shoulders as I lifted her leg and slipped through her arousal, denying myself the pleasure of penetrating her because I wanted to see her fall apart.

Her head fell back, her body grinding against mine. I wrapped my hand around the back of her neck and forced her lips to mine, devouring her kisses and her moans as she grew more soaked. I wanted to savor that moan, to slow down and build her climax so that she was trembling as it reached its precipice. But this wasn't the time for slow. It really wasn't the time to fuck, but I needed Eloise like I needed the blood in my veins. The desire to touch her was a constant, and now it was like a banshee screeching through my body. I tightened my grip on the back of her neck, my fingers threading between the strands of her hair and pulling what I could with it tucked away so firmly on her head.

"Gods, Garret, make me come," she moaned against my mouth.

"I don't think the gods have anything to do with you coming, El." I reached between her legs. "Is that a command, princess?"

"Yes, gods, yes it is."

I brushed my thumb over her clit, her grip on my shoulders growing tighter as her body quaked. I squeezed her neck, pushing her lips back to mine and thrusting my finger into her. Her cries stayed smothered as she came, clinging to me like she might tumble if my body and the wall weren't holding her up. My desire for her was like a howling wind tearing at my body, her quivering only intensifying it. I picked her up and thrust into her, groaning at the clenching of her muscles around me. Our bodies slammed together in a symphony of skin and moans until I could take no more and the ferocity of my climax washed over me. I held her tight as my release fled my body in wave after wave of pleasure that left me so spent that I dropped her legs and leaned against her. My breathing was ragged, my chest heaving in rhythm with hers.

She brought her hands down my arms, caressing my muscles, and I lifted my head from hers, looking into her eyes. They were hazy, and her cheeks held a rich flush. I kissed her trail of petals until I reached her lips. As our kiss grew more sensual, I wondered how I'd ever thought there was anything better than Eloise out there, kicking myself for not finding her earlier, cursing the gods for not putting her in my path before now. I would have been a different man with her in my life. A good man.

Her fingers traced my jaw as our lips separated and she cupped my cheek. "I love you, Garret of Southkent."

And as much as her words drifted through my soul, the reality that the man she loved was nothing more than a lie tainted them. Turning my face into her hand, I kissed it, thinking of all the lies I'd weaved that I wasn't so certain I could untangle now.

Those thoughts remained as I fixed her skirts before tucking myself away.

"Should I clean up before dinner?" she asked, smoothing her hand over my chest.

I stepped back into her space and tipped her chin to force her eyes to mine. "Leave it. It'll be reassuring knowing my cum is leaking out of you while your parents remind you they and this blasted kingdom own you."

Her eyes narrowed. "Why do you say it like that?"

"That my cum will leak out of you?" I teased.

"No," she said, pursing her lips. "That my parents will remind me they own me."

"Because no one owns you, Eloise. They stick you in this tower, only letting you out when they approve and once you're thirty years of age, there is no escape? That's not right."

"But it's the way of the vessel." I could hear the doubt in her voice.

I palmed her face, taking it in both my hands. "No one owns you, El. Not even me. I may own your heart and you mine, but I don't own you, nor does anyone else."

There were tears pressing behind her eyes and I thought of all the damage my lies would reap on her heart once she found out...

and if she found out from someone else. Like the parents who were waiting for her.

"El," I said, swallowing back my fear of that truth. "I need to tell you something."

My words stuck in my throat as she searched my eyes. The tightness in my chest was almost unbearable, but as I opened my mouth to tell her everything, to admit that I wasn't the man she thought I was, the door opened.

I stepped away as her features shifted to the timid, obedient vessel. I'd lost my moment, and I knew I wouldn't get it back. A feeling of dread sat on me like the heaviest of loads.

"My Lady," a servant girl said, averting her eyes just as I remembered my shirt was off. "The king and queen are expecting you."

Another servant laid clothes out for me as two men brought in a tub. Two others came in with buckets of water that barely filled the tub and I frowned, thinking of how I would wash my large body in such a small amount of water.

Eloise shooed them out, but a guard stepped into the room, waiting to escort her to her parents. I didn't want her out of my sight, and I didn't want to think of what might happen when she was.

"They didn't spare much water, did they?" she asked, ignoring the guard. "I don't think my father likes you any more than my brother does."

"I bet he doesn't. He definitely won't if he ever finds out what's between your legs," I whispered, giving her a wink.

With a laugh, she placed her hand in the water, bringing it up to let a few drops fall back in. Her markings glittered, the gold sparkling and spreading over the droplets. As each hit the water, the level rose until it was halfway full, steam now wafting from it.

"So you'll warm me a bath, but you won't use your magic to fight off Rikeri's men? Or those hounds at the border?" I asked, miffed as to how and when she used it.

She shrugged, then quickly looked away, and I noted the stress that now sat in the creases of her forehead. There was something about my comment that made her uncomfortable, and I didn't have time to question her about it. She gave me a kiss on the cheek and left with the guard, glancing back at me before the door closed, a hooded look in her eyes.

I stood there, looking down at the water that still sparkled with a golden dusting, and wondering what secrets she was still hiding from me and if I'd ever discover them before my own were revealed.

CHAPTER TWENTY-TWO

ELOISE

My legs shook as I walked the path down the circular stairs that led from my tower. Whether from Garret's touch or from nerves, I couldn't tell. But it was likely a mix of both. The way he broke me every time he was near left me weakened and craving more. I didn't want to leave him behind. Having him with me fortified me, reminding me of who I'd been during the years I'd been free from the confines of the title that defined me.

The bindings of my corset constricted my breathing, and I faltered, holding onto the wall to steady myself.

"Princess?" the guard behind me said, the word having such a different meaning when it wasn't coming from Garret's mouth.

"I'm fine," I said, regaining my composure and continuing my trek.

The stairs were never-ending, like the worry and fear that were whirring through my mind. I didn't know what to expect when I joined my parents, what lies awaited me. I'd been happy to see my father, running into his arms and momentarily forgetting what he'd done, part of me still believing it couldn't be true. But the stiff response, the distance that was clear in his embrace, reminded me of the truth and of all the times I'd denied his embrace was anything but loving. It never had been. I knew love now, knew the tight, protective sensation of arms that wanted to hold me. And what I felt from my father was anything but that. Only with Garret had I truly had that sensation...and with Tristan. I paused, realizing the truth in that thought. Tristan's hug had been emotional, tight, and relieved. His hold had always differed from my father's, and I'd never stopped to think of why that would be.

I continued my path until the stairs led out to the second door that sealed me in my tower, the first guard opening the door and ushering me through. I held my head higher, lifting my skirts slightly as my foot hit the landing into the castle. My instinct screamed for me to run back to Garret, to insist he walk with me, to shelter me from what I knew awaited me. The panic rose in my chest, heavy and uncomfortable, my breaths coming out shorter as we neared the great hall. My hands clenched my dress as my fingers tingled, my sight wavering.

Breathe, Eloise.

I pictured Garret with me, his strength bolstering me, his coy grin melting my insides, and the material loosened in my hands. Swallowing back my nerves, I stepped into the room, not expecting to find my parents and Tristan there. My father had said supper so the dining room would have made more sense, but spying my father's tense stance, I no longer expected food would be part of the evening.

I stopped halfway into the room, my confidence wavering as my mother's hard eyes fell on me. There was no love there, and I wondered at the few times she'd shown me that love, the times she snuck me into the kitchens, showing me how to dust my magic over the sugar on the rose drops to enhance the flavor. It was almost like she was another person because the woman who stood to the side, her eyes looking at me like I was nothing more than an annoyance she couldn't wait to be rid of, was nothing like that mother. I tore my eyes from her, meeting Tristan's and seeing the worry there as he approached me.

"Calm, Eloise," he said, reading the panic in my eyes, the emotion that was bursting through me like a storm I couldn't control. Like Garret, he knew without me saying anything. He took my hand in his. "It'll be okay," he murmured, and I wondered if he didn't want our parents to hear.

"Be done with it, Stefan," my mother said to my father.

"Done with what?" I asked, not really wanting to hear what he had to say.

"Where have you been all these years, Eloise?" he asked, not sounding like he really cared, but more like he was stalling.

"Do you care?" I asked. "You wanted me gone, and I went." I felt my strength returning, my anger at how they'd used me driving it.

His jaw clamped, the muscles twitching. "Yes, I sent Nilan to protect you and take you from Rikeri—"

"Stop lying," I said, pulling my hand from Tristan's. "I need the truth for once. Because I don't think anything in my life has been truthful. All of it has been nothing but lies and greed."

"Eloise," Tristan said, and I turned my sight to him.

"Don't, Tristan. Don't lie anymore. You all wanted me gone because..." I looked at my mother, seeing the disdain there. I was having a fit, and she didn't approve. She never had. "You didn't love me, Mother, and you, Father, only wanted me for my power. Neither of you cared for anything but what I am." Saying the words hurt so badly, I could barely get them out. "And you, Tristan, promised you'd protect me and that you'd continue to give me a taste of the world beyond that tower, but you broke your promise. Your lies hurt the worse."

I saw the flinch of pain at my words, the agony that contorted his features. His reaction was the only one that made no sense because my parents hadn't denied and they hadn't reacted.

My father rubbed his temples, his expression morphing with an anger I'd never seen in him.

"You had everything. More than any vessel before you, but you push and push, Eloise. You should have stayed wherever Nilan hid you. Where is that traitor, anyway?"

"Traitor?" I asked. "You sent him to take me away. Told him I needed to stay far from Bira to protect the magic and the people. That the night of my birthday, my actions had cursed the magic, and my presence would bring Rikeri back. That he would destroy Bira to get to me." I waited for my father to tell me that Garret was wrong, that they hadn't sent me away for their own selfish reasons, to protect their magic and not to protect me or the kingdom. But those words never came.

He laughed, the sound menacing and vicious. "Is that what he told you when he stole you away? The traitor stole you to weaken us more. Lies are all he fed you." He stormed over to me and grabbed my arm, rubbing his hand down my markings. "This keeps our magic flowing. You and every vessel before you. That power keeps us strong. I don't give a fuck if the people experience it." I cringed at his words, their acidity scalding me. The forceful grip he had on my arm grew more painful the tighter he squeezed. "It belongs to the king and those who serve him. And when you climbed the wall that night, sharing your gift across the country-side so that it touched that maniac in Duntraik, you cursed yourself. Drawing him like a beacon to steal what we coveted for centuries. Disrupting the balance of power, sending it cascading unreliably through us until he stole you away." He leered over me, causing me to shrivel back. "Nilan was supposed to bring you back as a bargaining chip. A tool to secure peace and stabilize our power. A trade to ensure your spoiled, misguided beliefs that you are anything but a vessel didn't damage our magic any further and risk this family's reign over Bira."

"That's enough, Father," Tristan said, jerking my arm from my father's hand and pushing me behind him.

"Enough?" my father screamed, smacking Tristan so hard the sound echoed through the room.

I cried out as Tristan held his cheek, glaring at him.

"Stefan!" my mother yelled, rushing to Tristan as if he was a toddler and not a grown man. He pushed her hands from him.

"You're not using her anymore," Tristan said.

"No, I can't because she ruined everything that night and because you're a fool who has squandered his destiny, choosing to avoid what needs to be done to ensure the blessings remain. You're as much at fault as she is, and I should get rid of both of you."

"Get rid of us?" I asked as he pushed my mother from Tristan and ordered her away. She scurried to the other side of the room, no longer as intimidating as she'd seemed.

"I've had years to think about how to keep your magic feeding ours. Three long years of dealing with no vessel to reinforce the kingdom and my power, three years of pretending it didn't weaken us and coming up with a way to ensure your recklessness never passes on to the next vessel and to punish you for pretending to be something you're not."

"Pretending? Pretending what? To be a normal woman? To live life like you get to live it? Like our people get to?"

"You are a vessel! Nothing more, nothing less! There is no life other than what you give to this kingdom and to our family!"

I stepped back, feeling the sting of his words like the smack of his hand. Garret had been right. That's why they'd locked me away, why the doors to my tower would have locked forever on my birthday when the full blessing of the gods coursed through my veins. I was nothing more than a thing to them, not a daughter, not a woman. Only an object to protect and use, to own, just like Garret had said.

"That's all I am?" I asked. "To all of you?" I looked at Tristan, hoping I hadn't lost all of my family in one night.

"Not all of us, El," he said.

"You're a fool, Tristan," my father said. "Given a gift that—"

"That what? Hurts those we love? Did you ever love your sister? Did you even know her before—"

"Enough! I will not have you bring that woman up, nor have you insult me with your questions. You are not king!"

"Nor do I want to be, if this is what it means to be one."

My father's eyes were deadly, and I backed up further. Silence followed, one that was so heavy I could almost feel it weighing upon my shoulders. Approaching footsteps echoed, and even the anticipation of seeing Garret and having him lend me his strength didn't ease the tension in my body. My life was faltering. The tower of lies it had been resting on was precariously unbalanced. I didn't know just how unbalanced it was or that the next truths would send it toppling so hard that it shattered into too many pieces to ever put back together.

CHAPTER TWENTY-THREE

GARRET

As soothing as the tub water was, I rushed through my bathing, a need to get to Eloise's side hastening me. The clothes provided for me were the finest I'd worn, and I snapped the lapel of the long jacket, missing the feel of my uniform and clean clothes. I'd brought the bare minimum with me when I'd left home and over the years I'd been hesitant to replace them.

Before leaving the room, I took the time to look around at the life Eloise had once led. The same life to which I'd foolishly brought her back. There was nothing in the room that spoke of the woman I knew, other than the paintings on the wall. These were pieces of a life she'd left behind, life changing her since that day. Just as it had me.

Her window cast a view far beyond the castle grounds, the mountains of Duntraik menacing in the far distance. She truly was in the highest tower of the castle, separated from the other parts of it. Locked away, but why? To protect her? Or to use her?

I was certain it was the latter, and I had my suspicions about the warm welcome she'd received when her brother had found her. If I was right, she was in danger. They wouldn't kill her because of who she was, but they could take her away from me, hide her, sell her off to another kingdom. My pulse quickened. They could bargain her off to Rikeri.

I hurried from the room, following the guard through the castle halls. My eyes surveyed the parts of the castle that I'd never seen when I was younger, only venturing as far as the servant's quarters, their ramblings as I'd pretended to be infatuated with them telling me the exact location of the quarters for each member of the monarchy. The princess in the tower in the far west wing, the prince in the east, and the king and queen in the south wing.

It was all Rikeri had needed to know as I'd detailed everything the girls had told me, trying not to think of how I'd used them, how I'd fucked them, spilling my seed on their bodies or their mouths, sometimes on the floors of those tunnels, Rikeri having warned me not to fuck it up by leaving one pregnant. As if he'd cared...as if he'd ever given any mind to me other than how to abuse me.

Swiping my hand down my face, I cleared the thoughts away, following the guard into the great hall where Eloise, her parents, and her brother stood talking.

Eloise looked uncomfortable, her brows knitted, and I wondered what had transpired before I'd walked into the room. Even her brother seemed on edge.

"Ah, if it isn't Garret of Southkent," her father said, distaste lacing his words. I liked him less each time I saw him. "Or should I say Hiranire?"

I drew a sharp breath through my clenched teeth.

"Hiranire?" Eloise said, turning her sweet eyes to me. I took them in, knowing it might be the last time they would hold anything but repulsion and hatred.

A servant stepped into the room with a flourished bow. "Sire, your guest has arrived."

I broke eye contact with Eloise and met the king's glare.

"Perfect timing. Send him in shortly." The servant hastened away. "It seems my guest has saved you the embarrassment of explaining the lies you've fed my daughter. As fate would have it, there are more important matters at hand than seeing you fumble your way through an explanation of how a dead man is standing in my hall."

My fists had bunched so tight, I knew the veins in my arms and neck were bulging. He motioned to the guards at the edge of the room. "Take him to the dungeon. Let him rot there until Hiranire's king gives me word on what to do with him."

Eloise's face distorted to a mix of emotions that I didn't like—fear, sadness, anger.

"Father, what's going on? You can't take him—"

Her brother moved next to her, standing protectively by as she grew more agitated.

"He's a criminal, Eloise," the king said, glowering at me before his head turned toward the front entrance of the hall.

I noticed how the marks on Eloise sparkled. Fear gripped me like an unwanted claw, ripping into my body and spurring the fight in me. I fought the guards, struggling to break free as an all too familiar heaviness permeated the air.

"Don't do this to her," I cried out. "She doesn't deserve this. Take me, kill me. I don't care, but don't do this to her."

Eloise's eyes grew wide, and she looked down at her hands, seeing the sparkle there. She took a step back but bumped into her brother, who put a hand on her shoulder.

"That's a bold statement coming from a dead man," her father said.

"Why do you keep saying that? And who's here? Please tell me." Her voice cracked on the last words, the emotion clear in it as she looked between the two of us. Panic sat in her eyes, and I remembered how she'd been when we first crossed into Bira, drowning in her emotions so she could barely stand. I wanted to go to her, to hold her and calm her.

I tried to talk first, but her father said, "He didn't bother to tell you how everyone in his kingdom thinks he's dead? That he died trying to kill their prince?"

I rolled my eyes at the mention of the beast, annoyed that her father was twisting this to bring the attention to me and not answering her question about the plague that was on his way to steal his daughter.

"Is that true?" Eloise asked, the disappointment in her eyes stabbing me.

I didn't answer. How could I? There was nothing to say in defense of myself.

"He's a coward, Eloise. Running from a failed attempt at killing the prince and stealing the woman who sits by his side." I'd heard the news of Beatrice's betrothal in my travels, each time grating my pride until one day it didn't. The day I'd met Eloise, her blue eyes shining in the afternoon sun, the rays shimmering in her silver hair.

"Did you do that?" Her voice held such pain that it hurt for me to look at her. All thoughts of who her father had invited into the castle were gone, her focus now only on me.

I wanted to defend myself, to tell her there was an explanation, a reason for my actions that validated them, but I couldn't because there were none. And I wasn't a good man. I was the villain in this story.

Her eyes reflected the fracture my lies had caused in her heart and that knowledge left mine devastated. "You ran...like you always do," she said, and I wanted to take back everything I'd ever done and fix the hurt reflected on her face.

Her words were like a slap, the sting not fading. Her markings were growing brighter, and the distinct aura of darkness was settling in my bones, my alarms ringing loudly at having been ignored.

"Eloise—"

"Did you do it?" she snapped, her eyes steely.

"Yes. I told you I wasn't a good man."

"Good man?" her father said, laughing. "You're not a good man. You're a villain."

"Eloise, please," I tried again, fighting the hold of the guards, desperate to reach her.

"I had my secrets but this...you hurt people. I know that story, Garret, the captain who turned on his king, the villain who coveted a woman he couldn't have, too vain to see she didn't want him." I felt each word like the snap of a whip to my skin, branding me over and over.

"Because that's all he is," her father said. "A villain."

I noticed how her mother stayed out of it, a strange observer to the commotion. Her brother stood vigilant, ready to protect her from me at any moment.

"That's not who I am now," I said, leaving my eyes locked with hers. "Not since I met you, El—"

"Don't call her that," her brother snarled.

I didn't bother looking over at him, instead continuing, "You changed me, El."

Her father glanced over at the door, and I knew he was looking for his guest. "Once a villain, always a villain. You can't change. If you had, you wouldn't have lied to her. You would have been honest with her from the start."

I knew the truth of his words and I'd battled with it as the lies had cascaded.

"Take him to the dungeons," he ordered.

The guards pulled me back, but I fought, wrestling with them.

"Eloise, don't trust him. I know who's coming. Run Eloise!"

I was fighting hard, Eloise's emotions rising as she tried backing up, her brother stopping her. He looked over at me, and I pleaded with him to stop this madness, but his eyes remained guarded. By now, Eloise's markings were so aggravated the gold had spread outside their lines, almost like they were bleeding into the rest of her skin.

"Get him out of here!" the king screamed, his finger pointed to stress the direction.

"Father," Eloise said, pushing against her brother to free herself. She stumbled from his grasp. "I need to talk to him." Hope bloomed again, and I paused my rebellion, the guards dragging me further from her.

"No, he goes to the dungeon, and you will forget him." A fracture formed in my soul, and Eloise looked my way. He grabbed her chin, turning her sight to him, and said, "You have other matters to attend to and company to receive."

"Don't listen to him, El. That's not any guest. That's Rikeri."

"Get him out!" His scream barreled through the room like a herd of horses.

"I demand to know what's happening! After everything you've done, you owe me that much!" Eloise yelled as her brother looked questioningly at her father, then back at me. There was something in the way his eyes were now creased that led me to believe he didn't know who was coming. He reached over and pulled Eloise closer to him and further from her father.

"We're fixing a mistake you started and Nilan fucked up," the king sneered.

I saw her brother's reaction, noticing only then that his hold on Eloise wasn't aggressive, it was only protective.

I called out again, but pain flared through my head and no matter how I fought it, my world went dark.

"Fuck," I muttered as I fought to open my eyes. My head was pounding even worse than it had been and I wondered at this point if I had a concussion.

The room was dank and cold, engulfed in darkness save for one lone torch that flickered across from me, providing barely any light. The dungeons. I'd like to have said I didn't recognize the sickening stench and the damp touch of lingering death, but I'd seen my fair share of dungeons in my youth. Punishments doled out by Rikeri were harsh, but the dungeons had been a reprieve from the sting of his magic and his fists.

When the room stopped spinning, I rose, albeit slowly and painfully. My legs were numb from the haphazard way the guards had thrown me into the cell, and it had been a full day since I'd had any sustenance but the touch of Eloise. At the thought of her, terror raked through me. I stumbled to the bars, tugging at them and cursing everything. There was no escape, no way to reach her, to save her from the wretched fate that awaited her.

I slumped against the cell gate, sliding to the floor as I questioned the gods. Questioned why they would bless her with such a curse. Why they would allow her parents to use her. Why they would stand to have someone so precious locked away from the land and the people the vessel should have been blessing.

Her face came back to me—the mistrust, the confusion, the fear. Of all my mistakes, this one hurt the most. My lies to her and my misstep in leading her back to the very people who wanted to hurt her.

"Why?" I asked the gods as I rested my head on the bars. I would have taken it all back to have her safe, but there was nothing I could take back. It was too late.

Footsteps echoed, announcing company I didn't want. Perhaps it was the guards coming to ship me off to Hiranire to face my demons. It wouldn't matter. I'd lost Eloise. Life didn't seem worth the fight without her.

"We all make mistakes," I heard her brother say. "El would say mistakes are the gods' way of making us strive to be better."

I didn't bother looking toward him. My desire to kill him was too high but stuck behind these bars, I couldn't satisfy that need.

"My father has sold her off to Rikeri in exchange for Bira's safety." His words confirmed my fear and the heavy twisted sensation of magic that I'd recognized in the air before I blacked out.

I turned my neck, seeing him slide down the other side of the bars, running his hands through his black hair. He looked distraught, his clothes rumpled as if he'd been fighting.

"I tried to stop him, to talk him out of it, to fight as Rikeri took her, but..."

"How can he do that to her?" I asked. "He's her father." Not that I held much stock in that given my own experiences, but from my travels I'd found that most fathers cherished their children, especially their daughters.

"Because my father only cares about one thing: power."

"But her mother—"

"She's not her mother, she's mine."

I turned my body toward him, creasing my eyes as that revelation hit me square in the chest.

"None of the vessels are legitimate and Eloise is not my full sister," he said in a relieved tone. "Gods, I've been holding onto that secret for so long it's good to finally let it out."

"How—"

"When a vessel is born, there's a ritual that binds her ability to have children. The family then treats them as holy, untouchable objects until..." He paused and I looked over at him, seeing the strain, the toll this had taken on him. "Until after the vessel has reached the age of thirty, when her power is at full blessing. Tradition dictates the prince will have married before then and had his firstborn, something I rebelled against, just as I've rebelled against all of this." He dropped his head to his hands and my chest thudded, nerves assailing me as I waited to hear what came next.

"What happens then, Tristan?" I said, knowing from his reaction that it was something traumatizing.

He dropped his hands, his head resting against the bars. "Vessels bear vessels," he mumbled. "The king severs their binding on their birthday and...and the king's son takes her virginity, using her until she conceives another vessel."

My stomach turned, and I gaped at him, his words unraveling everything I'd ever learned and everything Eloise knew of her existence. Anger boiled through me, a red-hot rage I couldn't stop. I reached through the bars and grabbed his neck.

"Did you touch her? Did you fucking touch her?" I'd never been so angry. The injustice, the immorality, the violations wracked me with a need for retribution.

"No," he choked out. "Why do you think I haven't taken a wife yet? I've delayed to avoid it, to protect her. I love my sister, regardless of the fact that she's my half-sister. I've done everything I can to protect her, to stop this madness."

I let him go, finding a new respect for him, one I did not have for his father. And remembering that Eloise had told me she'd been a virgin, that fact confirming the truth in his words.

"My father only cares about his power, just like every king before him. The vessel feeds that power. As wrong as it is, our family believes a new vessel can only come from breeding the living vessel with the firstborn of that generation, and so they forbid any outsider from touching her." Breeding was a heartless word that seemed fitting in this instance, and my stomach soured further. "The firstborn is always male, the vessel always female. There has never been a break in the birth order and that has been the defining proof that the gods bless the atrocity. No prince has ever challenged it."

"Well, I can tell you I've definitely broken that rule."

He laughed. "And I can tell you, my father is more than pissed about that."

"I wasn't the first," I said.

"Nilan?" he asked, his voice relaxing.

"Yes."

"Asshole. I sent him to keep her safe, to take her far from Rikeri's evil doings and my father's intentions. To break this tradition."

"Wait, you sent him?" There were so many lies twisted around Eloise that I wondered if she could handle how shattering the truth would be.

"I thought I had, but I think he was playing both sides, going for my father to retrieve her and on my behalf to run with her. Thankfully, he ran with her, even though I'm pretty sure I now know why, considering what you just told me and the fact that he was at least twenty years older than she was. Fucker."

I'd been jealous of the man before, but now I hated him. The idea that he had run with her just to get his hands on her didn't sit well with me. The only thing that softened the injustice was that he'd died protecting Eloise.

I ran my hand down my face, trying to piece everything I knew together, but still grasping to understand it all.

"So your father wanted Eloise back so you could both fulfill your duty to the kingdom?" I asked, the idea so disturbing my words came out in a growl.

"No. He knows I'll never follow through with it. Fuck tradition. I'd let the kingdom burn before I touched her."

I peered over at him, seeing the man who had been so instrumental in shaping Eloise and protecting her. "Then why? If what she did the night of her birthday disrupted the magic in the kingdom, why bring her back and risk further impact?"

He let out a long sigh. "My father locked her in the tower that night, debating on what to do now that our magic was faltering. No vessel had ever been beyond the barrier of the castle grounds before, even Eloise," he continued.

"Until the night of her birthday," I muttered, still trying to understand how the men in Eloise's family could do the things they did.

"The channeling needs to happen within the grounds. It's an extraordinary amount of magic that awakens in the vessels during the event. There is a boundary that keeps her magic contained—"

"Contained for what?" I asked, not understanding how anyone could keep a gift from the gods from the people. It was something that had bothered me this entire time, and my suspicion was that the king was hoarding it. I wanted to hear Tristan's confirmation of that suspicion.

"For my father, for me." He sighed and I could hear the heavy burden the secrets of his family had sewn. "Eloise is a constant source of magic when she's in Bira. It releases with no one even noticing. The gift of the gods, touching our people and our land with her every step, every breath, every laugh. It flows freely from her, like a river of blessings."

"With no one even noticing," I mumbled, repeating his words.

"Correct. Only when she purposely calls her magic do her markings glow, but that doesn't mean it's not there. The first kings realized this and used those vessels to form a boundary around the castle. The land and the people no longer enjoyed the full benefits of the gods' blessings."

"But the king still did."

"Yes, and his son."

I rubbed my hand over my head. The levels of deception were so dense that it was hard to truly understand the complexity. "But that night it went free, feeding the kingdom."

"Yes, and damaging our power. It was like a siphon, drawing it away bit by bit."

"Because her power was no longer caged," I mused. "Running free for the kingdom like the gods intended."

"Correct. My father was furious. His power is everything to him and Eloise had jeopardized it."

I scratched my chin, staring at the wall as I contemplated what he was telling me. "Why didn't your power stabilize after you brought her back inside?"

"We're not really sure," he said with a sigh. "I think it has something to do with the magic imbued in the wall by the first vessels and reinforced with their ashes. Either it happened when she climbed the wall and swung her feet beyond the spell, or it happened when the channeling occurred. Whatever it was, it's irreversible."

"Is it happening now?"

He flexed his hands in and out. "When I brought her back inside that night, the flow stopped, but the magic was no longer as strong or dependable."

Because she'd weakened it, changing history in that one move.

"The disruption delayed the ritual of removing her binding and since I'd been a thorn in my father's ass and not produced a male heir yet, there was no need for it, anyway," Tristan went on. "When Rikeri took her, our magic stabilized again. Sure, she was no longer feeding it, so it remained lessened, but it stabilized. My father was contemplating leaving her there. He didn't give a shit about Rikeri. But I did. I didn't want him touching my sister, hurting her, raping her." He ran his hands through his hair again. "Gods, the images that came to me while he had her wreaked havoc on my mind. I sent Nilan, knowing I couldn't go into Duntraik."

"Didn't your father know what Rikeri intended?" I asked, miffed at why he wouldn't see Rikeri as a threat.

"Not until the day we sensed him tap into her power." He rubbed his arms as if reliving that moment. "And that sealed her fate. It was a rush of power that fled through us, restoring what was missing and strengthening it."

I tried to think of why that would be. "Rikeri's magic sources from the Bira roses," I muttered. "Flowers touched by the gods and imbued with their power."

"Yes, when his magic connected to Eloise's, which comes directly from the gods, it affected everyone her power fed and everything beyond the castle boundary. The fields were richer the next morning, abundant and vibrant, even the air seemed fresher the next day."

"And your magic was stronger." I'd known Eloise was powerful, but never had I fathomed just how powerful.

"And my father's. Eloise stood no chance at that point. He sent a convoy into Duntraik on the grounds of accepting Rikeri's claim to Eloise and bartering a marriage proposal. He sent Nilan to steal her back to force Rikeri's hand, expecting Nilan would return with her before the convoy arrived, thus giving Rikeri no choice but to accept the proposal to get her back in his hands."

"Are you fucking kidding me?" I'd wanted to kill her father before, but now it was tenfold.

"No. The moment Rikeri tapped into her power, ours surged and my father knew what Rikeri's intentions were. With an unlimited flow of Eloise's power, one we could feel all the way into Bira, there was no longer a need to keep her locked up. Rikeri is powerful, and my father decided that if I wouldn't follow tradition, then he would use Rikeri to ensure the birth of the next vessel." Her own father wanted to sell her off like an animal to breed. There were no words for the anger that raged through me. "He thinks if he lifts the binds and she births an heir for Rikeri, the vessel will be born with even greater power. Power he could then steal back, letting Rikeri think we were in alliance with him."

"Your father clearly doesn't know Rikeri," I muttered.

"And you do?" he asked, peering over at me.

"Better than you can imagine." I rubbed my temples, trying to process all I'd heard. "If he's only using her, what was all that about letting her have her freedom when she was a child, because his sister...gods, no, his..." It was too hard to even voice, so I stopped, the bile rising in my throat.

"That was me," Tristan said. "I begged him to let her out,

promised that I would keep her safe. And I did. I was with her every time, as were our guards, and we never crossed the boundary of the castle grounds."

"Until that night," I said.

"Yes. Father had constricted her freedom more each year until it was mere minutes a day and with the channeling, she knew she'd never leave her tower again. She snuck out on her own and once she did, she unraveled everything our family had in place for centuries. And now my father thinks he has the solution."

"Because he's sold her off to Rikeri," I said, the words like lead from my mouth.

"Yes. They struck an agreement. Rikeri can use her as he wants as long as she produces another vessel and he returns that vessel to Bira at her birth. My father will release the binding once I marry and produce an heir to the throne. He's already found me a wife and is forcing my hand."

"Rikeri will never give him anything, especially a child." That I knew with certainty, because an heir with power was something he'd failed to produce.

"He's agreed to it and in return he can use Eloise as he wants, as long as it does not threaten the child's safety or Bira's."

"But she can't give birth. She'll die." The wrenching of my heart nearly doubled me over.

"No, he'll keep her alive to feed whatever it is he's doing to his power."

"But she'll die the minute she gives birth. Eloise told me all the former vessels died." The words came out hollow, the emotion too extreme to manage.

He shook his head. "Another lie. They were murdered... although there was some chaos the night Eloise was born. I remember a lot of guards running through the castle, a lot of worried voices until my mother took me back to bed. I was always suspicious that she escaped."

His disturbing answer only relieved my fear slightly. The

thought of Rikeri touching Eloise, of violating her, making it too eclipsing to remove.

"Why doesn't she fight back?" I asked, wishing she had. That she'd fought with all her might to run from them. "She has all that power. Why doesn't she ever use it?"

He stood, brushing his pants off, and I looked up at him, seeing the stress he bore, the love he had for Eloise coming through. "She won't because she thinks she can't."

"What does that mean?" I wasn't following, and when he opened the cell door, I was even more confused.

"She's been told her entire life that her magic is protective, nurturing. That it's only for enriching the land, the animals, the people. That's all she knows and so she believes that her magic will be useless if she uses it to harm any creature and the gods will curse her and Bira if she does."

"The stag," I said, thinking back to hunting.

"The stag?" His forehead creased.

"Yes, when she hunts, she waits for the stag to show her which animals she can kill. But she never uses magic, only her bow and arrow."

"My mother's doing. She always hated Eloise. I suppose knowing her husband was fucking his sister nightly until he impregnated her would spoil any love she could have had toward Eloise. She refused to let her eat with us, sending only scraps from our meals to her and rarely meat, saying the gods didn't approve of her eating it. The nights I could sneak a few pieces to her, she refused to eat it until I told her the gods had given their blessing to the hunters in the appearance of a stag. The stag is a myth—"

"One that guides her. I saw it with my own eyes. Giving her signs."

He stared at me, squinting as he comprehended my words. "Then maybe there is hope, yet."

He pulled the cell door open all the way and held his hand out. I looked up at it, unsure if this was some trick.

"I can't go after her. But you can. The special thing about Eloise is that she sees the good in even the worst of us. She saw something in you and regardless of what you did in the past, you can save her."

"You really believe that?" I asked, not convinced that I could.

"I have hope. Eloise is my sister, and I will do whatever it takes to ensure she's safe."

I took his hand and let him help me to my feet.

"There's a horse at the end of the old servants' quarters. It has provisions and weapons. You should be able to get to Duntraik within a few hours after Rikeri. I'll show you the way."

I didn't have the heart to tell him I knew the tunnels, that I was the one who led Rikeri to them and started this mess. Although, maybe it was good I had. If I could save her, she could live her life outside of that tower, free to live, free to love. With the thought, an ache swelled in my chest. She would live, but she would no longer love me.

Tristan easily took out the first two guards we met with his magic. After handing me their weapons, he led me down twists and turns through the castle until we emerged outside the kitchens.

"Don't be a fool, Tristan." His father stood at one end of the hall, his guards at the other.

I positioned my sword, ready to fight, my mind strategically thinking through our options.

"I'm not a fool. This needs to stop. You sold your own daughter off to our enemy." His words caused my grip on my handle to tighten.

"If you had done what you were supposed to, I wouldn't have needed to!"

I ripped my sight from the guards and glared at the king.

"It's sick—" Tristan said.

"It's necessary!" his father's face was red with his anger, his eyes were so dark they were almost black.

"Necessary? To bed my sister? I'm ashamed to be your son, to be any part of this family with its vile traditions and abuse of a gift from the gods."

He drew his hands up, magic trickling between them. "And I will stop this, Father. If it means overthrowing you, then so be it. I will not touch Eloise, and Garret will ensure Rikeri doesn't. It's time to give up the power and make things right."

"Is that how you want it?" The king took a step closer, golden magic dancing on his fingertips. Eloise's magic.

"Run, Garret," Tristan said. "Take this hall down to the right and you'll find the tunnels. Save my sister."

He struck his father with a stream of golden magic that flickered with shades of black. I turned away, facing the soldiers and engaging them. Taking them down easily, I ran down the hall, not bothering to see what was happening between Tristan and his father. Thinking my escape was too easy, I pulled out the dagger I'd stolen from a dead guard, keeping the sword gripped in my other hand.

My suspicion proved true when I rounded the corner. Another guard stood before me, this one carrying no weapons because he didn't need them. The magic of the vessel touched the citizens in Bira in different ways, some receiving the gift of magic abilities. From what I'd learned from Tristan, I doubted there were any beyond the castle gates whom the king hadn't rounded up and used to serve the kingdom.

Tristan's magic didn't flow as easily as it did for Eloise, and I suspected it would be the same for other magic bearers. There was a moment needed to summon it and given that Eloise's move had weakened Bira's connection to her, that delay gave me the opportunity I needed to fling my dagger into the guard's chest. He staggered, his concentration broken as he yanked at the knife. I charged him, cutting him down before he could stop me.

"You'll need to do better than that against me," I muttered, wiping my sword on his body before quickly turning and searching for the entrance to the tunnels. I was in a dead end, but I remembered the servant girl telling me the tunnels led to a one-ended hall near the kitchens, so the entrance had to be here. I groped around on the wall, knowing my time was ticking by too quickly. There was no sign of an opening anywhere. Turning in the other direction, a gleam caught my eye. I pushed the body of the dead guard aside, running my hand over the floor and detecting the wood surface hidden below a spell.

After finding the handle and lifting the door, I dropped into the tunnels. Pitch black surrounded me, but I knew where I was now. The memories returned as I ran through the darkness, the ghosts of my past deeds, my mistakes, my lies pounding against me with each footfall. I would have stumbled from their weight, but for the thought of Eloise.

When I burst through the boards that blocked the tunnel, seeing the horse waiting for me, my hope returned. I could make it to her, save her, and be the hero for a change. Not the villain who would have turned his back and run away, a man too fearful of losing her to even attempt to save her. This time I would do the right thing and show her how she'd changed me, even if she could never love me again.

CHAPTER TWENTY-FOUR

ELOISE

The saddle pressed uncomfortably between my legs, but it was a distraction from what pressed against my back. Rikeri had me in front of him, his arm around my waist, his other hand holding the reins against my leg. With each shift of the horse, the firmness at my back had grown. I was sure he was thinking of how he would use me now that my father had sold me off to him.

At the thought, my chest burned, the pressure of tears pushing against my eyes. My father had pushed me to Rikeri, telling him to take me and honor their agreement. He hadn't given me a second glance. My mother hadn't even blinked. She'd always been distant, except for the few times she would come to me at night. I could remember the nights when she would sit with me, holding me until I drifted to sleep. And the next morning she'd act like it had never happened, like even the thought disgusted her. Those moments with her were few and had stopped when I'd become a woman, but I missed them.

The woman who stood coldly aside and let a man older than

my father take me, knowing how he would use me, how he would bleed my magic, and hurt me, was not my mother. My mother was the gentle spirit who made rose drops with me and hummed a sweet tune as she comforted me on nights when I couldn't run to Tristan's room.

Tristan was the only one who had fought to keep Rikeri from me. The guards had held him back, my father's magic steady as it countered Tristan's. I should have fought, should have kicked and screamed to save myself, but the truth had left me too fractured. Garret was in the dungeons and my heart was in tatters. I'd known he was hiding secrets, but never would I have guessed he was the man who had tried killing the prince of Hiranire. The rumors had spread even as far as Troniere. Talk of the events, how the prince had been under a spell, all of us forgetting him for that time, the cobwebs of the memories clearing away. How his true love had saved him.

To think that the beast who had hunted him down and tried to kill him was Garret gutted me. Sure, Garret was vain and self-ish, a womanizer who had no respect for the women he'd had, expecting only to be waited on hand and foot, but that didn't make a man a villain, a killer. A coward who had run away and pretended he was dead so he wouldn't have to face the consequences of his actions.

The man I thought I'd loved was not that man and I couldn't reconcile the idea that the man who made love to me, whose touch burned through to my soul, could be that same man.

Rikeri's hand moved further along my thigh, pushing my skirts up.

"I can't decide if I want to bleed your magic or fuck you first," he said against my neck.

My skin crawled, and I moved my head to push his face back. He had my hands bound in front of me, so I couldn't use my magic or fight him. Not that I would. My fight had fled the moment the truth about Garret had come out and it hadn't returned as my father handed me over as if I were simply a thing he needed removed from his sight. And I couldn't use my magic. The gods forbade it. They would revoke my gift if I harmed another, and Bira would suffer the consequences.

"Or maybe I'll bleed your magic while I'm fucking you." He groaned and his hardness jumped against my back. "Gods, wouldn't that be stimulating?" His hand moved to my breast, squeezing it painfully. "I should have done that when I had you before, but I needed to discover the secret of your power first." His tongue slid over my cheek, and I shifted, almost sliding from the saddle. His hand squeezed my breast harder to keep me in place. "Now that I know the secret, I'm going to bring you so much pain, vessel, that you'll be coming on my cock while your screams fill the room." He shivered, his dick lunging this time.

I tried to contain my whimper. The memory of the pain he'd caused me last time he had me flashed in my mind as the bile climbed my throat.

"Don't worry, vessel. I'm sure you'll grow accustomed to it. We have an heir to produce. Another vessel. I thought I'd lost my chance to have an heir carry on my legacy, but with you, I have that again." His hand slid between my legs, and I bit back my scream. "And we have lots of time to practice, to get you used to the pain I'm going to bring you. Your brother has to produce an heir first. Just imagine how many years of fucking we'll have before I put a child in you."

I shuddered, pushing his hand away. I didn't know what he was talking about or why he thought I had anything to do with the birth of the next vessel. I didn't have the energy to argue or tell him I couldn't bear children. Somehow, letting him think I could seemed like a better idea. I needed to get it together and think of a way out of this before he violated me. Nilan had come to my rescue the last time, but I didn't think anyone would this time. I was on my own. My father had Garret locked up and even if he came, I didn't think I could look at him. I wasn't sure what he'd been doing all this time, if he was just using me and lying to me to get to his next opportunity. The thought sent a knife of pain slicing through my heart.

Rikeri shoved my hands aside and pushed under my skirts.

"Don't," I said, hearing how my voice shook. I needed to pull it together and remember who I'd been when I was on the run, when I had to be more than the coveted vessel. "You should wait until we're married," I said with my sweetest voice.

"What do I care about that? You're mine either way. If I want to touch you, I will."

Gods, I wished my magic could hurt him, but I had seen no sign of the gods, no stag to give me the approval of the gods and everything I'd ever been told forbade drawing my power for harm.

"But you should care. If you want the gods to bless our child, it needs to be done properly." I was making this up as I went and praying he would believe me.

"What do you mean?" he asked, his hand stopping its movement.

"I'm a virgin," I lied, somehow knowing that would turn him on even more. As if in answer, his cock flinched against my back. "The gods expect my first time with a man to be with my husband. They would not want me defiled without their blessing."

His other hand was still on my breast, and he squeezed it, slipping his fingers under my neckline.

"I don't much care for the gods," he said, cupping my breast, the feel of his skin against mine causing the bile to rise further in my throat.

"But you want their blessing on this," I said, trying to keep my voice stable. "Otherwise, they may not bless our child with my power."

His hand froze. "Is that possible?"

"Yes. Just like the vessel needs to be born second, after the next heir is born. We must abide by every tradition. You and I must wed before you take me." The lies were easy, and I was glad I hadn't mentioned my inability to have children. This would bide me more time to avoid his invasive touches.

He removed his hand, and I exhaled, wishing I could wash his touch from me. Then I remembered that Garret's touch was still on me, his cum still dried between my legs. My stomach somersaulted before I scolded it, frowning as I realized he had tainted his touch with lies.

"Fine, vessel—"

"I have a name," I grumbled. "And it's not vessel."

"I don't give a shit what your name is. You are here for me, for my power, for my pleasure, and for bearing me an heir. Nothing more, and as so, you don't need a name."

I bit the inside of my cheek, swallowing back the tears as utter helplessness drowned me. Setting my eyes on the terrain that moved by at a pace that seemed unnatural, I tried to think of anything about my circumstances that I could control. But no matter how I tried, I could find nothing.

MY THOUGHTS WERE a rapid flux I couldn't stop. Rikeri had locked me in a room after dragging me by the hair into the gloomy castle that had given me chills that climbed my spine, encouraging the hairs to stand on my neck. The last time his guards had brought me here, they'd left me bound and blindfolded, my mouth gagged the entire ride. I wasn't certain if having his hard-on at my back the entire trip was any better.

I stared at the bed, which was covered in black throws. The entire room was dismal, and I knew he'd locked me in his room. I backed into a corner and slid down the wall, praying he wouldn't touch me, that he'd continue to believe my lie about needing to be wed. I didn't know if I could handle it if he didn't.

Closing my eyes, I pushed the thought away and with it the panic that was building in me, the room closing in around me as the shards of lies that defined my life fell around me. Drawing my knees to my chest, I buried my face in them and held tight as my emotions overwhelmed me. No matter what I tried, I couldn't get them to calm. Garret had been my calm as my life had fractured more, but now he was part of the fissure that was pulling me into an endless gulf with no hand to pull me out.

He'd lied. I'd known he had secrets, we both did, but never had I thought his would hurt so badly. I turned my head, resting my cheek on my knee and staring at the stone wall. Flickers of candlelight illuminated the shades of gray within it. My magic had finally settled down, my markings no longer glowing in reaction to Rikeri's magic, and so the candle was the only source of light I had.

Garret had hidden his past, but the man I knew wasn't the one who had done those things. Maybe the man who had first asked me for a place to stay had been, but not the one who had brought me to ecstasy, whose voice murmuring the word princess left my legs weakened, whose grin melted me. That man was the Garret I knew and the same man who had fought three guards when he realized my father's intentions.

I picked my head up, staring at the bed and thinking of him. My heart still belonged to him. I wasn't sure there was anyone it would ever belong to but Garret. He'd hidden his past from me because he didn't want me to judge him, just as I'd hid my own. We'd both had our lies and our reasons and we'd agreed to overlook them. He hadn't left my side when my truth came out, yet I'd let my father drag him to the dungeons when his truths came to light. So he'd made a mistake...probably many mistakes. He hadn't been a good man, but he'd told me that. He'd never lied about that fact. My father had called him a villain, but did that matter to my heart? He wasn't a villain to me; he loved me, protected me, brought me more pleasure than I'd ever thought possible, pleasure enhanced by the love we shared.

The door opened, destroying the warm thoughts that had eased my fear. Rikeri walked in, the repugnant expression on his face curdling my stomach. He removed his shirt, and my insides twisted in fear. Throwing the shirt on his bed, he made his way to me. I braced for his touch, hating that I couldn't summon the side of me that Garret had fallen in love with. Hating how she'd surrendered to my father's domination and slunk away to leave me as the vulnerable girl who had cried herself to sleep in her tower.

Rikeri grabbed me and pushed me against the wall.

"Since you're denying me, vessel." I shrank back from his touch, trying to find that part of me, to be the fierce, mouthy bitch I'd been when I was free from my father's shadow, from the shadow of my purpose in life. "I'll give you a taste of what you'll get when I finally break you in."

"You're not touching me," I said, finding my voice even if it sounded meek.

He shoved me, pressing his body into mine. "No, I'm not," he breathed into my ear. "But you can watch me do what I plan to do to you once your power is flowing through my veins." He licked my cheek, his tongue following the path of my petals, just like Garret's fingers always did. But this didn't leave me with the same warmth in my belly.

He released me, rolling his neck and walking away as the door opened. A guard ushered two women in, both dressed in corsets that barely covered their nipples. They sauntered over to Rikeri, their hips swaying, their confidence not enough to cover the slight fear I could see in their eyes.

"Take a seat, vessel. While I'd rather have your virgin body, I'll bide my time with my whores until then." Vines slithered from the wall and encircled me, forcing me to sit as they twisted around my body in long, black, snakelike coils. Sharp thorns like the ones in the bramble that lined Bira's border jetted out, close to my skin like a warning not to move.

"You're disgusting," I said, trying to ignore how the vines were constricting my breathing.

He tore the corset from one woman, commanding the other to stay, then threw her on the bed. I looked away as he dropped his pants and climbed on her.

"That's an interesting term coming from you, vessel," he said just as the woman moaned. He grunted before the sound of skin slapping against skin berated my ears. I couldn't cover them, since he had my hands bound to my sides. But I kept my eyes closed, my head turned from them even as the noises of their fucking grew louder. At least he wasn't using me...for now. The shudder that scraped its way through my body was violent, and the vines bit into my skin.

Rikeri roared, and I fought not to laugh at the obscene display of his masculinity as he came. Roaring seemed such a showy thing to do. A growl would have sufficed and proven the point that he'd enjoyed himself. With that thought, a little of my old self returned, the witty woman who had bantered with Garret and his chauvinistic comments when she first met him. I tried not to think about how I'd never again hear his voice or see the look of surprise in his eyes when I made a comment he assumed only men would make. Instead, I thought of what he loved about me, forgetting that he was flawed, that he'd made mistakes. He'd told me he loved all of me, but I knew it was the spirited part of me, the one that had flourished outside of my tower, that he loved the most.

"You missed the show," Rikeri said, the vines forcing my neck to turn toward his voice. "On your knees, whore."

My insides squeezed, and I prayed he wasn't talking to me. The very idea of being anywhere near his flaccid dick was appalling. A little more of my fight returned, even as the thorns pressed at my eyelids.

"Open your eyes, vessel."

"I think I can infer that you enjoyed yourself after that loud announcement," I said.

His power dug into me, clawing under my skin and burning my body, the thorns pressing harder. "Open your fucking eyes now or I will rip them from you and feed them to my hounds."

"I can't open them with your thorns in the way," I snapped, trying to maintain my calm. The fear was creeping back in, but it had no place here. There was nothing my fear could do to save me, so why not shove it aside and be the woman Garret fell in love with. The fighter who had survived on her own for six months, who had killed the last of Rikeri's men before she discovered they'd mortally injured Nilan, who had killed the attackers the day Garret had discovered her secret. That was the woman I needed to be, not the one tempered by a life spent locked in a tower or a father who valued her power over her life.

The thorns retreated, taking the pressure from my eyes. I didn't want to open them, but I also didn't want to lose my eyes. Opening them, I spied Rikeri sitting at the end of the bed. The second woman was on her knees in front of him, her hand wrapped around his erection, which was an impressive size for a man who'd just come. I flicked my eyes away, spying the woman he'd just fucked on the bed still.

"Saving her for later?" I asked, eyeing the mess he'd made on her stomach. "Or just saving that for a treat in case you get hungry."

He narrowed his eyes at me, their brown so dull in the dim light that they almost looked like the night sky.

"Leave," he commanded.

"I would, but I'm inconvenienced." Gods, it felt good to have some spirit back.

The woman climbed from the bed and hurried from the room, much faster than she'd entered it.

"I should make you satisfy me, vessel," Rikeri said, jerking the one on her knees against him. Her gag hurt to hear. "Especially since you lied to me."

The vines constricted more, and I let out a strangled cry just as Rikeri moaned.

"There's no need to wed you. I appreciate your attempt to deceive me, but you failed." I stared at him, ignoring the flickers of pleasure in his features. "I'll give you tonight to think about how good it will feel when your body is writhing under mine as my seed is filling you. Think of all the fucking we'll do until your father releases the binding and you can bear me an heir."

My laugh came out haggard from the limited oxygen entering my lungs. "Did they forget to tell you I can't have children?"

I waited for his shock to show, but he only gave me a smug look and yanked the woman back by her hair, letting her take a heaving breath.

"Did they forget to tell you your father bound your ability to have children and will remove it once your joke of a brother bears him an heir?" he asked, shoving her back down with a grunt.

I couldn't stop my mouth from dropping. He'd mentioned bearing an heir when we'd been riding, but I hadn't cared enough to argue with him. This I would argue. "I think the joke's on you."

He closed his eyes as the woman's head bobbed faster, his hand tearing into her hair as his pelvis thrust toward her.

"Watch me, vessel, because once I leech your power and we're connected spiritually, I will take your body and make it mine as our magic surges from us. We will rule this world side by side and you will worship me on your knees every night."

"Never," I hissed.

He stood, stilling the woman's head and using her so viscously that I had to look away until I heard his grunts, thankful there was no roar this time. I peeked over, watching as he pulled from her mouth, her large eyes looking up at him. Her legs were shaking. No matter how they pretended, fear ruled these women. They were nothing more than things Rikeri kept for his pleasure, and I wondered how many he had in his castle. Tristan had taught me about the other kingdoms and their rulers, telling me the rumors of Rikeri's violent tendencies, the abuses on his people and his servants, the concubines he kept.

"Go," he commanded her, and she rose, bowing before she left, slower than the other woman had. He pulled his pants on, and I let out what breath I had in relief that he wasn't turning his used dick to me. But he walked over to me, and the vines loosened, my limbs tingling as the blood rushed back into them. He grabbed me by the neck, jerking me against his naked chest, and I thought of how different the action felt from when Garret had done it.

"You will bear my heir, but I will break you in first."

I tried pulling my head back, but he twisted his fingers in my hair. I cursed the stupid updo the lady-in-waiting had given me that was still holding my hair in place, even after the long ride. "I was told you were docile—"

"You were told wrong," I hissed.

He brought his face closer to mine, his grin diabolical, the chill it gave me reaching all the way to my toes. "I don't like spirited women, but I break them easily. And I will break you like a wild stallion."

The fear crept back in, threatening to unhinge the hold I had on my emotions.

"Too bad they lied to you about everything. That's what you get for listening to my parents."

His laugh sent fear prickling up my spine. "Parents. Funny you should say that. Your father, but not your mother. But they didn't tell you that, did they? Just like they didn't tell you about the binding on your insides, locking you down until you were rife with power and ready to pass that power to the next vessel. "

"I can't have children—"

"Not yet." He leaned close to my ear, saying. "Aren't you glad I get to steal your virginity instead of your brother?"

My stomach turned as he dragged me to the bed. I was trying to form the words, to ask why he would say such a disturbing thing when he continued.

"Oh, but they failed to educate you about how the vessel is conceived. How the power of the gods passes from generation to generation with no chance taken that it might fail."

"I don't know what you're talking about." And I didn't because nothing he was saying made any sense. "The vessel is the second born of each new king."

"True, but here's the part where I break that spirit of yours." His eyes danced with humor and it was disturbing against the seriousness of his expression and the pit that was forming in my stomach. "She's the firstborn of his sister."

"What?" The word came out like a high-pitched squeal.

He laughed again, vicious and cruel. "You are a contradiction, vessel. An abomination to the gods, an affront to their gifts. A child of incest just like every vessel before you."

The words barreled through me, ripping a hole in the foundation that remained and toppling me into an abyss from which I couldn't climb free.

"No," I said, pushing at him to free myself. "No, that can't be...I can't." But it explained so much—why my mother had been so cold, why she'd always favored my brother, why Tristan protected me, why he'd never married, never produced an heir, even as my father's anger with him grew. Even in my tower I knew because he would tell me how unhappy Father was, how he was pressuring him, but he would never tell me why because he was protecting me. But it left so many more questions, ones I didn't think I'd ever have the answers to.

Rikeri threw me to the bed and with my fight gone, I laid there, waiting for the inevitable that didn't come. "I'll wait to touch you, vessel. I'll take you when our power is at its fullest. When the full moon lights the sky tomorrow night, heightening my power with yours. I'll bleed your power, feeding my own as I mark you as mine. I own the vessel, I own you and everything you are belongs to me now." He hovered over me, and I closed my eyes as he said against my ear, "But you'll sleep in my bed with me, just like my queen should. And if you dare to move from it, I will blind you as I tear through your markings and let your eyes bleed with them."

I bit my lip, trying to hide the quiver as the rest of my strength fled, the spirited woman Garret loved swallowed so far below the ocean of emotions that I didn't think I could ever find my way back to the surface.

Rikeri rolled from me, wrapping his hand around my waist and pulling me against him. I didn't struggle, my eyes staring vacantly ahead as vines climbed from the bed and tangled around my ankles, another set slinking precariously around my neck as I watched the thorns spread from the ones in front of me, poised to strike if I dared rise from the bed. I wouldn't, because there was nothing to rise for, no past that wasn't a bed of lies, no future where my bed didn't belong to Rikeri, and no present that promised any bed but the one now holding me prisoner.

CHAPTER TWENTY-FIVE

GARRET

I rode my horse hard, letting him rest only when I'd run him too close to breaking. Tristan had left me a steed trained for distance, but even those horses needed to rest. Each time I stopped, it killed me as my mind played through every disastrous scene until I could barely think. I prayed Rikeri wouldn't touch Eloise, that he would wait, but I didn't know what would cause him to wait unless Eloise convinced him to. If he allowed her to talk. Rikeri had little patience for talkers, and Eloise had a mouth on her. Hopefully, she kept it controlled or he would gag her, and she would lose her chance to talk him out of anything he had planned.

It took a day to reach the border of Duntraik and I waited far enough away, waiting for dawn to ensure the hounds were nowhere near the border. It was risky to delay any further, especially when Rikeri was already hours ahead of me. I was certain he'd enchanted his horses to run faster and further, not one for being away from his castle for long. It surprised me he'd even left and dared step into Bira, which told me how important Eloise was to him.

There was little he valued, but a chance to have a child with power was one thing he would prize above anything. He'd had a son once, the firstborn in his line always inheriting the power, just as the second born in Eloise's did, even if their methods turned my stomach. Rikeri's son had died at birth with the mother. He'd tried for a second, but that son had left him disappointed when no power manifested. He'd killed the mother and raised the child in his shadow until he was convinced no power would present itself. Then he cast him aside like a servant. No other child had come, and so he continued to take his frustration out on the boy.

I wiped my hand down my face, watching as the morning sun filled the world, lighting the mountains of Duntraik and, in the distance, Rikeri's castle. It towered menacingly, casting a shadow that covered the lands behind it. His ancestors had built it close to Bira as if the gods' magic would somehow flow past the border and change the cursed magic that tainted their blood. Magic that gave them power but had corrupted their lands and infected their people. Magic that burned in their veins, turning their moods violent, and ensuring the touch of their power was far from the blessing the gods had given the vessels.

I patted my horse and mounted him, knowing the hounds had sulked off to wherever they slept during the day. They would be no trouble now. Rikeri's magic held more power at night, while Eloise's was stronger during the day, with one exception: a full moon. Only during a full moon were both distinct powers at their peak. It was a fact I'd overheard between Rikeri and his advisor, the door closing in my face, but not before I'd received a bloody beating for listening. I'd only heard bits of information as the two men had hovered over the ancient scrolls I'd fetched for him from Lapote, the kingdom south of Duntraik. It had taken me weeks to retrieve them. I'd thought of running away, but I knew he'd find me. There was no hiding from him and so I'd returned with them, expecting praise but getting only punishment for taking so long.

Urging my horse forward, I counted down the hours as I drew closer to the castle. I'd gotten past the soldiers stationed in the northern pass into Duntraik, taking them down easily in the glare of the morning sun. Each passing minute brought more fear that I'd be too late. That he'd violate Eloise before I could reach her or bleed her power, causing her immense pain. Neither situation was one I wanted to find, and I sent a prayer to the gods that I made it in time.

But the gods had let this happen, so I wasn't so sure they would hear my prayers. If Eloise was the vessel of their magic, surely they would have protected her all these years. Protected the first vessel and every one after her from the horrors they suffered, the lonely lives, trusting people who were using them, brothers who raped them, then birthing the child of that trauma only to be murdered after. How could the gods let that happen to their chosen daughters?

Unless the gods hadn't chosen them.

The power of my thought hit me squarely in the chest. If everything we knew of the vessels was a lie, it stood that the reason for their existence was a lie. I stared ahead, the castle not far now, and in my periphery I spotted the horns of a proud stag. The setting sun cast a glow around it as it stood regal and stoic, its black eyes looking at me as if in acknowledgement that I'd been right. The gods had never blessed the first vessel. I thought back to the story of the first, how the queen had struggled during her pregnancy, nearly dying. The gods had taken pity on the queen and sent their power into her, creating the first vessel. The gift of the gods for the queen of their favored kingdom.

But what if that wasn't the case? What if Bira's rulers had wanted to separate themselves from the other kingdoms, deeming themselves as the favored kingdom by attributing the vessel to the gods' blessing when that wasn't the case?

I stopped my horse to let him rest, seeing Rikeri's castle in the distance, as I tried to recall the rest of the story and the snippets I'd overheard as Rikeri had poured through the scrolls. As the birth neared, the queen could hold no food down, so the healer crushed rose petals from the thornless roses and fed them to her in a broth derived from the stems. It was a desperate attempt to keep her and the babe alive, and it worked. She craved the broth and since it was the only thing she could hold down, the healer continued to feed it to her. The king, fearing the gods' punishment, insisted the queen pray to the gods with each rose they sacrificed for her life and the child's.

On the day of the birth, the child almost died in her mother's womb. The healer made a salve from the rose stems and spread it over the queen's body to coerce the child to leave her womb. Magic wasn't new to our part of the world, but it was rare until the birth of the vessel. Before then, there were witches and healers scattered through the kingdoms, but their ancestors had come from different shores where magic was more abundant.

The stag was watching me intently, and I wondered if it knew my thoughts, if it was waiting as I unraveled the threads of lies that Bira's kings had woven to make Bira the pride of the realms. I thought back to the day we'd seen the stag standing in the field of roses. The roses were the key. The gift of the gods, when combined with the magic of the healer, had created something special: a vessel carrying the magic the gods had imbued in the roses.

That magic, then carried through each birth, had nothing to do with the superstitious birth order or the need for each firstborn son to touch his sister. Unless.... My stomach threatened to spill as the harsh reality of that first birth became clear. The queen had committed the first atrocity, her superstition leading the rest of her line to commit the same heinous act over and over. The child would have died, the mother likely as well, punishment doled out by the gods for the crime against nature.

But the king, or perhaps the queen's brother, had interfered, bringing magic into the scenario, magic harvested directly from the gods through those roses and manipulated by the healer, who had her own magic. Magic that saved the queen and created the first vessel, blessing the king, his son, and the kingdom as a byproduct of the child's birth.

The stag tipped its head before walking gracefully away. My eyes followed it as I scratched at the scruff on my face, trying to figure out why Eloise's birthday was significant. She'd said the channeling happened in each vessel, but maybe it wasn't an ultimate gift from the gods but only a delayed effect of the flower's magic, slowly building in the vessel until full power surged through her blood. Her markings stretched as she aged like an infection that took thirty years to fully spread. Thirty years for the body to fully embrace power the gods had never intended a mortal to hold. It was a miracle it hadn't twisted each vessel like it had Rikeri's ancestors, but perhaps the gods had intervened after all.

Whatever the reason, that surge of power had led to the next steps in securing the fate of every vessel after—each king then following the same pattern precisely to ensure the gift from the gods continued.

I swallowed back my bile, thanking the gods for Rikeri's bold move to kidnap Eloise on her birthday, sparing her from the same fate. Although, after meeting her brother, I was certain he would have been the first to rebel enough to change the course of history.

I guided my horse forward, my need to get to Eloise growing more desperate as the house of lies her life rested upon crumbled. I wanted to be there to catch her, to hold her as she unraveled the strings that had been holding her captive all this time. It didn't matter to me if she hated me, I would save her and take her far from Duntraik and even further from Bira.

When I finally reached the castle, dusk was falling. I jumped from my horse, grabbing my knives and sword. I knew every way in and out of this place, but I charged through the front gates, taking down the few soldiers standing guard before they even knew what had hit them. Rikeri was cocky, too proud of his power, too vain to worry about guarding his castle. And no one had ever dared enter it, too terrified of the man within it.

Taking down another guard after a fierce sword fight, I rushed into the throne room, punching the next guard and slicing his throat as Rikeri turned his attention from Eloise to me. He had her on the floor, her legs to the side, her hands tied. She looked defiant, but I could see her emotional strain in the tension that lined her face. Rikeri had gagged her and there was bruising on her cheek.

"Hello, son." His voice slithered through my body, stirring the fear years of his abuse had fostered. "I thought I warned you never to return to Duntraik."

"Did you lay a hand on my princess, *Father*?" I asked, emphasizing the word with as much venom as I could.

Eloise's brows stitched in confusion, her eyes pleading with me to say this wasn't true. But it was. As much as I hated to admit it, as much as I'd tried to forget where I'd come from, I couldn't. I was the second born of Rikeri, born after he stole my mother and kept her for his pleasure. He'd married her, hoping she would bear him a second son who would hold the magic his stillborn son had promised. But the gods hadn't favored me and so he'd let my mother live long enough for me to remember her and then he'd drowned her in front of me, his power holding me in place. The abuse, the servitude, had begun the day he gave up on his hope that magic would come late to me. Until the day I'd bought my freedom and never looked back.

"Your princess?" he asked. His eyes narrowed before he spat, "Did you touch my vessel? Did you defile her?" The rage was seething, his eyes wild.

"She has a name, and she's not yours. And yes, I touched her, and I will gut you and rip you apart for hurting her."

Eloise was yelling in the gag, trying to speak, her face growing red.

"Take the fucking gag off her," I demanded.

"Oh, I don't think I will. So you spoiled my virgin. I would say I'm surprised, but I have to admit I'm feeling a sense of pride." I wanted to gut him right then, but I gripped my handle tighter, waiting to hear what he would say. "You see, I heard what you did in Hiranire. Quite impressive, tormenting a young girl, hunting the prince down. Almost up to my standards, with one exception."

I braced myself, glancing over at Eloise and seeing the mistrust in her eyes again. It hadn't faded, even when I'd burst in. And I wondered if it would ever go away or if I'd lost her completely.

"What exception?" I asked, my jaw clenched.

"You fucked it up!" His voice boomed through the cavernous room. "You were this close to killing him and you fucked it up like some imbecile."

"Fuck you."

He ignored me and glanced at Eloise. "Did she know?" He moved his finger, and the gag loosened, dropping around her neck. "Did he tell you who he is?"

She glowered at him, remaining silent and stoic.

"Oh, but he didn't, did he? Did he neglect to tell you he's my son? Heir to my throne...well he was until he turned out to be a disappointment. Now I have you. You'll give me a legitimate heir with power he could never have."

"I'm not giving you anything," she spat.

"No? And what about my son?" He flipped his hand out and my sword dropped from my grasp, my knees going out on me. He had me immobilized in seconds.

"Eloise, don't listen to him."

"Don't listen to him?" she asked, her eyes hard. "And who

should I listen to? You? There's no truth to anything you told me, Garret. So why should I listen to you?"

Because I'm the one saving you, I wanted to say.

"Because I love you, El. You can hate me forever, but that won't stop me from loving you or saving you from this asshole."

"Love?" Rikeri said. "Love is for weak men." He stormed over to me, his magic tearing at me, constricting my airways, and invading me like an infestation that was eating me alive. I fought against it just as I had when I was young, but the more I fought, the more the magic attacked. "You don't love. I taught you that. You use, you take, you fuck, but you do not love!"

He grabbed my face, his power pouring from his hands and drowning me in its vileness. His soulless eyes looked into mine and, as I always did, I searched for any trace of a man who might have loved me, one who cared for anything other than power. And just as I had each time, I found none. The corner of his lip lifted, and I could see a plan forming to break me further.

Shoving my face back, he turned to Eloise.

"Do you love him?"

She looked at me, the hurt in her eyes causing more pain than Rikeri's magic ever could.

"I—"

"You hesitate," he said, walking closer to her.

"Don't touch her!" I yelled, but he ignored me.

"So let me help you." He stooped before her, and I could see he had her pinned with the same power that held me. She tried to move, but never gained more than a fraction of an inch. "Do you know how my men found you when I kidnapped you? How I knew the servants' tunnels were a weakness in your father's defenses?"

"He's not my father," she said, hatred burning through her eyes.

"Oh, but he is, and he's also your uncle." His maniacal laugh echoed through the room.

"You told her?" I said, my heart aching for her.

She whipped her head at me. "You knew?" Her voice cracked and I could see more mistrust growing.

"El, I didn't know until a day ago, I swear." But her eyes revealed her disbelief in my words.

"Another lie, son?" Rikeri said, twisting his magic further into me.

"You don't get to call me that," I growled.

He stood, his jaw clenched, his eyes lethal. "Tell her why you'll always be the villain, son. Tell her why men like us can't be the good guys. Why you can't be the hero who saves her."

Eloise creased her brow, her blue eyes so sad it was killing me. She looked defeated. Everything she'd known had been taken from her, and now Rikeri was sealing my fate, taking away any chance she could still have faith in me.

"I'm not a good man, El. I told you that. But you saw something different, you changed me—"

"Changed you?" Rikeri sneered. I kept my eyes locked on Eloise's, seeing the hope there and knowing his next words would crush it.

"Please, El."

"Tell her why I found her!" Rikeri commanded. "Why it was so easy!"

I dropped my head, my shame too great, my guilt too heavy.

"Tell me," she pleaded. "Please Garret, for once tell me the truth."

But I couldn't. It hurt too much to face the pain my selfishness had caused.

"Once a villain, always a villain, son."

I picked my head up, the tears in Eloise's eyes like a dagger twisting in my heart. "I didn't know, El."

"It wouldn't have mattered," Rikeri said. "Tell her how you bought your freedom in exchange for hers. How you fucked those servant girls to get me information."

Her lip quivered, and I wanted to look away, but this was my burden to bear and as heavy as it was, I had to face it now.

"I didn't know." My voice was barely audible, the crack of emotion splitting the words.

"Every detail of those tunnels, of how to reach the vessel. Of how many guards stood outside her door, how many stood outside her wing." He turned back to Eloise. "How many times do you think he had to fuck them to get those details? How many of them did he use and discard to ensure I captured you when I was ready? How many broken hearts did he leave to earn his freedom?"

"Shut up, Rikeri. You forced my hand, you—"

"Offered you a bargain. Your freedom for information on Bira. I never told you how to get it. Although I may have taught you how to use a woman and how easy they were to manipulate." He dropped in front of her again and took her face in his hand.

"Get your fucking hands off her!" I roared, fighting again.

"I taught you that women were only good for two things: fucking and breeding."

Eloise spat at him, and he smacked her, the move enraging me. I fought harder, the magic cutting further into my skin and digging into my organs. The pain was unbearable, but still I managed to move closer.

"You're going to be fun to break, vessel. So I ask you. What do I do with my son? Do you want to keep him? I can torture him for you as a wedding gift."

"I'm going to rip you apart with my bare hands," I snarled.

"I highly doubt that." He didn't look over at me, his eyes locked on Eloise. "Do you want me to kill him for you?" He stood, his hand coming out and the power coiling around my lungs. My breath stopped as it constricted in them. "Punish him for his lies." He walked toward me, his dark eyes burrowed into me as my chest burned. "Once a villain, always a villain, son. I should have killed you the day you were born, the first day you disappointed me."

The power tightened, and I struggled to breathe.

"No!" Eloise cried, and Rikeri swiveled his gaze to her. "Don't kill him."

The magic didn't stop, my lungs so pained now that I was blacking out.

"Do you love him?"

"I thought I did, but I don't know him now. The man I thought I loved was a lie. But he shouldn't die for that. Let him live with his guilt."

The air rushed back into my lungs as his hold on me released. I coughed as they filled once again, and my sight cleared.

"Take him away," she said, her voice trembling.

"Eloise," I croaked. "Don't do this. He'll only hurt you."

"That's all anyone has ever done. That's all you did." She looked away, my heart shattering into a million pieces.

The magical binds on me lifted, and I rose, leaping for Rikeri only to crash into his magic as it sent me sprawling across the floor.

"Run away, son. It's what you do best. This isn't your business anymore, and I'll only kill you. Run before she has to watch you die." The words brought the memory of my mother's death back, the horror of seeing her life fade when I was helpless to stop it.

"Please, Eloise."

She turned her face from me, driving the dagger through me and severing my heart in two. I'd done this to myself by not telling her the truth.

"Be the villain you are and leave. She no longer wants you and I have things to do."

"Eloise," I tried one more time. "Please, I can take you from here."

Rikeri's laugh was like the braying of an ass, and I wanted to punch him, but her response stopped me.

"You can't take me from here. You can't save me. No matter how much you lie to yourself and to me that you can. Take your lies and run, Garret. You're no less of a villain than he is."

"But he'll hurt you." I didn't recognize my voice. It sounded too broken.

"I'm already hurt. He can't do much more than you already have, than my father has. Go." She didn't look up, but I could see the tears that splattered on her skirt.

"Take him and dump him outside the gates," Rikeri ordered a guard before turning back to Eloise.

I didn't fight as the guard led me away, sensing the touch of Rikeri's magic on my skin as he prepared to do whatever it was he intended to do to Eloise. I remembered how she'd told me he would slice her marks open and drain the power, giving him a never-ending supply of magic. As much as I wanted to go back and save her, she had made her decision. There was no turning back, no happy ending to this story, no saving the damsel in distress who didn't want me saving her, no hero's ending for this villain. There was nothing but emptiness and futility.

CHAPTER TWENTY-SIX

ELOISE

I kept my eyes locked on my skirt, the binds of magic on me holding back the convulsive movements of my body as the sobs tried to escape. Rikeri had left me in his throne room without food, without water, with nothing but my thoughts and my struggle to hold it together. I'd tried fighting back, a bout of strength surging forth from under the pain that submerged it, but he'd only gagged me, saying I needed to shut up or he'd cut my tongue out.

My legs had cramped, and my back was in torment by the time he returned, telling me how the full moon was almost at its height, how he was ready to take what was rightfully his. I'd convinced myself no one was coming to save me, and I'd failed at saving myself. All I could do was question why the gods had given me so much power when I couldn't use it to protect myself and stop Rikeri from stealing what wasn't his to take.

I had accepted my fate until Garret stormed through the doors, his presence filling me with hope. He would save me. He would take me away and we would live our lives together, talking

OF PETALS AND LIES

through the secrets that had littered our time together, making amends to each other and growing old on a farm with our love to protect us. But that had been a dream, a naïve fantasy like the ones I'd had as a young girl staring out of her tower window and dreaming of the handsome prince who would save her from the fate the gods had in store for her.

Garret couldn't save me. He couldn't even save himself.

Rikeri's son. The truth had slashed through me like the thorns of Bira's vines. His son. He stood there with his thick, brown locks hanging on his forehead, his chestnut eyes bright with hope, their brightness fading as Rikeri revealed the rest of his secrets. The past layered with ashes of my world as it burned down at his hand. He had been the boy the servant girl had sneaked into the tunnels, the reason the tunnels had been closed off, the reason Rikeri had found me. Our lives intersecting in those moments but never touching.

The hold of Rikeri's magic was nothing to the agony the truth brought to my soul. Garret was the villain my father had said he was, and the truth hurt so badly I didn't think I could even look at him. But even with the truth in the open, he fought, trying to reach me, trying to save me. What if he was the villain? Did that change the man I loved? It hadn't when I discovered what he'd done in Hiranire. But that hadn't affected me. This had, and that fact hurt so much worse.

I heard the plea in his broken voice, the need for me to go with him even if I could no longer love him. But I did. Rikeri was still trying to break me, just like he had the prior night, and I wouldn't let him. He was a horrible man, and Garret was the result of what that horror did to those in his presence. A broken boy, a lost boy, a wounded man. And no matter what he'd done, I wouldn't let Rikeri hurt him anymore. My voice cracked, the tears spilling as I sent Garret away, hearing the desperation in his voice. He needed me to tell him to stay and fight, needed me to believe that he was something other than the villain Rikeri had shaped him to be. But I couldn't because in doing so I would seal his doom. And so I'd whispered the words my father had said, the same Rikeri had said. Calling him a villain. The wicked man that he'd told me he was when we first met. An irredeemable villain. And I sent him away, knowing it would seal my doom but ensure his safety. Rikeri had done enough damage. I wouldn't let him do any more than he had.

I saw the fight rush from Garret, his head dropping with his shoulders, the confident, powerful presence he was now stripped from him with my words. The sword in my chest twisted painfully, and I almost stopped him, almost called him back and begged him to take me away, to save me like he wanted. To be the hero I knew was deep inside of him, blackened and bruised by his father, trampled so far below that he couldn't find him. I knew the hero was there, perhaps in the guise of a villain, but he was there.

The doors shut, and I looked up from my lap, missing him dreadfully.

"That is why you will bear me an heir," Rikeri snarled. "That mistake was one I never made again. But you will bear me a son worthy of my name."

I picked my head up and glowered at him. "How can you say that about your own son?" I asked, unable to hide my disgust, for as disgusting as I found my father, Rikeri, was no better.

"He's a mutt, a failed attempt to pass on my power, one I should have killed when he was young."

I wanted to question him, to have him explain how a father could say such a thing, but my faith in those we called fathers had shifted. My father had raped my mother, his own sister, and conspired to have my brother do the same to me. I held little faith in what the term father said about a man. It was the actions that seemed to speak more. And neither of our fathers had proven their worth.

Rikeri's power dug further into me as his eyes glinted with

danger. "Don't make me put that gag back in your mouth, vessel."

He took a chunk of my hair in his hand and dragged me across the floor. I bit my lip, trying not to scream, knowing it would only bolster him. Pain raked through my scalp, his magic still burning into my skin with the invisible binds he had around me. He moved from the throne room down hall after hall and all the while I screamed internally, tears streaming down my face. Was this the fate the gods had intended for me? It seemed an unfair burden to bear. To be subservient to the men who used my power, to never use my magic to protect myself from them or stop the pain they brought to every one of us. If it was only my magic I risked losing by using it against Rikeri, I would have done it in a heartbeat. Even if he killed me in retaliation. But it wasn't. If the gods cursed me for using my magic to harm another and they stripped me of my abilities, my people and my land would suffer the consequences. The blessing of the gods would fade, the roses of Bira would once again become thorny, the thorny vines would retreat, and Bira would be nothing more than a weak kingdom. The fate of my people rested on my suffering, and I would not risk it to save myself.

Rikeri stopped, flinging his arm out and sending me careening across the floor of a large room with a glass ceiling, the full moon shining brightly upon us. His magic faded from around my body, and I brought my hand up to my scalp, which was burning dreadfully. I winced, wiping my tears away with my other hand.

"The full moon. The calling of our true power, the only time the power of the gods is at its strongest when the sun has descended. And the time when my power is strongest. This is it, vessel. Tonight we merge completely. You escaped me the night before the full moon the last time I had you, but there is no escaping this time. No fighting me. No one who is coming for you."

I didn't answer, knowing it was the truth.

His hand came out, his magic suffocating me before he threw me against the windowpane, the glass quivering against my back. I couldn't move, my body pinned by his power. He pushed his shirtsleeves up, rolling his neck before extracting a knife from his belt. I whimpered instinctively, remembering the agony of the knife tearing through my markings, his magic keeping them open. Jerking at my arms, I struggled to free myself as he stepped closer to me.

"Don't fight, vessel. You know what happens when you do. I hurt you more. I can cut slowly or I can cut quickly." He gripped my chin, forcing my head still so that I was looking at him. Only then did I notice the similarities between him and Garret, the same auburn hair only gray peppered his, the brown eyes tainted with the evil he wielded, but no less striking than his son's. But Garret had a softness in his features and no matter how villainous he had been, that softness reached down into his soul. Rikeri had none, his soul devoid of any goodness. An irredeemable villain.

"Let me hear you scream, vessel. The more you scream, the quicker I'll cut, but the more you fight, the more you hide your pain, the more pain I will bring to you." Fear clawed at my insides, looking for an escape as he brought the knife to my cheek. "Let's start with these annoying petals. It's a shame the gods cursed you with these hideous markings, you would have been a beauty." I braced myself as the knife dug into my skin, thinking of how Garret loved my markings, how his fingers would gently trace them as if they made me even more enchanting to him. With that thought, I lost hold of the scream as the knife sliced deeper, spilling the first signs of crimson and gold from my body.

CHAPTER
TWENTY-SEVEN

GARRET

The fire flickered inconsistently against the night sky as I warmed my hands. After riding from the castle a few miles, I'd stopped, the dull ache in my chest too distracting to go any further. Night had fallen, and I wondered if I was close enough to the border for the hounds to find me. If so, I wasn't so sure I would fight them this time. Death would be painful, but it would end the gut-wrenching agony that pulsed through my heart.

Dropping my head into my hands, I tried not to think about what Rikeri was doing to Eloise. How he was likely touching her or hurting her. Tried not to think of her screams, of her fear, of how I'd walked away and left her there. Running like I'd always done.

"Well, aren't you pitiful."

I looked up to find Leo, his arms crossed as he stared me down over the fire.

"What are you doing here?" I asked, the words slow and

unemotional. I barely had the energy to lift my head, let alone talk.

"Helping you get your head out of your ass," he said, taking a seat across from me. "Where's the vessel?"

My eyes widen, my mouth trying to speak but not working.

"I'm not an idiot, and it's hard to ignore the rampant gossip in town. Everyone is talking about her." He leaned forward, placing his elbows on his knees and folding his hands. His brown hair shimmered with red strands in the firelight, his green eyes almost black.

"She doesn't want me anymore." I flicked a log further into the fire, avoiding his gaze.

"Huh, did she find out your true side? Figure she didn't want to wait on you hand and foot and bear your children while you're out fucking other women?" he teased.

The truth hurt. The words had once been my own, the intentions mine at one time. Before all of this. Before Eloise.

"She discovered the truth. That I wasn't a good man like she thought I was. That I'm the villain like they all say."

He remained quiet and I could feel his eyes on me, seeing what only someone who had known me as long as he had could.

"Where is she, Garret? And why are you in Duntraik when you said you'd never return?"

"Why are you here, Leo?" I snapped back, not wanting to admit that I'd left her in Rikeri's hands. That she'd chosen him over me.

"Because I saw you fly past as I was collecting water and I followed you. Not an easy feat, I might add. I've seen you run away from things before, Garret, but I've never seen you so determined to run toward something. You weren't running away this time." He scratched his head. "Where is the vessel, Garret?"

"Gods, why does everyone call her that?" I yelled, tired of her being treated like an object. "She has a fucking name."

He put his hands up. "Sorry. Shit, what happened?"

I sat back, raking my hands through my hair. "Rikeri has her."

His mouth fell open, and he scrambled from his seat. "Rikeri?" he hissed.

Leo was the only one who knew the truth. The only one I'd ever let close enough to me to know where I'd come from and he'd never judged me, never reminded me of it. Maybe he should have, because it would have reminded me to be a better man and not my father.

"Why, in the gods' name, would you leave her with Rikeri? Fuck, when I saw you charge in there, I thought you'd lost your mind, but then you came back out...you left her there?" His voice rose a pitch, his fists bunching. "You left her with that madman?"

"She sent me away, Leo. She chose to stay. I went in there thinking I was someone I wasn't."

"And who would that be? The asshole who leaves a woman in Rikeri's hands?" The anger inflicted in his voice made me raise my eyes from my hands.

"I'm the villain. That's who I am. Just like her father said, like Rikeri said, like she said." The memory of that title from her lips tore at the seams that were holding what was left of my heart in place.

Leo stared at me, his eyes hard. I could see him chewing the inside of his lip, something he did every time he thought hard about something.

"So what?" he finally said.

I scrunched my brows. "What do you mean, so what?"

"So what if you're the villain? Does that change anything?"

Confusion set in my features as I tried to understand what he was trying to say. "Of course it does. It changes everything. I'm the villain who lied to her about my past, about Rikeri, about Beatrice and that prince, about everything. And no matter how hard I tried to be a good man, to change who I am, to become something she wanted me to be, it didn't work. I will always be the villain."

He tipped his head, studying me. "She wanted you to be? How could she want you to change if she didn't know the truth about you?" He sat back down and leaned toward the fire. "It seems to me you were trying to change, to fit something you thought she wanted, or maybe you didn't like who you were."

I shot him a look, pursing my lips as I waited for him to continue.

"Yeah, you're an asshole. A vain, foolish prick who thinks women are only here to serve him and treats his friends like garbage. An asshole who uses people to get ahead, who lies and cheats and never once apologized for who he is."

"You're not helping, Leo," I grumbled.

"What I'm trying to say is sure you can change some of those things and from what I've seen you have. Whatever El is to you, she's changed those annoying parts of you that made me question being your friend."

"I don't need to hear your opinion on any of this, you know."

"Yes, you do," he said with a smug smile. "You're not the good guy, Garret, but that doesn't mean there aren't some parts of you that are good. You'll always be the villain. It's in your blood, it's in your nature, but you can choose when that villain needs to be present and when he needs to step back. And right now, she needs you to be the villain."

I searched his eyes, letting his words sink in. Maybe he was right. I'd been trying for years to shed my past, to distance myself from my father and the man he was, but I couldn't completely. The things I'd learned from him, the pain he'd given me, the beatings that had shaped me, the terrible things he'd made me do were a part of me now. I'd never owned them, letting my vanity boost me, letting my pride be a shield that hid my wicked deeds. I'd connived and cheated and used all to be something better than my father had been. Always doing so in discreet ways so that no one would know. And they hadn't until I'd let my true side show that night in Hiranire.

"I am the villain," I said, sitting up taller. "It's who I am. It's who my father is."

"And it's who you need to be now. If El thinks you're the villain, show her what you can do."

"She sent me away," I muttered. "Dammit, no one sends me away. If I have to drag her out of the castle over my shoulder, I will, but I'm not letting my father touch her."

Leo frowned. "Isn't that a good guy thing to say?" He gave me a wink as he chuckled.

"Fuck off," I said, rising. I didn't give a shit if Eloise didn't want me anymore. I wouldn't let her suffer. I doused the fire and grabbed my horse as Leo mounted his. "What are you doing?" I asked him.

"Coming with you."

"This is too dangerous—"

"Since when do you care if I get hurt? You left me behind when you pretended you were dead. Don't start getting soft on me, my friend."

I gave him a smile and started to respond when the ground shook and a massive explosion of golden light burst from the direction of Rikeri's castle.

"That can't be good," Leo muttered.

"No, it's not. Time to show my father what his many lessons taught me." I spurred my horse into a gallop and headed for the castle, not knowing what I'd find, but hoping I'd arrive in time.

BY THE TIME we reached the castle, the golden flare from Eloise's power was a constant beacon. It was almost blinding. My father, being the arrogant prick he was, hadn't bothered to replace the guards I'd taken down earlier. We burst in and ran to the throne room, expecting to find them, only to discover it was empty.

"Fuck," I muttered, running my hand through my hair.

Leo came skidding to a halt beside me. "Where are they?" he asked. "Gods, does he decorate everything in black?"

I snorted, muttering, "Everything." I was wracking my brain trying to think of where he would have taken her. Eloise's power was tingling over my skin, sparkles of it in the surrounding air, but it had been shining into the sky. "The conservatory!" Eloise's power was stronger in the daylight, but he would have exposed her to the full moon based on the information in the scrolls. And tonight a full moon sat bright in the cloudless sky.

I ran from the throne room, coming to a halt when three guards emerged from the shadows. I'd written Rikeri off as arrogant, but he'd been calculating instead, knowing if I came back I'd go straight to the throne room where he'd been.

"Go," Leo said, swinging his sword in his hands. "I'll take care of these fools. It's been a while since I had to cover your ass while you protected your pretty face."

"Shithead," I grumbled. "You sure?"

He whipped his sword around in a flourish before taking on a defensive position. "I'm sure. Go show her why the girls all swoon for you."

He charged the guards, and I ran, shaking my head at his comment. The hall wasn't empty, and I faced the next guard with the backstabbing, ruthless moves I'd used to climb my way through the ranks, jumping over his falling body and barreling through the next two guards with one thing in mind: saving Eloise.

The castle shook, pieces of stone crumbling as I bolted to the conservatory. Memories rampaged through my mind with every step further into the castle I went. The terrors of my past, my mother's eyes as they stared lifelessly back at me when I removed her body from the water, and the years of verbal and physical abuse. All wrapped in manipulation, molding me into his servant, his spy, into the very image of him...without the magic.

The shaking stopped, the golden flickers of Eloise's magic fading and my heart pounded hard as fear careened through me. What had he done to her? I pushed harder until my feet hit the barrier of the conservatory, stopping as the memories overwhelmed me. Flashes of the beating he'd given me, thinking it would free my power, his magic burning through me, my screams filling the air. It had taken me weeks to heal completely, only to be punished again as he trained me on how a woman was to be used, taking one in front of me, forcing me to watch, then to take her myself. I'd hated him every minute and when he'd ripped me from her right as I was coming, my cum splattering her body, he'd screamed that I was to never come in a woman, that my seed was not meant for breeding. Then he'd beaten me while she'd watched, my hatred for him growing further, my respect for women further slipping with each laugh that escaped her plump lips. Now I understood it was her fear of him that had forced the reaction but at the time it had warped the only memory I had of women, taking the warmth of my mother's smile and replacing it until I'd only ever thought of women as something to use just as my father had taught me.

I closed my eyes, forcing the images, the memories away and reminding myself that they strengthened me. That I would not let them own me, just as I had the day I'd walked out of Duntraik and left them behind. I was not some weak man ruled by his past.

Opening my eyes, I remembered who I was. The villain. I squared my shoulders and walked past the doorway and into the conservatory, taking those memories and letting them feed my anger and my need for revenge. The moonlight lit the conservatory and against the glass panes was Eloise. Her skin was sparkling, the trails of her markings bleeding gold and red from where he'd cut her. I hardened myself to the sight and stepped further in, seeing no sign of Rikeri as Eloise lifted her eyes to me.

I gave her a coy grin, saying, "Hello, princess."

"Garret, no—"

"I know you don't want a villain, El. But that's what I am. It's who I'll always be. But that doesn't mean I don't love you and even if you no longer love me, I'm still going to save you. Even if I have to sling you over my shoulder and spank that ass to stop your complaints long enough to take you far from here."

"Once a villain, always a villain," Rikeri said, drawing my attention and his power. But this time, I was ready for him. I knew how he worked, and I braced myself for the impact, raising my sword to stop the flow of black magic barreling toward me.

"I am my father's son," I said, grimacing against the magic that was heating the handle of my sword. I wouldn't last long and once he had me pinned with his power, I stood no chance. But I had an idea, and I prayed Eloise would understand.

"Eloise," I grunted, my feet sliding back. "Everything you know is a lie."

"She knows, you fool." Rikeri looked proud, but I knew from earlier that he'd told her about her father. From his smug expression, I could tell he'd told her everything. "I told her the truth. I'm the only one who seems to know how to be honest."

My laugh was loud, and he pushed his power in a burst that tore my sword from me, sending it sliding across the floor. His power coiled around me, constricting my movement as he threw me against the glass. I heard Eloise scream, wondering why she would be concerned for me, knowing how she hated me now.

"Everything was a lie, princess," I managed, my teeth gritting against the pain as the coils tightened. "Everything. Unleash it, El, and show him what you're capable of."

My rib cracked, and I clenched my jaw from the pain, trying not to scream.

"The gods don't give a fuck what you do, princess," I wheezed as the pain increased.

"I should have killed you long ago," Rikeri snarled. "You're nothing more than a nuisance. You can't stand against my power, especially now that hers feeds mine. I am a god. Their power runs through me!"

"Yet another lie," I coughed out, noticing the tingle of Eloise's magic. "You're really going to regret not killing me when I drive my sword through your cold, twisted heart."

His laugh bellowed through the hall.

"Be the villain, princess. Trust me, it feels damn good," I mumbled, sensing her magic increase.

Rikeri's hold on me wavered, and he turned to her, raising his hands, his power flowing toward her. She tipped her head back and screamed, a blinding stream of gold flooding from her and barreling toward Rikeri, stripping the magic from him. I shielded my eyes from it, seeing him fly past me and slam into the glass, which shattered with the force. The sheer magnitude of power coming from Eloise shook the ground, the glass panes collapsing around us.

Rikeri lifted his head, trying to recover as Eloise's magic abated. I grabbed my sword and stalked toward Rikeri. The memories ricocheted through my mind like the pieces of glass scattering around us, and I stood over him. This time, I didn't look for any sign of love, knowing there was nothing in his rotted heart. In one swift move, I drove my sword into his heart, twisting it as his hands reached up to stop me.

"I told you I'd kill you for touching my girl, you fucker." I twisted harder, holding his fading gaze as his life fled his body. I felt no emotion, no remorse, nothing as his hands fell to the side, his eyes glazing with his last sputtering breath.

I backed away, a sense of relief overcoming me, closure to the past that had haunted me for years. Turning my back on him, I left him there with the memories and the past. Eloise was in a lump on the floor, and I ran to her.

"El," I said, taking her in my arms and brushing her hair back. Her wounds were extensive, but since Rikeri had cut only her markings, her magic was slowly healing them. I tenderly touched a healing petal, hating that my father had marred them. "El, please. I don't care if you hate me forever. If you never want to see me again. I'll give you up if you'll just open your eyes for me."

"You never want to see me again?" she mumbled.

She blinked her eyes open, the blue startling against the golden specks in them.

"I thought..." I couldn't say the words. The thought of losing her was too devastating.

"You thought because you're a lying bastard who made some really stupid mistakes, and had an asshole for a father that I wouldn't love you anymore?"

My heart somersaulted. "Yes."

"Well, you thought wrong, big boy. And it turns out my father's an asshole, too, and my life is nothing but one big lie."

"That's not true," I said, pulling her further into my arms. "I really *do* love you, princess."

"Do you?" she asked, bringing her hand to my face.

"Completely and irrevocably. I love you, Eloise."

Her smile sent a cascade of tingles through my body, warming every part. She pulled my face down to hers and kissed me, that kiss healing my heart and my soul and confirming her place in them for eternity.

CHAPTER TWENTY-EIGHT

ELOISE

The discomfort from my healing body couldn't distract from the intensity of Garret's kiss. It weaved through my body, encasing the magic and encouraging it, as if his kiss held its own magic. His powerful hands held me against his chest and again, that feeling of safety washed over me, leaving me with a sensation that told me his arms were where I was meant to be.

"I don't care who you were," I murmured against his lips. "I only care who you are now."

He drew back, our lips slowly separating. "And who is that, El?" I could see the pain behind his eyes, the broken boy he'd once been.

Sitting up, I took his face in my hands. "You're my villain," I said with a smile. "My protective, sweet, wonderful villain."

His chuckle swept through me like a kiss to my soul. "Let's go home," he said, turning his face to kiss my hand.

"But you are home."

He looked around, an auburn curl flopping on his forehead as he did. "This isn't my home. I left this place years ago." He dropped his head. "When I traded my freedom for yours."

The misery in his voice stung my heart. "I had already lost my freedom, Garret. I lost it the day I was born. You did nothing but make the first move in freeing me." And it was true. As much as it had hurt to hear, what he'd done had led me to this moment. To the truth. To my freedom. To him. "You did something you had no choice but to do."

"I'm sorry, Eloise." Gods, he sounded so devastated. The man who'd stormed into the room to save me with his wicked grin and cocky assuredness, owning his past and his title, was no more. That was the man I'd fallen in love with. The one with the witty humor, the disparaging remarks, the assumption that the world was there to bow to him. The villain with the heart of a hero was the man I loved.

My wounds had almost healed, the final tingles of magic swimming through my markings as I climbed into Garret's lap and picked his head up.

"Let's start over," I said, watching his brow crease adorably. "Hi, my name is Eloise. I'm a vessel of magic from the gods, my father is an incestuous creep, my mother is not my mother, I have a brother who I'm uncertain how to feel about now, and I am madly in love with a man as messed up as I am."

His lips twitched before they formed a sly grin that sent warmth flooding through my lower body. He raised a brow before he said, "Hello gorgeous, I'm Garret of Duntraik. My father is that piece of shit behind us who murdered my mother when I was five, then spent the next twelve years torturing me for not inheriting his corrupt magic. I sold my soul and the life of the woman I love to him for my freedom. I used a few innocent girls who weren't so innocent with their bodies—" I cringed, smacking his chest, which only made that sly grin bigger. He grabbed my wrist and pinned it behind me, shoving me into his chest. "And I thought I loved a girl who loved another man whom I thought was a beast. So I tried to kill him, then ran away only to discover that I was the actual beast." His eyes searched mine, growing serious. "Until I met a woman who was feisty and strong. Who had the most beautiful scars both inside and out, and who made me see there was more to me than the villain my father had shaped me to be."

I leaned closer to him. "So you love another woman?"

His grin turned lopsided, and I had to refrain from kissing him as I waited for his answer. "A gorgeous, stubborn, powerful woman who will probably kick my ass if she finds me flirting with you," he said with a wink.

"That's funny, because the man I love will probably gut you for touching me right now. He's a very protective brute."

"Sounds like a possessive fucker to me," he joked, weaving his fingers through my hair.

"Very," I said. "He can be quite the villain, but he's my villain, and he loves me."

"That I do," he said, encasing my neck and pushing my lips to his. This kiss was hungry, burning through me like a streak of lightning. I wrapped my hands around his neck, running my fingers through his hair as his other arm encircled my waist, bringing me flush against him.

After everything I'd been through, everything I now questioned in my life, this was real. Garret was now my starting point, and I knew everything from here on would be okay because he would be by my side.

"You two done in here? I'm tired of fighting and could use a cold mug of ale."

Garret chuckled against my mouth, and I pulled away to find his friend in the doorway. Blood splattered his clothes, his sword in no better shape.

He gave me a bow. "Princess, glad to see you're in one piece."

"Only I get to call her princess, Leo," Garret said, his words carving into my chest like a brand of ownership.

"Then what shall I call the woman who is more than comfortably positioned in your lap, not far from the body of your dead father? El doesn't sound right."

"That's mine, too," Garret grumbled. "I'll share it with her brother, but that's it. You can call her my wife."

My heart leaped so hard I could barely contain it. "Isn't that a little forward of you to assume?" I teased, trying not to show how that statement had gripped me. "We did just meet."

His coy grin stole my breath. "Seems like the perfect time, then. And no, it's not too forward to assume. I'm tired of everyone claiming to own you. Treating you like some object to be bartered and traded, imprisoned and used. No one owns you, El—"

"But if you call me your wife, then you assume ownership of me."

"No, I free you from the expectations that everyone else has of you." The assuredness of his words enveloped me like a protective blanket I didn't know I needed.

I dropped my forehead against him, and he kissed my head. "You already own me, Garret. Every part of me is yours. My body, my heart, and my soul," I breathed.

"I don't want to own you, El. But if you give those things to me, I will protect them and cherish them for the rest of our lives." He lifted my face, his thumb brushing over my petals. "And I will never hurt you again."

"I know." The moment was tender, reminding me of the man he really was, the one beneath the villain everyone else knew.

"Doesn't look so powerful now, does he?" Leo said, breaking the sweet moment.

Garret shook his head, kissed my forehead, then looked over at Leo, who was kicking Rikeri's dead body.

"Does this make you king of Duntraik?" Leo asked.

Garret went stiff, and my smile grew. "Yes, it does," I said. "King Garret, that's sexy."

He looked back at me, his eyes creased.

"You are Rikeri's son and only living heir," Leo said with a shrug, just as I saw a flood of soldiers enter the room. "Fuck, I'm not fighting any more of them." He flung his sword toward us. "You have that strange magic and Garret, you're better with a sword."

Garret untangled me from him and stood me up. I saw the wince of pain as he stood. Rikeri had hurt him, and he'd said nothing. His only concern had been for me. He stood tall, squaring his shoulders back, the roguish look I'd fallen for taking over his features.

"My father is dead," he said, addressing the soldiers. "Somebody take his body from here and burn it." He glanced around the room. "Damn, I hate this place," he muttered before saying, "Who's in charge of you lot?"

There was some confusion and grumbling before one stepped forward, saying, "You are now, sire."

"What the fuck? Don't call me that." He ran his hand through his hair. As confident as he was, he was out of his element. But I wasn't. I placed my hand on his back, and he glanced at me. It wasn't a woman's place to lead, and I knew from experience what place he thought women held. I hoped that had changed as I questioned him with my eyes, waiting for him to let me step up. His lip curved, and he gave me a mischievous look before he nodded.

I was thankful my brother had done more than let me play during my times of freedom. He had taught me about royal expectations and the politics of leading. Everything my father taught him, he passed on to me. I wondered why that had been the case if he was only planning to keep me locked in that tower until I conceived. The thought turned my stomach and threatened to derail me, so I pushed it away.

"Did Rikeri have an advisor?" I asked.

"Yes," one guard answered.

J. L. JACKOLA

I stepped forward, well aware that blood and remnants of my magic covered me, that Rikeri had left my dress in tatters, and I looked nothing like the coveted vessel of Bira. "What's your name?"

"Rodrick, My Lady," he said with a bow.

So they knew who I was, which helped our situation greatly. "Find the advisor and have him meet us in the throne room. All of you back to your posts and spread the word that Rikeri's son has claimed the throne."

"El—"

I snapped my attention to Garret, needing him to not argue that point or it would jeopardize our safety. A kingdom without a king and a kingdom with one whose legitimacy had yet to be proven was an unstable one.

"Go," I ordered Rodrick. "With haste."

He bowed again and ushered the others out of the room.

"King Garret," Leo said. "I like it. But I want to be your advisor."

"You don't know anything about advising, just like I know nothing about running a kingdom," Garret hissed.

"You don't need to know," I said. "But a declaration needs to be made or Duntraik will fall into chaos. Rikeri may have been a terror, but he was a king, and no one dared go against him. You they don't know and the faster we can provide legitimacy to your claim, the better chance we have of keeping Duntraik stable so we can deal with the mess in Bira."

I marched from the room, trying to remember which way the throne room was. Rikeri had taken me there first, but I'd been so disoriented by the time he moved me that I didn't know which way to go. I chewed my bottom lip as Garret grabbed my arm.

"Slow down, El. There are still some things you need to know about Bira—"

"I know enough, and it makes me sick to think about it. Now that I know they lied about my power so I wouldn't turn on any of them, I plan to pay them a visit and let them feel my wrath." Anger burned through me, mixed with repulsion and vengeance for all the vessels before me. For the mother my father had taken from me.

Garret smirked. "Damn, you're sexy when you're naughty. You might make a good villainess after all, princess."

I pursed my lips, not liking the sound of that. "Just show me to the throne room."

He led me down that hall, saying, "Your brother rebelled, El. He's not the bad guy you think he is. He sent Nilan to run away with you. While you snuck out to look at the moon, your brother was rebelling against the tradition that every prince before him had followed. He wouldn't have touched you. He loves you."

I stopped in my tracks, tears pushing behind my eyes. "But—"

"No, he set me free to come find you, El. Your father is the bad guy in this, as was every king before him. When Rikeri took you, your father realized there was potential if your brother didn't follow through. Rikeri was royalty, and he held power sourced from the same place as yours—the roses of Bira, the power of the gods."

I tried to speak, my mouth moving, but the words wouldn't form.

"He sent Nilan to return you, but Tristan sent him to take you far away so neither Rikeri nor your father would find you. Nilan sided with Tristan, although I'm certain I know why." His jaw tightened and I saw then what I'd failed to see as I'd handed my body to Nilan that first time and every time after. But I couldn't be angry with him. He'd taken care of me, taught me, and made me a woman who could fight for herself and knew what she wanted from her man.

"My father sent him to bring me back?" I asked, a sliver of hope forming that he'd been concerned about me, risking his unstable power to save me.

But Garret shook his head. "No, El. He sent him so he could

sell you back to Rikeri with assurances that he would return the next vessel to Bira. With you in Duntraik, there would be no further compromise to his power."

My hope crumbled like everything else, and I swallowed back my tears, giving him a nod and turning from him. "Let's get this sorted so I can pay my father a visit."

BY THE TIME we'd talked in length with Rikeri's advisors, several acknowledging that Garret was his son and had the right to the throne, it was past dawn. Leo was dozing in his seat, and Garret looked ready to pass out. I wondered how many hours he'd been without sleep.

I sent Leo out with an advisor who promised he'd find Leo a good bed, then I turned to Garret, loving how his eyes devoured me even with as sleepy as he looked. That exhaustion was lifting from me with every inch his eyes roamed, and I noticed he seemed more awake by the time he said, "You know you're pretty sexy when you're in charge."

He still sat on Rikeri's throne, where I'd instructed him to sit. He needed to look like he was in charge, even if he didn't want to be.

"But you'd look sexier without that torn and bloodied dress on." He sat back and watched as I slipped out of my dress, thankful it had held together enough to secure my breasts. Garret's eyes grew dark, the hunger in them causing my heart to pound. "Fuck, you're beautiful, princess."

A shiver worked its way down my body as I straddled him. He entwined his fingers in my hair, his eyes searching mine for something I hoped he would find. The love that burned in my core, the desire that raged within me, the undying devotion I now had for a man who had stumbled into my life, charming me with the smoldering looks and subtle signs of who he really was below the pride, the arrogance, the hurt child within protected by the façade he'd built.

"I love you, Garret," I said, my heart jumping with anticipation of the kiss that awaited me.

The corner of his lips rose, twisting the arousal in me so that he had me drenched within seconds. He pushed my head forward, our mouths meeting in a heated kiss that inflamed the embers of need flickering in my body. I came alive in that kiss, his love for me flooding through my every cell and claiming me in the way only Garret could. And no matter that he insisted he didn't want to own me, that I was my own person, not a thing to be owned and coveted like people had done to me my entire life, he owned me. That ownership sang through me like a brand on my heart that I never wanted removed because I wanted him to own me, to claim me for his.

He dragged his lips down my neck as I pushed at his shirt. Losing his touch left me cold when he removed his hands from my skin and ripped his shirt over his head. I dragged my hands down his chest, feeling the strength below and never wanting to be without it again. As he dropped his hand to my waist and he gripped it firmly, his other hand grasped my neck. The move made me so wet that I hastily grabbed at his pants.

"Damn, I love you, princess," he mumbled as I drew his length out, my body craving it like the air I breathed. He lifted me and I settled over him, sighing as he filled me. His moan lit the spaces the flames hadn't touched, my body a sensation of heated ecstasy. He gripped my hips, pushing deeper into me, his pelvis thrusting up to meet mine.

His name fell from my lips in an unrecognizable moan before he captured it with a kiss. His touches were firm, his kisses intense, and when he pushed me back, his fingers rubbing my clit as he sucked my nipple into his mouth, my climax tore through me like a storm battering the shore. The waves drowned me, and I gasped for air as it continued, shredding me to tatters that I knew only he could reform.

"Gods, El. You don't know how you destroy me," he mumbled, crushing his mouth against mine while I continued to shatter in his arms. He tensed, his body gripped in the rapture of his release as his climax joined mine. Our bodies became one, our breathing mingled, our lips entwined as he filled me, body, heart, and soul. The world turned to nothing but Garret and the way my body blissfully fell to oblivion with his.

When the last waves of release finished battering me, I dropped my head to his shoulder, his arms encircling my body in a protective hold, as if he never wanted to let me go. He nuzzled his face into my hair, his breathing ragged.

"I don't know who I was before you, Eloise. A lost soul, tattered and torn, wandering this world looking for his purpose. Until you peeked around those sheets that day and I found it. I love you, Eloise, and I will spend the rest of my life loving you as if every day was the first day I fell in love with you."

Tears burned behind my eyes, and I lifted my head, meeting his eyes and wondering how I'd ever existed before Garret had come into my life. Because before him, I'd only just existed. Now, I was alive.

"Take me to our room and show me all the ways you love me, big boy," I said, biting his lip, my smile too great to hide.

"And all the ways I worship you, princess?" he asked, his brow lifting.

"That, too. And then I'll show you all the ways I love you."

He slipped me from his lap, fixed his pants, and scooped me into his arms.

"Guess I'd better find us a room fast before I take you again in the hallway and have to kill anyone who sees you coming."

He walked us out of the throne room as I curled into his chest.

"You take one lingering look at her and I'll let you see why you should fear me just as much as my father," he shouted at the guard outside the door. "Now find me an empty room so I can finish ravaging my woman."

I giggled into his chest, the part of me that was soft and gentle, the side that had dreamed of escaping her tower for more than a few hours a day, of finding a man who would love me like the men in the fairy tales did, adored how possessive Garret was and how protected I felt in his hold. The part of me who had run from Rikeri, who had become a woman, a fighter, a survivor, and who was exhausted after years of being those things, quietly tried to reconcile what it would mean to no longer have to survive. And as he set me down on a bed of silk sheets and made love to me, she finally rested, letting her villain take control and treat her like the princess she was.

CHAPTER TWENTY-NINE

GARRET

Sweat dripped from my brow as I brought the axe down on the last piece of wood. The summer season had ended, autumn on the cusp of turning to winter, but the heat lingered today. Stacking the wood on the pile and satisfied we'd have enough for the winter, I walked back into the house.

A mop of chestnut hair ran between my legs, and I snatched his pants, lifting him up to give him a scolding look.

"Put me down, Papa. Esmine is going to get me."

"Is she?" I asked, pulling him into my arms and tickling him.

He giggled, his little feet kicking to get free.

A knock on the door took my eyes from his younger sister, who was spying from behind the banister, looking just as mischievous as her mother. Her blue eyes sparkled with the golden touch of her magic, the streaks in her curly ebony hair shimmering with the same gold.

"Esmine, leave your brother alone," I said, dropping Leon and patting him on the rump. "You know you can't use your magic against him when he doesn't have any."

"But he pulled my hair, Papa," she complained.

I gave Leon a disapproving look. "Don't pick on your sister. She's younger than you. You're supposed to look out for her. Remember what Uncle Tristan taught you."

His bottom lip pouted as another knock rapped on the door. I suspected Eloise was in the garden out back, working on the vegetables. I shooed the kids off, making my way to the door of our small house.

While I'd remained in Duntraik, I'd refused the legacy my father had left me. I wasn't a king, and ruling a kingdom was not something I wanted. Eloise turned her back on her father, she and her brother deciding they would let him stay in power until he died. Bira needed no more disruption than it had already suffered. I'd asked Tristan to take my place in Duntraik, to rule and guide the people to a gentler reign. They flourished under his rule, with Leo as his trusted advisor. Eloise would take over Bira when her father passed, but for now, she spent her time sharing the blessing of her power with the people of both kingdoms. And both had blossomed from the gift that hadn't come from the gods but from an innocent mix of god-touched roses and magic that had combined to bring the blessing of the vessel to each generation.

I reached the door, stepping out to greet the source of the knocks. An elderly woman, hunched with withered skin and white hair, stood before me, a basket of roses in her hand. She peeked her wrinkled blue eyes up at me.

"Kind sir, may I offer you a rose for your beautiful wife?"

She reached a shaky hand into the basket and picked one up before holding it out to me. The rose brought back memories of the day I'd seen Eloise turn the petals to a golden dust and of the roses I'd seen in the gardens of the castle the night I'd chased Beatrice, their petals floating in the water with me the next morning when I'd run.

Beatrice, who, along with her new husband, had forgiven my actions with Eloise's persuasion.

"Papa," I heard Esmine as she tugged on my pants. "Who is that?"

The woman's eyes turned with her smile. I glanced behind her, seeing no carriage, no horse or method for her to have traveled to our home, which was remotely settled in a valley between Duntraik and Bira.

"A guest," I said, taking the rose from the woman's shaking hand and seeing that it was no normal rose, but a thornless rose from the fields of Bira. "Tell your mother we'll be having company for dinner."

"Papa?"

I looked down at her. "Go, Esmine."

She scurried away, and I turned my attention back to the old woman, my breath catching as she transformed into the spitting image of Eloise, the distinctive petals staining her cheeks, the same flickers of gold sparkling in her blue eyes. Only the telltale signs of age in their corners differentiated her from my Eloise.

"You've done well, Garret," she said as I stood frozen with my mouth hanging open. "Tell my daughter I never stopped loving her. Keep her safe. I'll visit when it's time to teach Esmine to make rose drops."

"No, you need to stay. Gods, she'll have so many questions. She needs to see you."

I turned my head to yell for Eloise through the door, hoping she would hear me.

"Questions she knows the answers to as do you. She and Esmine are the future of our kind. Protect them."

I turned back, but she was gone, the rose the only evidence that she'd been there. I stared at the empty space, blinking my eyes as if it had all been my imagination. Movement in my periphery caused me to look away, and I spied the graceful buck before it sprang away, fading into the distance. The same buck I'd repeatedly seen, the same that had guided Eloise all those years. Not the gods watching over her, but her mother guiding her in the only way she could. My eyes remained locked on the horizon as I contemplated just how powerful the magic was that ran through my wife's veins and now my daughter's. Neither fully aware of the potential they held.

I walked around the house, finding Eloise looking over the garden with the baby on her hip. I took the time to stand and observe her. My heart filled as it did every time I saw her. She'd put on weight since the day I'd met her, her hips filling out with the birth of each child, and I loved that it made her even more seductive. I'd squeezed those hips so many times there should have been permanent marks on them.

Discovering she could have children had been a shock, one I gave her time to digest. Her father had lifted the binding on her when she was ready. Leon had arrived nine months later, named for the man who had been my loyal friend and who reminded me of that each time I saw him. Leon had been born without power, but then Esmine had come, her golden locks sitting brightly in her ebony hair. Rikeri had been right, Eloise's power mixed with his produced an even more exceptional child. But he'd been wrong in assuming I had no magic. It had carried on in my genes, lying dormant in me and passing through to Esmine, who was surprising us more every day.

Leon dashed past me, nearly knocking me over as Esmine chased him. I shook my head, knowing she hadn't told her mother of our visitor as I'd asked her to. With the rose gripped in my hand, I made my way to Eloise. Wrapping my hand around her waist, I kissed her neck, peeking at Trista, our third child, whom we'd named for her uncle.

"Hi," Eloise said, as Trista giggled in her arms, her hand reaching out toward me. I draped my lips down to Eloise's cleavage, which was swollen with breastmilk, something of which I reaped the benefits because I was a sucker for how her breasts filled out when she was nursing. Trista's small hand grabbed my hair, and I complained as the move pulled me from her mother's soft skin.

"I'll get my fill of that later," I said, giving Eloise a wink and taking Trista from her. I set her down, watching her teeter on her inadequate legs, which were still growing accustomed to walking.

"Oh you will, will you?" Eloise teased as I pulled her into my arms.

"Definitely, after my knees are thoroughly bruised from making you come, princess."

She threw her head back and laughed, and I nipped at her neck. I would have picked her up and carried her to our room if I hadn't remembered the rose in my hand.

"We had a visitor," I said, drawing back and showing her the rose.

"Is that a Bira rose?" she asked, taking it from me. As she did, it sparkled, the edges of the petals shimmering white like sugar as they slowly dropped into her palm. Her breath hitched, and she looked up at me, her eyes trying to find an answer in mine.

"She said to tell you she'd be back when Esmine is old enough to learn to make rose drops."

"My mother?" she said, her voice so soft I could barely hear it. "My mother is alive..." Her eyes grew wide. "The rose drops, the memories..." Tears spilled down her cheeks, and I brushed them away. "I always thought it was strange that my mother was so cold to me, so distant, but every once in a while she would be the mother I wanted her to be."

I took the rose drop from her hand, noticing how the stem of the flower had dissipated. Calling the kids over, I stooped and handed them the petals and the remaining bud, which Leon snatched and gobbled down. Rose drops were their favorite treat, along with the lemon brew Eloise still made. The magic she imbued in the sugar that laced the petals always fascinated me.

Rising, I brought Eloise into my arms and kissed her head. "She was always there, watching over you, guiding you and others," I said, thinking of the prince I'd tried to kill and wondering if she'd guided him just as much as she had me, and if he'd had to change, just like I had to see what was truly important in life. Perhaps we were all connected in some way by the petals that layered our pasts, ones swept away with the promise of the future.

I kissed Eloise on the nose, tracing my kisses down the trail of her markings until I met her lips. It was a gentle kiss, meant to give her my love and my strength. Strength I knew she only needed on occasion because she was her own force.

I rested my forehead against hers, saying, "She'll be back when she's ready, when you're ready, when Esmine is ready. Until then, I'm sure she'll be watching."

She glanced up at me, her blue eyes sparkling with the tears that remained. "Just like she always was." She kissed my cheek, resting her hand on my chest. "Thank you," she said.

"For what, princess?"

Her smile was like the sun on a winter day, its rays coursing through me to touch even the darkest parts. "For loving me."

"There's no way I couldn't, El. Not loving you would be like dying. You are the air that fills my lungs, the color that lights my sight, the sweetest taste that hits my tongue." I nuzzled her neck. "You are my everything, princess, and I didn't know life until I knew you."

Dropping my hand to her hip, I pulled her against me. "And you're the only one who can satisfy the raging need I have to constantly devour you."

"I love you, too," she said, kissing me and grabbing my hand. "Leon, watch your sisters. Your father and I have—"

I squeezed her ass, pushing her toward the house. "Just watch them!" I yelled, hearing him grumble. I wasn't so sure leaving a five-year-old in charge of a three-year-old and a one-year-old was the best idea, but I wasn't about to turn down a chance to touch my wife.

"You know, it's been a year since the last baby, and I love how sexy you are when you're pregnant," I said as she shoved me against the wall. She was in an aggressive mood, and it made my balls swell in anticipation.

"You need to work hard for that one, big boy, because these breasts are tired of being so full of milk. Aren't you tired of sharing them yet?" she pressed my hand against them, and I squeezed instinctively.

"Not when they look so fantastic," I replied, grabbing her hip and pulling her to me. "And when these are so sexy to grab onto."

"You're naughty," she said, playfully biting my earlobe.

"I'm a villain, princess. I'm always naughty."

She laughed, and I smothered her mouth, pulling her flush against me and reveling in the way she fit so perfectly there. She always did because she was my other half, the woman I'd never known I needed until she was there, opening my eyes. Eloise was my redemption, the second chance that was waiting for me to accept it. And as our touches grew needier, my body responding to her like it only did to her, I thanked the gods that I'd stepped into her path. That I'd taken that chance and she'd let me because there was no other place in this world I wanted to be and no other man I wanted to be but hers.

About the Author

J. L. Jackola is a writer of love stories with fantasy, darkness, feisty women, and morally gray men. She's an admitted sugar addict with a penchant for anything with salted caramel. When she's not weaving tales, snacking on sweets, or downing her morning cup of tea, you can find her logging miles in her running shoes, watching movies with her family, or curled up with a book.

She resides in Delaware with her husband and three children.

To learn more, visit her website at
www.jljackola.com

Made in the USA
Middletown, DE
08 March 2025

72258987R00182